The
BOY WHO
WEPT
BLOOD

Also by Den Patrick from Gollancz:

The Naer Evain Chronicles

Orcs War-Fighting Manual
Elves War-Fighting Manual
Dwarves War-Fighting Manual

The Erebus Sequence

The Boy with the Porcelain Blade

The
BOY WHO
WEPT
BLOOD

DEN PATRICK

GOLLANCZ

LONDON

First published in Great Britain in 2015 by Gollancz
An imprint of the Orion Publishing Group
Orion House, 5 Upper St Martin's Lane, London WC2H 9EA
An Hachette UK Company

A CIP catalogue record for this book is available
from the British Library

ISBN 978 0 575 13433 1

1 3 5 7 9 10 8 6 4 2

Typeset at The Spartan Press Ltd,
Lymington, Hants

Printed and bound in Great Britain by
Clays Ltd, St Ives plc

The Orion Publishing Group's policy is to use papers that
are natural, renewable and recyclable products and made
from wood grown in sustainable forests. The logging and
manufacturing processes are expected to conform to the
environmental regulations of the country of origin.

www.orionbooks.co.uk
www.gollancz.co.uk

For Juliet, who believed from the start.

'The best revenge is to live well'
STEPHANIA PROSPERO

'A raven who dives like a cormorant is drowned'
POPULAR LANDFALL PROVERB

Great and Minor Houses of Landfall

HOUSE DIASPORA

Araneae 'Anea' Oscuro Diaspora
reluctant ruler of Demesne, a learned woman who yearns
for a republic

Dino Adolfo Erudito
Superiore Maestro di Spada, bodyguard, and half-brother
of Araneae

Achilles
Dino's pet cataphract drake

Professore Falcone Virmyre
a scientist and friend to the Orfani

Domina Russo Maria Diaspora
Chief steward of Demesne

Fiorenza Giolla Diaspora
Housekeeper to the Domina

HOUSE FONTEIN

Duke Fontein
an elderly and conservative member of the nobility

Duchess Fontein
his notoriously bad-tempered wife

Maestro di Spada D'arzenta di Fontein
frustrated teacher of blades

Maestro di Spada Ruggeri di Fontein
laconic, to say the least

Capo di Custodia, Guido di Fontein
Duchess Prospero's consort

Isabella Gollia Esposito
the Duke and Duchess' reluctant housekeeper

Speranza di Fontein
a rarity, a woman messenger

HOUSE ERUDITO

Maestro Gian Cherubini
a bachelor of life, science, and the arts

HOUSE CONTADINO

Margravio Emilio Contadino
a noble of middle age, veteran of the Verde Guerra

Marchesa Medea Contadino
the soul of House Contadino, and of diplomacy

Lord Luc Contadino
just eleven, already the image of his father

Lady Isabella Contadino
a sparrow of nine summers

Massimo Esposito
the *Margravio*'s indispensable aide and rumoured assassin

Cook Camelia di Contadino
no-nonsense giantess of the kitchens

Nardo Moretti
a messenger and loyal servant

Maria Moretti
wife of Nardo, Housekeeper to *Marchesa* Contadino

HOUSE PROSPERO

Duchess Salvaza Prospero (formerly Fontein)
an ambitious and staunch conservative

Stephania Prospero
supporter of Anea, estranged from her mother, unmarried

HOUSE MARINO

Duke Lucien 'sinestra' Marino
Orfano, Kingslayer and ruler of San Marino, a town to
south-east

Duchess Rafaela Marino
a commoner made noble through marriage

HOUSE ALLATTAMENTO

Lady Allattamento
rumoured lover of Duke Fontein, governs a House of
varying fortune

Stella Allattamento
a devoted daughter keen to advance her station

Viola Allattamento
a theatrical and much spoiled daughter

Giolla di Allattamento
a niece and Lady-in-Waiting to Lady Allattamento

Angelo Allattamento
cocksure bravo and hothead

THE CULT OF SANTA MARIA

Agostina Desideria
self-proclaimed Disciple of Santa Maria

The Second Son of Allattamento

– 6 *Giugno* 325

Lady Araneae Oscuro Diaspora, formerly of House Contadino, known to her subjects as the Silent Queen, sat back from her letter-writing. Her nightgown was a pale grey silk that left her arms bare, alabaster skin almost luminous in the candlelight. As ever she wore a veil over the bottom half of her face, a neat triangle of matching fabric, a line of blue embroidery dancing along the topmost edge. Her kohl-stained eyes stared out of the lead-latticed windows; the town of Santa Maria slept in darkness beyond the glass. Blacksmiths slumbered, children snored faintly, while drunks mumbled and turned, beset by night terrors. Mothers and fathers dared dream of a prosperous, safer future.

The Silent Queen, known to those who loved her as Anea, regarded her reflection in the window. Just twenty-five, yet bearing a world of problems upon her slender shoulders. Her hair was a long and well kept mane of summer yellow, held up with a silver pin the thickness of her finger. Difficult to tell in this light if the beginnings of crow's feet were forming at the corners of her eyes. Her desk was covered in correspondence: an endless litany of complaints from newly formed guilds, lesser nobles clutching at the crumbling vestiges of yesterday's power. A glass of untouched red wine shone bloody in the twilight, reflecting light from thick, scented candles. Jasmine lingered on the air, calming nerves frayed by the day's debates.

Our Lady Araneae, the great reformer, known to her opponents as the *strega* princess, or witchling by braver souls. Not that she had ever evinced any magic in the ten years of her reign. Anea regarded the room: finely crafted furniture and woven rugs of bright wool. The candelabrum was a simple but fine example of what House Prospero artisans were capable of these days. A framed diagram of a human body dominated the fireplace. The bookshelf stood to her right, yet opportunities to read for pleasure were few these days.

A key clicked in the lock, causing Anea to stand and turn, hands pressed against the desk. The door opened on greased brass hinges. Even Russo, her most trusted lieutenant, knocked before entering. There were three of them, sporting doublets in black with gold thread at the collar. The shoulders were slashed, showing deep red silk beneath. Black and scarlet, the colours of House Fontein. All three were male, filled with impetuous swagger, young bravos in their twenties sporting the cropped hairstyle of Maestro di Spada Giancarlo, dead these ten years.

And they were armed. Each bore the short flat blade that was so in fashion at the moment.

'Good evening, my lady,' said the nearest of them, a sneer on his lips. 'Forgive me the late intrusion but I bring word from the *nobili*.'

His fellows stifled laughter at his mummery, Anea stared back, statue still.

'It seems they have decided your schemes to empower the commoners do not serve their best interests. While those in the fields have begun to worship you, it is a cruel irony you are less popular here, in Demesne.'

The leader took a step forward, closing the gap between himself and the defenceless ruler. She pressed herself against the desk. He wasn't much older than Anea. Likely half as intelligent, three times as pompous.

'We know you won't be turned from your dreams of a republic, so it falls to me to act. Still, hardly a reason we can't have some fun? It's not like you can cry out for help, is it, my Silent Queen?'

It was true. No sound had ever issued from behind the veil she wore. Some said she'd been born without a tongue, others claimed her witchery demanded silence, few knew the truth of it. The bravo stepped forward, hand reaching for the fabric hiding the lower portion of her face.

'There's no need for you to die with all your secrets, after all.' He had almost grasped the veil, a savage grin making him grotesque. Anea remained motionless, green eyes flat with hatred. The faint sound of snapping wood and breaking glass startled everyone.

'Time's up,' said a voice from behind them. The bravos turned as one, eyebrows raised in surprise. They quickly recovered themselves, retaining their swagger and bruised-knuckle nonchalance.

He'd been sitting in the deep leather armchair behind the door the whole time, listening to their petty theatre, enduring their poor intimidation. Deep brown hair swept to one side of eyes grey as a winter's day, face impassive. His boots were a deep weather-beaten umber, each adorned with seven buckles in muted brass. He might have been carved from stone, attired as he was in a suit of sober grey. The scabbard lay across his lap like a death sentence. Unfussy, unadorned, it was a work of function not art. It was a container, nothing more, promising a blade long and slender. An hourglass had broken under the predations of his long clever fingers, fragments of crystal and wood littering his hands, sand ran free.

'I should have known you'd be here,' said the bravos' leader, a second son of House Allattamento. He might have been called Angelo, or Antioco. He thrust out his chin and squared his shoulders, a curl to his lip. 'It is unfortunate for you the guards outside your door could be bought so easily. Three to one.' He flicked glances to his conspirators, who couldn't match his bluster, looking less sure of themselves. 'I dare say anyone in Demesne would choose such odds.'

'I am not "anyone".'

Dino Adolfo Erudito, Orfano and *maestro superiore di spada* of House Fontein, regarded the handful of sand and the broken glass with a look of dream-like introspection. A cataphract drake perched on his shoulder, staring across a flat snout with obsidian eyes. The lithe sepia-brown reptile scuttled onto the armchair and tasted the air. Dino set aside the broken timer, rising slowly, feeling the tiredness in his limbs, the itch of stubble left too long on his cheeks, the familiar icy calmness that seeped into him at times such as this.

'The wolf spider,' he said amiably, 'otherwise known as Lycosidae, belongs to the order Araneae in the class of Arachnida.'

The youngest of the bravos took a half-step back, incredulity crossing his features, a question frozen on his lips.

'It has a fine sense of vibration and particularly good eyesight, appropriate for a creature who hunts others by running them down.' Dino stood before them with the scabbard in his left hand, looking no more threatening than a shepherd with his crook.

'What *is* this shit?' said the youngest bravo. Another second son from a minor house with nothing to lose.

'However,' continued Dino, undeterred, 'many wolf spiders are content to wait for prey to pass their burrows, rushing out to attack them.'

Angelo Allattamento pulled on a grim smile and drew his sword.

'The *strega*'s lost his mind.'

Dino glowered at him, wintry grey eyes shining silver in the candlelight.

'You stepped in to my parlour. Fuckers.'

And then Dino was moving, coming forward without form, as if elemental. The scabbard darted out to one side, its tip hitting the door, which slammed shut. An outflung hand showered sand into the eyes of the bravo on his right. Curses fell from the man's lips as he stumbled back, clawing at his eyes. His torso hammered into a bookcase, a selection of literary works raining heavily upon him. The bookcase pitched forward, knocking him to the floor.

Angelo had already struck before his co-conspirator hit the floor. Dino blocked the blow with the scabbard, stepping sideways to buy himself the extra moment to draw. When Angelo pressed in again he found his blade stopped by steel, the sound ringing in the silence of the night, a spiteful bell.

A snatched glance confirmed Anea had retreated behind

her desk, putting herself beyond the immediate reach of the youngest bravo. He tried to follow, ashen-faced, blade held in trembling hand. She scanned the room for something, anything to fight back with. Her school days had been filled with more than just etiquette and sciences, but without a weapon she was greatly disadvantaged. Remaining empty-handed, she retreated further still, unable to call for help.

Dino struck low at Angelo, stepped in, taking advantage of the noble's poor parry and his stumbling step back. Then the Orfano thrust. He expected to be turned aside, of course, but this was just a feint for the kick to the side of the knee. Angelo swore and lost his footing. He threw up another parry, which Dino batted aside with the scabbard still clutched in his left hand. His blade flickered, opening a deep gouge across the young noble's thigh.

It had worked perfectly. He'd fought his way out of the corner and was now level with the youngest bravo, who was still summoning the courage to murder Anea. Dino mashed his pommel into the back of the young man's head even as Angelo limped back, cursing in the old tongue. Anea's attacker folded in on himself, clutching the back of his skull. The blade slipped from his fingers as he went down to one knee. Anea flipped the desk, the edge smashing into the bridge of her attacker's nose. The Silent Queen circled the table, drawing the silver pin from her hair, green eyes full of terrible intensity.

Angelo of House Allattamento knew he was bested. Too wounded to run, too proud to surrender, he assembled a series of hasty strikes. Dino let him come forward, stepping aside when he could, parrying when he couldn't, waiting, waiting.

Angelo's vigour abandoned him just as the blood staining his britches did the same. He stumbled, exposed and unbalanced. Dino wrapped his sword arm across his body, tensing for a second, unleashing a broad swipe that ripped through the other man's jugular. He felt the blade grind, grating against vertebrae. The second son of House Allattamento pressed a frantic palm to his undoing. His legs continued their duty for long seconds even as blood jetted hot and fierce.

5

'You stepped into my parlour,' whispered Dino, but it was regret rather than anger that gilded each word.

Angelo Allattamento hit the floor, eyes frozen wide in disbelief.

Dino turned to find Anea standing over her assailant, one hand clutching the top of his skull, the other a fist beside his throat. The man trembled and Dino stepped forward to help before realising Anea's hair hung long and thick about her shoulders. She withdrew her fist, revealing the silver hairpin, now a slender length of scarlet. Anea stood wide-eyed, shaking with shock, staring at her red-stained hand. Blood spattered her silver-grey nightgown as it jetted from the man's throat. The hem of her gown became a drench of gore as the man fell onto his ruined face.

The last of the bravos writhed free of the bookcase, regaining his feet amid a litter of books. He choked out an incredulous cry, eyes raw from the sand. The two Orfani turned to him, attired in the blood of his allies, gazes like flint and jade.

They hog-tied him in the end. Neither of the Orfani had the stomach for more death. The last of the bravos could wait until morning, when a sentence less final could be meted out. But the carrion stench and voided bowels of the fallen necessitated a change of quarters. The siblings haunted the corridors like shades, seeing assassins at every corner, lurking at every stairwell. This was not an unknown sensation; they'd shared a similar night ten years ago. Finally, they made the safety of Dino's apartment in House Erudito, an orderly sort of place where weapons hung above the fireplace. Achilles slithered down from Dino's shoulder, taking his usual perch atop the bookcase, where he stared down imperiously. Anea's fingers began to flicker and dance.

I have not had to leave that room since the night of the fire.

'I'd rather fight assassins than flames,' said Dino quietly.

Do you have anything to wear?

'Help yourself. Anything in the closet.'

She stalked out of the sitting room, head down, trying to still her nerves no doubt. Dino could still smell the iron tang of blood. Unsurprising, as he was evenly coated from the thigh down. None of it his own, fortunately. He shook his head, not able to believe the brazenness of the attempt. They hadn't even worn masks. It wasn't an assassination.

'It was an execution.'

Anea emerged from the bedroom in old hose and a cerulean doublet he'd forgotten he owned.

'Or a coup.'

She approached, slipping into his arms, pushing her forehead against his shoulder. She was shaking.

'House Allattamento is about to see a significant reduction in its influence.'

She pulled away, fingers moving tentatively: *The corruption of Landfall has spilled over into open violence. I suppose it was inevitable.*

'You need to send a message.' Dino scowled. 'We'll tolerate no more of it.'

Anea nodded, but her gaze was elsewhere, lost to shocked remembering.

This does not feel like politics any more. Has war been declared? Were we too distracted to notice? Were we too arrogant?

'The arrogance is all theirs.'

Spent and numb they approached the table where Dino took his morning repast on the rare occasions he wasn't sleeping in Anea's armchair. They sat at each end, feeling the distance between them.

Something was moving amid the dishes. Dino cursed. The maids hadn't cleared the table. Not unusual as he often slept until noon with instructions not to be disturbed. His room had clearly been passed over by the staff entirely. A column of ants trooped to and from the remains of yesterday's breakfast, carrying off fragments many times their own size. After the first wave of irritation Dino found himself quietly fascinated by their industry.

We're infested on all sides it seems, signed Anea.

'Looks that way. I'm not sure who are the worst pests, the ants or the *nobili*.'

At least the nobili *are less numerous.*

7

'And two less as of tonight.'

Dino supplied a bottle of Barolo and two glasses from a cypress wood cabinet. They sipped wine by candlelight until the dawn arrived, watching the ants march away with their breadcrumb treasures.

2

A Letter to Lucien

— 7 Giugno 325

'They made a pretty mess.' Massimo cast an eye over the damage to Anea's sitting room. Golden light filtered through the latticed windows, ablaze on the white plastered walls.

'Anea and I were at least partly to blame.' Dino looked down at the scattering of sand and the fractured hourglass. 'It was Anea who threw the table, believe it or not.'

'I can believe it.' The swordsman grinned. Dino was caught up in the man's expression. Being dour was its own challenge when Massimo was present. Margravio Contadino's personal aide and messenger was shorter than Dino by a slight margin but heavier set. Some whispered he was no aide; rather his role was more akin to assassin. Dino had trouble believing such a thing. A soldier with a gentle soul, Massimo's outlook was far from that of a jaded killer.

'You're awake early,' added Massimo.

'Not exactly. I couldn't sleep.'

Dino watched the swordsman pick over the devastation. He was darkly good-looking, wearing an embroidered scarlet doublet. The slashed shoulders revealed the white shirt beneath. White and scarlet, the colours of his house providing a proud uniform, Massimo was rarely seen in anything else. A rapier slept in a scarlet-enamelled scabbard; a stiletto hung from his other hip. Dino was grateful that House Contadino was sympathetic to Anea. He didn't relish the idea of facing Massimo should hostilities break out.

'You've nothing to worry from me, my lord,' said Massimo, face serious. He dropped his gaze to the pommel of his sword.

9

'People are going to start talking about witchcraft if you keep reading my mind like that.'

Massimo smiled, all trace of his previous formality gone.

'The only people accused of witchcraft are wilful women and Orfani.'

'Anea is unfortunate to be both.'

'Very much both.' Massimo smiled again. 'It's what I like most about her.'

At twenty-six Massimo was the darling of the court. His manners were impeccable, his wit easy, wardrobe perfectly chosen. Dino felt somewhat shabby by comparison. And yet Massimo remained unattainable to every girl who fluttered fan or lashes at him. The swordsman often said his first love was duty, the blade on his hip reinforcing the claim.

'Do people really think Anea can cast spells?' asked Dino. 'That's children's nonsense.'

Massimo shrugged. 'The *cittadini* are ignorant, uneducated – they don't know any better. I'd not be surprised if Houses Fontein and Prospero spread the rumours.'

Dino thought back to the three bravos and the guards who had abandoned their posts.

'I sometimes think we'll have to exterminate House Fontein down to the last drop of blood before we know peace.'

'The Fonteins probably feel the same about the Orfani.'

'I *know* they think the same about the Orfani.'

'Well, in that case it sounds like a fair match.' Massimo grinned again. 'Shall we start with the duke and work our way down?'

'You have no idea how tempting you are – I mean, how tempting that is.' Dino turned away to cover his blushes. If Massimo noticed the slip of the tongue he declined to comment on it. Dino had always been this way around Massimo, ever since they'd been children, marching off to the Verde Guerra, the only war in Landfall's patchy history.

Dino scuffed a boot at a bloodstain on the floor, recalling the previous night's melee. Anea had killed a man on this exact spot with a silver hairpin and a steely resolve. It was a long silver hairpin on account of her long blond hair, etched with a repeating thorn motif, the wider end featured the illusion of rose petals. Dino knew the details of the piece well; he'd been the one to commission it, a present at last year's *La Festa*.

'It must have been quite a fight,' said Massimo, noting the direction of Dino's gaze. The Orfano nodded but remained silent. The bloodstain on the floor would need scalding water and plenty of soap. House Fontein guards had removed the bodies, but death lingered, an unseen shade. One was never too far from that dark spectre in Demesne.

'I almost wish she did know magic,' muttered Dino. 'It might provide an answer to our problems.'

Massimo approached and clapped an arm round Dino's shoulder.

'Cheer up. I've not seen you this maudlin since Nardo sent that serving girl up to your apartment for your birthday.'

'Yes. Thanks for reminding me.' Dino shrugged off the aide's arm and fought down a moment's unease. The incident with the serving girl had left Dino facing some hard truths, truths he'd been avoiding ever since. Massimo grabbed his shoulder again and gave him a companionable shake.

'Come on, Dino! We'll get through this. I promise it on my life. And give yourself some credit. You defended her from three bravos who came here, key in hand. This was planned; this was a conspiracy.'

'She defended herself too. No mean feat when you're unarmed. Something I intend to remedy. I'm going to insist she carries a weapon and resumes her blade practice.'

'She won't like that much.'

'I dare say she'll prefer it to being dead.'

'In that case I'd best sign up for this practice too. Do you know any good teachers?' Massimo's grin was broad. 'I've heard the *superiore* is good.'

'As if you could learn anything from me.' Dino rolled his eyes.

'Best to not get complacent. I'll only keep my edge by prac- tising with equals.'

'Now you're flattering me.'

Massimo shrugged and looked away. 'What will you do about all this?'

'I just ...' Dino regarded the bookcase that had fallen on one of the hapless bravos. 'They had the key and they paid off the guards. All the skill in the world counts for nothing when corruption is this prevalent.'

'You've given word to question the guards on duty?' said Massimo.

'Of course, but they've not been seen since last night. Whoever paid them off did it well. They'll have absconded to the countryside to live on a fat purse.'

'Early retirement,' said Massimo.

'And all they had to do was abandon Anea.'

Massimo crossed to the door before glancing back over his shoulder. 'I'm going to fetch Virmyre. I suggest you meet us in the piazza for some sunshine and a drink. That's the only cure for this black mood of yours.'

'I can't, I should—'

'Dino, you protected her, you fought well, you have allies. Come and raise a glass to living another day. Who knows? Perhaps we'll invent a way to live a few more?'

'You make a lot of plans when drunk, do you?'

'Rash decisions, mainly.' The swordsman grinned again. 'But you can never predict when inspiration will strike.'

'I'll see you there. I promise.'

Massimo exited the room, Dino's gaze lingering on the doorway long after he'd left. Lord Contadino's aide was his closest friend since Lucien had departed, yet there was much that Dino could not bring himself to speak of. He dropped his gaze to the bloodstain at his boots and saw a scrap of parchment beneath a rosewood box. Curiosity demanded he retrieve it, then demanded he read the fine hand that formed orderly rows of looping letters.

Dear Lucien,

I hope things are peaceful in San Marino. How I envy the full support you enjoy. The remnants of House Fontein have become even more troublesome of late. Duke and

Duchess Fontein argue over every variable of the law. The remaining soldiery answer to Russo, the capo, *and Dino, but I fear the old loyalties still exist. I think I will be forced to recruit soldiers directly into my own house at some point, or create a new independent army. Russo is a commanding presence and has settled into her role better than I could have hoped for.*

House Prospero remains the most productive and yet the most fractious of all the houses. Stephania opposes her mother at every turn and is a worthy ally. The duchess continues to be an outspoken critic of a republic. She is still stringing Guido along but refuses to marry him. Rumours persist he grows restless.

More of House Contadino's cittadini *turn to the new religion with every passing week. I wonder if the king's abolition of religion was such a bad thing. The converts to the faith are an unknown quantity, and while their adherents do a lot of good in the town I worry at their agenda. How do you strike a balance with the Sisters of Santa Maria in San Marino? Are they as aloof there as they are here?*

Margravio *and* Marchesa Contadino *continue to aid me where they can. A small mercy. The children are growing all the the time and are delightful.*

If it weren't for House Erudito I might despair completely. Maestro Cherubini continues to win over the minds of the lesser nobles with concise and articulate arguments. And Virmyre, of course, has been invaluable in my research with the king's machines. Every moment I am away from my studies is a moment I fear I am failing the people who look to me. The secrets we have uncovered! Lucien, I know you distrust everything the king stood for, but if we could use that power to better everyone, rather than elevate a few ... the implications are breathtaking.

Virmyre has suggested we visit the coast and I would dearly love to. I know seeing you would lift Dino's spirits. The nine years since you left have passed all too quickly. Please give Rafaela my warmest affection. Tell your houses

that Aranea Oscuro Diaspora wishes them a fine summer
and a prosperous harvest.
  Yours ever faithfully,
    Anea

It was only as Dino reached the bottom of the page he realised the edge was red with dried blood. Two ants clung to the
thick paper, marching in opposite directions before turning,
unsure how to leave the island of parchment. Dino tilted the
letter, regarding the insects for a few moments. They were
larger than any ants he had seen before. He let the parchment
fall to the floor and looked up to find Anea standing in the
doorway.

I suppose I shall have to write a new letter now.

Dino nodded, feeling a pang of shame she'd caught him
reading it. No secrets existed between the siblings – there had
never been any cause for deception – but he felt wrong about
reading her missive all the same.

Perhaps I will just add a second page.

She looked tired.

'Did you come here alone?'

She shook her head.

'I'm going to need you to carry a weapon. And there'll be
blade practice.'

She nodded without energy, a resignation in the set of her
shoulders.

I saw Massimo. He told me he was taking you out for some air.

'Wine would be more accurate, but I imagine there will be
air involved too.'

*Be careful. Although I dare say you will be safer in the town
than you are in the castle.*

'Perhaps you should come too?'

I have too much to do. Go now. I will send if I need you.

Dino crossed the room and heard the crunch of glass as it
broke beneath his boots. Anea smoothed out his jacket across
the breast, then held him close for a moment.

'We should go to the coast. Let these fools rule themselves
– they all deserve each other.'

14

All?

'No, I suppose not.' Dino smiled. 'Not all of them.'

As long as good men serve Landfall I will remain here, Dino. Tyranny was the rule for three hundred years.

'I just hope it doesn't take three hundred years to amend it, you know?'

Anea held him close again, then shooed him away with a hand.

Off with you.

'I won't be long.'

And be sure to trade in that long face.

'I doubt I'll get much for it.'

Before leaving, he watched her enter her ruined sitting room and begin to re-order the books.

3

A Bad Vintage

– 7 Giugno 325

'And then the *figlio di puttana* had the audacity to claim diplomatic immunity, as if being the bastard son of Giancarlo would grant him some protection. *Buco del culo.*'

'I see you're in fine humour today,' said the *professore* in his usual deadpan. He was nearing sixty, movements slowed by the passage of time. Dino had thought the walking stick an affectation at first, but Virmyre had come to rely on it more heavily with the passing of the seasons. His blue eyes were just as sharp, but the black hair was now shot through with silver, his beard the same. The once fine eyebrows were now overgrown. Another sign of time's advance.

'What will Anea do with him?' said Massimo. The three of them had been sitting in the midday sun for an hour now, sipping white wine, picking at morsels of bread and ham, plucking olives from a bowl. The market on the piazza churned slowly, the shoppers too hot to move at anything more than a meander.

'She'll send him off to a farm to work off his penance, most likely,' said Dino.

'That is a fate worse than death.' Massimo grinned, suppressing a laugh. 'A *nobile* forced to do an honest day's work.'

Virmyre joined his laughter but it was cut short.

'*Porca miseria*, he's guilty of treason.' Dino's voice had risen. 'He tried to kill the queen.' This last through gritted teeth.

'But she's *not* the queen, is she?' said Virmyre, baritone gentle but insistent.

'She's the ruler of Demesne,' pressed Dino without conviction.

'This principle of refusing to take a title isn't helping anyone,' said Massimo quietly. 'Being Orfani meant something when the king was alive, but now? Well ...' He shrugged. 'No offence, Dino.'

'She can't make herself queen while pursuing a republic,' pressed Dino. 'It doesn't make any sense, you know?'

'True enough,' said Virmyre, 'but we can't deny the things we are, any more than we can pretend to be something we're not.'

'What do you mean?' said Dino, brow furrowed in confusion, his hands curling into fists. He was flushed with anger and not entirely sure why.

'I think Virmyre's trying to make you see that while Anea may not want to be queen she acts like one.' Massimo spoke in a soothing tone. 'Like it or not, Demesne needs a ruler with a title. Landfall needs a queen. Or a king.'

It was true. Being Orfani had been enough to keep the nobles in line in the past. Not just a title born of specific parentage, they were an actual caste of Demesne, a race apart. It wasn't that Dino, Anea or Lucien outranked the gentry, more that they remained outside it, afforded special treatment at the express wish of the king. But those times were a decade dead, along with the king and his many edicts.

'She'd enjoy an easier ride if she'd just assume a royal title and outrank the dukes and duchesses,' added Massimo.

Virmyre nodded soberly, but all three of them knew it was unlikely. Anea did not count hypocrisy among her sins.

'Easier ride?' Dino snorted a bitter laugh. 'Easier than having three thugs wander into her rooms at midnight? They were going to murder her. Do you really think a crown and a title would have stopped them?'

'Good point,' said Virmyre. He laced his fingers and looked away at the market. Dino's voice had crept up a fraction too loud. A small crowd of farmers at another bench had looked over, eyeing the weapons on display with unease.

'I'm sorry. I just ... Three of them. I'm just one person, you know? How am I supposed to defend her against that?'

'But you did,' said Massimo, obviously impressed.

'I wish she didn't spend so much time on those hateful machines,' said Dino after a pause. Virmyre cleared his throat and said nothing. 'Then she could concentrate on creating this republic she's so keen on.'

Finally Virmyre responded: 'Those "hateful machines" are doing a lot of good right now. The advances we've made in medicine alone are ample evidence of that.'

They lapsed into silence. Virmyre gestured for the bill, a distraction from the sombre tone that had settled over them like a dark cloud. They sat at the *taverna* watching the *cittadini* go about their everyday lives. The small town had flourished around the castle like the ivy that crept along its walls. The king had always kept the commoners far from Demesne, but Anea had adopted an entirely different stance. Santa Maria featured blacksmiths, tanners, carpenters, *dottori*, coopers, fishmongers, butchers, apothecaries and several potters. Each would have been sworn to one of the great houses just five years ago; now no longer, much to the chagrin of the nobles. Free men were forging their own destinies even as many remained wedded to the old loyalties.

The town's namesake stood at the north side of the piazza, a humble and kindly sculpture devoid of meaning, conjured from a handful of half-remembered myths. Dino noted she appeared to be holding a misshapen loaf of bread in the crook of her arm. Closer inspection revealed it to be an infant in swaddling clothes. Clearly the sculptor had enjoyed the challenge of the new saint far more that the representation of her fictional progeny.

'Thinking of praying to Santa Maria, Dino?' said Massimo, smiling.

She'd been created to soothe the anxieties of a population wanting to forget the dark centuries of the king.

'I thought people prayed to her when they wanted a child.'

'I heard she blesses the water in the wells,' added Virmyre.

'Some say she's the saint of lost children,' said Massimo. 'I doubt anyone really knows.'

Dino glanced at the statue again, a mystical placebo for all the spiritual ills of those beyond the castle walls.

'Perhaps she can absolve your captive killer,' said Virmyre in a tone confirming he believed anything but. 'Make him see the error of his ways?'

'I'd rather not have the little *carogna* sharpening his blades on a farm somewhere waiting for another chance to kill Anea.' Dino sipped the wine. It was dreadful and he was glad to be nearly finished. 'I'd rather see him dead. It's simpler.'

'Taking a man's life in combat is one thing, executing him is quite another,' remonstrated Virmyre. 'Lucien wouldn't approve of such a vulgar display of authority.'

Dino plucked at his lip. 'I'll never understand why he needed to found his house on the other side of the island.'

'I think it's perfectly understandable considering everything that happened,' said Virmyre, flashing an accusing gaze up at the old stones of Demesne. 'He never felt a part of the castle the same way you do, Dino.'

'I'm not sure if I feel a part of it; I just wanted to stay and protect Anea. That was my decision. I'd say I'd called it right, wouldn't you?'

Virmyre nodded at the truth of it. Massimo looked uneasy, the swordsman always preferring a conflict of blades to a conflict of words.

'Time for me to get back to my lord,' said Massimo, rising from the bench. Dino eyed him as he stood, wishing their time together had been happier.

'We'll walk you back to the gate,' the Orfano said, glad to be free of the vinegary wine. They stood, mouthing hollow platitudes at the innkeeper, who bade them come again.

'You might want to do something about the ants,' said Massimo with a friendly smile. He gestured beneath the bench, where dozens of shiny brown bodies milled around. The innkeeper looked embarrassed, assuring the swordsman he would take steps to stem the invasion of insects.

'I seem to find those things wherever I go,' complained Dino.

'Formicidae,' said Virmyre under his breath.

They set off through the narrow streets of the town. There were a good few dwellings mixed in among the shops, wooden shutters painted in vibrant blues, earthy reds and rich purples.

Women with heavy-lidded eyes looked down from windows. Occasionally a beckoning hand would emerge into the light. Massimo saluted with a wry smile on his lips.

'Not much work for them at this time of day,' said the swordsman. Dino shrugged and said nothing. He'd never understood the compulsion to spend money on whores, no matter how comely. He set his gaze at his boots and kept walking.

Paving stones had begun to appear at the edges of the roads. Soon there would be street lamps to turn back the night. The *cittadini* still told tales of horrors roaming the forests, an inheritance of the Verde Guerra, and stories of revenants and ghouls had returned to fashion. Lonely roads and cemeteries had captured the people's imaginations. Less fictitious were the accounts of the many abductions that besmirched the castle's past, although those fears at least were ended.

'Dino.' Massimo had edged closer, all but whispering in his ear. The Orfano dragged himself back from his bitter musing with a start. 'We are surrounded.'

Dino glanced around. There was a uniformed presence in Santa Maria that day. Not military garb but a unified attire all the same. The rags they wore were an ash-grey hue, faces concealed by hoods. Perhaps the tatters had been robes once, but there was little fine about them now. The hands that emerged from ragged sleeves were bound in grimy bandages. None of the loiterers looked whole in body. It was clear the *cittadini* of Santa Maria made them for beggars, giving them a wide berth.

Times are hard even here, thought Dino, but not as hard as they are out in the fields.

'Have you ever seen them before?' asked Massimo in a quiet voice.

'No. And none of our usual contacts have reported them either.'

Dino continued his surreptitious surveillance. Some of the grey men appeared hunched or twisted, yet all shared a poise he was all too familiar with. They were waiting. And what would come next would not be without blood.

Dino stepped close to Virmyre and took him by the elbow. 'Stay close,' he whispered, but the *professore* hadn't heard him.

He was staring at the wizened form of Angelicola, who struggled along the street with a large basket of food.

Dino blinked in astonishment. He'd not seen the bad-tempered *dottore* since the death of the king. House Erudito had made his expulsion a quiet affair. He'd slipped from memory as easily as he'd passed from the day-to-day running of Demesne. Always an unkempt-looking man, he had been sorely undone by the passage of years, iron-grey hair a ragged nest, cheeks sporting patchy stubble. His suit was beyond repair yet he still carried himself like a duke.

'I had no idea he was still alive,' whispered Virmyre.

'No time for the *dottore* now,' whispered Dino. 'We're in trouble.'

'What?'

'I fear Anea's enemies have singled you out. Be wary.'

The hooded figures made their move, as if cued by Dino's warning.

4

Death in Santa Maria

– 7 Giugno 325

Suddenly the street was transformed. A wordless panic rippled through the *cittadini*; uncertainty caused the hearts of every man, woman and child to skip a beat. Men and women looked aghast, realising they were unarmed. Rusted swords and pitted knives appeared in clenched fists, conjured from fetid sleeves. Someone cried out and the rush began.

A fleeing woman careened into Dino, not looking where she was heading, nearly knocking him from his feet. The Orfano stifled curses and drew his blade, his grey eyes flashing silver in the sunlight. Massimo drew his sword and stiletto and they closed up around the aged *professore*.

'Into the teeth of the wolf,' said Dino.

'And knock them out, every one,' replied Massimo.

The screaming began.

'All this for a glass of wine no better than piss and vinegar,' grunted Virmyre.

A figure in grey lunged across the street toward Dino but there was something wrong with the motion. More of a lurch than any considered movement, awkward and lacking the fluid assurance of a seasoned fighter. Dino met the charge with a strike of his own, slashing down at the man's knee with a force lent urgency by adrenaline.

His opponent blocked it. Almost.

A wooden club was smashed aside as Dino's blade bit deep into rags and flesh. The smell was overpowering, the cloying musk of an unwashed body, the acrid stench of urine. The attacker stumbled, momentum carrying him past Dino, who stepped in behind and neatly slashed across the back of his thigh. The man screamed for his severed hamstring, flopping down into the dirt. He proceeded to shriek and writhe as if on fire. Dino skewered him, feeling the tip of his blade catch on ribs before slipping through. The man coughed and trembled. Dino twisted the blade and tore it loose.

Massimo had also felled one of the grey men. He looked up from running his opponent through and locked eyes with Dino, a frown on his fine features.

'What in nine hells is happening here?' asked Dino.

'First Anea, now Virmyre,' replied the swordsman. But Virmyre remained untouched, shaken but unharmed.

'I don't think they even noticed me,' intoned the *professore*.

Two of the attackers were already departing through the crowd, hands full of plundered meat from the butcher. The last of them was wrestling with Angelicola, who gasped and sank to his knees, clutching his arm. There was a pitiful cast to his haggard features, part confusion, part fear.

Dino surged across the street, blade reflecting brightly in the sun, teeth bared, heart kicking loud and strong. Angelicola hinged forward from the waist, face down in the dirt. His attacker need no further encouragement, fleeing with the *dottore*'s basket hooked over one elbow. Dino followed, body bent low, sword parallel with the ground, eyes fixed on shoulder blades dressed in filthy rags. There was a dull roar in his ears, a bitter tang of adrenaline in the back of his throat that sang for blood like a dirge.

Suddenly the figure lifted off the ground as if plucked by an unseen hand, bounding up to an overhanging balcony. Dino snarled in frustration, turned the corner, taking the building's wooden stairs two at a time. *Cittadini* stared after pursuer and pursued, eyes glazed with shock, unsure of what they'd seen. Elsewhere in the town were occasional screams and shouts, becoming more distant with each passing second.

Angelicola's attacker had reached the end of an adjoining balcony when Dino caught up with him. A woman hanging out her washing had been knocked aside amid a scattering of garments. She looked up at Dino with unfocused eyes, nose a red ruin.

'Going somewhere?' Dino snarled, closing the gap with his prey. He fastened a hand on the basket, wrenching it back. The thief turned and lashed out with a knife, ripping through Dino's sleeve and the bandages beneath. Metal skittered from something hard, then snagged in the shorn material. There was a moment's confusion and then the basket fell apart, tumbling olives, vegetables and bread down into the street below. A clay pitcher of milk fell for long seconds only to shatter, a shock of white across the grey cobblestones. Angelicola's attacker slammed into the balcony rail and bounced back. Dino mashed the pommel of his sword into the grey man's face on instinct, hearing the wet snap of something beneath the hood. The momentum of the strike lifted the man over the rail, pitching him head first to the street below.

Dino gasped, watched the descent, heard the muffled thump. Silence.

The Orfano hopped over the rail and landed nimbly, rolling as the fall stung the balls of his feet. The chase was at an end. Dino looked down at the broken man, knife in one hand, remains of the destroyed basket in the other. The head, still obscured beneath a hood for the most part, rested at a cruel angle. A few urchins were already prowling close to the fallen food. Dino shivered as sweat cooled beneath his doublet. He forced his breathing to a slow crawl, calming himself. Something about the way the man had come to rest reminded Dino of a body he'd found many years ago. A body discovered at the base of a spiral staircase when he'd been just eleven years old. Demesne had not been kind to him during his eleventh year.

'Dino?'

He jerked back as if stung. Massimo stood by his side.

'Are you hurt? Your sleeve is—'

'No, I'm ...'

'You were just standing there, staring into space.'

'I was ...' The food had been neatly stolen, the urchins long gone. A crowd composed of respectful silence and hand-wringing anxiety had gathered without his noticing.

24

'He fell from the balcony ...' Dino gestured with one hand as if this might conjure further explanation. 'I didn't mean to ...'

'You've no need to justify yourself to me.' Massimo frowned. 'A death from a balcony is just as good as one from the blade. They were dangerous and they were armed.'

Dino composed himself. 'Is Virmyre ...?'

'He's fine.' Massimo grinned. 'It will take more than a few ragged paupers to give Virmyre pause.' The swordsman looked back up the street. 'The old *dottore* didn't make it. Seems his heart couldn't take the strain.'

Dino's gaze had returned to the crumpled man. Massimo sheathed his sword and took a step closer, dropping his voice.

'What's troubling you, Dino?'

'This wasn't assassination. This was starvation. They were after food.'

'I can believe that. None of them look much like assassins.'

Dino continued to gaze at his quarry, a broken tangle of limbs beneath the crude collection of rags. The bright sunlight spared no detail. Naked filthy feet, a hunch in his back, dull black nails on fingers that clutched a short rusted blade.

'Dull black fingernails. Just like—'

'Come on,' said Massimo gently. 'Let's get you and Virmyre back to Demesne. We can let the guards clean this up.'

'Clean *him* up, Mass. It's a person. A man like you or me.'

'Just not so well dressed.'

Dino curled his lip. 'He's a person, Mass.'

The Contadino swordsman studied him a moment, concern clouding his dark eyes.

'I'm sorry, Dino. I didn't mean anything by it.'

The Orfano's anger subdued, then withered altogether. Dino had always found it impossible to stay angry at the swordsman for long. He sheathed his sword, unable to meet Massimo's eye.

'Bad wine and starving peasants,' said Virmyre, leaning heavily on his stick. 'This is one hell of a town we're running.' He'd pushed his way through the crowd, dabbing at his brow with a kerchief.

'I'm sorry about the *dottore*,' said Massimo.

'Don't be,' replied Virmyre. 'He was dead the moment he

25

left Demesne. He was probably glad to have an end to it all. If the people knew what I know, he wouldn't have lasted ten days, let alone ten years.'

'I didn't realise he was still alive,' said Massimo quietly.

'Well, he's no loss to us then, is he?' said Dino.

Virmyre nodded and stalked off.

'Your sleeve, it looks bad,' said Massimo with obvious concern. Virmyre stopped, turned and flashed a glance at the fabric. Beneath the rip were the telltale cream bandages. Dino held his forearm up to his chest, covering it with his free hand.

'It's fine. My ... my deformity protected me from the blade. There might be a little damage but nothing that won't grow back.' Virmyre nodded to him, stern face more serious than usual. 'They always grow back.'

The walk through the town took too long, Virmyre's pace an idling stroll compared to Dino's urgent stride. The swordsman and the Orfano flashed looks over their shoulders, wariness in every step. Virmyre rattled off an articulate series of complaints about the town, the wine, the *cittadini*, the economy and the weather.

'You've never really told me what's wrong with your arms,' said Massimo as they approached the Contadino gatehouse. 'Even after all this time,' he pressed when Dino made no effort to provide an explanation.

'Surely you've heard the rumours,' said Dino, eyes fixed on the cobbles at his feet.

'Something about spikes or stings?'

Massimo missed the warning glance Virmyre spared him.

'Tines, we call them tines.' Dino was stifling hot, and it had very little to do with the midday sun.

'We don't have to speak of them if you—'

'It's fine. I just ... Golia had them too.'

They lapsed into silence. Dino could almost sense Massimo searching for something to say, anything to provide a change of subject.

'It seems my simple need for wine and sunshine has drawn attention.' The swordsman jutted his chin toward the gatehouse, where Lady Stephania Prospero waited with her retainers. Dino had seen the way men at court regarded her. Olive-skinned, she possessed an hourglass figure that set pulses racing. Never without a fan, her dark hair often piled atop her head, spilling ringlets framed her eyes. Her choice of attire was always in good taste, never gaudy or flamboyant.

'I cannot understand why a woman like that is going to waste,' said Massimo.

'Perhaps you should propose to her,' said Dino.

Massimo missed the dangerous edge to his tone. 'A lowly swordsman does not propose to the daughter of a major house.'

'And there is your answer, young masters.' Virmyre paused and wiped his brow for a moment. 'There are few who possess the correct standing to make such a proposal. And so Demesne's most exotic flower withers in the sun.'

'I know how she feels,' replied Dino. 'Can we get into cover before you die of old age?'

'Impatience is ever the folly of youth,' replied Virmyre. 'But yes. Onward.'

They walked the final stretch of road in silence, presenting themselves to the noblewoman with the requisite bows.

'I'm so glad you're safe,' she said with a smile. 'I came as soon as I heard. The messengers are spreading the word even as we speak. We all feared the worst.'

'We're fine,' replied the Orfano, 'I had Massimo to look after me,' making a lazy salute at his friend.

'I live to serve.' Massimo grinned. 'But we both know you could have protected the *professore* alone.'

They passed under the arch of the gatehouse and into the House Contadino courtyard, crowded with wagons. Chickens clucked and strutted, the sweet smell of straw and manure obscuring all others.

'It seems people have been trying to finish you your whole life,' said Massimo, 'and yet here you are. Dino the Untouchable.'

'Not quite,' replied Dino, gesturing to the ripped sleeve.

Stephania's eyes widened. 'Should I send for a *dottore*?'

Dino shook his head. 'I'll attend to to it myself, thank you.'

27

Stephania nodded, then turned and headed into the cool corridors of the house.

Massimo clapped a hand on Dino's shoulder as the Orfano gazed after her. 'What's on your mind?'

'There have been other days like this,' replied Dino, 'other ambushes.' Other times he'd felt ashamed of his difference.

5
Recollection
– Settembre 314

Dino had progressed no more than a dozen steps from his apartment when he heard the now-familiar scuff of feet. It was Stephania, of course, clutching her school books to her chest, attempting to run in a dignified fashion. Not easy given the increasingly elaborate gowns her mother insisted upon. Duchess Prospero had eyed Stephania, just seventeen, and made a challenge of her ripening figure to any man with a pulse. Dino, fast approaching twelve, couldn't see what all the fuss was about. Camelia assured him that in just a few short years he'd notice girls, and then he'd have difficulty noticing anything else. Boys of his own age made various comments that ran the gamut of inappropriate to crass; Dino remained none the wiser. That Stephania had become fascinated by an Orfano six years her junior was a constant source of annoyance to the young blades among the nobility. Dino, however, had not been fooled for a moment.

'I'm sorry I'm late.' Dark hair fell in a confusion of ringlets about her face. She wasn't of course. Dino had left early but omitted to mention this. He also failed to mention there were more direct routes to the classroom.

'It's wonderful you receive private lessons,' she said.

'Hmmm.' The syllable was non-committal at best. 'I was expelled.'

'Really?'

'There was a brawl. One boy's nose was broken, another suffered a fractured rib.'

'How is that your fault?'

'They were attacking me when it happened.' Dino shrugged. 'Cherubini decided my education might progress more smoothy if I don't have to best every other boy in the class.'

This was how Dino found himself being privately tutored and in turn being escorted by House Prospero's dark-eyed daughter.

Stephania's campaign had started innocently enough with random encounters in the halls of House Erudito. The young noblewoman always took time to greet him, and Dino was glad of the exchanges. Few if any in Demesne made an effort to put the Orfani at their ease. At best he could hope to be insulted a minimum of three times a day, although never to his face. *Strega* or witchling were the preferred terms of disparagement, but harsher terms were never far from the lips of his tormentors. Lucien had no better time of it, nor even Golia, who was not to be riled for sport. Only Anea seemed to escape the worst of the whispered unkindness. Many in Demesne believed she wielded arcane power and were loath to insult her lest she look on them with the evil eye. Stephania by contrast hadn't succumbed to the prejudice. And for good reason. Her mother intended her to marry an Orfano, which in turn had precipitated her interest in Dino.

What had begun with ever more frequent meetings after classes in House Erudito evolved to include a sudden interest in his fencing lessons at House Fontein. Next were unannounced visits to his apartment. He'd been baffled at first, then oddly complimented, before confusion combined with a dose of irritation. Finally he'd accepted his new companion, developing patience when questioned by Stephania on her favourite subject.

Lucien.

Where was he? How was he performing with weapons? Why did he have such awful pets?

'Does he spend an unseemly amount of time with Anea?'

Dino laughed until he was quite breathless, pausing in his haste to reach the classroom.

'No one spends "an unseemly amount of time with Anea".' Dino suppressed another round of laughter. 'She's almost a recluse, more enamoured with books than people. She tolerates Professore Russo. And me, I suppose, but only just.'

Stephania's questions regarding Lucien continued. She had the wit to bury them within innocent conversations, but sooner or later the topic always focused on Demesne's most wayward Orfano.

Lucien 'Sinistro' di Fontein.

Duchess Prospero had not concerned herself with anything as delicate as subterfuge. She intended Stephania, blood of her blood, to wed the most troublesome of boys her own age. Dino wondered what the duchess's true agenda was. Lucien rarely refused to spend time with Stephania, largely to keep the peace with the duchess, but neither did he seek her out. Now, so close to his his final testing at eighteen, Lucien had volunteered for additional lessons from Maestro di Spada Ruggeri, which took up a great deal of his time. The rest he spent with Professore Virmyre, whom Dino was journeying to see himself.

'Master Dino.' Virmyre had not commented on Lady Stephania Prospero's appearance. She'd no need to be there. The women of Landfall did not study the sciences. At least until Anea had come along. The silent Orfano had almost pulled House Erudito down, stone by stone, during one of her trademark rages. Maestro Cherubini wisely changed policy at that juncture. So now not just Orfano ladies, but all ladies, were allowed, if not encouraged, to study the intricacies of physics, biology and chemistry, should they so wish.

Virmyre's classroom was a dusty place of solid workbenches with a high ceiling that saw pupils freeze in the winters and boil in the summers. The wooden floor was unvarnished, threatening a host of splinters to any who tripped. Virmyre had built a backdrop of oak shelves that were monolithic in scale, home to minutiae and oddities beyond counting. Books in languages known only to a handful of scholars competed for space with broken timepieces and jars of specimens. The worst of these were organs rank with corruption, bloated in cloudy fluid, promising only noxious fumes should they be opened. And there was the urn full of ashes that none dare ask after. The centerpiece of the numberless curios was a cat shark which lay at rest in a tank of preservative. Virmyre was obsessed with sharks. He never failed to use them in some metaphor or other that only the truly eccentric can ever achieve with any aplomb. It was after one such lesson with Virmyre that Dino almost lost his life.

They had come for him in a rush; this was the first difference. Beatings were always presaged by posturing. It was the ritual of bullies everywhere, the mark of aggressors, even petty ones such as these. One did not simply do violence without verbal escalation.

'*Strega.*'

'Witchling.'

'*Figlio di puttana.*'

'What are you looking at?'

'You think you're better than us?'

Dino had learned it all by rote, knew the boys would only commit to the physical once the verbal assault had provided the vanguard. It made the attack that day all the more shocking. They approached from behind, catching the Orfano and the noblewoman in a stretch of seldom-used corridor. The attackers were older than him by a few years and spoke coarsely, jackets unbuttoned, shirts untucked. Their close-cropped hair indicated allegiance to Maestro Superiore di Spada Giancarlo, or simply that they aspired to the levels of thuggery he espoused. They drew closer until it was all Dino could do not to walk backwards so as to be able to keep watch on them. He didn't see the third of them until he'd been punched in the stomach. The boy had emerged from a side corridor, obviously having lain in wait for some time.

The strike knocked the air from the Orfano's lungs, and was accompanied by an unexpected sting. He staggered and reached for his blade. Reluctance to draw his weapon conflicted with numerical inferiority and his duty to protect Stephania. He got no further than closing his hand over the hilt. The trio ran off, not laughing or jeering, instead committed to fleeing the scene. Stephania shouted after them but Dino urged her to pay them no mind.

'I've suffered worse beatings.' A single punch to the stomach was no great hardship after all. Stephania pressed one hand to her mouth and fell silent, eyes widening. A dark stain of deepest red was spreading from a tear in his jacket.

'It was only a punch,' said Dino. A frantic moment to unbutton the garment revealed a white shirt soaked with blood. The sight of it staggered him, shock undoing his knees, ushering a cold sweat. The floor lurched toward him. A hand struck out for the wall, clawed for purchase on a side table, then darkness.

The rock and sway of walking. His legs motionless. Being carried. Dino forced his eyes open and saw ash-grey robes. There was a smell of dust. The arms that held him were like iron. And above the vast slab of a chin, weathered skin, the ragged hood concealing eyes.

'I ...' His throat was too dry for other words, mind stumbling.

'Hush now,' droned the Majordomo. 'Be still, rest.'

Dino did just that.

Dottore Angelicola's face greeted him, all too close, shaggy eyebrows fixed in a frown beneath a bird's nest of wiry grey hair. The man's breath was an affront; a light dusting of white clung to the shoulders of his threadbare suit. There was a litany of complaint and half-whispered grievances, silenced every so often by a sharp word from the Majordomo. A damp cloth tended to Dino's brow, provided by Stephania, her face taut with worry. Her immaculate gown was now smeared and unclean. The *dottore* mumbled something, reassuring him the wound was not fatal in anything but soothing tones. Somewhere in the confusion he'd lost his shirt, and in losing it had been exposed. The tines. He could feel her eyes on them in the scant moments she allowed herself to look. They began just after his wrist bones, tines of deep blue chitin that punctured the skin and angled back along the limb, pointing toward the elbow. There were thirteen of the tapering barbs on each forearm, some almost as thick as his smallest finger; all wept with a clear tasteless fluid that required him to bind them up before bed each night.

This was Dino's mark, his heritage as Orfano. His tear ducts were also affected, causing him to weep blood on the rare occasions he gave himself over to tears. Golia had the same tines, combined with great size and strength. Lucien lacked ears and his fingernails were a shiny midnight-blue; he also benefited from agility and a certain resilience. Dino hoped he might develop these same benefits in time. He'd certainly have use for resilience if today foretold his future. Only Anea's marks remained hidden. That she was never seen without gloves made Dino suspect she had the same blue-black fingernails as Lucien. Few if any knew the nature of the deformity she hid beneath the veil, and none spoke of it. When people did pass comment they discussed her great intellect.

The Orfani, twisted children of Demesne, strangelings of Landfall.

How Dino hated those tines. How many hours had he spent binding them? How many shirts had snagged and torn on their points? They grew longer with each year: soon he'd need to bind them during the day, or else walk about with sleeves rolled back to his elbows, his disfigurement plain to see.

There was a fiery pinprick of pain as the *dottore* began to sew the wound.

'Take this.' Stephania proffered a thimble of brandy, which burned all the way down his parched throat. Dino lost track of how long he lay there, the ill-tempered *dottore* working at his gut, the pull of thread closing up the slender wound. Lost count of the times Angelicola told him how fortunate he was the blade had missed his entrails. Lying there with the full extent of his otherness revealed, Dino felt anything but, only a deep and excruciating shame. A shame that would in time harden to a cruel hatred of House Fontein. He felt the corners of his vision grow red with blood. He would not cry.

The only thing worse than tines were tears.

6

To Speak Ill of the Dead

— 13 Giugno 325

'Don't you think it's hypocritical?' Dino was unpleasantly warm as he plucked at the collar of his formal attire. So much black on such a humid day. The dark interior of the carriage was stifling. 'No one spared him a thought until he died, now this clamour to attend his funeral. It's horse shit.' A pothole in the road caused him to rock forward on his seat.

Anea stared at him, jade eyes immaculate amid the fine lines of kohl. The Silent Queen looked especially imposing behind the black veil she wore.

'And I suppose we're paying for the bastard's casket?'

Anea's hands flickered, the movements short and sharp. *Virmyre is paying for the funeral, if you must know.*

'Why does Virmyre care where the old bastard is buried?'

He said something about closure. He and Angelicola have history.

'What history?'

He declined to elaborate. Perhaps you should ask him?

She picked up her fan and pulled back the curtain to look through the carriage window. Dino clenched his fists, then stretched his fingers with frustration. Demesne was riddled with secrets. Legions of pretty deceptions and unwholesome inventions, all huddling together and breeding more of the same. He wondered if they inhabited the deep places below the castle, threatening to erode the foundations.

The day had started brightly enough but sombre clouds had drifted in from the east. There had been a storm in the small hours, haranguing the grey sea.

'Did the thunder wake you last night?'

Everything wakes me.

'Did you get any sleep at all?'

A little.

Dino found himself hoping for rain, anything to leach the humidity from the sultry air. The carriage slowed and drew to a halt. The driver tapped on the roof. Dino opened the door and jumped to the road, looking around with a hand on the hilt of his blade. Anea stepped down, taking his free hand as she did so.

'Angelicola was always a complete bastard to us,' said Dino, voice subdued, 'Lucien particularly.' His anger had departed, leaving him maudlin. She caught his eye then pulled him close, the embrace all too brief. They were seldom given the chance to be siblings; the isolation of being Orfani weighed on them keenly.

I promise we will head to San Marino when things are more stable.

'There's no guarantee I'll come back if we go.'

The same thought had occurred to me. Her jade eyes twinkled with amusement.

Another two carriages stood empty at the side of the road, horses bored and restless, tails switching at flies. The coachmen idled, smoking moondrake leaf from pipes. One of their number spotted Anea, prompting them to remove their three-cornered hats. Deeps bows were made across the dusty road. Dino nodded back to them, noting the wariness in their eyes.

They do not trust me, signed Anea. *Even after everything I have done, I am still the* strega *princess.*

'Don't let it concern you, they're Fontein men.'

I will have to win them over one day if I am going to survive.

'We could always bring back hanging.'

Anea rolled her eyes and her shoulders shook with a giggle.

Time to bury Angelicola, she signed, then resumed a poise of rigid formality, green eyes alert, bronze headdress creating a halo above her corn-blond hair. Dino presented a hand and she rested her own atop it, looking straight ahead, confidence emanating like a nimbus. Her gaze was set on the black iron gates of the cemetery, yellowing bindweed clinging to the metal.

36

The hinges had long since rusted, the portal yawning open, death's invitation to the living. Anea's black silk fan beat a steady rhythm as they walked. Numerous gravestones awaited them inside, each a monument to one who had served Demesne – and had the coin to pay House Prospero stonecutters.

'What do *cittadini* do if they cannot afford headstones?' asked Dino solemnly.

Wooden markers. But not here; these plots come at a premium.

The lesser houses opted for delicately pointed slabs or morose angels sporting pious wintry gazes. The great houses had mausoleums in which to inter their dead, as befitted the nobility. Those who had stood against Anea were buried at sea, an edict she had passed soon after taking the throne. Dino found himself admiring the elegant simplicity of her thinking. There would be no shrines for assassins.

'I didn't expect so many mourners for an outcast *dottore*.'

Many of these people owe Angelicola their health. Some were even delivered by him.

'There's a terrifying thought. Imagine if Angelicola was the first person you'd seen as you came into the world.'

Anea began to sign, thought better of it and stopped. The Orfani walked on.

The mourners were by the graveside on the far side, in positions appropriate to their station. All waited for the Silent Queen's arrival, a hushed reverence upon each of them. Only Lady Stephania had lingered at the the centre of the cemetery to greet Anea, a retainer at each elbow. Stephania wore a gown of lavender silk with black lace detailing, the colours declaring her for House Prospero. A matching fan occupied her hand, poor insurance against the heat. Her hair was concealed beneath black gauze, suitably solemn for the occasion.

'My Lady Diaspora.' She bobbed a curtsey to Anea, her maid did the same. She'd taken on a personal messenger of late, an unsmiling man who sketched a deep bow.

'Lord Erudito,' said Stephania, another curtsey. Dino forced himself not to roll his eyes, the veneer of titles and dusty ceremony made his teeth ache.

'My lady,' he nodded, 'Are you well, Stephania?'

She favoured him with a smile from behind her fan. 'Yes, my lord. Better than Angelicola at least.'

Dino smiled. Perhaps Stephania wasn't so dusty after all.

The two women and Dino conversed as they approached the grave. Lady Stephania had taken pains to master the silent language the moment Anea and Dino had finished devising it. Booted feet crunched in the white gravel, the grass neatly trimmed on each side of the path. The oak and willow of the woodland behind the cemetery whispered and swayed while the sun maintained its golden vigil amid the clouds.

'It's strange to think he's been living outside the castle walls this whole time. I'd not seen him since ...' Stephania trailed off, unsure how to finish.

'Since he nearly lost his mind keeping the king's unholy secret,' said Dino. Anea glared at him.

Virmyre stood with Russo, the Domina. Ten years ago they'd been the bright stars of the House Erudito. Now they were the right and left hand of the Silent Queen. Russo was dressed in deep scarlet, shunning the drab grey of the old Majordomo along with his title. She'd retained the staff associated with the office; hers was silver and unadorned. She was a striking woman, long-limbed and auburn-haired, lips painted a sombre purple.

She looks especially sad today.

Stephania nodded

'It's been a long time since I've seen her smile,' said Dino.

Duchess Prospero, Stephania's mother, fanned herself under a parasol, attended by her consort Guido, the *capo de custodia*. The *capo* had been in thrall to her mother for over a decade despite being a similar age to Stephania. It was widely agreed he was the most attractive and vapid man in Demesne. The *capo* smiled without humour, favouring Dino with an insincere salute. The Orfano stared back, returning neither. The duchess caught the men's exchange and murmured to her consort, breaking the spell.

Do not let the idiot rile you, signed Anea.

'I like being riled.'

Fine, but not today.

38

Dino smiled, spotting Maestro Cherubini in the crowd. A heavy man, he dabbed at his brow with a purple kerchief, his teaching robes a burden in the heat. Cherubini nodded to Dino, a smile playing about his bow lips. Dino had grown up in the safe keeping of House Erudito, retaining the name even now. A childless bachelor, the *maestro* had always looked upon Dino as a favourite nephew.

Sombre *professori* lurked behind the *maestro*, raven-like in black robes. Irritation and eccentricity spilled over into a rumble of complaint. There were new faces among the scholars that Dino didn't recognise, something he'd need to remedy. Not that there was much chance of corruption or betrayal among the faculty; Anea was feted for her cerebral nature and for her fondness for education at all levels of society.

Duke and Duchess Fontein were conspicuous by their absence. Petty breaches of etiquette were the favoured mode of protest of late, but to miss a funeral marked a new level of impertinence. They had sent their maid, Isabella, in their stead. The woman waited alone, face dour, clinging to her shawl despite the heat. The *maestri di spada* arrived, attending at Dino's insistence. They were tardy but had the good grace to look apologetic about it.

'Better late than never,' said Dino quietly.

Ruggeri and D'arzenta exchanged a look. 'Some of us have to teach,' said D'arzenta.

'I'd give my wolf's teeth to get back to teaching, I can assure you,' replied Dino with a frown. Ruggeri pursed his lips and said nothing.

'Surely there are others who can guard your sister?' pressed D'arzenta.

Anea's eyes narrowed.

'You mean the Lady Diaspora,' said Dino, stepping closer.

'I think what my colleague means,' said Ruggeri, standing between the two men, 'is that you are often engaged as a bodyguard these days. Perhaps it would be for the best to appoint a new *superiore*, one who could give the position, and the students, the full attention they deserve.'

Anea took Dino by the arm and signed. *Tell him I will consider it. We do not have time for this now.*

Dino passed her words on and they continued on their way, leaving the *maestri di spada* to stand with Isabella.

'D'arzenta is in a particularly poor humour today,' said Stephania.

'He was as dutiful as any,' said Dino, 'but he's never forgiven me for being appointed *superiore*. He'd decided he was next in line.'

'Succession rarely works out the way we hope,' replied Stephania, glancing at her mother.

House Contadino had arrived en masse. *Margravio* and *Marchesa* Contadino were attended closely by Massimo, who glowered at anyone stepping too close. His hand rested none-too-subtly on the hilt of his blade. Word of the attempted assassination had left a sour taste in the mouths of the mourners, the tension shared by all a hangover from the violence. Despite this, the Contadinos' children were in attendance, Luc and Isabella, transparently bored and unimpressed – understandable given they were too young to have met the old *dottore*. Luc Contadino was just eleven but already the image of his father, minus the beard and scar. Isabella on the other hand had features from both her parents. A sparrow of just nine summers, she was spare of frame in the same way as her mother. Their cook, Camelia, stood at the back of the party. She gave a tiny nod to Dino and a tight smile. Her eyes shifted back to Virmyre.

Russo began the ceremony, which was mercifully short. The people of Landfall lacked much in the way of religion; the king had seen to that in a ruthless purge that had seen piles of books lost to conflagrations. The nobles were wedded to stoicism and spiritually apathetic since the purge, Angelicola included. The nascent cult of Santa Maria was the domain of the *cittadini* for the most part.

'Who's reading the eulogy?' whispered Dino.

Anea shook her head.

The rites for the dead had been prescribed by the king, who had insisted on a panoply of funerary statuary: headstones and urns for the majority, angels for those who could afford them, crypts and sarcophagi for the very rich. No one alive knew the significance of these symbols, which were as ageless as they were meaningless, any religion the people adhered to a relic of the past. The disciples of Santa Maria searched for texts that had not fallen prey to the king's attentions, archeologists of creed, cobbling together their faith from scattered remnants.

'You look tired,' whispered Stephania.

'I feel tired.' Dino smiled.

'How is your arm?'

Dino looked down at the point where the dagger had slashed his jacket only to be turned aside by his tines. He swallowed and frowned.

'It's fine. One snapped off. It'll grow back. They always do.'

Russo grated out hollow platitudes while Virmyre remained silent. No one had much to say: few had paid Angelicola mind, outcast this long tumultuous decade. Duchess Prospero manufactured some tears but genuine sorrow from the mourners was in short supply. Anea placed a lily on the coffin lid and bowed her head in respect. The undertakers lowered the casket into the ground by means of thick ropes dyed black. The sad spectacle concluded almost the minute it commenced. Dino watched the crowd.

'Now comes the difficult part,' whispered Stephania.

'How so?'

'There's always someone wanting to make themselves the centre of attention on a day like this.'

'I hope not,' replied the Orfano, little knowing he'd find himself at the very centre of that attention, willing or not.

7

Strange Weather

– 13 Giugno 325

'It's a pity we don't have a few more like him in the castle these days,' complained Duchess Prospero just loud enough to turn heads. Anea was still paying her respects at the graveside. The duchess's words roused her like the sound of clashing steel. Dino saw her flinch then straighten her spine.

'He spoke a deal of sense and knew that real leadership comes from …' The duchess trailed off as Anea turned, favouring the woman with a look that could wither grass.

'Not now, Duchess,' said Russo frowning.

'I merely meant to say—'

'Not now, Duchess.' Russo stepped closer to the woman, imposing scarlet robes and silver staff silencing the outspoken noble.

Anea had brought two lilies to the cemetery. One remained, cradled in her clever fingers. The crowd parted as the Silent Queen stalked forward, the eyes above the veil offering sufficient warning to any potential obstacle. Dino followed, wondering at Anea's next move. The mourners watched her passage through the cemetery to the mausoleums at the rear.

'You're full of surprises,' muttered Dino.

Just a small act of kindness and remembrance.

'Or a ploy to keep Stephania allied with us and at odds with her mother.'

That is one feud that requires little reinforcement. I simply wish to remind the people what a cheating puttana *Salvaza is.*

The Prospero mausoleum was a short walk, baroque and ridiculous in a halo of light spilling down from a gap in the sodden clouds. Anea entered the dark confines of the mausoleum and paid her respects to the duke. Dino lingered at the doorway, remembering the duke as a terrible bore but three times more tolerable than most of the nobles. Anea laid the lily on the stone sarcophagus.

'Do you really think he slipped and fell down all those stairs?'

That truth died with him, unless someone feels compelled to confess to murder.

'And you don't think Salvaza—'

No, I do not. She may be many things but a murderer is not one of them.

'That's why she has the *capo*.'

We have been over this before. You know if I had a scrap of proof I would bring his killer to justice. Anea stopped signing and gestured to Dino to look over his shoulder. Stephania waited outside at a polite distance. Dino waved her over.

'How I miss him,' she said with a twist of her lips that lent weight to the understatement.

I'm going back to Demesne with Russo and Virmyre. Anea glanced out through the door and then at Dino, clearly distracted. *The rest of the day is yours. The coming week will be difficult with the conclusion of the Allattamento business.*

And with that she was gone. The mourners parted around the Silent Queen, heads bowed until she had left the cemetery. She climbed into a carriage with Virmyre, keen to be at work. Dino plucked at his lip. Those damned machines and their secrets.

'She's all work lately.' Stephania was watching the carriage depart along the road toward Demesne.

'I worry her ambitions aren't aligned with her function,' admitted Dino. 'Lucien wanted to discover the south-east coast of Landfall.'

'But Anea desires scientific discoveries when she should be leading.'

Dino nodded.

'I must return. I've matters to attend to.' Stephania forced a smile. 'Take care of yourself, Dino.' She stepped forward and rested a hand on his shoulder, brushing his cheek with her lips.

43

He watched her leave, surprised by such an informal display in public. She mounted the steps of her carriage and then she too was gone.

Dino sighed and let the day's tensions drain out of him. The interior of the mausoleum was a cool balm. He regarded the single pale lily resting on the duke's sarcophagus. Other dukes and duchesses were also laid here, but Duke Stephano lay alone. Just as he'd been the night Dino had found him.

'You'd barely recognise the place now, my lord,' said Dino addressing the sarcophagus. 'Anea has converted the King's Keep into her court, the Ravenscourt she calls it. She still has the same quarters in House Contadino. I think they remind her of her childhood, you know?'

He traced fingers along cool stone.

'The *sanatorio* was made into a school by Lucien for a while. The lower floors are a library where the *cittadini* can read. For free. Anea's idea, of course. You'd never believe how many books the old king had. Anea has her laboratory on the upper floors, packed full of those awful machines.'

He unfastened his sword belt, squatting down and laying the scabbard across his thighs.

'Your daughter's all grown up, but in truth I think she's as lost and lonely as the rest of us.'

He rubbed a speck of dirt from the crosspiece of the sword with a thumb.

'She does you proud, my lord. She's her own woman, knows her own mind. A touch formal perhaps, but, ah, what do I know of women?'

'A good question.' It was the *capo*, appearing like smoke at the doorway. The Orfano made no hurry to rise to his feet, piercing the man with a look. He made no attempt to reattach his sword belt but one hand curled around the hilt of worn leather.

'Did you want something particular, or did Duchess Prospero send a message?'

The *capo* clenched his jaw, nostrils flaring. As her consort he had no real standing at court, the duchess's refusal to marry him keeping him politically impotent. He was an ornament at best.

44

As *capo de custodia* he might have once had some power, commanding the men of House Fontein. Now he was required to answer to the Domina and to Dino, another of Anea's changes to Demesne.

'I bring no message, but you should be warned: there will be friction if Anea maintains her course.'

'Which course would that be?' Dino enjoyed watching the *capo* grasp for words.

'Her desire to neuter the *nobili*.'

'Neuter? You walk into this mausoleum and talk about neutering while he lies there?' He indicated the dead duke.

The *capo* ignored him.

'I should neuter you for fucking other people's wives.' Dino felt the anger come to him quick and easy. A few inches of steel had eased out of the scabbard.

'What do you know of passion?' replied the *capo*, trying for defiant, managing a limp petulance.

Dino had no answer for him, distracted by an unbidden thought of Massimo.

'Tell your sister there have been changes enough to our way of life. The nobles have worked tirelessly to support her, and yet she undermines them at every turn with her desire for a republic.'

'Tirelessly? You pompous—'

'Tell her, Lord Erudito. It's in everyone's best interests.'

'And what if I don't pass on your warning?' Dino imagined how good it would feel to break that perfect nose. He'd pay the price in bruised knuckles willingly.

'Then other messengers will come.'

'Like the *messengers* last week, I take it,' spat Dino, eyes hard as flint.

'That's not for me to say.' The *capo* broke eye contact, aware he'd said too much.

'You send them. Send your second sons and your dispossessed. Send your morons and your fanatics. I'll be waiting, you pathetic motherfucker.'

The *capo* went for his blade.

Dino struck him in the face, the crosspiece of his undrawn

sword smashing into the perfect lips of Demesne's most hand-some man. The *capo* stumbled out into the graveyard, holding one hand up to his mouth. Those mourners who'd lingered by the graveside looked up, curiosity making them bold. A few gasped when they saw the *capo*'s bloody fingers. More gasps and a call of alarm as Dino emerged from the mausoleum, grey eyes flashing silver with hatred, blade drawn, jacket unbuttoned.

'This won't take long,' he whispered.

The *capo* drew his own blade and jutted his chin defiantly.

'You arrogant Orfano swine,' he sneered and lunged. Dino stepped into the swing, parrying the blade and catching the *capo* in the face with a hasty elbow. Guido stumbled, swore, lashed out. Dino stepped beyond range and flicked his fingers from beneath his chin.

'First blood to me.'

'Your funeral next, I think,' said the *capo* with a bloody grimace.

'Why don't we stop talking and find out?'

Dino prepared an attack he hoped would disarm the mewling *capo*, but instead felt something lodge in his eye. Guido spotted the hesitation, stepping in to press his advantage, but something alighted on his face. He swept a hand across his cheek, then blinked and flinched back.

Dino felt more soft impacts on his skin, something crawling at the corner of his mouth. The mourners, who had been engrossed in the fight, now swatted and batted the air. Dino looked up and saw the sky was speckled with black, swarms of bodies adrift on the afternoon wind, emitting a drone that made his blood run cold.

'Get them off me!' shouted the *capo*, wiping his face and running fingers through his hair, dislodging a score of winged insects. Dino stared at the sky, trying to understand the rain of black bodies. He withdrew to the mausoleum as mindless panic enfolded the graveyard.

A few screams. People dashing to the mausoleums for shelter. Someone lost their footing, almost tumbling headlong into Angelicola's open grave.

'They're in my mouth!' someone shouted. Dino ran a hand across his face on instinct and was glad he did.

'What in nine hells is this?' he whispered. Tiny black bodies writhed in the palm of his hand.

The *capo* fled, sprinting across the graveyard before clambering into a carriage with a handful of his retainers. Dino could hear him yelling at the coach driver over the hum of winged bodies swarming the cemetery. The carriage started, stopped, then careened away, the horses confused and skittish.

The swarm moved on, heading toward the town and the looming stone of Demesne itself. Dino surveyed the graveyard wordlessly, feeling as if he were in a dream. The remaining mourners had fled to the cover of the trees. Gravestones were upholstered in black bodies which crawled or took to wing at intervals.

'No good will come of this.'

Dino turned and found himself face to face with a young woman, eyes bright above a cream veil. One eye shone icy blue, the other glinting green. The simple shift had matched the veil once but was muddy from the road, the fabric stained brown to the calves, the ragged hem almost black. Lank hair lay plastered to her scalp and an unwholesome vapour lingered. Dino had seen women like this before. Disciples of Santa Maria. Gutter prophets and *taverna* seers, telling fortunes for a few *denari*. He'd not seen her at the funeral or sneak into the mausoleum.

'Black rain.' She gestured to the skies, the roiling wings. 'No good will come of this.'

'It hardly needs saying. A swarm of locusts is never good.'

She knelt down to retrieve a squirming body, pinching it between forefinger and thumb without killing it.

'Not locusts, ants.' She held the creature before him and Dino saw the truth of her words.

'I didn't know they grew wings,' he admitted.

'They are attempting to create more colonies. They will grow in strength until we are overrun.'

'Overrun? They're only ants.'

'It's easy to dismiss something so small, but didn't they just stop you killing that man?'

47

'The *capo*? Yes, I suppose they did.' Dino brushed a few lingering bodies from his hair and shook his head. 'This is disgusting.'

'Another symptom of a deeper sickness.' She crushed the ant between finger and thumb. 'Of Demesne's deeper sickness.'

Dino shuddered. Her fingernails were chewed down to the quick, the skin on the backs of her hands cracked and dry. There was a feverish cast to her features.

'This is a portent of things to come.'

'What do you mean?'

'Difficult to say. We all interpret signs differently. What do you see?'

'I see a woman in need of a bath with a squashed insect on her fingers.'

Dino backed out of the mausoleum, reattaching his sword before heading toward the cemetery gates and the road beyond.

'Portent,' he grated from clenched teeth. 'As if I need anything else to go wrong.'

8

Myrmica Rubra

– 15 Giugno 325 ·

Sleep was fitful, the thunder had seen to that. A violent clamour over the very rooftops of Demesne close enough to rattle the glass in the windowpanes. Lightning etched the landscape in luminous white, fading to black seconds later. The *cittadini* would face the day bad-tempered and longing for rest, those in the castle much the same. Dino sat in Anea's apartment counting the long hours until dawn, waiting to return to the warm forgetfulness of his own bed. No assassin had been so bold to attack during the day, and never in the morning.

Anea had retired early that night, leaving him with his own company. Books failed to interest him; exercise was a chore, his appetite a stranger. Achilles dozed on his shoulder, surrendered to the arms of sleep, leaving Dino jealous of the slumbering reptile. The candles in the room had burned down to stubs, leaving him with the darkness of his thoughts.

Tell your sister there have been changes enough to our way of life.

The *capo*'s words echoed in his memory, whispers between the thunder.

What do you know of passion?

Again, the image of Massimo came back to him – at practice, sipping wine, smiling in the sunshine.

The hours dragged on until the long-case clock in the hall tolled out five mournful chimes. It would be light soon. Anea's maid would arrive and begin the lengthy ceremony of running her bath, preparing the towels, arranging her clothes and brushing her hair. The Domina would present herself, briefing

Anea for the day ahead. It was a meticulous existence, every minute accounted for.

Dino did not envy her in the slightest. He woke with a start as Anea's bedroom door opened. His hand grasped the hilt of his sword on instinct.

Asleep on the job, are we? Amusement filled Anea's eyes, tousled hair falling to her shoulders. She crossed the room and placed a hand on each of his shoulders, pressing her forehead to his. She'd adopted the gesture in lieu of kissing him on each cheek, as was common among families in Landfall.

'What time is it?'

Anea shrugged and crossed the room to the table, now replaced. Dino watched her inspect the floor. The bloodstain was covered by a rug of startling cerulean.

'I've been your bodyguard for three years now.' Dino regarded the crosspiece of the sword. 'More than three years.'

She looked at him, head cocked one side.

'I dislike admitting it, but D'arzenta makes good a point. We need a new *superiore.*'

I will think of something, Anea signed. She looked around the room, as if some clue to their predicament might be concealed on a shelf. *I wish I could release you from these duties, but I can trust no one.*

'Being Orfano carries a high price.'

Exactly. Dreams of a republic more so.

'Speaking of trust. We need to create a core of soldiers that don't have old ties to House Fontein – new blood, people who understand loyalty and can't be bought. Perhaps in time we can employ new bodyguards?'

I agree. I do not enjoy asking you to stand watch over me night after night.

'I know. But what other choice is there?'

Is there no one else we can trust in the interim?

'Virmyre is too long in the tooth.'

Massimo?

Dino swallowed at the mention of the man's name. He cleared his throat. 'He'd be honoured, I'm sure, but it may cause some friction with Lord Contadino. He'd be reluctant to leave Medea and the children unguarded.'

I can ill afford to sour the Contadinos. Not in light of… She gestured to the floor, at the stain beneath the rug.

'What do you propose to do with the Allattamentos?'

Anea shrugged. *I spent all of yesterday thinking on it.* She sat on the edge of the table and her regal poise sagged. *What would you do?*

Dino flicked a finger twice against the scabbard in his lap. Anea shook her head.

I think an execution might send the wrong sort of message.

'You worry too much.' Dino grinned.

One of us should. She sighed, breath making her veil ripple. *I can hardly kill Lady Allattamento because she gave birth to a idiot son.*

'Two actually. Three if you count the one who cut ties with her.'

She must have known about the plot. I cannot believe Angelo put this scheme together by himself.

'He admitted as much. He said he brought news from the *nobili.* And I doubt he would have been able to lay his hands on enough money to pay off both guards.'

Only a great house could afford that sort of money.

'Or he had help from other minor houses.' Dino fell silent a moment and tugged at his lip. 'You need to send a message, a firm message, that even being associated with treason results in dire consequences.'

I had hoped to win people over with reason, not fear.

'That time is past. You should be furious with them, furious they could even conceive such a plan, let alone recruit agents to carry it out.'

Anger gets you so far…

'And then it gets you dead. I know. But you're likely to end up dead if you don't get angry.'

I think you are angry enough for both of us.

'True, but I'm not the one in charge.'

Dino rose from his chair and stretched, hiding a yawn behind a fist before unlocking the door. Anea crossed the room and drew him into an embrace.

'I'm not going to let anything happen to you, big sister, but you've got to start taking the fight to the enemy.'

She nodded and looked away, uncomfortable with the prospect. Dino opened the door and stepped into the corridor beyond. A guard stood on each side of the doorway, halberd in hand, maintaining a vigil over the lonely stretch of corridor. Achilles roused himself, lifting his blunt snout and inspecting the men with obsidian eyes, scaled tail swishing impatiently. It was cool in the corridor and the cataphract drake would fidget until he was somewhere more temperate. Dino nodded to the guards and they saluted in response, neither of them much older than he.

'Not long now,' he said, eyes straying to the long-case clock further down the corridor. The guards mumbled their agreement, forced cheerfulness and stoical duty.

'That was some bad business the other night, my lord.'

Dino nodded and fought the urge to drop a few coins into the man's hand, anything to quell the disquiet he felt, anything that might make the guard think twice before accepting a bribe from their enemies.

'It's bad business every week of late,' replied Dino.

'Aye. Assassins, ants, pests all over.'

Dino took his leave, thoughts of loyalty and possible betrayal dragging at every footstep. All men had a price and the guards of Demesne were no different. He chided himself for such thoughts and pressed on, back to his own apartment in House Erudito, lit sconces guiding his way. The castle was rousing itself. Bakers would be at their ovens, kitchen staff stumbling to their stations, bleary-eyed. The muted sounds of industry and preparation drifted along corridors, summoning all to wakefulness. Strange to be a part of Demesne and yet so separate from it. His nocturnal vigils removed him from so much of life in Demesne. Belonging to the nobility removed him from the people. Being Orfano removed him from everyone bar Anea and Lucien, far to the south. Achilles curled about his neck, seeking warmth.

'At least I'll always have you.' Dino smiled as the drake pushed his cold snout into the collar of his jacket.

Sleep did not come to him. The storm abated and still he could not surrender consciousness. The gale exhausted itself, leaving the land scoured fresh by the downpour, the grass verdant and lush in the morning light. Gentle hills rolled on the horizon, cypress trees standing to attention, clusters of them watching over Landfall, green sentinels. Clusters of birch and oak huddled together in the distance, clouds of green scudding over the landscape.

Dino endured a restless hour in bed before washing and changing. The bandages that concealed his tines had come loose and he set about rewrapping his forearms. Achilles formed a loop of scales at the foot of the bed. The drake looked affronted by the interruption to his rest.

'Count yourself fortunate you don't have to wrap your tines each day, my handsome friend.'

Achilles yawned, hissed and slid from the bed.

'Try and give someone a compliment ...'

Dino killed time with a shave, noting the haunted expression that stared back from the looking glass. Achilles clambered up one leg and took his perch on a bare shoulder.

'I hope she knows what she's doing,' Dino said as he towelled his face dry, but the reptile offered no reassurances, spoke no words of suggestion.

Dino dressed and placed Achilles in the sitting-room window so he could sun himself with a few dead crickets for company. The reptile would get round to eating them in his own good time. The idea of food had some appeal and Dino headed out, wondering if he looked as bad as he felt.

It was a long walk from his apartment in House Erudito to the House Contadino kitchens. A few scholars were stumbling toward their classes. They nodded to Dino as he passed, sparing him kind words and asking after Lady Diaspora. The Orfano reached the gatehouse joining Erudito to the Central Keep, the wide circular corridor linking the great houses. There were no windows here, the air thick with smoke from the braziers that burned at each gatehouse. The guards looked bored and unkempt, prompting Dino's thoughts to stray to Anea, attempting to calculate the cost of paying off a guard.

The Contadino courtyard was teaming with life and industry. Dino watched it for a moment before crossing to the kitchen porch. Nardo appeared from within, tucking his thumbs into his belt, and leaned against the door frame.

'Hell of a thing,' said the House Contadino messenger.

'Don't speak of hell around the *cittadini*, you know how superstitious they are. They'll be no end of trouble now that we have a plague of ants.'

Nardo was a good ten years older than Dino, dark in the way common to the peoples of the Diaspora. His horseman's boots were dull from the road, his starched white tabard muddy. He'd recently replaced his short sword and a new scarlet feather adorned his hat. Nardo always looked in need of shave, a deep shadow of stubble on his firm jaw.

'Huh. True enough.' The messenger pursed his lips. 'Still, hell of a thing. The *cittadini* didn't care for them too much.'

'What did they do?'

'Lit torches, drove them off with smoke. What did Anea make of it?'

Dino was long acquainted with Nardo's lack of formality, even when discussing Lady Diaspora. It was one of the reasons he liked the man so much.

'She said something about "meteorological conditions" and "geographical displacement" then something about "preventing inbreeding".'

'Pity she couldn't tell some of the houses about that last one a few generations ago.'

Dino cracked a smile and and shook with silent laughter. Nardo grinned, taking out his pipe and stuffing it with moondrake leaf, more commonly known as *luna*.

'I expect she'll discuss it with Virmyre and they'll come up with a theory. None of us will understand and we'll all be no better off than if nothing had happened in the first place.'

'Sounds like science,' agreed Nardo.

'Sounds like a waste of time.'

'It's happened before,' said the messenger. 'Long time ago.

When I was a boy. I don't remember there being so many though. Made all kinds of folk anxious. Not just the superstitious ones.'

'A gutter priestess told me it was a portent. No wonder people are so skittish with that kind of nonsense being peddled around.'

Nardo smiled again, then lit the pipe. 'Huh. Out of sorts today?'

Dino released a breath and massaged the back of his head and neck with one hand.

'There's too much going on. Anea doesn't know how to conclude the Allattamento business, then there's the mass theft at the market. Now ants are falling from the sky. *Figlio di puttanta*. What next? How much more of this can we take?'

Nardo had the sense to leave the question hanging between them. In time it dissipated like his pipe smoke. Sounds from the kitchen intensified as more workers arrived.

'And you?' said the messenger.

'Me?' Dino shrugged. 'I just want things to be simpler. I'd like to get back to teaching. Three years I've been a bodyguard. Three years not knowing if it's safe enough to leave her unguarded.'

'I'd say we've not reached that day yet.'

'That's an admirable talent for understatement you've got there, Nardo.'

'I learned it from you, my lord.' The messenger winked. Dino sniggered. 'I'd best be getting on,' said the messenger. 'Send for me if you need me, eh?' He clapped the younger man on the shoulder and departed, leaving the Orfano in the shade of the porch with his thoughts. It wasn't long before he sat on a barrel and felt his eyelids grow heavy.

9

Fictional Deities

– 15 *Giugno* 325

Dino woke to a tangle of voices, interrupting and contradicting each other, punctuated by the odd laugh. 'And then a girl fell into his grave.'

Dino smirked as the legend of Angelicola's funeral began to grow. He remained in the kitchen porch, shielded from the sun as it climbed into the sky.

'It was Mea di Leone,' added a second voice. 'I heard she had a heart attack. The shock, you see. Terrible it was. She was so young.'

'She was afraid of spiders.' The first voice again.

'But they were ants.' Another voice – deeper, male.

'Well, she didn't know that, did she?'

'Aye, terrible.'

'I heard it was a haunting. Duke Prospero getting his own back on that wicked wife of his.'

'Aye. Slut. And at her age. Makes you fear for your sons.' Dino stifled a smile and continued to listen.

'Duke Prospero summoned a plague of ants?'

'No!'

'I thought he was dead.'

'He is dead!'

'Still, I wouldn't say no to the *capo*, eh?'

'You wouldn't say no to anyone in a uniform.'

Raucous laughter. And so on.

The elaborations and retellings amused Dino at first. There was something that reduced the shocking arrival of the ant

56

swarms to the merely prosaic when overheard like this. But gradually he tired of it.

'Wouldn't be surprised if the duke rises from his tomb and comes back to the castle to cause some mischief.'

'I hear Little Luc was in the mausoleum, talking to himself.'

'Ah, shame.'

Little Luc was an appellation given to Dino by the staff. They'd chosen the name long before, when he'd emulated Lucien's long hair and choice of clothes. That the two Orfani looked similar also played its part. He'd not heard the name for some time, years perhaps.

'Wants to get himself a women that one. *Porca miseria*, if Lucien can manage it with no ears then Dino will have no trouble.'

'Aye, I reckon there's a few here that wouldn't mind a chance with Lord Erudito.'

'Perhaps he can get cosy with Lady Stephania.' A male voice. 'I hear she's in need of something beneath her skirt besides her own hand.'

More laughter.

Displeasure spiked through Dino like a stiletto, forcing the air from his lungs. He lurched upright and stalked into the kitchen, grey eyes flat, fists clenched.

'It may interest you to know,' he boomed, 'that Mea di Leone did not fall into Dottore Angelicola's grave.' The kitchen staff were abashed, avoiding eye contact with the Orfano. 'Nor did she suffer a heart attack.' He glared at them, feeling his frustrations finally given vent. 'Furthermore, there will be no haunting, from the duke or anyone else.' The pot washer had not looked up from his task. Dino ran him through with a gaze. 'And Lady Stephania's courtship, or lack of one, is no one's business but her own.'

The staff remembered themselves, managing nervous curtsies or stiff bows before pressing on with their chores. Dino had spent a lot of time in these kitchens as a child, being watched by Camelia when very small. The long table was the same, the cypress timber smoothed to a satin finish by countless tasks. Knives hung from hooks at the far end, dull glints of steel.

Produce sat in barrels; sacks were propped against the walls. The faint smell of flour and garlic was present on the air, soothing him. The heat, always welcome in winter, was stifling at this time of year.

Dino's eyes fell on Camelia and his anger fled him, replaced with a feeling of sheepishness. She approached, broad honest face unreadable. She was a tall woman, eclipsing Dino in height, close to fifty and showing no sign of slowing or stooping.

'Thank you so much for coming to the kitchens to discipline my staff, Lord Erudito. Is there something we can get you, or were you just passing through?'

Dino swallowed and looked at his boots. 'Camelia, I'm sorry. I shouldn't have ... It's just I was out on the porch and I heard, you know?'

'Will you take coffee then?' she said, breaking into a slow smile. It was like watching the sun come up.

He passed a hand over his face, pushing fingertips into the corners of his eyes. The staff were hard pressed not to stare as he talked with Camelia. None dared speak following his outburst, which made what he had to say seem so much louder.

'I only came down for a bite to eat and to help you make gnocchi.'

'It's been a while since you did that, or was that Lucien? I get confused.'

'Both of us, I think,' he said plucking at his lip.

'Well, there won't be much gnocchi made today: we're having a hard time keeping the stores free of ants.'

'Because of yesterday?'

'No, no. Every summer we have the same problem. And it's been getting worse. They come in from the courtyard. Some even come in from outside the castle. They're in everything.'

'And this year they've taken to wing.'

Camelia nodded. 'They've not done that for a while, since before you born, if I'm remembering rightly.'

'What do you normally do, with ants?'

'Most times we get pans of boiling water and pour it in the nest, but it doesn't seem to make any difference this year.' She shook her head. 'They're in the sugar, and the jam; they're all over the fruit. And they love breadcrumbs. The corners of the kitchens are filled with the brutes. And they're bigger this year, I'm sure of it.'

Dino declined the offer of coffee for some watered wine, settling on a stool at one side of the kitchen.

'You look terrible,' Camelia said, concern showing in her eyes. She stepped closer and brushed a stray a hair back from his face.

Dino smiled. 'I'm not a child any more,' he said, smoothing back his fringe.

'Sorry, my lord. Old habits die hard. So what's troubling you?'

'A great many things. I'd rather not speak of them here.'

'And you can't sleep?'

'No.' Dino shook his head. 'I was guarding Anea last night. When I got back to my room I couldn't settle.' His gaze came to rest on a woman in a white shift with a ragged hem. She wore an apron, but her attire put him in mind of the disciple at the cemetery.

'There was someone peculiar at the funeral.'

'Duchess Prospero?'

'More peculiar than that.' Dino grinned. 'She was in the cemetery when the ant swarms flew past. I think she was one of those disciples of Santa Maria. She was talking about portents and—'

He got no further. Camelia ushered him out into the courtyard, face serious.

'Why are we out here?' He'd spilt wine over his sleeve in the rush to leave the kitchen. It was already warm outside despite the previous night's storm; by midday it would be stifling. Camelia took his arm and began a stately but determined walk away from the kitchens.

'A good deal of the *cittadini* in there are enthralled with the church of Santa Maria. If they hear you talking disparagingly about one of the disciples, well ...' She snatched a glance over her shoulder at the kitchen doors. No one had followed them out.

59

'Santa Maria, really?' Dino rolled his eyes. 'I thought it was just popular with the *cittadini* on the rural estates.'

'Well, you're wrong.'

'But here? In Demesne?'

'It'd do you good to appreciate that the *cittadini* need something to hold on to. We don't have apartments and clothes and drakes and titles like you do.' *Cittadini*. Anea's gift to the people. They were no longer commoners, but citizens. Camelia never said 'common folk' or 'country folk'; after all, she was one of them.

'But all of that Santa Maria stuff is just a concoction,' whispered Dino. 'It's odd bits of myths found in the library welded to old stories and—'

'Exactly. Two different things joined together to make something better.'

'But it's all horse shit, Camelia.'

'Your sword.' She tapped the scabbard with an index finger. 'It's not made from one type of metal, is it?'

'Well no, but an iron core welded to a steel blade are hardly the same thing, you know?'

'*Porca miseria.*' She threw her hands up. 'I wish I'd had all the answers at twenty-three the way you so clearly do.'

'I'm twenty-two.'

She stopped walking and closed her eyes, pressing one hand to her forehead.

'Sometimes you're so much like Lucien it's as if he never left.'

'But Santa Maria is horse shit.'

'Look, *my lord*, there's plenty about the *cittadini* believing in Santa Maria that makes your life easier.' Dino opened his mouth to speak but Camelia silenced him, one index finger held up in warning. 'If you'd only just pipe down and see it.'

'I am an ear waiting to be filled with your wisdom.' He sketched a bow.

'You're not so big I can't give you a clip round the ear.'

'I'm sorry. You were saying?'

'You need to appreciate people are still confused about all the business with the king. For a long time he was like a god.'

'Camelia, he was not a god, He was a motherf—'

60

'Dino! I didn't say he was a god, I said he was *like* a god, at least in people's imaginations. He's gone now and people have started wondering what it all means, why we're here. All of those things.'

'So they've invented a new god. A female one.'

'You can't blame them.' Her voice was quiet. 'Not after the things the king did. The *cittadini* want to believe in something again, something nurturing.'

'I see your point.' Dino looked around at the staff in the courtyard. 'But that still doesn't excuse the fact this stuff's just made up.'

'Well, they've found references and added in some morality and symbolism. Now they're saving up to build a church.'

'I'd rather they were loyal to Anea than to some fictional deity.'

'They revere Anea just as much. Look at everything she's done for the *cittadini*: the library, better medicines, better prices for the farmers, shorter hours, no more disappearances. Some even whisper Anea is the herald of Santa Maria. An avatar or something.'

'That's insane,' he grunted. 'They'd say different if they'd seen her killing an assassin with her hairpin.'

'Perhaps. Did you know they sell veils in the market now? Some women even take vows of silence so they can be like her.'

'Anea isn't silent. She never stops talking; it's just that she uses her fingers to speak.'

'But they don't know that; they just hear about the Silent Queen behind the veil.'

'I'm still struggling to imagine Anea as a divine entity. What does that make me?'

'Too clever for your own good.' Camelia smiled. Their walk around the Contadino courtyard had almost led them full circle. Camelia's eyes strayed to the kitchen door.

'I should let you get back,' said Dino. 'I've caused enough disruption this morning.'

She turned to him, pushing his hair back from his face again, brushing lint from his shoulders. He felt very young at that moment, pining for times when life had been simpler.

'The thing is, Dino, most people just need something to believe in. Might be a god, might be Santa Maria, might be the goodness of people or the beauty of nature. People are likely to start causing trouble if they don't have anything to believe in. People are fallible, that's why they need something bigger.'

'I think I understand.' He now realised how long he'd been away from the kitchens and how much he'd missed Camelia.

'You're such a good boy, Dino,' she said, patting his cheek with calloused hand. That smile again, like the sun coming up. He wondered when he'd become so busy he'd not had time for this.

'What do you believe in, Camelia?'

'I believe it's way past your bedtime, young man. You can't stay up all night watching over Anea and not pay a price for it. Go and get some sleep.' She kissed him on the forehead and went inside. A good deal of shouting and some colourful language followed. Dino waited in the courtyard for a few moments feeling the sun on his face.

'The goodness of people, the beauty of nature,' he said to no one in particular before heeding Camelia's advice. He managed four hours of dreamless sleep before Nardo called for him, telling him to attend the Ravenscourt. The Allattamentos were about to discover the extent of Anea's displeasure.

10

Demesne Adjourned

– 15 Giugno 325

The Ravenscourt was at the heart of Demesne, a vast circular chamber with a domed and coffered roof. Windows allowed shafts of sunlight to stream in, stilettos of white piercing the dark. A viewing gallery framed three quarters of the circumference where *cittadini* could view the proceedings, another of Anea's ideas. Few *cittadini* attended; the gallery was the domain of merchants and untitled bravos clinging to ambitions of power. Doric columns supported the gallery, lending the chamber further vastness and solemnity.

Dino remained by the double doors, watching the assembly from the rear. Lady Araneae Oscuro Diaspora waited on the wide oak chair that served as her throne, a decidedly mundane affair on a broad dais at the far side of the chamber. She wore her usual turquoise gown. A headpiece of golden crêpe and lace sat atop her head like a fan, sweeping back from her brow. She'd retained the same black veil and gloves that she'd worn to the funeral, eschewing the crisp white she usually favoured. Few if any could miss the intent, gravitas painfully evident. Anea sat, chin raised, shoulders back, while the nobles on the floor whispered among themselves. Five banners hung from the wall behind her, one for each of the great houses, her own turquoise and gold banner at the centre.

The Domina slammed her staff against the dais floor three times. 'This session of the Ravenscourt is now in progress.'

Maestro Cherubini stepped forward, struggling to overcome the bulk of his gown and doublet, sweating freely in the heat.

'If I may,' said Cherubini. The Domina gave a curt nod. The

63

maestro swept his eyes across the room, addressing the many nobles: 'I would like to condemn the recent attack against Lady Diaspora. This stains our reputation as a democratic, intelligent people.'

'But we're not democratic,' whispered someone close to Dino, who glared toward the source, unable to determine the speaker in the crowd.

Cherubini hadn't noticed the heckle and continued:

'These actions serve no one. I appeal for unity among the *nobili* at this difficult time. Let us come together and resolve our differences amicably.'

The *maestro* bowed toward the dais and withdrew, taking up a position alongside Lady Stephania, who patted his forearm. She whispered something from behind her fan. The other nobles shifted in the heat, exchanging wary looks.

Lady Allattamento stood on the far left of the chamber, flanked by her daughters, fans thrumming like hummingbird wings, enjoying a sliver of shade provided by the gallery above. Lady Allattamento was a mature woman, spare of frame and feature, olive-skinned and well preserved. She had worn her hair down since her husband's death. It fell in oiled black ringlets about her high cheekbones. There was a good deal of gold about the woman – fingers, ears and neck – but her gowns were many seasons out of date. A self-satisfied smirk played about her lips that roused Dino's temper.

Anea used the pause in proceedings to tap on the heavy wood of the throne with her fan. The Domina turned to her and the room caught its breath. Anea stood, flicking open the fan before moving to the front of the dais. Russo took this as her cue to begin.

'Lady Araneae Oscuro Diaspora, ruler of Landfall, has come to a decision regarding the recent attempt on her life.' Anea's eyes drifted to Lady Allattamento and her entourage, but not before casting a glance toward Duke and Duchess Fontein. Few if any could have missed the insinuation.

'Please, my lady,' said Lady Allattamento in warm tones, forcing a smile, 'do not punish me for the actions of one wayward

64

son, now dead by the cruel consequence of his actions. I have already lost one son to tragedy and the other to estrangement.'

'It has been decided,' continued the Domina, 'that House Allattamento is to give up the three farms it owns as reparation to Lady Diaspora.'

Hissed intakes of breath around the Ravenscourt, a cry of dismay from near the back.

'These farms shall become the property of the families who work on them.'

The chamber filled with full-voiced disapproval, angry voices silenced by three shuddering booms of the Domina's staff on the dais.

'I will have order!'

The discord abated.

Lady Allattamento's younger daughter, Viola, chose this as her moment to faint. Dino watched the collapse with cynicism. More theatre to embellish the scandal. The viewers in the gallery were ecstatic with the performance. Laughter echoed from above.

'There is no proof Lady Allattamento colluded with her son,' shouted the *capo*.

Dino stepped forward, shouldering his way past a few minor dignitaries, taking up a position alongside Margravio Contadino. He felt the eyes of the chamber follow him. There were a few whispers, mainly from behind fans. The men stared with open disdain or vestiges of proud approval. Massimo nodded to him, looking handsome as ever, immaculate and alert.

'Perhaps the *capo* knows where Angelo Allattamento secured the funds to pay off the two guards?' Dino looked around to make sure he commanded the attention of everyone present. 'Guards who should have been outside my sister's door.'

'I know nothing of the sort,' said the *capo*.

'Lady Diaspora, please,' protested Lady Allattamento, 'I had no idea. Surely the loss of my son and the shame he has brought my house is reparation enough?'

Anea dropped the black fan, which hit the floor and lay like a struck raven. She stepped down from the dais, green eyes dangerous, skirts hissing across the flagstones in her wake. Lady

Allattamento shrank from her like a creature hunted. Anea's hands began to flicker.

'Your son told me he brought a message from the *nobili*,' translated Dino, 'a message to put an end to any dreams of a republic.'

Anea had drawn close to Lady Allattamento now, within arm's reach. Those nearby melted away, afraid they too would be feel the heat of Anea's wrath.

'You may retain your apartments in Demesne and the family estate,' continued Dino, watching Anea's fingers. 'I may be persuaded to return one of the farms to you should you come by any information regarding your son's fellow conspirators.'

'This is outrageous,' blurted the *capo*.

'Hold your tongue or I will remove it,' growled Dino.

The room settled into uncomfortable silence as the two men glowered at each other. Two porters struggled to carry Viola from the Ravenscourt with dignity. Anea retook her place on the dais and Virmyre appeared behind the throne, lurking over her right shoulder. Margravio Contadino coughed politely into his fist and stepped forward. The Domina favoured him with a curt nod while Anea took a moment to settle herself on her seat.

'My Lady Diaspora, I regret to inform you that we are seeing a rise in prices from the farms.'

'A spike in prices would be a more adequate summary,' drawled Duke Fontein. He was wearing leather armour despite the heat and bore an elaborate blade on his hip. Sashes of scarlet and black were tied on his sword arm. His hair and beard were entirely white, a contrast to his deep brown eyes.

Margravio Contadino stared back. The scar through his right eyebrow made the already severe-looking noble seem uncouth and dangerous.

'The high prices are due in part to the ant infestation. I'm sure everyone is aware that we are heading toward drought. Crops will become more expensive in the coming months.'

A murmur of disapproval, the shuffling of feet; some half-hearted retorts were lost in the noise.

'The reason food is so expensive is because the farmers

'themselves are dictating the prices,' said Duchess Prospero, fanning herself.

'I'd imagine your many servants eat better than their children do, my lady,' replied Margravio Contadino. His lips were drawn thin behind the strip goatee and moustache he wore.

'Well, if the farmers are not receiving the money then who is?' This from Duke Fontein again. It was a common scene at court: Prospero and Fontein shoulder to shoulder against any reforms, all too ready to complain when laws or economics went awry.

'I assure you, Lord Fontein, my house takes a very small percentage after the farmers have taken what is rightfully theirs and taxes have been paid,' said the *margravio*.

'I've never really understood how your house earns its keep,' replied Duke Fontein, eyes still intent on Margravio Contadino. 'I'm sure it would make for fascinating reading.' He crossed his arms and smiled without warmth.

'Perhaps you should cart your own turnips in future if you object to the fees,' said Dino.

A few giggles from one side of the room and the gallery above, a histrionic intake of breath from behind Duchess Fontein.

'Let us not forget the population has increased considerably of late,' added Cherubini, keen to provide facts. 'The cost of all food is at a premium.'

'Enough,' said Russo. 'Lady Diaspora wishes to make a further announcement.'

The nobles turned away from the dispute between Fontein and Contadino to Russo, who looked as curious as the rest as to what would come next

'*Nobili* of Demesne, leaders of houses great and minor, messengers, *professori*, artisans, merchants, it has not escaped my notice that there have been many changes in the last decade.' Murmured agreement, most of it bitter. Anea's hands continued to sign; the Domina continued to translate. 'And so I declare a period of consolidation. The Ravenscourt will adjourn for three months.'

Dino noted the genuine astonishment in the faces of everyone in the chamber, not least the Domina.

'During this time I shall be working closely with Professore Virmyre. As many of you know, we have made significant advances in the sciences recently, not least in the prevention of diseases, the delivery of our young and providing clean water.'

This was undeniable. Part of Demesne's recent population swell was due to secrets gleaned from the king's machines.

'Perhaps you can do something about the ants!' shouted someone from the gallery, prompting a round of laughter. Dino clenched his jaw.

'We will reconvene in three months' time,' continued the Domina, still translating, 'when I hope I can count on your support. It would be unfortunate if you continued your current course of internecine bickering.' A pause. 'To safeguard against any misunderstandings –' Anea dared to look directly at Duke Fontein, who stood taller and raised his chin defiantly '– I will be entrusting the Domina with the day-to-day affairs of the castle. You will give her your full and unflagging cooperation.'

Anea stepped down from the dais, cutting a route through the slack-jawed functionaries and courtiers. The nobles had the good grace to bow their heads as she passed. Virmyre followed, face inscrutable.

There was a minute of hushed incredulity in the Ravenscourt following Anea's exit. Russo looked pale on the dais, gaze unfocused, attempting to keep the frown from her face. Duke and Duchess Fontein wasted no time in retiring from the chamber, locked in animated discussion with Duchess Prospero. The *capo* trailed after them, apparently too stunned to speak. Maestro Cherubini imparted a few words to Russo before he too left. Stephania approached and curtsied to Dino.

'Did you have any ...'

'None at all.' Dino shrugged. 'An adjournment does make a certain amount of sense.'

'But now? And for three months?'

'There's nothing here that can't be done by Russo. I can't say I blame her. Not after the other night.'

Stephania nodded. 'No wonder she wants to lose herself in her work.'

'She always wants to lose herself in her work; Angelo Allattamento just provided the excuse.'

'Keep safe, my lord.'

'You don't have to call me lord.' Dino struggled not to roll his eyes.

'We are in the Ravenscourt: we should act accordingly.'

'I'm sorry. You're right.'

'Send word if you should need me.' Stephania curtsied and withdrew.

Gradually, in groups of threes and fours, the chamber emptied. Even the guards departed after a time, until only Russo and Dino remained, flanked on every side by thick white stone columns. The Ravenscourt darkened as the sun passed behind a cloud. Dino drifted toward the dais and retrieved the dropped fan.

'Judging by the look on your face, I'd guess Anea didn't tell you about the adjournment beforehand?' He opened the fan slowly, noting tiny prints of birds in dark silver. Ravens, of course.

Russo shook her head. 'Even after all this time she's still unpredictable.' Every syllable was weighted with anger barely held in check. 'Did you know?'

'Of course not. We briefly discussed recruiting new soldiers but ...' Dino folded the fan, sliding it into his sleeve.

'Ten years I've been working for her, Dino.' Russo's brow creased. 'Ten years I've been working *with* her. You'd think she'd keep me informed of something this important. Suddenly I have the whole of Landfall entrusted to me.'

'It's *because* she trusts you that she's turned Landfall over to you.'

'Really? Because I don't feel trusted.' Russo bowed her head as if humbled or shamed. 'She tells Virmyre everything. Some days I'm not even granted an audience, just messengers bringing me hurried scrawls.' Russo looked down, fingers squeezed tight around the silver staff, lips pressed into a thin line.

'She's obsessed with those machines,' said Dino softly. 'She always has been'.

'And now with the attempted assassination ...' said Russo, meeting his eyes for the first time.

'What are you going to do?'

She looked at him blankly, then cast her eyes across the chamber and up to the gallery. For a second he'd thought she'd calmed down.

'I'm going to make sure none of those bastards disturb her work. I already have an idea forming.'

'Is that so?' Dino forced a smile. 'Anything I can help with?' He looked up to the dome. The clouds had thickened, the room descending into a deeper darkness.

'No.' There was a faraway cast to her eye. 'But I have other uses for you. You're going to keep an eye and an ear on those self-serving pigs.' She indicated the doorway through which the nobles had departed. 'I want to know where they sleep and what they eat.' She stepped down from the dais, addressing the double doors: 'I want to know where their money goes and who they employ. I'll have copies of their accounts and access to their correspondence. They won't be able to bed their mistresses without me knowing. I'll make them regret plotting against Demesne. I'll make them regret being born.'

She turned to him, breathing hard, the silver staff in her hand looking less of a symbol of office than a weapon. There was a steely look to the Domina's eyes that Dino hadn't seen before. Tiredness had etched deep lines into the corners of her eyes and mouth. The hem of her red robe was frayed at the front, its sleeves worn.

'You're going to help me rid Demesne of treason and corruption, Dino.'

'That sounds like a good deal of work,' he replied, uncomfortable with the low monotone she spoke in, 'and more than I can do alone.'

'We have money, and everyone has their price. I'll stop any plots against me before they've even begun.'

'You mean Anea. You'll stop plots against Anea.'

She turned to him, took a breath and blinked a few times.

'Yes, that's what I said.' The Domina nodded once and swept from the room, robes flowing behind her. Dino retrieved the fan from his sleeve and opened it once more, regarding the silver ravens on the black silk.

'No, that's not what you said at all,' he whispered.

11

A Lesson Remembered

– 22 Giugno 325

'You're in bright spirits today,' said Stephania looking out across Landfall. They stood on an old balcony projecting from the outer wall of House Prospero. Dino followed her gaze to the gentle swell of golden fields. Far beyond were the thatched buildings of the Di Toro estate, tiny smudges of white and fawn in the distance. Dino cast a glance over the edge of the balcony, marvelling at the town beneath. In just ten short years Anea had conjured a halo of townhouses nurturing numerous shops and tradesmen around Demesne.

'It's an impressive view from up here,' he said.

'Strange to think the town didn't exist when we were children.'

'And it's not just change down there, either,' said Dino with a meaningful glance at the doors they'd passed through. Stephania had renovated the abandoned seventh floor of House Prospero a room at a time. She'd opened offices and created workshops for tailors and seamstresses, all free of her mother's influence. It was a house within a house, and she was proving just as adroit at business as her father had been.

'I'd guess it's not the view that's making you smile.'

'A week in one's own bed, at night, is nothing short of a miracle.' Dino cradled a cup of coffee in both hands, regarding the dark richness of it.

'They can only grow it on one estate, you know.'

'What?' said Dino, looking up. It was still early.

'Coffee. They can only grow it on the House Previdente

estate far to the south. The right mixture of climate and soil and skill, apparently.'

'They have the monopoly, then?'

'Yes, so make sure you finish it. It's much too expensive to waste.'

Dino sipped, enjoying the bitterness and the fresh morning air. 'Did you have a reason to send for me, or did you just want to show off your good taste?'

Stephania smiled. 'I do have *very* good taste, but I wanted to ask you a few things.'

'If I know I'll tell you.' He paused. 'Within reason.'

'How is the adjournment going?' She stepped closer.

'I don't know.' He shrugged. 'I've resumed my role as *superiore* for the last week. It's been bliss. No politics, no breaches of etiquette, no endless carping from Duchess Prospero.' He stopped and his eyes widened a fraction. 'Sorry, I forget sometimes that she's your mother, as strange as that sounds.'

Stephania smiled. 'She does carp. Long and loudly.'

'Why do you ask?'

'People are claiming the adjournment will ruin them if it continues.'

'Is it ruining you?'

'Me?' Stephania held her coffee to her mouth, savouring the smell rather than sipping it. 'Well, no. Not at all.'

'Because?'

'Because people always need clothes, and uniforms. Those are my main lines of business. Just because a few dozen nobles aren't apoplectic in the Ravenscourt doesn't mean life around Demesne stops.'

Dino smiled. 'So is it possible the people complaining about being ruined are ...'

'Carping like an old duchess.'

Dino sniggered and Stephania looked pleased with herself.

'But three months?' she said after a pause. 'Is that wise?'

'That's three months of stability without any laws changing, three months without Fontein buying up votes to overturn whatever displeases them.'

'You have to admit it's strange.'

'The king adjourned the court for over a hundred years; I don't think three months will hurt.' Dino drank the coffee, wondering just how much it cost. 'I think the adjournment will focus people's minds. We can get on with running Demesne rather than arguing about it. And I can get on with doing what I do best – teaching.'

'I thought you were best at fighting?' Stephania smiled.

'I have many talents. And I need to be on my way. It's bad form if the teacher arrives later than the students.'

'Perhaps you can teach me one day?'

'Perhaps, but your wits are sharper than any sword I've seen.' He flashed a grin. 'I dare say you can survive with those.'

'Flattery, my lord?'

'Flattery is insincere; I was paying you a compliment. Thanks for the coffee.' Dino bowed and headed from the balcony.

He hoped Massimo would be at practice, even if Lord Contadino could only spare him for an hour. 'Back again, my lord?' D'arzenta stood to one side of the training yard with the *capo*. Mornings were given to the novices, who were drilled en masse outside during the summer. Intermediate and advanced students were trained in smaller numbers during the afternoons in one of the many circular training chambers.

'Did you miss me, Maestro?' Dino tried for an insouciant smile, but in truth he was tiring of D'arzenta's barbs. They'd been easy to ignore at first but a week of them had worn at Dino's patience.

'We've not had the chance to miss you – you were here just yesterday.'

'And the day before, and the day before, and so on,' said Dino, shedding any pretence at friendliness. 'Lucien always spoke most highly of you, Maestro, yet I'm having trouble deciding why.'

'You've no right to speak to him that way,' said the *capo,* squaring up to the Orfano, puffing out his chest.

'And you've no right telling the *superiore* his business. I'll kindly ask you to leave my training yard, unless you've come for an early lesson?'

The *capo* drew five inches of steel before D'arzenta pressed a hand down on the man's forearm, stalling the motion. The *capo* looked affronted but turned his attention back to Dino.

'I've not forgotten the day of Angelicola's funeral,' he sneered.

'And I've not forgotten you threatening the life of my sister,' said Dino, taking a step closer. They were at a range to trade blows, only D'arzenta's presence prevented them. 'We call that treason, you know. Perhaps you'd like to excuse yourself to the library and look up the word's meaning.'

'I know full well the meaning—'

But the *capo* got no further. The doors to the training yard disgorged the students, a rabble of smartly dressed, arrogant, spoilt boys. A few girls formed a knot among them. Dino didn't take his eyes from the *capo*, his countenance wintry. A hush settled over the novices as Ruggeri followed the last of them into the yard.

'Shall we begin?' said Dino to D'arzenta, 'or would you prefer to stand in the shade, conspiring with your friend?'

The pupils looked from one teacher to the other, surprised at the *superiore*'s rebuke.

'I'll be back for that lesson soon.' The *capo* slunk from the training yard with a sour look.

'I'll look forward to it,' said Dino, flipping him a lazy salute.

It was just before noon as they prepared to dismiss the last class of novices when the question came. The boy was a thickset oaf from House Di Toro. He'd spent the greater part of the class wiping his nose on his sleeve or pushing the other boys around when he thought Dino's back was turned. He had heavy shoulders and a stoop that put Dino of mind of Golia.

'Who is the best swordsman in Demesne, Superiore?'

'We don't know for sure.' Dino glanced around to find D'arzenta within earshot. 'I'd say there are perhaps ten men who are equal to the *maestri*.'

'But you're the best; you're the *superiore*.'

'All have their strengths.' Dino glanced at D'arzenta again. 'All have their weaknesses, just as you novices do.'

'But who is the best?' persisted the boy.

'The best is whoever is left standing when steel is drawn in anger.' Dino approached the boy. 'Until that time everything else is just theory and practice.'

A bell chimed from a high tower of Fontein, ringing over and over. The boys and girls fell into rows, almost neat, waiting for their teachers to give the order. Dino nodded to Ruggeri and the pupils were dismissed, chattering and pushing toward the doors and the promise of food.

'I'd have thought you would claim to be the best swordsman, Superiore?' said D'arzenta. Dino couldn't miss the hint of challenge in his voice. 'Better than even the *capo*.'

'I suppose we'll never know –' Dino wiped his brow with a cloth '– until we draw our blades in anger, will we?'

D'arzenta nodded and exited the yard, stepping around Massimo, coming in from the opposite direction.

'You're late for class,' said Dino, mock stern.

The Contadino swordsman embraced him and laughed. 'Seems like D'arzenta is in need of a lesson more than most.' He had clearly caught the last of the exchange between the two men.

'Are you here to give it to him?'

'No.'

'Shame,' said Dino.

'I'm here under orders. I'm to escort you to House Contadino.'

'Is there trouble?' Dino's mouth went dry.

'Yes. It's serious.' Massimo grinned. 'There's a large quantity of lunch that needs consuming. Virmyre says you're just the man for the job.'

Dino sighed. 'Well, that does sound serious. Lead on then, faithful escort.'

It was too stifling to eat inside comfortably, yet the sun was strong enough to force people under cover. Nardo had pulled up some barrels, forming a crescent at one side of the Contadino courtyard. A spare wheel from a wagon had been pressed into service as a table, resting atop a larger barrel. The high walls provided shade.

'It's a touch rustic for my refined tastes,' intoned Virmyre, 'but I suppose I shall dine with you ruffians.'

'I think you'll find we're the very finest of ruffians,' replied Dino.

'The finest in all of Landfall.' Massimo smiled as he poured the wine.

'I think I'll promote myself,' said Dino.

'To what?' asked Virmyre, hands resting on his stick.

'High Scoundrel.'

'Huh. Sounds about right,' said Nardo, eliciting a few chuckles.

'Gentlemen,' said Virmyre, 'your health.' The men raised their wooden cups and took a sip. 'And to Dino. It's good to have you back among the living, not sequestered away each night and sleeping by day.'

'I'll happily drink to that.' Dino removed his jacket, shirt still damp with sweat from the morning's trials.

'The thing I don't understand,' said Massimo after the hungry men had eaten their fill, 'is that Anea is just as at risk in the old *sanatorio* as she was here in Demesne. Shouldn't you be guarding her?'

'Anea told me to go back to teaching.' Dino picked at the last olives. 'So that's what I did.'

Of the meats and cheeses there was nothing left; only breadcrumbs remained of the two loaves. The single bottle of wine had not stretched far between four men.

'The old *sanatorio* is rather chaotic on the upper levels,' explained Virmyre. 'Our Silent Queen has hidden herself in a maze. One she knows exceedingly well.'

'And there are guards at the entrance,' said Dino, 'at least until someone buys them.'

'Fonteins,' grunted Nardo.

Virmyre gestured to his sleeve and Dino shook his head, confused. The *professore* made the same gesture again and raised his eyebrows.

'Dino,' whispered Massimo. 'Your tines. One of them has pierced your shirt.'

Dino looked down and saw dark blue chitin poking through the fabric of his sleeve.

'*Figlio di puttana.*' He covered the tine with his spare hand and felt himself grow hot, unable to make eye contact with Massimo.

'Do you need help wrapping your arm?' offered the swordsman. Dino shook his head but said nothing.

'Careful not to hurt yourself,' warned Virmyre.

'It's not as if I can poison myself, is it?' Dino snapped. There was an uncomfortable second of silence. 'Sorry, Virmyre. Excuse me.'

Dino left the improvised table and his friends, cursing his Orfano heritage as he headed into the Contadino kitchens. It took a while to rewrap the hated tines in a quiet pantry, free from inquisitive glances. Dino's mood darkened as the afternoon dragged on with class after class of sword-wielding boys and girls. The students asked questions warily when they did so at all. The day's teaching ended and the Orfano began the winding walk through Demesne from House Fontein to Erudito, a nagging tension in his muscles he longed to be rid of.

He pushed the key into the lock of his apartment to find the door already open. Grey eyes flashed silver as he kicked the door wide, sword free of its scabbard. He was already lunging across the sitting room before he realised it was friend rather than foe who had infiltrated his quarters. Dino flicked the blade to one side before sheathing it with a flourish.

'Are you trying to get yourself killed?'

The Domina looked at him, haughty and unimpressed. It was clear she didn't blame herself for the brush with mortality.

'Perhaps if you were a little less hasty.'

Dino took a step back and closed the door. 'Hasty?'

'I'm merely saying—'

'Key.' He held out a hand. 'Key, Russo. No one gets in here except me.'

'I am the Domina!'

'You'll forgive me for being sensitive on the subject in the light of what's happened.' He crossed to a sideboard and poured wine, not offering the woman in crimson a glass. 'Why are you here?'

'I need you, Dino, and I need your secrecy.'

'Too bad. I teach novices the sword now. I'm not interested in spying.'

'I can't protect Anea without spies.'

'We have dozens.'

'Not like you.'

'I don't care. I teach the sword.'

'Dino, I need to protect Anea; I need to protect her rule.'

The Orfano glowered at the woman, took a gulp of wine and held out his hand. 'Give me the key and I'll consider it.'

12

No Honour

– 16 Luglio 325

'You look dreadful, Lord Erudito. You're not becoming a revenant, are you?' Massimo smiled and for a moment Dino could forget his troubles, amused at the mock formality. They were sitting on a stone bench in the House Contadino rose gardens, one of several enclosed courtyards in Demesne. Gleaming windows looked out from under pointed arches on all four sides, each a looking glass to some part of House Contadino itself: kitchens, bedrooms, sitting rooms, offices.

'I said you're starting to look like a revenant,' pressed Massimo.

'I'm beginning to feel like one.'

'Perhaps you should stop lurking in the cemetery trying to avenge the dead.' Massimo smiled again but it was a forced thing, like the joke, undermined by the concern that ghosted across his blue eyes. Dino's mind strayed to the argument between Duke Fontein and Margravio Contadino in the Ravenscourt before the adjournment.

Contadino wielded the least power of the great houses. It lacked the commerce of House Prospero or the prestige of Erudito. House Fontein boasted a small army, whereas Contadino could only count cooks, maids, porters and messengers among its ranks, although Dino would have taken any of them over the guards of Fontein, trusted all of them with Anea's life if put to the question.

'This is probably my favourite place in all of Landfall,' said Dino, his gaze far away, tone distracted.

'Mine too,' agreed Massimo. 'Sometimes I think it's the only place I can get any peace.'

'I think I'm going to buy an estate,' said Dino. 'I'll have a gardener put a rose garden in, just like this one. I'll pay the people who work my fields a good wage and retire quietly.'

'How old are you?' said Massimo with a raised eyebrow.

'Don't spoil this; it's a perfectly good pipe dream.'

'We have a few decades before we see any rest.'

'I said, "Don't spoil this,"' said Dino shaking his head.

In the centre of the garden, reached by white gravel paths, was a stone dais. Numerals had been etched upon it corresponding to the hours of the day. A statue of a robed man stood at its centre, his shadow dictating the passage of time. His poise was proud, his bearing regal, but the statue had been defaced – nose smashed, cheeks shattered, hands broken off at the wrists. Once a monument to the king's ego and vanity, it was now testament to the hatred people felt for his memory. The *marchesa* knelt in a flower bed singing to herself happily. She had spent the last hour watering the plants and was deadheading roses of blood red and delicate white.

'If only it were so easy to remove the conspirators,' said Dino. Massimo followed his gaze. 'How is Medea doing?'

Massimo shrugged. 'She's adjusting to the adjournment – I think all the houses are. There are plenty of meetings with representatives. No one ...' The swordsman paused. 'Almost no one wants to suggest talks. The thinking is that such a suggestion shows weakness.'

'No one except Medea, you mean,' said Dino.

Massimo nodded and looked toward the *marchesa* with an expression somewhere between admiration and sadness, or perhaps it was just the way the shadow caught his face. Dino struggled to take his eyes from the man by his side, then turned away, suddenly self-conscious.

Marchesa Medea Contadino was well liked throughout Demesne. Twelve years younger than her husband, she possessed a delicate, diplomatic touch absent in the man she loved. Maestro Cherubini had already passed through the rose garden that afternoon, entering into a hushed yet intense discussion with the diminutive noblewoman. He'd gone off looking worried, not noticing Dino and Massimo in the shadowed corner of the gardens. Nardo had made a brief appearance, delivering messages from distant parts of the castle.

'I've barely seen you the last three weeks. What's Lady Diaspora had you doing?'

'It's not Anea, it's the Domina.' Dino sighed and sat forward, resting elbows on knees, lacing his fingers. 'I've not seen Anea since the adjournment. You know how absorbed she gets with those infernal machines. She's in the laboratory morning, noon and night.'

Massimo said nothing. Dino plucked at his lip before continuing.

'The Domina sees plots everywhere. She's running herself ragged chasing phantoms and rumours.'

'And it's not just herself she's running ragged,' responded the swordsman.

'The stewardship of Landfall doesn't suit her; managing a pack of seething *nobili* suits her less. I barely recognise her any more. It's as if some poison has changed her, or she's under a spell.'

'Is there another conspiracy?' Massimo looked as grave as Dino had ever seen him. 'Is Anea in danger?'

'No.' Dino shrugged. 'Not that we know of. That's my job now. The Domina's eavesdropper. I used to spend my nights in Anea's sitting room, waiting for the scrape of blade on scabbard, willing the fuckers to come and fight face to face. Now I don't even have that.'

'What is it Russo has you doing exactly?'

'I lurk in dark corners and on windowsills; I dress as kitchen porters and messengers. I listen and I watch. It's like a game.' He sat back and blew out a breath, crossing one ankle over his knee, casting his gaze over the sea of red and white blooms. Marchesa Contadino's head bobbed gently as she worked, as if she were swimming among the flowers, not tending to them. Dino hoped she wouldn't drown. 'There's no honour to it, Mass. Sneaking around at night, hoping to catch someone out, see something people would rather I hadn't, hear things I shouldn't.'

'Sounds like it could be fun,' offered Massimo hopefully. 'There's plenty of men who would give a week's wage for the sight of Stephania in her small clothes.'

Dino stared at him, a frown starting to form.

'Sorry, just trying to lighten the mood.' Massimo looked away to hide his embarrassment.

'It's just …' Dino almost growled with frustration. 'It's no way for a man to live. And I lack the patience for it. If people oppose Anea they should come. I'll champion her and I'll cut them all down. Every last crooked one.'

'Doesn't sound too much like this democracy Anea's trying to win everyone over to.' A playful smile etched itself onto Massimo's fine lips and Dino found himself caught up in it. They shook their heads with the ridiculousness of it all, settling into a restful silence, but Dino's unhappiness soon returned.

'You know that the *margravio* and *marchesa* would stand by you if you were in any sort of trouble,' said Massimo.

'I've never doubted them.' Or you, thought Dino. You might even fight alongside me, perhaps give your life for me. Dino stared into his companion's eyes and had his thoughts confirmed. The sun shone with fierce intensity; the pool of shadow they occupied shifted and shrank.

'I'd give a king's ransom for a single day of rain,' said Dino, plucking at his lip again.

'I'd give a king's ransom for a single day of peace,' countered Massimo. 'Just one day where I didn't have to wake up thinking, Will this be the day I die protecting them? Will this be the day they die because I fail?'

'That's quite a debt we're running up.'

'True enough. But worth it.'

'I need that money for my estate,' complained Dino.

'The fictitious one with the rose garden?'

'Exactly.'

A messenger from House Fontein entered the garden, and Massimo was on his feet, striding toward Marchesa Contadino in the space of a heartbeat. Dino trailed after him. The messenger was a woman called Speranza, an oddity in the castle, dressed like man in a man's britches, doing a man's job. She bowed to Marchesa Contadino, nodding to Massimo and favouring Dino with a broad smile.

'Good morning, my lady, my lords.'

The messenger produced a note for the *marchesa* and went on her way. Massimo didn't take his eyes off her until she disappeared through a doorway.

'So much for my time among the flowers,' said the *marchesa* wistfully after reading the note. She stood and looked to the men. 'Sorry to break up your conversation, Dino. I'll need Massimo close by for the next few hours.'

'Is there anything untoward, my lady?' said Dino.

'Duke Fontein hasn't been seen for four weeks. It's making my husband suspicious. You can hardly blame him.'

'But wasn't the note delivered by a House Fontein messenger?' asked Dino.

'Speranza? Well, I suppose she is one of theirs. But you can trust her. The note was still sealed when it arrived.'

'I understand, my lady,' replied Dino, stepping forward and kissing her hand, ignoring the muddied fingertips and the faint smell of earth.

Massimo nodded to him, expression grave. 'Try and get some sleep,' was all he said before turning to escort Marchesa Contadino from the garden, chest out, shoulders back, hand resting on the pommel of his blade. It would be a foolish assassin that attempted the life of Medea Contadino.

Dino stood before the statue of the old king and noted the fractured cheeks, the missing nose. He wondered how much it would cost to commission a statue of Anea. He was lost in his thoughts until the *crunch-crunch* of gravel announced he was no longer alone. A glance over his shoulder confirmed his suspicions.

'You're a difficult man to find.'

'I would have thought that was a good quality in a spy.'

The Domina forced a smile. 'You know I wouldn't ask you to do this, but you're one of the few people I know who is absolutely loyal to Anea.'

'As you keep telling me, but all I've discovered so far is a number of affairs that were widely rumoured and a pregnant maid in House Erudito. You could have confirmed the same facts by paying a few known gossips.'

'Tonight may change that.'

84

Dino curled his lip in distaste and clenched his jaw. 'What is it I have to do this time?'

'Duke Fontein—'

'Has been missing for a number of weeks.'

'We knew that already.' The Domina flushed with annoyance. 'I've just had a message from a source who expects him to return to Demesne. Tonight. I need you to find out why he's been away and what he plans to do next.'

'At least he's not one of the most heavily guarded men in Landfall.'

'Spare me the sarcasm, Dino. This is important.'

'It will be significantly more important when I'm caught spying on Duke Fontein.'

'So don't get caught.'

'Have you considered inviting him to dinner and asking him?'

'He'll sign a full confession before dessert, will he?'

Dino shrugged. 'Depends on the dessert.'

The Domina turned on her heel and hurried away, no doubt keen to be free of the sun.

'I think I preferred it when you were still alive,' said Dino to the shattered statue of the king. 'Subterfuge seemed more honest back then.'

The rest of the day passed in a languid malaise, the humidity unbearable to all except Achilles. The drake trotted around Dino's sitting room, hunting down crickets released to keep the reptile entertained rather than fed. The sun began its inexorable descent, staining the eggshell sky vermilion as it waned. The citizens of Demesne clustered about the kitchens and great halls to take their evening meal. Dino waited in his room, having no wish to join the many *professori*, assistants and scholars of House Erudito, and took his food alone, waiting for the dark blanket of night to smother the land. He dozed fitfully, scabbard across his thighs, shirt untucked, boots unbuckled. Achilles kept watch with a restless onyx eye.

In time darkness came, and the Orfano slipped away in dark clothes, his destination House Fontein, his objective its many secrets.

13

Over Rooftops

– 16 Luglio 325

Dino set out from his room attired in scarlet and black. A three-cornered hat perched on his head, the peak pulled low. Achilles was stubborn, refusing to give up his perch on Dino's shoulder.

'Fine, you can come with me, but if the fighting starts you're on your own.'

The drake yawned and gripped onto his shoulder more tightly. Dino had taken rooms up on the sixth floor after he'd become Anea's bodyguard.

The Orfano slunk along corridors on the lower floors, where he would be mistaken for a messenger. He'd made his skin darker with a touch of make-up, and the fake beard would prevent immediate identification.

'If only it didn't itch so much,' he whispered. Achilles stared off into the distance. 'You're not exactly helping my disguise.'

Dino had become familiar with the layout of the great houses during three weeks of spying for the Domina. He'd memorised their trackless corridors, the endless maze of corners and curves. There were locked doors with missing keys, secret ways that led nowhere, tumbledown dead ends and loose flagstones. Each floor of the castle was subtly different, just as each house was distinct in its architecture and lighting.

The seventh floor was largely abandoned, a secret kingdom of dust rented only by decay and atrophy, House Prospero the exception, colonised by Stephania's rooms. Moths feasted on drapes and curtains that had cost riches in their day, while paintings bleached with the passing of each sun. The seventh floor was all but a myth to most who lived below it, a place given over to time long passed. Here and there maids and pages slept entwined, the heat of their passion cooling on their skin. This was forbidden but a reprieve from the overcrowding of the servants' quarters on the floor below. Cooks, cleaners, porters and messengers slept four to a room. Tailors, scribes, and chefs enjoyed less crowded quarters. The fifth floor was given over to minor houses and the few *cittadini* who'd won status or celebrity. The corridors between these apartments were not always empty.

'As much business is conducted between the sheets as it is in the offices on the floor below,' explained Dino to the drake. Achilles yawned again. 'I was just making conversation, you know?'

The third floor of each great house consisted of the apartments of the ruling families guarded by loyalists and ex-soldiers. The second floor contained great halls, offices and meeting rooms. In House Erudito this was a maze of classrooms, while in House Prospero it was workshops. At night the second floor was abandoned by all but a few brave mice and the occasional cataphract drake. The first floor was home to the kitchens of the great houses, rarely quiet even at night. When they were not staffed by cooks and porters they were patrolled by guards.

'Only House Fontein is different,' whispered Dino. 'I can't get a feel for it. It's as if it was built to defy memory.'

House Fontein possessed training chambers and storerooms, armouries and forges seemingly at random. Dino was least confident in the corridors of the martial house. Even a messenger in the attire of that house would provoke difficult questions from the guards. 'But there are other ways to move between the houses.'

Achilles hissed as Dino pressed his back to the cool stone of an arch leading to another staircase. He listened a few moments before ascending. An iron key and a shove from his shoulder opened a long-forgotten door. Wood grated on flagstones, disturbing deep dust, gathered like drifts of snow. The rooftops were a landscape of slanting horizontals and crumbling walkways. Countless pantiles, fired in kilns across Landfall, lay in orderly rows. Stars looked down with wavering silver light, one among them blinking amethyst with a baleful intensity. Only the slim crescent of the moon, spared the impediment of clouds, banished absolute darkness. Rusted weathervanes emerged from spires, threatening to snag his messenger's tabard. He wondered after the ravens that had lived here during Lucien's time, long gone these nine years – yet another shift in Demesne's character. The journey across the rooftops was a treacherous affair. He worked at the route, mindful and without haste. He had become more acquainted with the terrain over the last weeks.

'I may as well just live up here,' he complained. 'Sneaking about like thief or a—'

His foot slipped, eliciting a grunt. Achilles hissed. Something moved in the darkness ahead. Dino crouched on instinct, removing his tricorn with one hand and pressing his shoulder to a chimney. A few seconds passed. Dino dared not breathe. Achilles curled his tail about the Orfano tightly, snout pressed against Dino's cheek.

The sound of voices. Dino struggled to decipher the words, which were clipped and gruff in a dialect he'd not heard before. The speakers edged into view. Five men in grey rags, each bearing a knife or cleaver or club. Dino knew that these were not seasoned fighters, but five to one were odds sought by the very brave or the very foolish. He clutched his hat a little tighter and covered the crosspiece of his sword lest it shine in the moonlight, then pressed his face to the corner and risked a look at the men in grey. Their path lead them away. Dino knew with certainty he'd be killed should the men detect him. Hot prickles of sweat broke out across his brow and under his arms. The voices faded in the distance, the night silent once more.

'Why were they up here?' whispered Dino to the reptile. 'And why at this late hour? Certainly there's no food to steal.'

As ever, Achilles said nothing, onyx eyes inscrutable, a frown in the set of his scales.

'Perhaps they've been sent to spy, just as we have?'

The climb down was harder than he remembered. The walls of Demesne offered few handholds, requiring exacting strength and precision at every move. Achilles detected the difficulty and scuttled free, descending on four legs, claws finding easy purchase. The ivy was hard, withering due to the drought; Dino didn't trust it to bear his weight. Finally he arrived and settled down, resting his aching fingers, resisting the urge to spasm from the growing spike of cramp he felt in his calf. He kneaded the offending limb, stifling curses. The windowsill was just broad enough, squatting with his back to the glass, one ear pressed against it. He breathed. The drake clambered onto the sill beside him, curling up in his lap.

Golden light spilled from the windows and doorway of a *taverna* below his vantage point, the *cittadini* inside sharing wine and song. Figures hurried home along the curving streets of Santa Maria.

Dino found a gap in the curtains wide enough to gain a view of the room inside. Duke and Duchess Fontein's sitting room.

Speranza stood near the door, upright and stiff. There was nothing of the smiling messenger Dino had seen earlier that day. A wariness lurked in her eyes, despite the impassive mask of her face, pale with tiredness. Dino adjusted his position on the windowsill until he could see the couch. Achilles clambered up onto his shoulder and pressed in close to the nape of his neck, a scarf of sepia scales.

Duchess Fontein sat fanning herself. The day's end had done little to reduce the oppressive heat, and the duchess's discomfort was evident. Her pinched and lined face betrayed the meagre affection she showed anyone. There was a sour cast to her painted lips, and few if any could remember her smile.

'Where can he be at such an hour?' she said irritably. 'How long can it possibly take?'

A maid refilled her wine glass. Dino recognised her from the cemetery – Isabella Esposito, no relation to Massimo, the last name common among the *cittadini*.

'Not long now, my lady,' said Isabella in hushed tones. Speranza said nothing, eyes fixed straight ahead.

Dino shuffled his feet on the windowsill trying to get comfortable, but it was to little effect. The faint chime of bells could be heard from a distant part of Demesne. Dino didn't bother counting; he knew all too well they ushered in the eleventh hour.

The wait was long and uncomfortable. Twice he cursed the architects; if the windowsills were just an inch wider ... Three times he shifted his weight and regretted it, boots slipping at the edge. Achilles abandoned his shoulder, taking up refuge inside the messenger's tabard.

Then Isabella approached the window. Dino felt a moment of icy panic as the maid gripped the handle. If the window opened in she'd need to pull back the curtain, revealing his place of concealment. If the window swung out he'd be swept off the ledge, falling to his death.

'Don't open that!' said a gruff voice. The window remained closed and Dino pressed his eye back to the glass.

Duke Fontein stood in the doorway, dusty from the road, a frown fixed on his face. He smoothed his white beard and cleared his throat.

'Well?' pressed the duchess, wasting no time on greeting or reunion. She folded her fan, clutching it in one fist, knuckles turning white. She remained seated, spine straight like a spear shaft.

'He said no.' The duke turned to Speranza. 'Leave us.'

The messenger did so, Isabella following, almost tripping over herself in her haste. The door made no sound as it closed behind them.

'*No?*' The duchess threw the fan at the duke, who batted it aside with a deft hand.

'Keep your voice down!'

'What right has he to deny us anything?' she continued in a seething whisper. 'After everything we did for him? All those long years.'

The duke removed his riding gloves and snorted. 'Everything we did for him? How much wine have you had?'

'He still holds a grudge?' The duchess pressed one hand to her scrawny throat. 'After all this time?'

'He wanted to know why you were so keen to leave. He wasn't taken in by my telling him you were ill. He all but called me a liar.' The duke threw his gloves onto a side table, the frown on his face deepening.

'Did you not tell him the *dottore* said I should have sea air?'

Dino grinned. Sea air could only mean House Marino. The duchess hoped to visit Lucien's bustling town. A silence descended on the room, the quiet of desperation and despair.

'I want away from here,' sobbed the duchess finally. 'I want no more part in this. It's only a matter of time until things come to a head.'

'And what use will going away be?' thundered the duke, long past weariness or exasperation. 'You'll be implicated along with everyone else, and Lucien will hand you over. And he'll do it smiling.' The duke stalked to the sideboard, where a *caraffa* waited, and poured brandy into a glass. 'It's too late in the game to lose your appetite, my *darling*.'

Dino blinked.

Suddenly the long wait on the windowsill didn't seem a wasted one.

The duchess rose from her seat and crossed the sitting room, her pinched face drained of blood. Her lips pulled back from her teeth. 'How many more minor houses can we recruit for our cause? How many more can we expend before everyone loses their stomach for it? How many more sons of the *nobili* will be cut down just so we can hold on to what is rightfully ours?'

The duke pressed a hand to his forehead, shielding his eyes from the woman who stood before him, pressing for answers.

They were a ghastly pair. Dino wondered if they'd ever loved each other. He doubted it. More likely they'd married for politics and gain rather than affection. Certainly no children had been born of this sour union. All they had was each other, their lands and their titles, and Anea's dreams of republic were steadily eroding the latter.

'Calm yourself,' said the duke, attempting a soothing tone. 'She's still playing scientist with Virmyre. We've another two months. Perhaps I can purchase a small estate from House Contadino. We'll hide you there.'

'They'll never agree to such a thing.' She was all but shaking now. 'Never.'

'I'll go through a minor house. They'll make the purchase. You'll move in secrecy with a small staff.' He laid a hand gently on each of her shoulders. She didn't return the embrace. 'When Contadino falls we'll get the money back. It's perfect.'

'And what then?'

'And then you wait until Anea is dealt with.'

Dino nearly slipped from the windowsill. The town's rooftops stared up at him, blank faces willing his fall. He swallowed in a dry throat. Suspecting treason was one thing, hearing it spoken aloud quite another.

'You won't be there long,' continued the duke. 'I doubt you'll have to winter there. This business will be concluded soon enough.'

Sooner than you think, thought Dino.

14

Thorny Intentions

– 17 Luglio 325

'I'm not concerned with what I already suspect, Lord Erudito; I worry about what I'm unaware of.'

The Domina stood in the shade of the Contadino rose garden, pale skin and scarlet robes complementing the blooms behind her. The silver staff occupied her left hand; her right was clenched in a fist. Dino flushed at the rebuke, dipped his chin. The *margravio* and *marchesa* exchanged a look, faces impassive, but Massimo made no attempt to hide his frown.

'Isn't the point that I heard them plotting with my own ears?' replied Dino, the words coming to him slowly. 'Before, we only guessed their intent, but now we have proof. Me. I'm a witness.'

It was early. The sun had yet to climb the walls of Demesne and flood its light into the garden. No breeze stirred the roses but Dino felt a chill all the same. The statue of the old king stared after them, an eroded gaze from smashed features.

'Merely knowing intent is not good enough,' said the Domina. 'I need details, I need co-conspirators.' The Domina had recently taken to wearing a circular biretta. Dino supposed the headdress marked a new chapter in her office, but he couldn't say it suited her. Nor the waspish, impatient delivery of her interactions.

Where is the Professore Russo of my childhood? he wondered. What tight-lipped imperious impostor is this?

'If you'll excuse me, I have matters to attend to.' Russo sketched a half-bow to the Contadinos and began to turn.

'Domina,' it was the *margravio*, a note of displeasure in the word.

'My lord?'

'You failed to bow to Lord Erudito.' The moment stretched between them. 'I believe he outranks you.' The *margravio* stared at her coolly. 'Perhaps you forgot in your haste.'

The Domina regarded him, struggling to keep her features neutral, a tiny flare of the nostrils, a twitch of her brow. Her alabaster features turned red, almost matching her robes.

'Forgive me, my lord.' She turned to Dino. 'It has been many hours since I slept. I meant no disrespect.' She nodded curtly and went on her way, crisp footfalls loud in the early-morning quiet.

'Strange,' said the *marchesa* after a few moments, 'That's not the Russo I used to know.'

'I was just thinking the same thing, my lady.' Dino pulled at his lip.

'She needs to be reminded that we're allies in this,' said the *margravio*, an icy command lingering on him.

'I fear she suspects disloyalty and betrayal in every house,' replied Dino.

'But the Contadino have always supported Lady Diaspora's rule,' said Massimo. He cast an angry glance toward the doorway the Domina had departed through.

'As the *marchesa* said,' replied Dino, 'the Domina is not herself of late.'

'Or yourself, Lord Erudito.' The *margravio* favoured the Orfano with a direct look.

'My lord?' Dino suspected he wouldn't like what would come next.

'First a *superiore,* then a bodyguard, now a spy. Can we still trust you?'

'Emilio!' said Marchesa Contadino, frowning. 'I'm sorry, Lord Erudito. My husband forgets himself.'

Dino pressed a fist to his mouth and took a moment to think. 'Can we dispense with the titles? I want to speak with you honestly, and this pomp is driving me to distraction.'

'Dino,' said the *margravio,* 'I apologise. I have no right to doubt you.'

The Orfano shook his head. 'I am a spy, and I hate it, but

given the gravity of recent times I have no choice. My focus is on House Prospero and Fontein, as you can imagine. House Contadino has nothing to fear from me.'

'Is there anything I can do?' asked Massimo, earning himself a stern look from the *margravio*.

'No. The Domina has placed this task before me. I can't involve you.'

'We're very fond of you, Dino. You know that.' Medea smiled at him and sighed. 'We were never very good at making Lucien feel welcome, but we'd never betray Anea, or yourself.'

'I know, but it's a comfort to hear it.'

'I have matters that require my attention,' said the *margravio*. 'Send messages to let us know you're well, Dino.'

'My lord,' Dino almost whispered, 'there was something else – the reason I asked you here.' The Orfano looked around the garden. Six men struggled under the weight of a great burden wrapped in canvas on the far side.

'Please, go on,' said Marchesa Contadino.

Dino recounted Duke Fontein's scheme to buy a small estate through an intermediary.

'And he means to hide his wife in this purchase?' The *marchesa* had drawn closer, words hushed, fan beating a steady rhythm.

'Yes. The duchess is frantic to put distance between herself and the events that will unfold here.'

'She doesn't believe they'll succeed,' said Massimo.

'No, she doesn't.' Dino looked to the *margravio*. 'Do not sell any of your estates or villas, my lord, no matter how tempting the price or how trustworthy the buyer.'

Massimo caught Dino's eye. There was a hint of admiration in the swordsman's gaze, a tiny glimmer of cheer on a gloomy day.

'You've done me a great service with this information, Dino. I owe you a debt of gratitude,' said the *margravio*.

'We should investigate this,' added the *marchesa*, taking her husband's arm gently. 'Farewell, Dino.'

Massimo stepped toward him, clapping one arm about his shoulder.

'Seems you're just as good at spying as you are at being a bodyguard.'

'That's well and good but I'm a *maestro di spada*, you know?'

'I'd completely forgotten.' Massimo grinned, then cast his gaze at the men, who had now got the bulky canvas-shrouded object to the centre of the garden. There was some colourful language on display as tempers rose with the heat.

'What's going on there?' said Dino.

'They're replacing the statue of the old king with a new one.'

The porters were struggling to remove the king, grunting with the effort.

'It's that ridiculous saint, isn't it?'

'Santa Maria. And keep your voice down. Marchesa Contadino herself is quite taken with the new religion.'

'I thought she at least might have some brains.'

'She does. Take care, Dino. Try not to become too cynical, lest you end up like Russo. All duty and no sense of humour.'

Dino flicked his fingertips from beneath his chin but couldn't stop the smile overtaking his face.

'Into the mouth of the wolf.' Massimo sketched out a mocking salute.

'And knock his teeth out, every one,' replied Dino, giving a salute of his own.

He'd meant to have a night to himself. Due in part to tiredness, but also a response to his treatment by the Domina that morning. The ungrateful *carogna* could uncover Demesne's miserable secrets alone. But the evening meal at House Erudito was always a long and cheerful affair, the many academics remaining afterwards to gossip and argue. Good company was much needed after a day of study or teaching. They crowed and cackled like dark birds, their robes making them raven-winged. Dino joined them, entering into conversations with old acquaintances, drinking rather more than he should. Through it all was the nagging memory of the Domina's words: *I'm not concerned with what I already suspect, Lord Erudito; I worry about what I am unaware of.*

'And how fares the most famous prodigy of House Erudito?'

asked Cherubini, settling down on the bench beside the Orfano. Dino smiled in return.

'Some prodigy of House Erudito I am. Shouldn't I be the scourge of the sciences, rather than a *maestro di spada*?'

'Well.' Cherubini shrugged his large shoulders. 'House Erudito is not short of scholars. It never hurts to diversify, especially with talent.' He gestured to the hall, where the *professori* discussed various subjects, alchemical to metaphysical. 'And you are *maestro superiore di spada*. Impressive at any age, more so given your youth.'

'Yes, for all the lessons I teach.' Dino rolled his eyes. 'Ruggeri treats me like a stranger; D'arzenta can barely stand the sight of me. Hard to believe I learned from them. Those days are long gone.' Dino swirled the wine in his glass.

'Hard indeed. You've grown so much.' Cherubini grinned with obvious pride. 'I barely slept a wink when you left for the Verde Guerra. I barely had a full night's sleep the whole time you were away.'

Cherubini's gaze flicked to the side of the room, where a single Fontein guard stood by the door, a formality rather than any serious security.

'Well, I returned.' Dino sipped from the glass. 'How are you sleeping these days?'

Cherubini stared at him with a quizzical look, and a blush crept across his broad face, although whether it was from wine or heat Dino couldn't tell.

'Aren't all these frictions with the other houses keeping you up at night? I'm finding it difficult to enjoy any rest.'

'Ah, I see,' replied Cherubini looking relieved. Dino was confused by the *maestro*'s discomfort. 'Well, you know me. I'm not happy unless I'm worrying at some problem or other.' The large man grinned. 'That's why I'm so proud of you – you never give me any headaches. You've always looked after yourself.'

'Except for the Verde Guerra,' Dino reminded him.

'That was war, Dino. Any parent would be concerned.'

And then Cherubini really did blush. Dino drank from his glass again, simply to spare the *maestro* his moment of embarrassment.

'I think of everyone in House Erudito as my children, is what I meant to say.'

'But that's not strictly true, is it?' Dino caught Cherubini's eye.

'No. You're right, I don't. I've often wondered at the joys having would children bring.' The *maestro*'s eyes were pensive. 'But I never married, and old age is harder to bear when you can't lavish attention on the young. Perhaps that's why I'm so fond of you. All these years watching you grow.'

'You could still marry; you're not so very ancient.' Dino smiled and sipped his wine.

'I'm not sure I could. Ah, look at me being all maudlin. I think I shall order some coffee to lift my spirits. Keep safe, young prodigy.'

'Good night, Cherubini,' said Dino, standing up. 'Sleep well.' He patted the *maestro* on the shoulder and took his leave.

Dino emerged from the great hall of House Erudito, jacket unbuttoned, boot buckles loosened, shirt stained with spots of wine. He'd removed his scabbard, carrying it like a walking stick. It put him in mind of the sword cane Lucien had given him, along with the order to protect Anea. He'd been doing just that ever since. The sword cane's location eluded him, some cupboard of half-remembered things, no doubt.

A shadow fell across him, startling him from introspection. '*Porca miseria*. You scared the life out of me.' He released the hilt of the blade, felt the surge of adrenaline.

'Apologies, Lord Erudito,' said Nardo, stiff and formal. A small scroll appeared from a leather case.

'It's fine. I'm more on edge than I thought.' Dino took a breath. A message at this time of night would not contain much cheer. He read the scroll by the light of a guttering candle and gave a sigh. 'Do you know what this is?'

'The Domina told me it was for your eyes alone.'

Dino thrust the parchment before the messenger, a reluctant moment passed and Nardo read the contents. 'Back to being a bodyguard.'

'Is there really no one else who can do this?'

Nardo shrugged. 'Seems the Domina has decided for you.'

'Tell her to go f—'

'I'm not sure that's wise.' Nardo looked around to check they were not overheard. 'And if you won't be persuaded you can tell her yourself.'

'This is horse shit.'

'It is strange, I grant you. You should do it.'

'Why?' Dino sounded like a spoilt teen and loathed himself for it.

'People will put more pressure on if they realise you're at odds with the Domina.'

'You mean I have to make a show of unity.'

'Yes.' The messenger's frown was one of concern.

'Tell her I'll do it.'

'Take care of yourself, Dino.'

The messenger departed into the gloaming of Demesne.

The assignment was neither difficult nor dangerous, yet Dino couldn't help feeling it was punitive. The Domina's neat flowing handwriting instructed him to keep watch over one of their own 'in case of assassination'. He had no wish to skulk along Demesne's corridors another night, and bodyguard duty suited him better. Or it would have without the added stipulation: 'Maestro Cherubini must not know he is being guarded. Remain unseen unless attacked.'

Dino headed to his rooms, changed into darker clothes and splashed water on his face in the faint hope it might sober him.

'It's going to be a long night,' he whispered to his reflection.

15

Behind Locked Doors

– 17 Luglio 325

Gaining entrance to the *maestro*'s chambers was a simple matter, although Dino knew first hand that the door would be locked at all times. Only Cherubini possessed a key, even denying his maid the same privilege. Famously private, others sneered he was overly suspicious. Dino thought him prudent given his increased political importance. Less well known was that the *maestro* struggled with his breathing. He'd claimed to be allergic to dust for as long Dino could remember and always left a window open, even in the cruellest depths of winter.

Dino looked out of his window on the sixth floor, casting an eye over his chosen route. Achilles scuttled to the sill and tested the air with a dark tongue.

'One day I'll spend some time in the town, rather than just looking down on it.' Achilles turned away and plodded back to the bed. 'Well, thanks for wishing me good fortune, you ingrate.'

The Orfano began the climb down, the alcohol and the height conspiring to set his head spinning. The rooftops of Santa Maria awaited him should he fall. Or perhaps he'd land in the street on his face, cobbles mashing his brains to soup.

The windows of House Erudito showed dim lights, but Dino kept his eyes fixed on the wall. He had no wish to see more than he was required to. These were the rooms of people with lives, private lives. Not every aspect of a person's affairs affected the running of Landfall or the birth of a republic.

Dino pulled himself through the *maestro*'s window, sucking down lungfuls of air, then lost his balance, almost knocking over a low table in the dark. He cursed himself and looked around. He'd had no cause to call here for some time, yet it was much as he remembered. Cherubini had invited him for dinner often as a child, offering private tutoring when Dino had been at odds with his classmates. There was a feeling of luxury here. The couches were deep and soft, the pillows numerous, the curtains and drapes of rich fabric. The walls were crowded with oil paintings and framed sketches. Such furnishings might have been expected in House Prospero; to find them in Erudito was surprising. A smell of old red wine and fresh flowers hung on the air, adding to the feast of the senses.

Dino didn't have to wait long.

No sooner had he regained his composure than a key scraped in the lock, announcing the *maestro*'s return from the great hall. With no other obvious solution at hand Dino sought concealment behind the purple drapes at the window. Mercifully they were floor length.

Oh, good work, Dino, he chided himself. Even a five-year-old knows to look behind the drapes.

But the *maestro* had more pressing matters on his mind than his sitting-room curtains. His were not the only footsteps that reached Dino's ears. A soft murmuring of voices. A stifled laugh. An overloud 'Shhhh' followed by another laugh. The voices passed through the sitting room without pause, to Dino's relief. He took a furtive glance around the edge of the rich brocade. The sitting room was empty, the door to the bedroom ajar. Only the steady glow of a candle broke the gloom, a rectangle of tawny light. Dino approached on hesitant feet, hoping the floorboards would not betray his passing. A sigh reached his ears, followed by a low moan.

Dino's mind raced.

The *maestro* was famously single, a bachelor in every sense. Perhaps he'd lured a young maid back to satisfy himself? He'd been noticeably maudlin on the subject of marriage, after all. Dino froze just a foot away from the door. Sounds of gentle rhythmic movement increased in volume. Another moan, unmistakably male.

Then a hushed voice keen and urgent: 'Yes, yes.' Also male.

Suspicion unfolded in Dino's mind. He willed himself forward, one half-step at a time, drawing closer to the door. He was trembling, daring himself to look past the door's edge. A terrible reluctance seized him. He'd no wish to see such an intimate act, and yet a terrible curiosity burned within him. He stepped forward.

Dino swallowed, almost flinching back to the safety of the sitting room. They were naked. Young men about his age, bodies hardened by training or labour, olive-skinned with a hint of dirt. He thought he recognised one of them, a low-ranking guard from House Fontein; difficult to tell in the candlelight. The other was kneeling on the floor, his head bobbing in the lap of his companion. The guard on the divan was thrusting his hips to meet the eager mouth. He grasped the man by the hair and became more insistent, forceful. Dino stared at the hair entwined about the strong fingers, watched the man's thighs tense and strain like ropes pulled taut.

A grunt and a shuddering sigh.

Dino realised he'd been holding his breath. And also that he was painfully aroused, his groin aflame with a deep ache he'd not thought possible. Entranced, he kept watching, unable to take his eyes from the hard bodies bathed in candlelight. The men stood, kissing hungrily for a moment. They laughed together before the guard turned, kneeling on the divan.

Dino turned from the doorway, keen that he remain unseen, the urge to leave a fierce one. He told himself he remained out of duty, but the lie was all too sour even as he persuaded himself. He'd never seen such a thing before, not with man and women nor this unusual pairing. He turned to leave but remembered the Domina's order. He was to remain in case assassins attempted entry.

It's not as if he's unguarded, Dino thought bitterly, eyes drawn back to the men in the bedroom. The men on the divan were now joined. The guard bent over, his firm buttocks shuddering with each impact from the man who stood behind.

Surely I am mistaken, thought Dino. The *maestro* has merely lent his room to these two lovers so they can ...

A soft moan issued from elsewhere in the bedroom. Dino

pressed himself up against the wall, his eye seeking the narrow gap between door and frame where the hinges joined both. Maestro Cherubini sat in the opposite corner from the two men. Always overweight, he was grotesque in his nakedness, the deep shadows doing little to hide his bulk. One hand fumbled weakly in his lap, stroking himself beneath the expanse of his stomach. His eyes glittered drunkenly in the dim light, a look of pained desperation frozen on his features.

Dino drew back from the gap in the door, shock settling into his bones like a chill. His eyes were drawn back to the two men. Powerful hips beat a constant rhythm, narrow waist stretching up to broad shoulders, strong arms reaching down to hold the hips of the man in front. Dino could only stare in mute fascination, stomach knotting, cheeks flaming scarlet. His length strained and ached beneath his small clothes. The *maestro* called out encouragement from the corner in a husky rasp. Dino pressed his eye to the sliver of space between door and frame once more. The *maestro* lay back, thighs glistening with his spend.

Dino could bear no more of it, moving through the sitting room in a daze, past the litter of academia and objets d'art. He turned the key in the lock, desperate that it not click. The sounds in the bedroom became more intense. Dino opened the door and passed through, closing it behind him in silence. For a few seconds he stood in the corridor, shocked and breathless, then fled for the stairwell, losing himself in the ever-present darkness of Demesne.

Massimo was waiting outside Dino's apartment, leaning against the wall with his arms crossed. His look of boredom shifted to one of concern.

'You look as if you've seen a ghost.'

'If only that were true.' The Orfano unlocked the door and pushed his way inside, Achilles scuttled across the floor to him. He reached down to gather the reptile in his arms. 'Miss me, did you?'

Achilles yawned and coiled about his master.

'I just called by to see if your spirits had improved since this morning.' Massimo closed the door behind him and turned the key in the lock. 'Marchesa Contadino is concerned about you.'

Dino nodded, forcing a smile. He'd known Cherubini his whole life; now he felt as if the man were no more than a stranger. His stomach lurched, eyes prickling with the onset of bloody tears he'd refuse to shed. A terrible weight occupied his chest, making each breath a labour. Achilles looked up, tail curled about Dino's arm, black liquid eyes reflecting the light. Dino lit more candles, buying time to compose himself. It didn't help.

'What's wrong, Dino?'

'Only you could call at a time when I'd rather be alone,' whispered Dino.

'Alone? Why do you wish to be alone?'

'I ... I saw ...' His throat was swollen with words that he couldn't bear to speak.

'Has Russo had you out spying again?'

The Orfano nodded, eyes fixed on Achilles – anything to avoid meeting the swordsman's eyes.

'Cherubini,' was all Dino managed before he choked up.

'What about Cherubini? Not dead?' said Massimo, suddenly grave.

Dino shook his head, the image of the naked *maestro* surfacing in his mind, painfully unwelcome. He looked away from his friend, squeezing his eyes shut, willing the memory away.

'I was supposed to be guarding him. He came back with two men.'

Massimo raised an eyebrow.

'They ... He was watching them, in his room. They were ...'

Dino pushed a hand to his mouth to stop the words leaking out. Massimo crossed the room, laying one hand tenderly on his shoulder.

'Dino, what the *maestro* gets up to behind his own door is his own affair. He's not hurting anyone.'

'But it's not right,' whispered Dino.

'What consenting men and women do after dark isn't your concern.'

'But it's not men and women, it's men and men.'

'Consenting men?'

'Well, yes. Two men. Together.'

'Mention this to no one,' said Massimo. 'No good will come of it. He'll be ruined if word gets out. He's one of Anea's most vocal supporters.'

Dino nodded and looked away, plucking at his lip.

'Dino, you've killed men, you've trained alongside them.' Massimo narrowed his eyes, strangely intent. 'You're aware of what they're capable of. It matters not who they lie with or what they do behind locked doors.'

Dino stepped back. He wasn't used to being lectured like this – by the Domina perhaps, but not by Massimo.

'Why does this upset you so?' asked the swordsman, tone suddenly soft.

'Landfall isn't the garden of tolerance and forgiveness we think it is. Even here, in Demesne, people sneer and curse *invertiti*. Men are beaten and sometimes killed out on the estates. It's taboo.'

'Well maybe it shouldn't be. It's long past time Landfall started accepting difference. Take you, for example.'

Dino felt a moment of horror. He clutched Achilles and the reptile hissed, favouring the Contadino swordsman with a pugnacious stare. 'What do you mean?'

'Well, you're Orfano. That's different, and yet the *cittadini* can never decide whether to fete you for being a defender of the people or despise you for being a creation of the king.'

'They despise us for bearing deformities,' intoned Dino.

'Orfano, *invertito* – is it really such a problem?'

Dino shook his head, unable to answer, remembering the lingering ache of his own powerful arousal. 'I wish it were otherwise too,' he admitted, 'if only for Cherubini's sake.'

'You can't report this to the Domina. If word reaches House Fontein or Prospero—'

'I know. Cherubini will be ruined and Anea will lose her most articulate ally in the Ravenscourt.'

The heat of the discussion dwindled, and neither Orfano nor swordsman knew the words to fill the aftermath. Massimo soon left, Dino sighing with relief as the door closed.

He spent the night awake, willing the sun to appear on the horizon. He'd constructed arguments against his preference many times: it wasn't seemly, it wasn't what real men did, it didn't become a soldier, what would Lucien say? His desire was a pain he was used to, like the ache of an old wound on a damp winter day. Finally he lurched from his bed and lit a candle, then another. Anything to escape the darkness of the night and the images of hard bodies etched onto his memory. Anything to escape the suffocating shame of his denial.

16

A Letter from Erebus

– 18 Luglio 325

Dino walked the corridors of Demesne, dazed and restless. People passed him on their way to their morning chores. Their faces were indistinct to him, like fleeting phantoms or figments from dreams. Some few greeted him, but his responses were muted. Something had broken within him – a lantern of fractured glass, the flame extinguished. The walk from House Erudito to House Contadino was a long one, made longer by a detour to House Fontein. The *maestri di spada* regarded him with wariness, then resumed their lessons, taking care to stick to the syllabus. The *capo* was also teaching and didn't deign to acknowledge Dino's presence, who didn't mind the impertinence, content to be spared another hostile interaction. The pupils struggled to concentrate, self-conscious under Dino's unwavering but vacant gaze. The *superiore* sat on a wooden bench with his fingers laced in his lap, felt the itch of stubble under his jaw.

'Is something amiss, my lord?' grunted Ruggeri over the din of sparring students. Wooden blade clashed with wooden blade.

'Just checking on the next crop of trained killers.' Dino regarded the students, not meeting Ruggeri's eyes. 'Imagine if all of these children were training to be *dottori* instead.'

Ruggeri looked at the students, then back to Dino, a puzzled look on his lined face.

'Pardon me for saying so, but you look unwell, my lord.'

'There's much that's unwell in Demesne today.' The Orfano pushed himself to his feet and drifted on. Back through the Central Keep toward House Contadino.

The kitchens beckoned but his stomach was an acid ache, appetite a faded memory. Camelia would know something was wrong and demand to know the truth of it. Better to avoid her until he'd slept. He dragged himself up spiral staircases, distracted by the echo of footfalls. Sounds of life from the castle were muted under the weight of the ancient stones. Dino rapped on the stout oak of the Domina's door with chalk-white knuckles. Fiorenza answered, a slow smile passing over her features.

'My lord.' She bobbed a curtsy. 'Please come in.' Fiorenza wore a grey skirt that reached her ankles, a clean crisp white blouse and a fraying black bodice, undoubtedly a hand-me-down. 'Some wine, my lord? We have fresh water also.' Fiorenza was the Domina's maid of five years. A scholarship to House Erudito had escaped her by a tiny margin. Dino suspected her exclusion had more to do with gender than exam scores.

'No wine.' The words came out a hollow croak. He shook his head, dropping his gaze.

'Are you unwell, my lord?'

'Very tired.' He tried for a smile.

The Domina's apartment was a shambles. There was no couch, only an armchair overrun with books from the library. Books sorely missed by Simonetti the archivist, no doubt. A long table was obscured by scrolls and missives, ledgers of accounts, wax and seals. Five chairs had been pushed to the margins of the room, also stacked with papers and books, the last of these standing near the table. The Domina's circular biretta rested on it like a cushion. Clumps of candles sprouted on saucers like fungus placed on high shelves to grow. Deep brown brocade drapes bore a look of disease, afflicted by moths, weighted with dust.

'And I thought my rooms were in poor repair.'

Fiorenza stifled a smile behind her hand.

'There you are.' The Domina entered from the bedroom, still wearing her nightgown. Black silk from ankles to neck, bare arms pale in contrast. Her auburn hair fell to her shoulders in tousled disarray. Yesterday's make-up stained her lips bruise purple. Her eyes were deeply lined and red-rimmed.

'Well? Did anyone attack Maestro Cherubini?'

'Don't you think you'd have heard if they had?'

'And you stayed there all night, keeping watch?'

'I've not been to bed yet.' This much at least was truth.

'And nothing untoward occurred the whole night?'

Dino crossed the room to the window, Massimo's warning ringing in his ears. *Mention this to no one.* He turned back to the Domina, locking eyes with her. *No good will come of it.*

'Nothing happened.' But the lie stuck in his throat. 'I'll have that water now, please,' he said to Fiorenza.

'Wait here,' said the Domina. She retired to her room, emerging thirty minutes later, a column of scarlet, the biretta lodged on her head, silver staff in hand. Dino's temper prickled in the rising heat. He wasn't some lackey with time to waste waiting.

'Explain to me, Lord Erudito,' began the Domina, 'how you failed to miss Maestro Cherubini's two guests last night?'

'I don't know what you mean.' The words faltered on his lips.

'Maestro Cherubini's maid entered his apartment this morning. Evidently the *maestro* thought the door locked. His maid has no key.'

Dino's stomach lurched. He saw himself, as if in a dream, fleeing the apartment. He'd not been able to lock the door behind him.

'The maid was horrified to find two men in the *maestro*'s chamber.'

This is my fault. He all but said the words aloud.

The Domina crossed to her table and stood in front of it, tilting her head slightly. Dino realised he wasn't reacting, not feigning surprise or even attempting to hide the lie.

'However,' continued the Domina, 'they'd not been sent there to kill him.'

This is all my fault. The words burned on his lips, begging to be released.

'I'm not sure I follow you,' he managed from gritted teeth.

'Then perhaps you'll follow this.' Her eyes flashed angrily.

'I received this information from a maid this morning. A chambermaid. And you were supposed to be in that very apartment. In the adjoining room, Dino. How in nine hells do you miss something like that?'

Dino clenched his fists and drew in a breath.

'I was in the sitting room. The *maestro* must have retired for the night before I arrived.'

'And you failed to overhear three men fucking?'

'I heard nothing.'

'You have to be the most half-witted spy in the whole castle.'

Dino fought the urge to strike her, woman or not.

'I was on bodyguard duty last night, not sent to spy on anyone.'

'If you can find work with another house I suggest you do so. Perhaps Margravio Contadino can lend you a scythe to get the harvest in.'

'And perhaps we can demote you back to school teacher.'

They faced each other, a fraying rope of silence straining between them.

'What will happen to him?' Dino took a step forward.

'Who?'

'Cherubini, of course. What will happen to him?'

The Domina looked at him incredulously. 'He'll be asked to retire. What parent in their right mind would send their child to him for schooling following this?'

This is all my fault. The words ached to be free.

'Retirement? That's ridiculous.' He'd taken another step toward her. 'Think of the political consequences.'

'The news will be all over Demesne by now,' she said, waving one hand casually. 'This isn't *my* doing, Dino. You may as well blame the maid.'

Or yourself. She hadn't said it. She hadn't needed to.

'We can't lose Cherubini,' Dino pressed. He's one of Anea's greatest supporters. He's one of *our* greatest supporters.'

'I don't need a lesson in politics from a *failed* spy.'

His fingers curled around the hilt of his sword, jaw clenched, anger a thick and bitter bile in his throat.

A knock on the door broke the stalemate.

Fiorenza emerged from the bedroom to answer it, a worried look crossing her face as she snatched a glance at her employer. She opened the door, peering through the gap.

'I bring news for the Domina.' Nardo's voice from the corridor. The Domina crossed the room, all but pushing Fiorenza aside.

'Well? Out with it.'

'It seems Lady Allattamento is looking to move to the countryside. She's making enquiries to purchase a villa. The Contadinos have a scheme they'd like to discuss with you in the great hall.'

Dino rolled his eyes. Didn't I just tell them not to sell? he wanted to shout. Didn't I just say that Duke Fontein plans to conceal his wife elsewhere?

The Domina turned to Dino. 'We'll finish this later,' she said, every syllable loaded with threat. She left the room, her voice audible down the long corridor as she demanded answers from Nardo. Dino listened to the voices dwindle in the distance.

'Are you sure you're well, my lord?'

Dino looked up to find Fiorenza regarding him, concern plain in her gaze.

'I'm fine. But what of you? It can't be much fun to work here.' He stabbed a thumb over one shoulder, indicating the departed Domina. A smile blossomed on Fiorenza's face. She looked away and regained her composure.

'I only work in the mornings. She doesn't like me cleaning the place.'

'Hmmm.' He looked around. 'Can't say I didn't notice.' This earned him another smile.

'I just change the bedclothes and clear away the plates.' She clasped her hands in front of her. She was a generously proportioned woman, well turned out, obviously trustworthy and with some humour. A thought occurred to him.

'I could use someone like you for my own apartment.'

'My lord?'

'Bedding, plates, a little cleaning. You don't have to feed the drake; he's my concern.'

'Oh, my lord, that's a generous offer but I'm—'

'I'll match whatever the Domina's paying you. You don't even have to stop working for her. My rooms can wait until the afternoon.'

'I should probably ask her for permission ...'

'And I'll see if we can get you into a few classes.'

Her eyes went wide.

'No point working for Lord Erudito if you can't enjoy privileges of the house.'

'My lord, you are too kind.'

'Not really.' He cocked an eyebrow. 'I'm a lousy spy, a poor diplomat and bad dancer. I should do one useful thing this lifetime, you know?'

'You're too hard on yourself, my lord.' She beamed, clearly not believing her good fortune.

'Call me Dino. Formality brings me out in a rash.' He sketched a mock bow. This earned him a giggle. It was a good sound, one he needed to hear more of.

'Now get out of here. Take the rest of the day off.'

She dropped a curtsy and was gone.

'Shame your motives weren't entirely selfless, my lord,' he muttered, crossing the room, turning the key in the door. The click of the lock satisfied him intensely. The Domina would be gone for some time.

'I'll show you *half-witted spy*, you scrawny *carogna*.'

He examined the table meticulously, starting at one end, carefully setting each item down as he'd found it. There was nothing particularly interesting or out of the ordinary: records of taxes, the incomplete results of a failed census, complaints from Lord Fontein. Plenty of the latter.

He continued looking, anger fuelling his desire to uncover something on the sour-faced Domina. The bedroom door was ajar, just as Fiorenza had left it. He edged into the room, eyes settling on the bedside table.

'And now I have you.'

He'd hoped to discover some personal embarrassment, something he could use, something to hold over her. But what he found far exceeded his imaginings. The script was in a disjointed and spidery hand, hard to read and full of pomposity.

The parchment was uneven, as if water-damaged, but what unnerved him the most was the rich ruby-red ink.

My dear Domina,
    I have a simple request following my generous donation to the House Diaspora coffers. It has come to my attention that Maestro Cherubini is in grave danger. There are those in Demesne who are not fooled by his corpulent and avuncular ways. Make no mistake, the maestro is a formidable political opponent, perhaps even the equal of yourself. It stands to reason that weaker minds seek to undo him in a more direct fashion.
    It is my recommendation you assign someone to watch over him. Do this without his knowledge else he be alarmed unduly. I'm sure you have someone in your employ you can spare. It is no great chore, nor does it require much skill.
    I look forward greatly to meeting you, but am currently indisposed. Know that I am bending every effort to attending the Ravenscourt when it reconvenes. I hope to prove a staunch ally to your endeavours. Forgive my penchant for secrecy, but rest assured my agents are already among you, keeping you safe from harm. It will be a fine day indeed when we return Demesne to her old glory.
    Sincerely yours,
    Erebus

Dino sat on the bed and placed the note back on the table, puzzling over this new player. 'As if I needed further complications,' he whispered to himself.

The Orfano all but collapsed when he returned to his rooms, but not before locking the door into the corridor. He wedged a chair under the handle for good measure. Achilles watched with his usual indifference but grew increasingly agitated as Dino moved the furniture, scuttling under an armchair with a loud hiss. Dino shifted a small wardrobe across his bedchamber and placed it in front of the door to his sitting room. Finally, he slept.

17

Prospero's Star

− 18 Luglio 325

Noise.

Dino rolled over, hunger and the burning desire to make water competing for awareness.

'Hold on,' he shouted through a sore throat.

The small wardrobe took a moment to shift. The banging on the apartment door continued urgent and loud. Achilles hissed.

'I said hold on, damn you.'

Dino went back to the bedchamber and drew his sword, then stormed back to the sitting room. He kicked the chair from the door and turned the key in the lock, flinging the door open.

'I said hold on, you donkey-raping halfwit.'

An intake of breath, a grimace.

'Ah, it's you. I'm only just awake and not in charge of my humour.'

'No mean understatement.' Massimo nodded and suppressed a smile.

'Did you not think it possible I might be out?'

'I was more concerned you might be dead. People have been looking for you all afternoon.'

'Dead tired is all.' He sheathed the sword and frowned, trying to mask the foolishness he felt.

'Why don't you find your manners, and some clothes,' Massimo raised an eyebrow. Margravio Contadino wishes to speak with you in the rose garden.'

'I'll be there as soon as I can.'

Dino closed the door, pressing his forehead against the ancient wood, squeezing his eyes shut.

The Orfano emerged into the rose garden, the dregs of sleep weighing on him. He was unsure of the time, knowing only that he'd retired before noon. It was cool in the garden, the sun absent, dirty white clouds littering the sky like rumpled bedsheets. The shock of the Fonteins' scheme and the undoing of Cherubini lingered on his nerves. He felt outside time somehow, in a fugue state.

The *margravio* stood beside the statue of Santa Maria, one hand in the small of his back, the other holding a rose, testing its prickles with a calloused thumb. Massimo haunted the double doors on the far side of the garden, deterrent to any who should intrude on the conversation. Dino flicked him a salute and the swordsman returned it, but no smile appeared on his face. The Orfano hurried to the *margravio* and bowed.

'My lord, please accept my apologies for keeping you waiting.'

'Do not concern yourself with it, Lord Erudito. I know you keep unusual hours and must take your rest when you can. Are you well?'

'The business with Cherubini has put me in poor humour.'

The *margravio* nodded and regarded the rose.

'You're not alone in that. Medea has been inconsolable.' If the *margravio* felt any sadness he refused to show it, his face a mask of formality. 'My wife has been greatly concerned about you. I sent Massimo to your door because we knew you'd take the news badly.'

'Cherubini has been my constant.' Dino crossed his arms and looked away. 'Even before I discovered Lucien and Anea were my brother and sister there was always Cherubini. And now ...'

'And now they're sending him away,' said the *margravio*. Dino's eyes returned to Massimo.

'Who watches your children, my lord?'

'I have two men,' said the *margravio*, 'trusted men, veterans of the Verde Guerra. Abramo and Marcell.'

'That's good,' said Dino without much inflection. 'Forgive me for being forward, my lord, but I heard you were planning to sell a villa, despite my warning.'

'Yes.' Margravio Contadino almost smiled. 'Another reason for calling you.' He set off at a gentle pace around the garden, boots rasping in the white gravel. 'I've decided upon a scheme and it's all thanks to you.'

'How so, my lord?'

'You mentioned that Duke Fontein wanted somewhere in the country for his wife. She assumes she'll be safe there.'

'That's true, my lord.' Dino's eyes narrowed.

'I'm going to turn that to my advantage.'

'My lord, I do hope you're not—'

'Our supporters are more depleted that ever following the scandal with Cherubini. Duchess Prospero and Duke Fontein grow more daring all the time—'

'My lord, I've reason to believe that the shaming of the *maestro* was a plot, but not by Fontein or Prospero.'

'Nonetheless,' continued the *margravio*. He'd settled into a rhythm now. Dino could see he'd spent the day thinking his plan over. 'With Cherubini retired we'll be underpowered at court. But if we could hold the duchess hostage …'

'My lord, Anea would never agree to such a thing.' Margravio Contadino stopped abruptly and turned. The fencing scar through his eyebrow made his frown all the more furious.

'We're fighting for our very existence. You and I will be the first of those executed if Prospero and Fontein overthrow Anea. You of all people *know* this.'

'My lord—'

'Let Allattamento buy the villa,' snarled the *margravio*. 'I need the money. Let Fontein send his duchess from Demesne.' He stepped in close to Dino, eyes hard. 'If they harm one hair on Medea's head I'll have my vengeance in kind. By my own hand.'

Dino stared, not trusting himself to speak.

'Mention this to no one, Lord Erudito. I regret informing you of my plans. Forget this conversation ever occurred.'

'Anea would not want us to conduct ourselves like this, my lord.'

'Good night to you, Lord Erudito. Perhaps you'll see the sense of my actions in the morning.'

Dino watched the man walk away, past the statue of Santa Maria, on through the double doors into House Contadino.

Massimo hesitated, then approached. 'He's been like that all day,' said the swordsman.

'Can you speak to him?'

'You think I haven't tried? I'd hoped you'd be on hand to help. What happened?'

'I was exhausted, you know. And after the business with Cherubini I—'

'A little old to be hiding in your room?' Massimo smiled, but the words stung all the same.

'I wasn't hiding,' he replied, too quick to temper his displeasure. 'I was sleeping. Something I do precious little of.'

The first stars had appeared in the sky above the garden. Dino walked over to the stone bench in the corner, the swordsman trailing him. They sat and watched the night unfold.

'Do you remember saying I should ask for help if I was in trouble?'

'Of course,' replied Massimo.

'Can you ask the *margravio* to release you tomorrow night?'

'That might be difficult.'

'Ask Medea.' Dino wasn't used to begging. 'She wouldn't begrudge me one night, surely?'

'I can't just drop my duties to come and drown my sorrows at the *taverna*.'

'We're not going to the *taverna*.' Dino sat forward and laced his fingers.

'And I can't come spying either; the *margravio* was very clear on that.'

'That's not going to be a problem,' said Dino.

'Because?'

'Because I'm no longer Russo's spy.'

'You resigned?' Massimo had dropped his voice to a whisper.

'Not exactly. Sufficient to say the Domina and I had a difference of opinion over the Cherubini scandal.'

'So what then?' pressed Massimo.

'The night I went up to the rooftops, the night I went to House Fontein, I saw more of the grey men.'

'The raiders in the town?'

'Exactly.'

'And you want to hunt them?'

Dino nodded.

'But shouldn't we go tonight?'

'I can't. I'm having dinner with Stephania.'

'Oh.' the swordsman looked crestfallen, unusually so. 'Well, until tomorrow then.'

Massimo stood, hesitated as if he wanted to say more, then left. Dino watched him go, content he'd recruited the right ally for the job. Now he'd need to convince another ally to face another of Demesne's ills.

Dino's pulse was racing by the time he arrived on the seventh floor of House Prospero, but it wasn't the prospect of seeing Stephania, rather the many stairs that had induced the effect. Her sitting room was an artful sprawl of books and paintings, odd pieces of unfinished tailoring and swatches of fabric. A likeness of the late Duke Prospero watched over them. He had not possessed a profile that suited being captured in oils, but the duke appeared kindly and jovial, a refreshing change to the many dour portraits around Demesne.

Stephania had dressed especially for his visit, a gown of vivid cyan declaring her loyalty to House Diaspora, as if Dino had ever doubted it.

'Did you know?'

'No. Not a clue.' Dino sighed with the full weight of his sadness. 'I always assumed he was an eccentric old bachelor. House Erudito is full of them.'

'He's not that old,' Stephania said with a smile.

'An old soul, that's what Camelia would say.' Dino pulled at his lip. 'She'd also say live and let live, but that won't stop the Domina asking for his resignation.' He couldn't keep the bitterness from his voice.

'How have you been?' said Stephania, crossing to the table. 'Since the news broke, I mean?'

'Sleeping.'

She poured two glasses of wine from a *caraffa*.

'It wouldn't be so bad if he was an Orfano.'

'What do you mean?' said Dino, struggling to keep the pique from his voice.

'He'd be accepted if it came to light he were an Orfano, but as an *invertito*—'

'He's ruined.'

'It seems to me they have something in common.' She extended a glass to him. Dino took the wine but didn't meet her eyes.

'How so, exactly?' He didn't really want to hear the answer.

'One doesn't choose to be Orfano any more than one chooses to be *invertito*.'

Dino nodded and sipped the wine, letting the thread of conversation slip away. He blinked, and for a moment he could see the two men performing for Cherubini's pleasure, bodies golden in the candlelight. He flinched, causing his wine to slop over the lip of the glass.

'What's wrong?'

'Sorry. Just on edge. I've not been awake long.' He sucked a droplet of wine from his knuckle.

'Come, let's have dinner and speak of something else.' She favoured him with a brave sort of smile and led him him into a small dining room.

'I so rarely have guests, this is a treat really.'

There was a joy to Stephania that forced a smile from him, but in truth he simply desired to be back in his apartment, trying to make sense of an unravelling world.

The meal was a series of small courses: soup that failed to rouse his interest, spinach and tomato tortellini, partridge stuffed with shallots, garlic and potato, and so on. Dino's appetite was greatly diminished by the shaming of Cherubini; the wine at least was welcome. In time they retired to the balcony, where Stephania had servants bring them black coffee.

'There's something I wanted to discuss with you,' said Dino in a small voice, feeling the heat of the mug on his fingertips. Stephania adopted a look of interest; there was hope in the faint smile that touched her lips.

'Of course. You can always turn to me.' She stepped closer until he detected the light musk of her perfume.

'I stumbled across a name during my investigation of Anea's assassins.' It was only a small lie, he told himself. 'Erebus. Do you know it?'

Stephania looked surprised for a second, then shook her head.

'I've reason to believe this is someone operating from outside the castle, yet he has agents within. He also has access to a fair amount of coin.'

'Who has he compromised?'

Dino paused. It was easy to dismiss Stephania as a spoilt rich girl with nothing better to do than commission elaborate gowns, but her political insight was matched only by her acuity for intrigue.

'The Domina. Not directly; rather he's paid money into the House Diaspora coffers, but only to further his agenda.'

'He's paying for influence. What's his agenda?'

'I'm not sure. But Erebus requested Cherubini be watched because his life was in danger.'

'And was it?' Stephania frowned.

'No, I don't believe so.' Dino looked away to the dark horizon and the smattering of stars. 'I think this Erebus knew about Cherubini and his preferences; I think he wanted him unmasked for what he is.'

'Did you accept the duty?'

Dino nodded. 'I stood guard.' He sighed and set his coffee down on the parapet. 'I didn't betray him but I failed to protect him. I left the door to his apartment unlocked ...'

'And when the maid arrived the next day ...'

Dino nodded, felt the corners of his vision turn pink. He would not shed tears for the *maestro*. He looked away and cleared his throat.

'I've searched the map of Landfall for a House Erebus, one of the distant estates, but ...'

'None exists.' Stephania sipped her coffee and looked pensive. 'Let me look into it. I don't have a network of spies but I do have sympathetic ears. They tell me things.'

'Ears?'

'My mother's messengers loathe her for my father's treatment. They're loyal to me. Cherubini and I have long shared information, and the Erudito messengers tell me things from time to time.'

'And Fontein?' Dino's tone was incredulous. 'Surely not Contadino?'

'No, those houses are closed to me, not that I fear the Contadinos.'

'All this time and a whole network of spies right under my nose.' Dino grinned and shook his head in disbelief.

'Not spies.'

'Sympathetic ears.' He rolled his eyes.

'If I hear anything about this Erebus you'll be the first to know.'

'If I'm right, then Erebus has just removed a significant player from the board, one that leaves you, me, Anea and the Contadinos at a severe disadvantage.'

'I hope you're wrong,' said Stephania.

'So do I, but if I'm not ...'

'Then we'll get this bastard together.'

A single star far above the balcony stared down with an amethyst light.

'What is that?' breathed Dino.

'My mother said it was Prospero's star. Should it ever fall then so will my house.'

'I'm not sure I have much influence with stars.'

'Let's hope it remains up there a little longer then.'

Dino bade her good night. She pressed a kiss to each of his cheeks, and he descended the stairs, hand never far from his blade.

18

Drunk and Negligent

– 18 Luglio 325

Dino reached the Central Keep joining the great houses but felt no inclination to retire. The guards at the main gate let him out despite the hour, and he wandered the lonely chasm between Houses Contadino and Prospero. The triumphal arch loomed in the darkness, resplendent with heraldry and the colours of the houses. He passed under the tapering towers and sloping roofs, lost to his thoughts. The stars looked down from their appointed places, one shimmering amethyst, the rest silver.

'House Prospero's star,' he murmured. 'Look after Stephania, won't you?'

He pressed on through the town, reaching the old *sanatorio*, home to the library and his sister's laboratory. The iron-bound double doors were guarded by four soldiers in House Fontein colours. He climbed the few steps and saluted, nodding to the men and their *sergente*.

'You arrive to us late, my lord.' The man had a broken nose, bloodshot eyes, and possessed a unique odour.

'Not exactly the warm welcome I was hoping for.'

'We're under orders not to admit anyone.'

Dino squared up to the man. 'Do I look like "anyone" to you?'

The *sergente* nodded to his men, one of whom hammered a fist on the doors. It was unbarred from the other side after a few moments.

'Apologies, my lord, but orders are ...' Anything else the man had to say died on his lips as Dino glowered at him.

*

It hadn't been used as a *sanatorio* for a long time. The first three floors were fitted with vast oak shelves, extending from the centre like spokes of a wheel. Books nestled against each other in the dusty darkness. Tomes lay in piles and waited on desks, waiting for the attentions of Archivist Simonetti. Turquoise carpets, the house colour of Anea, lest any forget who opened the library, ran like garden paths between shelves and desks. Stepladders loomed by shelves, brass handrails gleaming.

It had been difficult luring people in at first, as the building was steeped in bad associations, and its gargoyles and buttresses, the black iron bars on the windows did little to welcome visitors. Anea had persisted all the same, removing the bars and fitting stained glass. And yet the *sanatorio* was not completely changed: the top three floors remained out of bounds.

He found her on the third floor, sitting at a desk surrounded by books. She was dressed in her nightgown, a triangle of silver silk covering the lower half of her face, blond hair falling in disarray around her shoulders.

'Couldn't sleep?'

I was about to ask the same question.

'I'd assumed you'd be in the laboratory.' He flicked his gaze up.

The top three floors are somewhat basic; the library is a nicer setting. I needed to check a few things. She patted the books in front of her by way of explanation. Dino frowned. She moved with a dream-like grace, her gaze not quite focused.

'Anea, we need to talk.'

The Silent Queen nodded and got to her feet, then beckoned with a finger, the gesture languid. Dino wondered at the distant look in her eye and that she hadn't embraced him. She led him to the far side of the library, pausing to draw back a thick tapestry that concealed a door.

'I'd actually forgotten where the door was.' He shook his head.

Anea produced two keys on a length of cord around her neck, using them to open a pair of locks in the centre of the door. The Orfani slipped into darkness, the smooth stone of a spiral staircase passing beneath boots and naked feet until they emerged on the fourth floor.

'I take it your studies are going well.'

She nodded but didn't slow her walking in order to sign, ushering him along the corridor, past workshops filled with the king's machines. He glimpsed benches covered in ledgers and scraps of parchment. Ten long years she'd been trying to decode the secrets of the infernal machines. A decade of simultaneously ruling Landfall and researching the king's sciences. Dino had watched her through the passing of the seasons, only admitting it was not time wasted with some reluctance. At first there had been soap and disinfectants, then analgesics and cataract surgery. Then unexpected advances in astronomy and metallurgy, followed by leaps in chemistry and pharmacology.

Some of the machines summoned ghostly words on surfaces of obsidian, displaying endless essays and complex instructions. Other machines spoke in stilted antiquated dialects. Dino hated these most of all. They were mindless things chanting recherché theories and unproven practices, not responding when questioned, dry echoes from ghosts unremembered. Most of the machines took the form of charcoal-grey rectangles no longer than a forearm, like portable gravestones. Each bore a single beady eye, staring at the world with an amethyst glow.

And there were apparatuses: microscopes and cold devices in black leather cases, cardio-this and retino-that, fine needles attached to syringes, scalpels and clamps. The old steel instruments looked cruel and unfathomable. They made his skin crawl.

Anea's rooms were small. Two battered armchairs faced each other across a hearth. It had been a long time since a fire had burned there. The room lacked all decoration: it was clear she had no use for the place besides sleeping.

What news? Do I still rule? Has Lady Allattamento staged a coup? Has the capo *finally come to his senses and married Stephania?*

'Don't be facetious; it doesn't suit you.' He slumped into one of the chairs, hand straying to his lip, stubble on his chin firm against his fingers. Anea sat patiently, waiting for him to fill

124

the silence. He'd longed to speak to her these last few weeks, but now the words wouldn't come.

'Demesne is going through changes,' he began, feeling foolish. And once more a flash of memory brought the image of hard bodies moving against each other in the darkness, sculpted in candlelight.

That is nothing new, Anea signed before pouring a glass of wine.

'Not like this. It's more serious this time.' His mind drifted to Massimo.

Her fingers flickered. *You know I would come back if I could, but Virmyre and I are close to a breakthrough. We may be able to extend longevity.*

'Margravio Contadino has set himself on a course that I can't turn him from.'

He will come to his senses. Medea will act as his conscience, just as she always does.

'Maestro Cherubini is being forced to resign.'

I heard. Regrettable but...

'You knew?' He shook his head, incredulity making the words sour. 'How could you know and not come to help? He needs you.'

What can I do? My being there would have changed nothing.

Dino looked away to the empty fireplace. There was nothing on the mantel. A pair of glass vials lay forgotten in the ashes of the hearth, missing their stoppers, empty vessels. The bookshelves behind were barren, the rug threadbare.

'And you know the Domina has had me creeping around spying?'

Anea nodded almost imperceptibly.

'She's not herself, and I'm not the only one who thinks so. She seems intent on uncovering secrets but unwilling to do much with the information.'

She is doing what she believes she must. She knows the stakes better than anyone. I sometimes thinks she knows the cost of things more than I.

The pronouncement of that uncomfortable truth sat between them.

'I overheard the Fonteins plotting against you, and she demands proof, but what more proof do I need than my own ears?'

The Fonteins will always plot against us. We need physical proof in order to move against them, legally. You know this, Dino.

He shook his head, frustrated and exhausted. 'There's something else.' He felt a tightness in his chest, the anxiety of saying words he'd not been able to whisper to himself when alone.

'I'm …' His courage slipped away. 'I'm looking for someone called Erebus. Are they an old family, one of the distant estates?'

Anea shook her head.

'Does Lucien have an Erebus serving him?'

A shrug. *I could ask Russo to make enquiries—*

'No.'

Anea blinked at the force of his interruption.

'I'd prefer you didn't mention it to her. This is a personal matter,' he lied. 'There's something I haven't told you,' he said after a pause, keen to change the subject. Anea leaned forward in her chair, into the light, revealing how drawn she was, dark rings beneath her eyes, hair pulled back with a simple tie. There was a gauntness to her frame he'd not noticed before.

'I drew steel on the day of the *dottore*'s funeral. The *capo* and I …' Another diversion from the secret he had meant to tell her. She sat back, crossing her legs at the knee, rubbing her hands palm to palm. Dino drank the wine, more for something to do than slake his thirst.

You and the capo *have been testing each other's patience for years. It seems inevitable you'll cross blades at some point. I would prefer it if you did not kill him this year if it makes any difference.*

Dino grunted in amusement, regarding the contents of his wine glass, blood red in the dim light.

Still, it is not like I have any control. Just make sure you are the one left standing when the fight is done.

Dino nodded again and plucked at his lip. Anea appeared more focused than when he'd encountered her in the library.

Are you going to tell me what is really upsetting you, or shall we continue talking about treason, nobili *and petty politics.*

126

'Hardly petty. They want you dead. And Margravio Conta-dino fears for his life. And rightly so.'

What is wrong, Dino? There is a strange look about you. Hunted. No. Haunted.

'You hardly look yourself either. Are you eating? Do you sleep?'

What is wrong, Dino?

He tried to swallow, then pulled at the collar of his shirt. He was suddenly much too warm.

'I'm ... I think I'm different.'

Well of course. Anea paused, then blinked. *You are Orfano – different by birth, by ability, by the way we conduct ourselves.*

'Yes, but I've always been more different than you and Lucien ...'

Because you have spines that grow from your forearms? Or be-cause of your eyes and the bloody tears you weep?

'No, nothing like that.'

I can make you a duke if it makes you happy. Is that it? You want more recognition, more status?

'*Porca miseria*, no.'

Well, what then?

Memories of standing in the doorway of Maestro Cherubini's bedroom flooded through him: the shock of his own arousal, the embarrassment, the desire to keep watching, the fear of being discovered and the shame. Shame had been the greatest of these, following at his heels like a faithful hound. It kept him awake when he needed rest, troubling him in the quiet hours of the night.

'Anea. When I went to Cherubini's rooms ...' He faltered.

What?

'I was there. Acting as his bodyguard on the Domina's orders. It was me. I left the door unlocked. The maid only discovered them because of my mistake.'

You were there? But not to ... not in his bedroom?

'No, but that's what I'm trying to tell you. I saw what was happening inside ...'

The sound of footsteps in the corridor. Dino started from the chair, wine glass shattering across floorboards in the deep quiet of the small hours. Dino's sword was free of its sheath before he'd drawn breath. He turned with a snarl frozen on his lips.

Virmyre faced him, hands raised, his usually stony demeanour apologetic. 'Easy. I didn't realise you were here, Dino.'

'Ever heard of knocking?' he grunted, sheathing his sword.

'It's not as if we're inundated with visitors, Lord Erudito.'

Dino glowered at him and dropped his gaze. 'I'm sorry, Virmyre. I've been on edge lately.'

'Perfectly understandable.' The *professore* turned to address Anea. 'Sorry to interrupt but the vials of *tinctura* are ready.'

Dino caught Anea glancing at him, saw the concern in her eyes turn to indecision and then resignation. Her fingers began to move but he already knew what was coming.

Can we finish this another time? I am sorry. Tomorrow perhaps?

Dino nodded and watched them leave, disappearing into the lantern-lit workshops. He drifted along the corridor, down the stairs and back through the secret door. The guards outside nodded to him, different to the ones before: a changing of the guard had occurred with the coming of midnight.

'My lord,' said the relief *sergente* cheerfully. The scent of wine was strong.

'Are you all drunk or simply negligent?'

The men stared at him, sullen and silent in equal measure.

'Not drunk, my lord, just something to help through the small hours.'

Dino stepped back and appraised the men. They were hardly fighting fit, nor were they in their cups.

'Very well. Try and stay alert, Sergente, you know?'

The walk back to Demesne was a lonely one. Robbed of the chance to unburden himself, he visited the kitchens instead.

'Just something to help through the small hours,' he whispered to himself. A vintage Barolo and Achilles were his only companions until sleep claimed him, but his dreams were heady and explicit, leaving him more desperate than ever to confide in someone.

But who could he tell such a secret to?

19

The Underneath

– 19 Luglio 325

'And this is where you saw them?' Massimo regarded the uneven landscape of roofs and towers pointing toward the star-flecked sky.

'I hid behind this chimney.'

The day's heat had cooled, a breeze drifting in from the north. Heavy cloud occluded the moon, making the difficult footing treacherous.

'What in nine hells were they doing all the way up here?' said Massimo.

'The same thing I was doing, I expect – spying.'

'It's a good way to get from one side of Demesne to the other without being seen,' admitted the swordsman.

'It also provides access to a lot of windows and balconies if you've the stomach for the climb.'

'So what now?' Massimo pulled his collar up. He wore a charcoal-grey three-quarter-length jacket, so different to his usual attire. 'Are we just going to lurk here all night and hope they pass by?'

'Unless you have a better idea?' Dino smiled. 'Advice on tracking mysterious bandits is hard to find, you know?'

'I can believe it. Where do you want to stand watch?'

Dino pointed to the vast swell of the Ravenscourt and the steep curve of the dome. Swordsman and Orfano picked their way across the rooftops on silent, if hesitant, feet.

'I'm glad we're not trying to do this at night, without torches,' said Massimo after he'd slipped the second time. Both times he'd regained his balance. 'How are we supposed to fight them if we can't see them?'

'Your eyes will get used to the dark.'

'Can't you ask Anea to cast a spell for moonlight?'

They settled at the base of the dome on the south side, looking down at the triumphal arch and the town below. Squares of golden light spilled from doorways; a dog barked; the tinkle of broken crockery drifted up to them.

'We could be in a *taverna*,' said Massimo. 'Good company, good wine—'

'You said you couldn't simply slip away from the *margravio* to come drinking, if I recall.'

'We need to work on our social lives.'

'You'll get no argument from me on that topic.'

The time dragged, and when Massimo spoke he was grateful to have something to concentrate on, if not for the subject.

'Have you spoken to Cherubini yet?'

'I've not had the chance.' Dino grimaced as the lie fled his lips, glad the darkness hid his face.

'Is Anea really going to let the Domina accept his resignation?'

'Yes, she is.' Dino sighed, remembering how distant his sister had been the previous night, only warming to him after they'd spoken for a time. 'Have you ever heard of *tinctura*?'

Massimo shrugged. 'Sounds like something you'd buy from the *dottore*. Are you unwell?'

'No, just a word I heard that made me curious.'

A shout of alarm sounded from the streets below, followed by a scream. The swordsman and Orfano lurched to their feet and squinted into the darkened town.

'Come on. We'll not see anything from here.'

Dino led them along the edge of House Erudito. Progress was slow. They alternated between checking their footing and trying to discover the source of the disturbance. A slender tower emerged from the gloaming, dark grey against the blue-black of the sky, tapering to a fine point.

'We can use this to reach the ground,' said Dino.

'How do you know that?'

'I've been doing this a while, you know? Mind your feet, though; the steps are wooden and I don't trust them.'

A crowd had gathered by the time they reached the streets, many of the *cittadini* carrying torches, a few brandishing cleavers.

'Care to tell me what happened?' Dino enquired of a *cittadino*.

'What is it to you?'

'About two *denari* if you mind your manners, the back of my hand if you don't.'

The man wore a grubby tunic and his slippers were all but worn through. He blinked a few times, reappraising the two bravos before him and the blades they wore.

'Apologies, my lord. We've had a scare is all. More of those men in grey. They took yesterday's bread from Luca's bakery. Normally he'd give it to the Sisters of Santa Maria. They hand it out to the poor, you see?'

Dino nodded. 'Which way did they go?'

A lank-haired blonde girl of around seven pointed, saying nothing.

'A little late for you to be awake, bambina?' said Massimo, settling on his haunches.

The girl sniffed. 'They went that way. It happened last week too. Papa says no one at the castle cares because the people in the castle always have enough to eat.' She sniffed again and looked at the swordsman with sleepy eyes. Dino and Massimo shared a look.

'Come on,' said the Orfano and began walking in the direction indicated, but not before pressing some coins into the girl's hand.

They tracked the grey raiders across the town, questioning each person they encountered. Startled *cittadini* lingered at street corners, complaining. The events had already succumbed to embroidery.

'I heard they took an entire leg off a pig.' The woman standing before them was as round as a barrel and had trouble standing still. Her eyes drifted in and out of focus.

'You mean a ham, and it was bread, actually.' Dino's frustration was growing. 'Stale bread.'

'Well, they went that went way, through that arch there.' The smell of wine was overpowering. 'It's not the first time either.'

'Thank you,' replied Massimo.

The courtyard was small, smells of straw and manure declaring the wooden structure on the left a stable. A well covered with a tiled sloping roof occupied the opposite corner. Three buckets had been stacked with care. The backs of townhouses made up two sides, a blocky building with narrow windows formed the fourth. The darkness was near absolute.

'We should come back in the morning.' Dino couldn't miss the weariness in Massimo's voice.

'Just give me a moment,' said Dino, approaching an iron-bound door. He knocked hard and lights appeared in the narrow windows.

'A little late for house calls, my lord,' said Massimo.

'Not when the safety of Landfall is at stake.'

'I have a hard time telling when you're mocking me of late.'

'You'll learn to love it.' Dino grinned. The noise of sliding bolts announced the door would soon be open and then light spilled out into the courtyard.

The disciple of Santa Maria stood before him, the woman from the cemetery. Her shift was new, her hair clean, the skin on her hands and arms less angry. Only her mismatched eyes remained the same, cool blue and jade green.

'You?' Dino was open-mouthed with astonishment.

'My lord.' She crossed her arms and frowned. 'Why do you come to the chapel so late?'

'Chapel?' Now it was Dino's turn to frown.

'This is the chapel of Santa Maria, and I am her disciple. What are you seeking?'

'Raiders,' said Massimo. 'Grey raiders. They stole bread from a nearby bakery.'

'Again?'

'How many many times has this happened?' said Dino.

'We didn't see them for a week or two after the first attack. Since then they've shifted their visits to nights.'

'Makes a certain kind of sense,' said the swordsman.

'We were told they came this way,' said Dino. 'Can I step inside?'

'This is a chapel!'

'I simply need to be sure. I mean no disrespect.'

'This is consecrated ground! We don't take in thieves and murderers!' Her voice had crept up, indignation making her bold.

'It's only consecrated if you believe in it,' snapped Dino. 'Now get out of my way.'

'I will not—' But Dino grabbed her by the arm, thrusting her out into the street, where she all but collapsed at Massimo's feet.

'*Porca miseria*, Dino. What's got into you?'

The place was modest, two candelabra shedding light from a dozen candles. A two-handed sword suspended by iron pitons hung on the wall. No one fought with such weapons, favouring faster, lighter blades. Dino pressed a gloved finger to the edge and felt it score the fabric. There was a blue tint to the steel, polished to a mirror finish. The disciple and Massimo entered behind him.

'What are you going to do with that?' said Dino, jabbing an accusing finger at the weapon. 'I doubt you could even lift it.'

'One day our order will have templars.' She lifted her chin and anger shone from her mismatched eyes.

'You need a temple in order to have templars.'

'The saint provides and keeps us,' whispered the disciple.

Dino searched the cells of the building, six simple rooms with narrow beds, and a small shrine at the rear, the smell of incense heavy on the air. Four Sisters pulled their bedclothes up to eyes filled with worry.

'Dino,' hissed Massimo. 'If you're quite finished I'd like to abandon this charade and get some sleep.'

The Orfano was about to reply when a voice called from the courtyard, 'What is the meaning of this? Come out at once!'

Dino rolled his eyes and Massimo broke into a weary incredulous grin.

'Oh good,' grunted Dino. 'The *capo*, just as I thought this night couldn't be any more pointless.'

Guido di Fontein stood in the courtyard with four men, two clutching halberds while the others held up lanterns. Dino recognised them by sight if not by name: House Fontein loyalists, hard men who hadn't let themselves grow soft since the Verde Guerra.

'Dino?' blurted the *capo*.

'Touch informal for my tastes, but your gifts of perception are as acute as ever.'

'Are you here to take your vows?' sneered the *capo*. 'I think you'd suit a wimple and veil.'

'Did you want anything in particular or are you just here to brighten my day?' Dino crossed his arms.

'A disturbance was reported, men forcing entry into the chapel.'

'It's true,' said the disciple. 'This man threw me out into the street and entered without permission.'

'We were looking for the raiders,' said Massimo.

'I hardly care about a few beggars.' The *capo* flashed an impish grin. 'Shame about Cherubini.'

'I imagine you're devastated,' said Dino. 'I'll be on my way now.'

But the Fontein guards made no move, obstructing the passage back to the street.

'I've not forgotten your slight in the cemetery, Dino. Perhaps we can settle that issue here?'

'With odds of five to one?' Dino nodded to Guido's escort. 'That sounds about your style.'

Massimo drew his sword slowly and without flourish. 'That's five to two.'

The Fontein men took a step back, and a look of disgust laced with disappointment crossed Guido's features.

'I can't fault your boundless arrogance, either of you,' sneered the *capo*.

'Will you *carogne* be quiet? Some of us are trying to sleep,' shouted a voice from a darkened window above. Lights appeared at windows and shutters were thrown back, faces gazing down at the armed men. There'd be no fight now, not with so many witnesses.

The *capo* muttered, and his men backed out of the courtyard, leaving sour glances in their wake. The disciple retreated behind her door, slamming it for effect, the bolts slipping into place.

'What a waste of time,' growled Dino.

'No,' replied Massimo cheerfully. 'It wasn't.'

'Care to tell me why exactly?'

'The grey raiders. They're not in the town.' He pointed to the well in the corner of the courtyard. 'They're underneath it.'

'How can you be sure?' asked Dino.

'Just a feeling. It's why no one can find them, and how they escape with such ease. They're underneath the town, perhaps beneath Demesne itself.'

'Like a nest of ants,' whispered Dino, 'spreading their colony.'

20

Learned Denial

– 26 Luglio 325

Cherubini had drawn a small crowd for his departure. Always a kindly and jovial man, he struggled to mask the pain. Emotions chased each other, passing across his broad face in quick succession. Embarrassment for the cause of his expulsion. Shame for the vicious rumours that circulated in Demesne. Gratitude for those who had come to bid him farewell.

Dino watched from afar, heartbreak welling in his chest like blood from a knife wound. He stood on a street corner of Santa Maria, viewing the scene through the broad arch of the Erudito gatehouse. The red ivy covering so much of Demesne had withered, the drought turning leaves brown like an affliction. Just two hours after sunrise and the day threatened a sultry heat, torpid air beneath dirty clouds. The sun's glaring copper disc gilded the pale blue of the sky.

'If only it were me being expelled,' the Orfano said to Achilles, perched on his shoulder. The drake sunned himself, eyes closed as if in deep contemplation.

Cherubini thanked the stable boy tightening the straps on the two ponies he'd acquired. The *maestro* was a man of some means, never a spendthrift, so the simple cart he'd bought was piled high with possessions he couldn't bear to leave. Dino guessed there had been some hard choices. The *maestro* owned a great many books, most no doubt given to the care of Simonetti. The archivist stood amid Cherubini's well-wishers, taller than most by a head, sun reflecting from the corrective optics he wore.

Exquisite furniture had been sold off to fund the journey ahead along with a selection of paintings. Two of the last hung in Dino's apartment, delivered without warning by Erudito porters that very morning. The paintings would be a constant reminder of his failure.

One moment.

One key. One lock left unturned.

Many of the *professori* who owed their livelihoods to Cherubini were absent. A quiet majority of Demesne's inhabitants had refused to be seen in the same room as the disgraced *maestro* since the scandal had gone public. All of Cherubini's good work, all the favours he'd given, the help he'd supplied, all forgotten. Preoccupation with the scandal bordered on obsession.

The days between Cherubini's discovery and departure had been cruel ones. Dino had watched him from afar, sometimes trailing him. Awkward crossings on staircases with other scholars. The averted gazes of servants. Mumbled greetings in corridors from other nobles. Long days enduring whispering behind his back from the guards. Half-heard unkind words from every dark corner. Cherubini had taken his meals in private, a week of cruelty for one who had been as sociable. Dino told himself he followed him in order to protect the former *maestro*; in truth he was simply trying and failing to approach, desperate to offer some small apology.

Camelia stood alongside Fiorenza. The cook and maid gave the rotund man supplies for his journey, sadness about their shoulders like heavy shawls. Nardo stood to one side, offering a firm salute but nothing more. Speranza was more invested, double-checking the straps on the ponies. Dino's eyes widened when she removed her scabbard and pressed the short sword into the *maestro*'s hands. Cherubini made a show of refusing the gift, then accepted. Speranza knew well what Cherubini did not: Landfall's roads were far from safe, especially through the Foresta Vecchia. There was every chance he'd need the messenger's blade.

The Contadinos emerged from a side door. The *cittadini* bowed and curtsied on instinct. Watching this act of obedience at a distance stirred embarrassment in Dino; nobility was an accident of birth, chance and station made grotesque. The feeling passed as he laid eyes on Massimo, wearing a look of profound concern on his handsome face. The nobles conversed with the former *maestro* briefly, and something changed hands between Margravio Contadino and Cherubini. Achilles scuttled from one shoulder to the other, restless and agitated.

'I know how you feel,' said Dino.

Virmyre presented himself, appearing like a thunder cloud in charcoal grey. Stephania accompanied him with a solemn cast on her features. Virmyre hugged the disgraced man, pressing his mouth close to Cherubini's ear, words intended for the former *maestro* alone. Then Virmyre turned and limped away, back to Anea, no doubt, and the king's machines.

'Too bad she didn't have the decency to come herself,' said Dino to the drake. Achilles fixed the castle with a stony stare.

It would have taken Virmyre a long time to journey from the old *sanatorio* on account of his limp, Dino realised. He felt a deep pride for the taciturn *professore*. There was something incorruptible about the man, a rare quality within the walls of Demesne.

Stephania kissed Cherubini on each each cheek, a tearful smile on her face as the former *maestro* said something amusing. He climbed up on the cart and shook the reins, tears tracking down his round cheeks, leaving a subdued crowd of waving hands in his wake. None expected to see him again. Dino waited in the heat, forcing unwelcome images from his mind that angered, aroused and confused in equal measure. The cart proceeded across the cobbles, then beneath the arch of the House Erudito gatehouse. Dino stepped into the centre of the street, mouth downturned, feeling the sun beat down on him. The *maestro* drew up beside him in the cart; the din of creaking wood and hooves ceased.

'Oh dear. Barely a minute into my journey and I'm beset by highwaymen.' Cherubini's forced cheerfulness was heartbreaking.

'Just the one, I'm afraid,' said Dino, feeling the corners of his vision swim pink with diluted blood. He would not cry, he would not allow it. 'This is all my fault,' he blurted. The ponies stamped, flicking their ears impatiently. Achilles ran down Dino's back and curled around one boot, hiding in the shade of his leg.

'Whatever do you mean?' said Cherubini, barely composed after his send-off.

'It was me. I'm sorry. I need you to know. I left the door unlocked.'

The former *maestro* looked down on him from the cart, perplexed.

'The Domina sent me to be your bodyguard. I see now that was just a ruse. She said I couldn't let you know I was protecting you.'

Realisation dawned on Cherubini's face. He trembled and swallowed. 'My dear boy. I'm so sorry. Had I known …'

'The fault is mine. I came in through the window, I should have left the same way. But I was shocked and—'

'I imagine you were,' said Cherubini in a whisper. He pressed one plump hand to his mouth, eyes brimming with new tears. 'How much did you see, Dino?'

'Everything.' He looked down at his boots, dusty from the road. 'I spoke to no one. Save Massimo. I …' He choked up at the memory of the night, confronted by the stark reality of his own arousal. 'I'm so sorry, Maestro. I wish I'd locked the door.'

'So do I, but it's done now, my boy. And you must remain here to defend Anea from these jackals.'

Dino nodded fiercely. 'What will you do now?'

'Oh.' Cherubini rolled his eyes and dabbed at his cheeks with a purple kerchief. 'I've heard that traders band together and venture down to San Marino every few months. There's an estate allied with the Contadinos before the forest proper – House Albero. I'll wait for the traders there, then I'll hire some men to act as porters and bodyguards. I can finally discover what Lucien has been up to all this time.'

'I think I'd rather come with you, if you'll let me.'

Cherubini leaned forward and took a deep breath. 'Many think me learned, my boy, but if there is one lesson the last several days have taught me it is this: you must be true to yourself. I watched those men because I couldn't bear the idea I was like them. Not participating was an act of denial, and yet here I am, cast out all the same.'

'I don't understand,' said Dino, feeling young and foolish.

'I persuaded myself that if I didn't touch another man, if I didn't love another man –' Cherubini paused, a pained frown crossing his brow '– if I didn't fuck another man, then I wasn't truly *invertito*. But I am, and there's the shame of it.'

'The shame is ours,' said Dino. 'Shame that Landfall is losing someone like you at such an important time.'

'Don't get too maudlin; I'm sure Lucien will find a use for me. They're not nearly as squeamish about sex in the south. I'd have moved there years ago if I hadn't lied to myself this whole time.'

Dino nodded, heart cold lead in his chest.

'Are you disappointed in me?' Cherubini's voice was a broken whisper, barely heard.

'I should ask you the same thing.'

'But are you?'

'I didn't want to believe it.' Dino couldn't meet his eyes. 'Not at first, when I was in your room. I …' The Orfano shrugged. 'Then I was angry. I didn't understand. It was Massimo that talked me round, of course. I've spent the whole week trying to think of anything I could do to make this right – I even sought out Anea. All week I've followed you, ghosting along corridors and standing watch. I wanted to be sure you were safe, but I couldn't speak to you. I …' The Orfano shrugged again, his lips twisting in misery.

'I don't blame you, Dino.'

'Well maybe you should. I left the door unlocked.' Achilles hissed and scuttled around his boots.

'You'll survive this, Dino, just as I will survive this. You have to accept it.'

'Well I choose not to!'

'But you must. Accept that this is done, just as I must accept my time as *maestro* is over.'

Dino blinked, willing away the film of red that slipped across his eyes.

'Don't cry for me, Dino. You set me free in a way. I can go to San Marino and be myself, finally, after all these years.'

'Is there anything I can do?'

Cherubini looked down, his broad face showing only affection. 'Yes, there is something. Always be true to yourself, Dino. No matter what.'

The *maestro* flicked the reins, and Dino watched the cart recede. It would be many miles before the contents were unpacked, many weeks until Cherubini had somewhere new to call home.

The Orfano turned toward Demesne, Achilles perched on his shoulder once more. Stephania was waiting for him at the Erudito gatehouse.

'It's done,' said Dino.

She held out a kerchief.

'What am I supposed to do with that?'

'Your eyes.' Her voice was lighter than the breeze.

'Thank you,' he managed, abashed. 'Cherubini was the closest thing I had to a father.'

'I know,' replied Stephania. Dino held the kerchief to his eyelids, ignoring the stains when the fabric came away bloody.

'Cherubini is not the only one to suffer.'

'What do you mean?' said Dino.

'My sympathetic ears have been telling me things: a handful of men have been accused of being *invertito*. There have already been beatings.'

'*Porca miseria.*'

Achilles hissed, blinking in the sunshine, scaly face deeply affronted.

'And a cook from House Fontein failed to appear for work yesterday morning.' Stephania sighed. 'The rumour persists he's fled south.'

'How is it that I'm only hearing of this now?'

'The Domina's been keeping these events from the eyes and ears of the majority, but ...'

'Your sympathetic ears.'

Stephania nodded, her gaze tracking Cherubini's progress. She linked arms with the Orfano, pulling him close.

'I'm going to find this Erebus,' said Dino. 'I'm going to introduce him to the full force of my displeasure.'

'I hope you do, Dino. I really hope you do.'

Together they watched the *maestro*'s cart edge toward the horizon.

21

The Bloody Task

– 26 Luglio 325

The Ravenscourt was well attended. Maids, cooks and porters of every rank and stripe looked down from the gallery, gossiping in whispers. The nobles clustered together in groups, each an island of hostility. Dino positioned himself at the back of the room, leaning against the wall.

'Are you sure you won't stand with me at the front?' said Stephania.

'I don't trust myself not to speak out; I'll wait here.'

The noblewoman nodded and moved across the Ravenscourt with a determined stride, fan fluttering in the heat. Achilles remained perched on Dino's shoulder, head turning in precise, small movements as he regarded the drifting nobility. Dino scoured the attendees with eyes of granite. Speranza was close by. He summoned her with a flick of his head.

She was a slight woman but moved with assurance, and riding had put muscle on her bones. There was something boyish about her, not least the men's britches she wore and the tricorn sporting scarlet and black feathers.

'That was a kind thing you did for Cherubini,' he said quietly, not taking his eyes from the dais, where the Domina waited for Anea.

'Thank you, my lord.' Speranza tucked her thumbs into her sword belt, now bereft of the weapon she'd given away.

'I took the liberty of retrieving this from a wardrobe.' Dino presented a short sword he'd concealed along the line of his leg. 'It needs sharpening and there are a few notches from where I trained with it.'

The scabbard was enamelled black, its locket dull but would polish nicely given time. The chape had seen better days and was loose.

'My lord, I can't ...'

'You can't *not* have a blade at a time like this. And you can dispense with the *my lord.*'

She drew the blade slowly, noting the basket hilt, the elegant lines of steel circling her fist. A smile worked its way onto her lips.

'Now tell me: what makes a low-paid messenger give up a sword for a disgraced *maestro*?'

She didn't get the chance to answer.

'Lords and ladies of Landfall.' The Domina's voice filled the room, silencing all.

'So it begins,' whispered Dino, lip curling to a sneer. Achilles scuttled across his shoulders, tail switching back and forth. Anea entered, pale, gaunt, distracted. Virmyre was notable by his absence, a considerable breach of etiquette. Anea was followed by a much shorter man. He would have looked like a child if not for the stick he used, the weight of years so obviously pressing down on him. Watery blues eyes stared at the room over an aquiline nose that dominated his lined face. His wife hovered behind him, nearly as wide as he was tall.

'After long consideration and a series of recommendations,' Russo gestured to the man beside Anea, 'I present to you the new *maestro* of House Erudito.'

Polite applause.

'Nice to see they found someone who isn't scared of his own shadow,' growled Dino. Speranza looked uncomfortable.

'House Diaspora recognises Maestro di Fidelio, and will aid and advise him in all ways,' continued the Domina. 'It is the wish of everyone that his appointment will herald a new period of cooperation between the houses, ushering in an era in which all can live peacefully.'

A susurration of whispering sounded from the front of the room. Dino spotted the *capo* muttering to Duchess Prospero, who smiled and fanned herself, unbearably smug. Across the room, standing in the shadow of the gallery, was Stephania.

She looked thoroughly alone, accompanied by her maid and messenger as she was. Her eyes were fixed pointedly on the dais, as if ignoring the other nobles might banish them.

The new *maestro* limped to the front of the dais and began to speak, but his words were swallowed by the great chamber. His was a thin reedy voice that cracked often. Dino's mind drifted, thinking of Cherubini on the cart with only ponies for company. He wondered at the journey ahead, through the Foresta Vecchia and down to San Marino, perched on the cliffs above the sea.

'My lord,' whispered Speranza. He looked up, noting the ceremony had droned to its conclusion without his attention. The other nobles made small gifts to the new *maestro*. He was now attired in scholarly robes and a ridiculous velvet hat that conspired to make him look like a gnome. 'Thank you for the sword,' said Speranza. She exited the Ravenscourt ahead of the crush.

Dino maintained his slouch at the back of the chamber, searching the faces of every noble as they left, looking for traces of guilt or anxiety. Could it be possible that the author of Erebus' letter was among them?

Duke Fontein took care to avoid his gaze, while the duchess offered a cold stare. Of all the houses it was Fontein that could make free with their funds. Were their coffers the source of the donation with which Erebus had secured the Domina's favour?

Margravio Contadino was deep in conversation with his wife. Medea managed a brief nod in Dino's direction before leaving. Massimo trailed behind his lord, offering a smile and the kindness of his eyes. The Contadinos were no more the author of the letter than Achilles. Duchess Prospero sneered and fanned herself while the *capo* did his best not to trip over the train of her elaborate dress. She had the wealth and the motivation. Adopting an alias to screen her intentions would be wise indeed.

Dino watched them depart in twos and threes. Anea had taken her leave through a concealed door at the back of the room. Her absence at Cherubini's departure continued to rankle. Dino nodded politely to the new *maestro*, who smiled as he passed with his rotund wife. Achilles hissed and turned his back.

'Behave yourself,' muttered the Orfano to the drake.

Golden motes drifted on the air of the Ravenscourt, stirred by the nobility's exit.

'You could at least stand like a man of the court.' The Domina stepped down from the dais, shielding her eyes from the sun with the palm of her hand. 'Instead you lounge like an upstart in borrowed finery.' It was noon. Dino felt sweat beneath his arms and between his toes. The heat paled in significance when compared to the anger inside him. 'You should stop attending if you really can't mask your contempt,' continued the Domina. 'The Ravenscourt won't miss you.' She'd come closer, strides short and measured, grip on the silver staff tight. 'This has to stop, Dino. I know you were close to Cherubini, but his position was untenable. It's all for the good.'

'Is it?' Dino pushed himself off the wall and rolled his shoulders. Achilles scuttled off, skulking at his boots, looking pugnacious. 'Because as far as I can tell, we're losing. Cherubini was our voice of reason. Anea's barely here, and when she does attend she's dead on her feet. Virmyre's much the same. That leaves us Margravio Contadino, who's long past the point of diplomacy.'

'Perhaps we can help him in this regard.' The Domina sighed, passing a hand over her features, pushing tension from her brow with ink-stained fingertips. For a fleeting second there was the ghost of the Russo he'd once known, the Russo that had existed before duty scoured her down to function. Before the Domina.

'How will you help him?' asked Dino, seizing on the thread of hope.

She composed herself. Suddenly the command was back, spine straight, dark eyes serious, mouth betraying nothing. She looked around the chamber as if hearing voices, then raised her eyes to the galleries. They were quite alone.

'Margravio Contadino seeks to keep Duchess Fontein captive on an estate to ensure the duke's good behaviour. I'd rather the duke was made to answer for his part in the plot against Anea more directly.' She'd inched closer, words dangerous and low.

'We need proof,' said Dino. 'Anea said we need proof, something to show the court.'

'The duke's no fool,' whispered the Domina. 'Do you really think he'd leave a confession lying around.'

'We can hardly pit my testimony, eavesdropping from a window ledge, against the word of Duke Fontein. We need something irrefutable – you said the same yourself.'

'I'm fully aware of what I said,' she snapped.

Dino clenched his jaw and tucked his thumbs into his sword belt. 'Sympathy for Anea will dwindle if word gets out that we're spying.'

'They know,' snarled the Domina. 'Stop being such an ingenue. They all have people inside the other houses, previously loyal retainers taking bribes for secrets or favours.'

'Perhaps.' Dino thought of Stephania and her sympathetic ears.

'They're all at it, Dino. You need to face facts. Childhood is over.' Her voice was a droning bitter thing that unnerved him.

'I don't need any lectures on maturity.' Dino had stepped closer, only a hand's width separating their faces.

'We're not giving the duke a trial,' said the Domina in a whisper.

Dino stared at her, eyes narrowing to slits. 'Assassination then?'

The Domina nodded. 'If you have to give it a name, I suppose that's as good as any.'

Dino crossed his arms and snorted with disgust. 'I won't do it.'

'Be practical, Dino. This is how things are now. They struck first.'

'And we're to stoop to their level?'

'You heard with your own ears that he ordered the attack; now be a man and make him pay for his insolence.'

Dino grimaced and shook his head. 'Anea would never—'

'This is precisely why Anea put me in charge. I can do the things she can't.' The Domina's mouth was a cruel sneer. 'She longs to be rid of the wrangling in court. This is an elegant solution. And you're perfect for it, Dino. The perfect killer.'

'I kill when combat is joined; I don't hunt people.'

'Then perhaps I'll ask Massimo.'

Dino glowered at her but said nothing, then clicked his fingers twice, causing Achilles to scuttle up his leg and across his back to the perch of his shoulder. Man and drake passed between the double doors of the Ravenscourt, down the stairs and through the king's library. He emerged into the circular corridor of the Central Keep, into the mass of porters, cooks, messengers, scholars and aides marching about like ants. Stephania lurked by a buttress. She gestured him over with a wave.

'The Domina has asked you to start spying for her again.'

Dino nodded, then swallowed, plastering a smile over the lie.

'Is there really no one else?'

'Not for the task she has in mind.' A task a good deal more dangerous than lurking on window ledges or dressing up as a cook.

'Do you want me to speak to Russo?' pressed Stephania, eyes full of concern. She reached out and touched him lightly on the forearm.

'No. If I don't do it then she'll make Massimo, something I want to spare him from.' He pressed a hand to his face. 'I'm sorry, Stephania. I've said too much.'

'You're a good person, Dino.'

He nodded again. 'I have to go and prepare a few things.'

She kissed him on each cheek and went on her way, back to the sunny balcony of her apartment, no doubt. How he envied her.

Dino walked the winding corridors deep in thought, guessing likely outcomes, worrying at consequences. He spent the day drifting through the deep shadows of Demesne. Each corner he took, each doorway he passed, brought him closer to the awful truth.

'There's not a single soul I can depend on to finish what Duke Fontein started,' he whispered to the drake. Achilles wrapped about his neck, nudging his cheek with a cool snout.

'I have to spare Massimo this bloody task, spare him this war of assassins.'

22

Retrospect
– Settembre 318

I have always loathed this occasion, signed Anea. There was a measure of flint in her jade-green eyes, tension in the set of her shoulders.

'Something else you have in common with Lucien.' Dino smoothed down the front of his jacket. 'I can think of better ways to kill three hours.'

La Festa del Ringraziamento was held at the end of summer each year. The great houses took turns hosting the event, trying to outdo each other.

The Orphani stood beyond the double doors of House Fontein's main hall. Anea wore a gown of cream brocade with elegant flowers embroidered in turquoise. Matching silk gloves reached past her elbows. The headdress resembled a profusion of turquoise leaves, swept back from her forehead, her hair an intricate plait. A veil completed the outfit in matching cream. She'd applied a smear of kohl to her eyes that he'd not seen before. Now eighteen, Anea's curiosity had turned to any number of subjects, cosmetics being the least of them. Her main passions were biology, chemistry and democracy, which made her popular with House Erudito but resulted in few allies among the remaining nobles. House Contadino were obedient more from loyalty than shared gain, while Duchess Prospero saw the silent Orfano as a threat to her economic power.

The doors to House Fontein opened and the room turned as one to regard the siblings. A brightly dressed popinjay bellowed their full titles.

'Got them right for a change,' whispered Dino, not that he

was overly concerned with heraldry and etiquette. Anea by contrast was meticulous.

The great Hall of House Fontein was as dour as those who ruled it. White marble, always in short supply on Landfall, had been passed over in favour of dark granite tiles. Many joked that Fontein would rather spend money on swords than interiors. Others pointed out that blood would not stain granite half as noticeably as it would white marble. An army of servants had polished the floor until it not only gleamed, but promised to upend any who hurried on its surface. It was for this reason there was seldom any dancing when House Fontein hosted *La Festa*, adding to its dour reputation.

'Just like the Fonteins to enjoyed keeping people off balance,' muttered Dino as he escorted his sister into the room.

The duke and duchess were immaculate. He was in dress uniform, complete with duelling blade featuring a swept hilt chased with precious stones. A broad scarlet sash encircled his waist; a matching sash was tied about his sword arm. The duke regarded his guests as if they were an inconvenience. The duchess wore a high-necked gown in purple, a fan of black lace occupying her hand, a none-too-subtle display of the alliance between Fontein and Prospero. The gown was long in the sleeve with a corset that looked to do her harm.

'Do you think there's any truth to the rumour she spends her nights in a vat of lemon juice sucking wasps?'

Anea stiffened and flashed him a warning glare.

'Surely that's the only explanation for the look on her face.'

Dino advanced the length of the room with his right hand raised, Anea's resting upon it. They presented themselves to the hosting couple and quickly excused themselves. There were no pleasantries to be exchanged; such things had long since withered on the vine. Anea had done many things to change the nature of Demesne since coming to power, chief among these that the soldiers now reported directly to the Domina. House Fontein had been reduced to a training academy. The duke had since gone to great pains to lure away any number of smiths and armourers from House Prospero. If this antagonised the mercantile house it didn't show. Dino suspected an agreement had been reached between Salvaza and the white-haired duke. Houses never relinquished staff without histrionics.

Anea took up residence in one corner of the hall, where she communicated through the medium of the Domina. Virmyre was ever close at hand, sipping wine while keeping other guests at arm's reach. He nodded to Dino pleasantly before being accosted by Mistress Corvo, the dance teacher. Age had not been kind to her, and speculation was rife regarding her retirement. Dino for one wouldn't miss her; he'd long since dropped such lessons from his schedule. The dance mistress wore her customary black, her hair pulled up into a bun that only served to make her visage more skull-like, papery skin ever thinner with each passing year.

The Contadinos remained apart from the throng, attended by a cluster of courtiers. Dino found his eye lingering on Massimo, who'd recently risen to the rank of adept under Ruggeri. Nardo was there too, uncomfortable in his finery. Dino had decided some men were made for the road, some the court, but rarely were such men the same person.

Maestro Cherubini shouldered his way through the crowd and clapped a chubby arm about Dino's shoulders, favouring him with a broad grin. 'And why have you two arrived so late?'

'There's only so much excitement Anea can stand,' replied Dino. 'She has a fragile heart.'

'So droll.' Cherubini laughed, a touch too loud perhaps, then launched into spirited debate with a *dottore* regarding the finer points of biology. Dino noted the *maestro*'s eye was drawn time and again to a servant bearing a tray of wine.

Stephania appeared, a fan of fluttering silk in her hand like a captured butterfly. She'd also attired herself in turquoise, an open statement of continued displeasure and estrangement from her mother. The gown left her shoulders and arms bare, while tightly cinched at the waist. Stephania drew a wealth of attention from the men in the room, some old enough to be her father. Dino could admit she dressed well, but felt nothing else, certainly not the stirring promised by Camelia.

'I swear you get taller each time I lay eyes on you,' said Stephania.

'I had the cobbler put heels on my boots.'

The Orfano took two glasses from a tray and handed her one, earning himself a few dire looks in the process. Dino wondered if he were missing some vital attribute. His fourteenth year had ushered in a broadening of the shoulders and a downy fuzz on his top lip, which he duly scraped off once a week. And there'd been other changes he was less inclined to speak of. His interest in women as such remained zero; certainly he'd no interest in Stephania other than as a friend. They danced a slow and careful gavotte for fear the polished tiles leave them sprawling.

'Let's take it slowly,' she whispered.

'On a floor like this, there's no other way.'

Stephania didn't mention the fact he was shorter than her, and he kept his opinion that she'd applied too much rouge to himself.

Over a year and a half had passed since Lucien had departed for the coast with an entourage carried in many carts and wagons. Stephania, keen not to be regarded as a sad jilted fiancée, had entertained a number of suitors. She'd settled on one in particular.

'I can't see your beau here tonight,' said Dino.

'Ah. We decided to part.' She cleared her throat. 'I decided we should part.'

'Did he do something wrong?'

'No, nothing.' She paused as they danced. 'He's kind in his own way, but as sparse spending coin as he is giving compliments.'

'You're not telling me something.'

'We argue. He's intimidated by my political successes.'

In short, she'd yet to meet her equal. Dino felt a pang of sympathy for her. Stephania smiled sweetly, passing off the end of her courtship as no more than a minor irritation. The tightness around her eyes confirmed the contrary.

'I see Duke Fontein is taken with Lady Allattamento,' said Stephania, keen to change the subject. The minor noblewoman was famously fertile, littering Demesne with a profusion of noble children. Now, with her husband in the grave, her gaze hunted the steps of other men, usually ones bearing wedding bands.

'I heard she'd made a play for the *capo*. He nearly took the bait, but your mother intervened.'

'It must have taken five servants just to get her down from the ceiling.'

'Six.'

This petty *commedia* had thrown Dino's own lack of lust into sharp relief in his mind. Was it some quirk of being Orfano? And if so, why had Lucien remained unaffected? Did Anea feel any stirrings toward men? Or did she share his affliction, a deadened yearning? Did they both lack some anima or essence? All these worries tripped and stumbled across the breadth of his thinking, and in doing so caused Dino to slip on the polished floor. He regained his balance without undue fuss. Mercifully the music ended.

'Thank you.'

'I dare say you'll be asked to dance by any number of men before the night is over.'

'I expect so.' A look of sadness crossed her face before she disappeared back in to the crowd, a rustle of skirts, fan already a blur in her hand.

Duke Fontein loomed over Dino's shoulder with a gleam in his eye that said he'd sampled his cellar too keenly. Dino by contrast always remained sober. The stabbing he'd endured four years ago still haunted his dreams. He was never without a dagger in each of his boots and a sword cane to hand. There were few things he cherished more.

Duke Fontein rumbled some inconsequential sourness that Dino failed to interpret. He never had much interest in what the duke had to say and rarely feigned it. Tonight however was *La Festa,* and Dino felt the inclination to set aside the grudges and feuds of the past. He nodded and tried for a smile, always an able parry to the drunken conversational thrusts of old men. He gleaned the words *maestro superiore di spada* from the duke's wine-soaked grumblings, and also the word *capo*. It made sense, Dino supposed. Guido di Fontein was old enough for the position, although younger than both Maestri di Spada

Ruggeri and D'arzenta, who were surely more deserving of the role. It was then that Dino realised he was being warned not to contest the *capo*'s claim. He struggled to keep the humour from his face. And the incredulity. Who in their right mind would appoint him, a fourteen-year-old, *maestro superiore di spada*? It was unthinkable; no one in Demesne would do such a thing.

Unless of course an Orfano sat upon the throne.

Dino took a step back and prepared to make his excuses, tired of the duke's drunken warning. Lady Allattamento swept in, a gust of autumn in brown silk. A proliferation of gold jewellery decorated every finger and lobe. She whispered something to the duke, whose interest in the Orfano dwindled as she lavished her attentions on the old man. Duke Fontein turned on his heel, hand straying to the small of the noblewoman's back. Dino watched the duke lurch off suspecting his rest would be taken in Lady Allattamento's chamber.

'But why shouldn't I be *superiore*?' he said under his breath. 'I'm already twice the swordsman Guido is.'

'What did you say?' Stephania had returned.

'I want to be *superiore* after my final testing. I'm going to spend my every waking moment making it happen.'

'I've heard Duke Fontein has other ideas.'

'Duke Fontein can go to hell.' A smile stole over Dino's lips, mischief twinkling in his grey eyes.

'*Superiore*', he whispered to himself as Duke Fontein exited the room.

23

Vecchio Bastardo

– 28 Luglio 325

Dino sat on the windowsill, back to the glass, the lead lattice-work a stark black against the day to come. His legs were crossed, one ankle resting on the opposite knee, while his hands turned over a stiletto, fingers tracing the hard lines of the weapon. The Domina's request weighed on him, along with the knowledge of Margravio Contadino's plot against Duchess Fontein. His course had been decided with doubt and reluctance, but in the end he simply desired to keep Massimo clear of the dishonourable task.

Santa Maria slept, held fast by the soft embraces of blankets or the arms of lovers. A solitary cockerel strutted in the streets, ready to declare the day begun. The taverns hosted those too drunk to walk home, labourers in the main, hard at work on the new church. Burly men slept under tables that had been piled with flagons just hours earlier. Wretches slept on street corners, clutching begging bowls, dreaming of full stomachs and better days. Bakers commenced their chores, preparing the ovens and dough for the daily bread. Soon the market would fill the piazza, the air sullied by the boasting and harangues of traders, wagons would creak along narrow roads, filling the town with the smell of horse, but for now the majority were abed.

But not Dino.

It would be dawn soon, the last dawn Duke Fontein would see. The old man turned in his bed and grumbled, words throaty and half formed. What torments pursued the slumbering duke? Surely he was beset by subconscious phantoms, made manifest by the guilt of old crimes. Perhaps he simply suffered indigestion. There was no need to wake him, no need to rush this final act. Death, while rarely dignified, never succumbs to haste.

The chamber was furnished with paintings on each wall. Dino guessed the stern patrician in oils for the previous duke. He wore his beard in the royale style, looking out from the portrait beneath shaggy eyebrows. The family resemblance was strong. Both men had snow-white hair, shared the same inscrutable brown eyes. That both men would die in their sixties was another resemblance they shared. For now the current duke slept on, unaware of his impending destiny.

The well rounded yet sour-faced woman could only be the previous duchess. Her once black hair was shot through with grey and fell to her shoulders in oiled ringlets. She wore a gown in house colours and stood for her portrait, a wolfhound by her heel, all pricked ears and lolling tongue. If only all the subjects of House Fontein were as obedient as that. Still, thought Dino, even the most loyal of hounds could turn rabid.

The duke growled something in his sleep, beginning to wake.

And there was the nude, tasteful yet informal. This painting stood apart from the others, its frame markedly less impressive. There was a hurried, almost unfinished feel to the brushwork. The woman was young, and had not been born with aristocratic features, but possessed an earthier beauty. A sadness haunted her eyes, matching the bouquet of lilies she clutched.

'What?' The duke was awake. Sunlight had bled into the chamber, curtains tied back neatly. This was Dino's final gift to the duke.

'What?' The duke repeated. Any other enquiries died on his lips as he recognised the Orfano perching on the windowsill. He dragged himself up from the bedclothes into a sitting position.

'Do make yourself comfortable,' he grunted.

'I already did,' replied Dino, not taking his eyes from the stiletto. It possessed a tapering triangular blade coming to a turned ricasso before the perfunctory parrying guard. Each side of the blade bore an inscription in the old tongue. *Tempo. Velocita. Misura.* The script had been inlaid with gold. The weapon was exquisite. Not made to slash, only to pierce, deep wounds to puncture lungs and kidneys, hearts and stomachs.

'Where are my guards? You'll not get away with this.'

'But I already have.' Dino ran a thumb across his lips, pensive. 'The first of them is probably asleep. He's been balls deep in one of Lady Allattamento's girls. Courtesan is such a strange word, isn't it? It's fascinating that the upper classes can make a word for whore sound sound so appealing. Expensive though, you know?'

The duke swallowed but remained silent, eyes narrowing.

'You've been patronising them rather heavily of late, so I hear.'

The duke shook his head and opened his mouth to remonstrate but quickly abandoned the notion.

'So much so your guard couldn't resist the opportunity to discover what all the fuss was about.' Dino turned his attention back to the stiletto.

'What of Leoncarlo? He's been my man for thirty years. You don't buy off loyalty like that with expensive skirt.'

'Leoncarlo was loyal. Unfortunately for him, a consignment of weapons was found in his home a few hours ago. We had no choice but to arrest him for treason. We suspect he might be planning a coup. He's being questioned by the Domina as we speak. You know how she likes the sound of her own voice. The investigation could go on for a while.'

Dino let this sink in, watching as the old man became aware of just how impossible his situation was.

'But the door was locked,' mumbled the duke.

Dino laughed, a brittle, unpleasant sound.

'Gaining entrance was the easy bit. Do you remember spilling that *caraffa* of red wine over the rug in your sitting room? It must have been three years ago now.'

'What in nine hells has that to do with anything?' The duke coughed, then coughed some more.

'Do you remember losing your temper at your maid, Isabella? She failed to remove the stain.'

The duke swallowed and had the good grace to look guilty.

'Do you remember chasing the girl out of your apartment,

shouting at her as she left? She was so scared she slipped and fell down the stairs.'

This provoked a fresh round of coughing from the duke, who reached to his bedside table for the glass of water there. He drank noisily, paused only to fix Dino with a hate-filled look, then drained the rest of the glass.

The event was well known throughout Demesne. The serving staff had nicknamed Duke Fontein the VB following Isabella's tumble.

VB.

Vecchio bastardo.

The maid had broken her wrist and the bone hadn't set right. She'd not had the money to pay a *dottore* and the wrist remained crooked. The duke kept her on out of shame, so they said.

'That was regrettable,' admitted the duke

'How hard do you think I needed to persuade her?'

'She'd never give a *strega figlio di puttana* the key.' The duke thrust out a thick finger. 'That's treason.'

'She didn't have to give me the key, just leave the window open.'

Dino tapped on the glass behind him, then smiled, savouring the impotent fury of the *vecchio bastardo*. The duke snapped, reaching under his pillow, finding nothing. In his rage he threw the pillows aside, fingers searching.

Dino gave low whistle. 'Looking for this?' He held up the stiletto. The dawn light caught the gold and sent bright reflections around the room.

The duke cursed under his breath.

'It's nice.' Dino held the weapon up to the sunlight. 'I may keep it. Was it a gift from your father?'

The duke said nothing, all but shaking with fury.

'Maybe I'll give it to the maid. It won't help her wrist any, but I'm sure she could make a coin or two if she sold it to the right person. I might buy it from her myself.'

'So is this level we're stooping to now?' muttered the duke. 'Killing old men while they are abed? Hardly the stirring victory a real swordsman yearns for.'

Dino shrugged, then allowed himself a smile at the duke's goading.

'Well? Have you nothing to say for yourself?'

'If I stoop it is only because you brought the roof down, my duke. Sending three bravos to my sister's chamber. To kill her.' He regarded the point of the stiletto. 'Hardly the stirring victory a real swordsman yearns for.'

'You have no proof.'

'I have my own ears. I heard you and you wife plotting against the throne. Against my sister. Against me. I know you bought the villa on the Contadino estate to hide your wife there. Just until the castle was safer. You'd be surprised how much I know.' He'd been enjoying this until now, but suddenly his mouth was filled with sourness. The memory of the three bravos entering Anea's chamber swept away any vestiges of compassion. There would be no last-minute change of mind, his conscience silenced in the shadow of his anger. Only vengeance remained.

'You have no right,' muttered the duke, 'no right to come here and judge me. You don't know what we've endured. You don't know the sacrifices I've made! Forty years I've served Demesne, forty years I've been its watchman. A proud defender.' He actually beat his chest with one fist at this last remark.

Dino clapped his hands slowly, lip curled. The mock applause died out.

'Forty years? You must have seen much during that time, must have been party to a lot of secrets. Secrets like all those abductions. Every three years or so, by Lucien's reckoning. I make that at least ten girls under your watch. Ten daughters abducted.'

The duke's eyes strayed to the picture of the nude.

'Not so much the proud defender on those dark nights, my duke.'

'We had no choice,' he whispered.

'There's always a choice,' replied Dino from between gritted teeth.

'The king ... the Majordomo had spies everywhere. There

was nowhere we could go without his knowing. We objected, of course. So many times we tried to break the agreement.'

'What agreement?'

'The hecatomb agreement.'

'Who else knew?' pressed Dino. The stiletto felt heavy in his hand, and he had a terrible keenness to use it.

'Fontein, naturally. Usually a *maestro di spada,* but sometimes the *capo.*'

'You mean Guido?

'*Porca miseria*, no. I wouldn't trust Guido to find his arse with both hands. We appointed him as a favour to Duchess Prospero. He's the worst *capo* I've ever seen. Simpering ponce.'

'That's one thing we can both agree on at least. Who else?'

'A dozen guards. Ones we knew we could trust, often *sergenti.*'

'And the other houses?'

'No.' The duke shook his head. His eyes looked glassy and unfocused. 'Can you imagine if Erudito had known? Cherubini and his limp-wristed intellectuals would never have had the stomach for what needed doing. And Contadino? They'd never have stood for it. That Medea has some fire in her. I would have liked to have burned my fingers on that flame.'

'I'd say you've played with more than enough fire.'

The duke nodded. 'If you had a wife as cold as mine you'd welcome the chance to burn.'

The sun continued its ascent. The day would be beautiful, cloudless and long. The roosters set to their din, and Santa Maria woke with grumbling voices and stomachs.

'So how do we do this?' said the old man finally. 'You could slash my wrists and call it suicide.' He grinned, but there was no humour to it, just a sick resignation.

'That's the trouble with a good stiletto.' Dino fingered the point of the weapon. 'They're only good for stabbing.'

The duke nodded again. He'd known as soon as he saw the weapon. 'Stabbing, eh? I always wondered how it would feel to die like that. Drowning in your own blood as it fills your lungs. Do you know, I've always secretly wanted to die in my sleep. Isn't that strange?' He looked away from Dino, staring into the distance. 'All the weapons I can use, all the men I've trained, all the death I've seen. The wounds. The blood.' The duke turned his eyes back to Dino. 'What a load of shit. And for what? For nothing. I'm glad it's over, to be honest. Ten years ago, well, that would have been a different story.'

'I'm not going to stab you,' said Dino. His anger had fled him, burned off by the rising sun perhaps, like mist.

The duke frowned at him.

'You were dead the moment you finished the water. I had something made, something that would loosen your tongue as you died. I was worried you'd take all your secrets to the grave.'

'I see,' said the old man. He took the glass and turned it over in his hands. 'So it was all down to this?'

'That glass. A spilled bottle of red wine. Plus a score of abducted women.' Dino sighed, 'And three assassins sent to kill my sister.' He concealed the stiletto in the sleeve of his jacket. 'But in the end it was just a glass filled with water.'

'And poison,' added the duke. And then his eyes rolled back in his head and he slumped against the headboard. The glass rolled from his fingers, becoming lost among the cream folds of the bedding.

24

Drinking Alone

– 28 *Luglio* 325

The Domina's chamber was in the same state of cluttered disarray. Fiorenza opened the door, flashing him a smile.

'You look exhausted, my lord. Can I offer you some refreshment?'

Dino shook his head. He wanted nothing save to return to his room and fall deeply asleep. Maybe he could forget this awful business if he slept long enough. Perhaps a *dottore* could slip him a preparation, ensuring a dreamless slumber. He'd much need of it.

'Lord Erudito for you, my lady.'

The Domina remained at her desk, hat discarded to one corner, hair matted and tousled about her shoulders. She scratched at parchment with a quill, not looking up. He stood there for a handful of seconds, feeling the weight of the stiletto where it lay along the inside of his forearm beneath his jacket sleeve. Another source of shame stored alongside his cuffs and the bindings of his tines. Taking the blade had been a mistake; he should have slipped it beneath Duke Fontein's pillow.

'It's done,' he said, looking out of the window and watching the *cittadini* go about their work. Somewhere below, children laughed, but the sound was foreign to Dino, like another language. The Domina continued her correspondence, seeming to ignore him.

'I said it's done.'

'Fiorenza, leave us.' The maid flashed a look of concern at Dino as she left, pulling the door closed behind her with care. The Domina looked up from her work. There was a gleam to

161

her eye he didn't care for, and a vitality that had been absent for some time.

'How?'

'Poison.'

The Domina laughed, but it was loaded with bitterness, as hateful a thing as Dino had ever heard. She reached up with both hands and massaged her temples, a contented sigh as her eyes slid closed and reopened.

'The most formidable swordsman in Demesne and you employ poison?' Her voice was a sleepy drone. Another laugh. 'Did you lose your stomach for killing? Were you afraid the old bastard might best you?'

'More elegant that way. Less mess. Fewer questions.'

'Until the *dottore* examines him.'

'I took the precaution of leaving half a *caraffa* of wine and two glasses on the dresser. His maid will find a whore's small clothes when she strips the bed. Rumours will spread. They'll say he died with his cock inside a courtesan. Too much excitement for an old heart.'

The Domina stared at him, eyebrows raised. 'Impressive.' She nodded with a begrudging respect.

Dino shrugged. It had not been easy – many things to set up, feints and distractions. He didn't enjoy lying for a living but he'd managed it.

'It seems I underestimated you, Dino.'

'You address me as Lord Erudito. And yes, you did.'

He swept from the room, leaving the door ajar, struggling to keep the sneer from his face. The duke's stiletto weighed heavy in his sleeve. And on his heart.

'Come in,' he shouted, too loud. He was amused to find himself slurring. Nardo stepped into his sitting room, hat in one hand, the other gripping the hilt of his blade. Always a serious man, Nardo looked on the verge of anger. Massimo entered close behind, the look of concern on his handsome face turning to one of curiosity. Dino was slouched in an armchair, feet up on a low table. A *caraffa* of red wine stood close at hand, accompanied by a glass empty but for dregs. A spare glass on the table reflected the dying sunlight as it dwindled. His boots were unbuckled, shirt undone, jacket hanging from one corner of the bookcase. The couch was occupied by his sword belt and scabbard.

'Huh. Unlike you to leave the door unlocked. Expecting company?'

'Not really,' said Dino, eying Massimo with a broad grin. 'But you'll do. You'll do just fine. Join me for a drink?'

'I think you've had enough,' said Massimo with an embarrassed smile. Nardo eyed Dino warily as the Orfano turned a long stiletto over in his hands.

'Suit yourself,' replied Dino.

'Margravio Contadino said I should bring you the news.'

'News?' said Dino, distracted by Achilles. The reptile had scuttled up onto the couch and was staring at Nardo from beneath a scaled brow.

'Duke Fontein is dead,' said the messenger in a quiet voice.

Dino nodded twice as if he were hearing an appeal in the Ravenscourt. He passed the stiletto to his other hand, then proceeded to pour another glass of wine.

'Did he fall down a staircase?'

Achilles yawned and continued to look at Nardo with a baleful eye from the couch.

'Huh. Speranza said he died in his sleep.'

'I imagine the duchess is *overcome* with grief,' said Dino, taking another sip.

'You don't seem very surprised,' said Nardo, his gaze lingering on the stiletto.

'There's a rumour he wasn't alone when he died,' said Massimo from beside the door, which he closed and locked. Dino shrugged and took another sip of wine as Nardo took the chair opposite, removing his gloves. Massimo remained standing, hand on the hilt of his sword as if expecting trouble.

'Sit down, Mass,' said Dino. 'You're making the place look untidy. Untidier. Is that even a word?'

'They're saying he was with a woman when he died,' said the swordsman.

Achilles chose this moment to hurry over to the armchair

and take up a position on Dino's shoulder, tail curving around the nape of his neck.

Nardo tossed his gloves onto the table and rubbed at his temples with one hand.

'Hell of a thing.'

'Poor girl,' muttered Dino. 'Imagine having to ride that sour bag of bones, just for the fucker to die inside you.'

'Huh. This girl, this whore. They say she took something from the duke – a knife or something.' Nardo's gaze lingered on the stiletto even as Dino slid it inside his sleeve to lie flat along the inside of his forearm. 'It has gold engraving on it. Quite a piece apparently. Very recognizable.'

'Well, I reckon she earned it,' said Dino, a drunken scowl on his features. 'Don't you?'

'Not for me to say,' replied Nardo.

Dino set his glass on the table and stood, swaying. He steadied himself on the mantelpiece and took a deep breath. 'Virmyre always said drinking alone was … something. Something bad.'

Massimo stood and crossed to the mantelpiece, regarding the swords in their scabbards suspended by black iron hooks from the chimney breast: a rapier with a swept hilt, a saber from the Verde Guerra, a court sword with the pommel fashioned after a raven's head.

'Quite a collection.'

'Most of them are blunt,' said Dino. A terrible dread closed its fingers around his heart. 'Just dangerous bits of old metal really.' He took out the stiletto and placed it on the mantelpiece. What did he care if they knew? He'd done them both a service. If it were not for him Massimo would find himself asked to kill for the Domina. Nardo's life would surely become easier now that House Contadino had one less opponent.

The red light of evening shone from the golden letters on the blade. *Misura.* Massimo looked away, oblivious to the proof of Dino's guilt, turning to regard a painting that had belonged to Cherubini. The scene was a nocturne, great pine trees reaching up to the stars, a slash of purple lightning descending from the heavens. Dino had always thought it gaudy and fanciful.

'What are you celebrating?' asked Nardo in a disapproving tone.

'I'm drinking to Cherubini's departure.' Dino scowled again. 'He always knew a good vintage.'

'You can have too much of a good thing,' said Massimo.

'Virmyre always said drinking alone was ...' Dino eyed the collection of weapons, then stretched out one arm along the mantel to obscure the stiletto.

'We have to get back to the *margravio*,' said Massimo. 'He's worried for Medea and the children.'

'So soon? But you've only just arrived.'

'We have other people to see, I'm afraid,' said Massimo, who smiled and shook his head. 'Marchesa Contadino wanted us to warn you there is an assassin abroad in Demesne.'

'There's no assassin,' Dino replied, but the word evaded him, came out horribly slurred. 'The handsome swordsman and the loyal messenger, what a pair.'

'How are you so drunk?' asked Massimo.

'With the liberal application of this,' replied Dino, waggling the wine glass, his head drooping forward.

Nardo stood and crossed to the door, opened it, taking a moment to check the corridor was empty.

'You go on,' he told Massimo. The swordsman left with a quick salute.

'Do you know what you're doing, Dino?' said Nardo. The Orfano turned to him with a gaze as pointed as any weapon, the grey of his eyes transformed to silver for a second, a trick of the light.

'Do any of us?'

'It's one thing to go looking for trouble,' said Nardo; 'it's another to welcome it into your home. Have a care, my lord.'

The Orfano nodded, eyelids heavy with the wine. When he opened them he was alone save for Achilles. He locked the door and stumbled to bed. The room spun unkindly in the darkness, forcing him to light a candle and keep his eyes open. Somehow the stiletto was back in his hand, an unwelcome weight, a cold reminder. He'd given the duke a painless death at least.

Tempo. Velocita. Misura.

'Virmyre always said drinking alone ... *Porca miseria*, what did he used to say?'

25

The Vine-Choked Divide

– 4 Agosto 325

The castle bustled with its usual fervour, members of the houses going about their business. Students of blade and book went their separate ways, guards stood to attention and saluted Dino's passing. He chewed his lip as he paced the flagstones, acknowledging them with curt nods. A week had passed since Duke Fontein's death, four days since the great and the good had paid their respects, sincerely or otherwise.

'My lord?' Speranza appeared from a side corridor in House Erudito bearing a bouquet of lilies, an anxious smile troubling her lips.

'What have I told you about addressing me like that?'

She fell into step, struggling to keep up with his stride. 'I've not seen you recently.'

'I've been teaching. The *nobili* pay a fortune to have their sons trained to be effective killers. Pity they don't spend the same money to educate them.' He flashed her a look. 'I hear your own lessons are progressing admirably.'

She blushed, hand straying to the blade and scabbard he'd given her. She'd fixed the chape, and the locket gleamed. They scaled the steps up to his apartment in silence. Dino gestured to the couch once they were inside.

'Excuse me for a moment.' Speranza nodded and removed her hat, laying the flowers on the low table. Dino emerged moments later in a clean shirt to find her standing at the fireplace, admiring the craftsmanship of the engraved stiletto.

'Was there something you wanted, Speranza? Or do I have a

secret admirer.' He gestured at the flowers, a tiny smirk tugging at his lips.

'The flowers are from the Domina.'

'*Porca miseria*. This is how rumours start. First flowers, then a private dinner.' Dino raised an eyebrow. 'She's somewhat old for me though, you know?'

Speranza hid a smile behind her hand and shook her head.

'She would have you take them to Duke Fontein's mausoleum.'

'*Maledetta puttana*,' he grunted. Speranza placed the stiletto back on the mantel, favouring it with a look of curiosity before turning to face him.

'You appear in very poor humour of late, my lord. People are saying—'

'Stop calling me that!' He pressed thumb and forefinger into the corners of his eyes and let out a sigh. An awkward moment passed before he spoke again, more quietly. 'What? What are people saying, Speranza?'

'They're saying things aren't the same any more.'

'Masters of understatement, all.' He rolled his eyes.

'Lady Diaspora is never seen, Maestro Cherubini is sorely missed and Margravio Contadino is all but unapproachable.'

'I can't fault them so far – accurate and fair,' he threw himself down on the couch and stretched out a coaxing hand for Achilles. The drake remained perched on the windowsill, sunning himself contentedly. 'Fine,' grumbled Dino. He turned back to Speranza, who had taken a seat in the armchair facing the door. 'What else are they saying?'

'That Duke Fontein died in bed with a whore. Although some refute this. They say there's some other force at work. Her eyes strayed to the mantelpiece, then returned to the lilies on the table. 'There's a good deal of anxiety about the next Duke of Fontein. The old duke has no heirs and the duchess is very old. Some say the *capo*—'

'The *capo*?' Dino almost shouted. 'I'd rather give a drunk swineherd the title of duke than that simpering, perfumed ...' He was out of his seat, pacing the stretch of floor behind the

168

couch. Did people say the same of him behind his back, he wondered.

'There is no one else,' said the messenger.

'There's always someone else. There must be someone else.'

'Now you mention it, I suppose …' She smiled at him.

'Me? Duke Fontein?' He considered it, plucking at his lip.

'I'd happily swear my sword to you, my l—' He glowered at her. 'Dino.'

'Well, that's something. Although I fear my problems would double overnight if I became duke.' He looked down at the flowers. 'Do I really have to go through with this damned charade?'

'The Domina said you'd react this way.'

Dino said nothing, crossing an arm over his chest, the other hand straying to his lip as he regarded the lilies. Speranza stood and crossed the room. Her fingers grasped his.

'If you ever need anything, Dino. The colours I wear aren't the colours of my loyalty. Demesne always comes first, Demesne and its sons.'

Speranza pushed up onto the tips of her toes and brushed her lips against his cheek. And then she was gone. Dino blinked and took a breath, a frown of confusion on his brow. The drake regarded him from the windowsill, unmoving.

'I didn't see that coming, you know?'

Achilles flicked out his black tongue and scampered off.

'Well, you would say that, wouldn't you?' muttered Dino.

The walk from the castle was a warm but pleasant one. He didn't wait for a stable lad to saddle a mount, opting instead to take his time. The evening was well under way when he finally set out, the task at hand less odious once he'd committed himself to it. The *cittadini* of Santa Maria saluted, curtsied or bowed, complimenting him on the flowers as he passed. They all knew what the lilies were for, but none mentioned the duke directly.

In truth it was a blessing to be free of the castle, beyond the beck and call of messengers, out of reach of the Domina, away from the stench of the town and the sour reek of politics.

Farmers on wagons greeted him cheerfully as they delivered their produce to the granaries of House Contadino, shire horses plodding the dusty earth. A brewer's daughter occupying a precarious perch behind two dozen barrels waved to him from the back of a wagon. She flashed a coy smile at the young bravo bearing wilting white flowers. Dino guessed her for eighteen summers. She was nut brown from the sun and full of life.

What agreement?

The hecatomb agreement. His conversation with the dead duke whispered in his mind. He recalled the night the women had got free of the *sanatorio,* shorn wraiths who hobbled and haunted the meadow.

Not so much the proud defender on those dark nights, my duke.

The cemetery waited with rusted gates and a profusion of bindweed. Dino entered, boots stained chalk white by the gravel. It didn't take long to find the Fontein mausoleum. It was a curiously undecorated affair, constructed from a black glossy stone found rarely in Landfall. There was a sombre weight to the building, imposing and imperious. It needed no gargoyles or angels, settling instead for unadorned menace. Dino entered, tracing his way past decaying dukes and their crumbling wives. He located the newly dead and placed the lilies on the top of the sarcophagus.

'At least you had the courtesy to die without a fuss, you old bastard.' He looked around the spartan chamber. 'I doubt my own death will be so bloodless.' He flicked a lazy salute before turning on his heel. The door to the mausoleum stood open, a rectangle of golden light, pink at one corner. He paused a moment to lean against the jamb and savour the evening.

Two horses were tied to a tree in the far corner of the cemetery. A break of tradition; mounts were always left by the side of the road where a trough had been placed. The horses were of good pedigree, but he recognised neither of them. Dino glanced around the cemetery. No sign of the riders, assassins or otherwise. The trees sighed, mocking him with whispers in the late-evening breeze. He stepped out from the mausoleum, drawing his blade as a precaution, pulse quickening. Grey eyes searched every headstone and silent angel, potential cover for crouching killers. He crossed to the horses, who received him warmly, whickering.

'And what are you fine ladies doing unescorted on a night like this?' One hand smoothed the powerful neck of the nearest steed. Something delicate shone underfoot. Dino stooped, careful not to startle the horses, retrieving the curio with a deft hand. A pearl earring sat in the palm of his hand, bathed in the last of the sun's light.

'You aren't the only ladies taking the air, it would seem.'

The wind picked up, setting the trees swaying. A compelling susurrus filled his senses. He didn't deny it, following the cemetery wall to a tumbledown vine-choked section. He mounted the stony debris and crossed into the woodland beyond. The smell of dust, so pervasive in the castle, so cloying on the road, was absent here. Willow trees filtered out all but the smell of lush greenery, the musk of gentle decay. It was a world away from the endless stone corridors of Demesne.

The appearance of the man in grey took him by surprise, rapt as he was in the verdant maze of willow branches. Dino dropped to a crouch, breath held in protesting lungs. The stranger wore rags and a hood much like the attackers in the market place. That same feeling of tension, of attention, despite the stooped frame. That same impression of not being whole, something festering beneath the coarse cloth. The ragged man stood gazing intently. Dino followed the line of his interest to where more figures had gathered.

The majority were dressed the same, all bar one, who wore a veil much like Anea. Strange that a man cover his face in the way of the sisters. Keen eyes stared from under a pointed hood and he clutched a short blade in a reverse grip. His left hand was held out. Two people in black riding cloaks stood nearby. One had a sword belted underneath the velvet; the other produced a note. The grey men stirred and Dino feared he'd been seen. There was some conversation, but he was too far away to glean any word of it. Frustrated, there was nothing for him to do but retreat, taking care not to attract attention, putting the trunks and boughs of the willows between himself and the eyes of the conspirators.

Dino lost track of the number of times he swung a cautious gaze over his shoulder on the walk back to the castle. He cursed to himself when the riders failed to appear. The sun was now heading toward the horizon, bathing the sky in a shocking vermilion. He arrived at the gatehouse to the Contadino court-yard famished and thirsty. The guards on duty favoured him with a curious glance.

'Just went to place some flowers on the duke's tomb.' Dino jerked a thumb over his shoulder at the road leading to the cemetery. The guards nodded and cast furtive glances at each other. Word would soon spread, adding to the undertow of rumour and speculation. Dino imagined the currents of confu-sion eddying about him as he passed beneath the arch. He was halfway across the courtyard when Camelia struggled out from the kitchens with a sack of flour. She sunk a knife into the cloth and ripped at the fabric.

'That sack giving you trouble?'

'Oh! Dino. You scared the life out of me.'

'Is this some tradition I was unaware of?'

'Not exactly. Look.' She pointed at the flour, which was speckled with grey. Dino dropped to one knee and pushed a hand into the sack, taking out a handful of the powder. Black ants dusted to a dirty grey writhed, legs working a mindless churn.

'More ants,' she muttered. 'I think it's getting worse.'

'Is it ruined?'

'No.' Camelia shook her head. 'But we have to sieve them out. We can't afford not to.'

Dino nodded, saying nothing, watching the creatures attempting to escape the landscape of his palm.

'They look peculiar in the flour,' she said, voice low. 'Like they're dressed in rags. And they're big.'

Dino flung the contents of his hand to the cobbles.

'You may want to keep that knife with you at all times, Camelia. I think we've bigger problems than ants.'

26

Length of Service

– 5 Agosto 325

'And it was here that they attacked you?' asked Dino. 'You said about thirty of them?'

'Yes, my lord.' The farmer rubbed at his shoulder, the arm in a sling. They were just over three miles away from Santa Maria, a copse of cypress offering shade nearby. The sun had yet to reach its apex.

'What were you carrying?'

'Vegetables, some flour, a pair of suckling pigs. They took everything.' The farmer looked at the cart, now stuck in a ditch at the side of the road. 'They even took the horse.'

'That's ridiculous,' the *capo* sneered. 'Horses can be recognised; horses can be found.'

'Difficult to find a horse once it's been eaten,' said Dino, chewing his lip.

'No one eats horse,' countered the *capo*.

Dino yawned and rolled his shoulders. 'Have you ever been hungry, Guido? I doubt it. People will eat anything when forced to, and if they have more mouths to feed then they'll take whatever they can, even if it's still walking around.'

'It's obviously bandits,' said the *capo*. He looked at the farmer and sniffed. 'I dare say this damn fool is in on it, splitting the proceeds.'

The farmer's face darkened. He was a heavyset man, stripped to the waist and olive brown. There was a hardness to him. Dino doubted few if any called him liar to his face, among the *cittadini* at least. The dozen guards that lined the road looked away or inspected their boots, each one sweating beneath a tabard of scarlet and black. Speranza, who had escorted them for no reason Dino could discern, stood to one side holding the reins of the horses.

'Bandits?' Dino smiled. 'Split the proceeds? You really are out of touch. When was the last time you had to buy anything, Guido? This man could earn more than half of your so-called proceeds at market.'

'Less than half actually, my lord,' said the farmer, 'after taxes and feed for the horses.'

'He doesn't deny it,' crowed the *capo*.

'And I suppose the fractured arm is part of this elaborate ruse?' The Orfano glowered, causing the guards along the road to stiffen.

'I wouldn't put anything past—'

'Stop flapping your fucking mouth, Guido.'

The *capo* stared back, face flushed purple. The farmer busied himself inspecting the ruin of his wagon while Speranza produced a brush from a saddlebag and attended to her steed.

'You would do well to remember who you are talking to,' said Guido, dropping his voice to a harsh whisper.

'I know exactly who I'm talking to.' Dino took a step closer. 'Some popinjay, suckling on the tit of a sinecure. How can you have survived with so feeble a brain?'

'You talk to me of sinecures?' Guido was was just an arm's length away, lips peeled back from his teeth. 'It wasn't my sister that made me *maestro superiore di spada*,' he seethed. 'That role was meant to be mine!'

Dino stepped closer, almost nose-to-nose.

'Perhaps it escaped your attention, but Anea doesn't promote people for length of service; she promotes them for ability. Your conduct during the Verde Guerra put paid to any hopes you had of advancement. You should be grateful you're still *capo*.'

'Grateful?'

'The only reason you've come this far is because Duke Fontein paved your way as a favour to Duchess Prospero.'

'That's simply not true!' Guido di Fontein took a step back, a look of injury in his eyes before he recovered and regained his anger.

174

You're a member of the guard,' said Dino. 'I suggest you start acting like one.'

'This man is swindling us.' The *capo* raised an accusing finger at the farmer, keen to change the focus of the dispute.

Dino took a step back, drew in a breath and released a long sigh. 'You're dismissed, Guido. Go away.'

For a second there was only silence. The *capo* stared, incredulous, staggered at the slight.

'You'll look back on this day and regret crossing me, Lord Erudito. I won't be the *capo* for ever.'

'Fancy your chances as the next Duke of Fontein, do you?' Dino allowed himself a smile; only Guido would be idiot enough to show his hand so early. The *capo* swallowed, eyes darting toward the guards standing nearby, aware he'd said too much. Again.

'Think you can claim that title without a struggle, do you?' Dino smiled with malice. The *capo* spluttered a moment, shut his mouth, then turned on his heel. He mounted his steed and mumbled something to Speranza before setting off at a gallop. Dino watched him go, not taking his eyes from the man for a moment. *'Figlio di puttana.'*

The nearest guard failed to keep the smile from his face.

'There goes your new duke,' said Dino, unable to resist the dig.

'Santa Maria save us,' replied the guard. Dino shook his head and approached the farmer.

'I suppose these bandits were clad in grey rags, hooded, bearing rusty weapons and wooden clubs?'

The farmer nodded, brow furrowed.

'They were led by a man wearing a veil, carrying his sword like this?' Dino drew his sword and held it in a reverse grip so the blade pointed back toward his elbow.

'How did you know, my lord?'

'You don't have to address me like that. The half-wit has gone. What's your name?'

'Bruno.' The farmer stood a little taller, smiled, still clutching at his wounded arm.

'Make a note of how much you lost, tell Speranza when

you get back to Demesne. I'll see to it that you're reimbursed.'
He took a step closer to the farmer. 'Tell no one about this,
understand? It's our little secret. If word gets out I've become
soft-hearted I'm as good as finished, you know?'

Bruno nodded. 'Most kind, my lord.'

Dino smiled. 'We've got a team of horses on the way to
pull the wagon out. We can have it repaired – not everyone
in House Prospero loathes me.' Bruno offered his good hand.

Dino shook it. 'You have honoured me, my lord.'

'And you've forgotten my name again.'

'My apologies.' Bruno nodded, then winced on account of his
arm. Dino flicked out a salute and made his way to his horse.

Speranza carefully avoided looking at him but struggled
to keep the smile from her lips. 'Will you escort me back to
Demesne?'

'Of course.' They mounted and wheeled their horses toward
home. Dino shouted back over his shoulder, 'Sergente! You and
your men are to guard Signore Bruno until the horses arrive.
Then escort him back to Demesne. Understood?'

The *sergente* nodded, saluted and smiled.

'I'll see you in the Contadino courtyard later, Bruno.'

The farmer waved as the Orfano and messenger set their
heels to their horses' flanks, surging along the road to Demesne.

'Much more of this and people will think Lord Erudito has
regained his good humour.' Speranza and Dino were halfway
back and it was close to midday. Dino decided he would have
a bath on returning. Dust clung to him where it met the sweat
of his body. Summer continued to fall like a golden hammer.

'Goading Guido is the only sport I get these days. I might
as well enjoy it.'

'That was a good thing you did for Signore Bruno.'

'After all the things Demesne has subjected the people to ...
Well, it's the least I can do.'

'The guilt of the king isn't yours to bear, my lord.'

'Do you know, I've changed my mind,' Dino said after a
pause.

'How so, my lord?'

'I'm not going to ask Anea to make me a duke; I'm going to ask her to strip me of a title altogether. Then you'll have to call me Dino.'

'You're an Orfano, you're entitled by birth. You can't forget who you are or where you come from.'

'I'm not asking to forget, only that you do once in a while.'

'It's not easy,' she admitted with a smile. 'When you've had as many etiquette lessons as I have, certain things become ingrained.'

'There's plenty of ingrained things in Demesne that I'd change in a heartbeat.' He grinned at her. 'Come on, let's get back in time for lunch.'

They put their heels to their horses and thundered along the road in a cacophony of hooves.

The *passeggiata* was a custom that had emerged since the king's passing. The youths of the houses, major and minor, would congregate in one of the four courtyards to share wine and wander in an aimless circle, strutting, preening, each step a casual declaration of braggadocio. In time the promenade had spread to the piazzas outside Demesne's walls. Its popularity was not limited to those in their teens: people could be found walking and chatting until after midnight. Small deals were conducted, kisses stolen, gossip exchanged. Most were keen for the company, others keener still to attract potential suitors. The summer nights were the perfect backdrop for the sultry, often raucous promenade.

'It's a rare night that the mighty Dino Adolfo Erudito graces us with his presence at the *passeggiata*,' said Massimo with a teasing smile. 'Do the wonders of Demesne bore you, my lord?'

They were sitting around the improvised table in the corner of the Contadino courtyard, a wheel of a wagon long since gone to firewood. Massimo and Bruno had struck up an unlikely friendship and had been drinking before Dino had arrived. The swordsman had bought a *caraffa* of wine and made free with it. Dino wasn't sure what the wine was, didn't care for it much, truth be told, but he'd no wish to spend the night locked in his rooms with only Achilles for company. And it was hard to resist Massimo's company, despite the surge of shame he felt when in the man's company.

'Won't you join us, Camelia?' The Orfano raised a mug to the cook with a wry smile.

She raised her eyebrows in response. 'I've a husband to get back to and a child that's not seen me since dawn. Enjoy your wine, gentlemen.' She curtsied and left.

'As fine a woman that ever walked,' rumbled Bruno.

'The tallest woman that ever walked might be a better description.' Massimo grinned, drinking more of the nameless wine. 'Are you on the lookout for a woman, Bruno?'

'Not me no. Married, with a grown son I'm very proud of and a daughter I'd do anything for. And she knows it, unfortunately. And you, my lord?'

'No.' Massimo forced a smile. 'Not yet anyway.' The words were strained and the mirth behind them rang hollow.

'I'd take this whole place apart if anything happened to her,' said Dino, watching Camelia leave the courtyard. 'She's the closest thing I have to family, after Lucien and Anea.'

'No need to gain the wolf tonight, Dino,' replied Massimo. 'Take a few hours' rest from that ill temper you're so taken with. Speranza told me you cracked a smile today. I'd not thought the girl dishonest. Was she?'

'Speranza is ever trustworthy,' said Dino, standing, allowing himself a smile as he stretched. 'Even if she is employed by that dreadful Fontein crone.'

'I'm sure someone with your unique title could arrange to have a girl like that added to your staff.' The corners of Massimo's mouth curved up. 'I dare say she could be useful in any *number* of ways.'

'I don't want staff. Fiorenza is more than adequate—'

Bruno and Massimo burst out laughing.

'I didn't mean like that.' Dino came close to blushing.

'What in nine hells *did* you mean?' asked Bruno.

Dino cleared his throat and grasped for something to say, but his mind only conjured what he'd seen in Cherubini's chamber. 'I think I've had a little too much sun and much too much wine. I'll leave you gentlemen to finish the bottle.'

178

Dino turned and headed toward the nearest door before Massimo could protest. The sounds of laughter and companionship rang loud in his ears, making the quiet of his apartment stifling by comparison.

27

Casualties

– 7 Agosto 325

Dino was waiting on the balcony for her just after sunrise.

'Did my front door stop working?' said Stephania.

The Orfano smiled. 'Not at all; yours is the most functional door in all of Demesne. It was just quicker for me to come over the rooftops.'

'And you didn't want to be seen.'

The Orfano nodded. Stephania wore a high-necked night-gown of grey silk. Intricate embroidery decorated the neck, cap sleeves and hem, where pale naked feet emerged. The fabric looked like steel, conspiring to make her look older.

'You heard about the farmer? Robbed on the road to Demesne?'

Stephania nodded, hair spilling from the hasty ponytail she'd tied. 'More of your men in grey?'

'Massimo thinks they live beneath Santa Maria or Demesne itself.'

'So why not seek them out?' Stephania stepped out onto the balcony, resting her hands on the parapet.

'There are so many tunnels down there.' Dino turned and followed her gaze to the streets below. 'You could dispatch a detachment of men, lose half of them, and still not find anything worth looking for, you know?'

'At least tell me you tried,' pressed Stephania, frowning.

'Margravio Contadino sent a few men last night. They came back empty-handed, eventually.'

Stephania said nothing. There were dark shadows beneath her eyes, a wrinkle of irritation at her brow.

'Are you unwell? You seem on edge, if you don't mind me saying so.'

'I'm fine.' She sighed. 'I know why you're here. I can't locate Erebus. It's possible he's only using House Fontein messengers, where I have least influence.'

'I thought they were closed to you. You have someone inside now?'

'You should know, Dino; she spends enough time attending on you.'

'Speranza?'

Stephania nodded and turned her face toward the Di Toro estate in the distance. Dino regarded the woman and glanced at the apartment doors.

'Am I keeping you from someone?'

'What?' She crossed her arms.

'I mean, do you have company?' he whispered, gesturing toward the apartment.

'Who would call at this time of morning? Ah.' She smiled. 'You mean do I have a guest from last night?'

Dino swallowed. Stephania shook her head and sighed.

'Is that why you think I'm being short with you?'

'I'm struggling to think of another reason.'

'You really don't know anything about women, do you?'

'A little more than I know about Erebus.'

'I'll keep trying, but I think the Domina has found another way to receive her letters. Come and see me in a few days.'

'Thank you.'

Dino sprang onto the parapet and climbed the wall, reaching the top of Demesne with ease. He turned and looked down at the woman in grey silk, the tips of his boots hanging over the lip of the roof.

'Is there anything I can do for you, Stephania? Do you need anything?'

For a second Dino thought she might reply; instead Stephania Prospero shook her head, retreating to her apartment and her thoughts.

*

181

Dino spent the morning in the Fontein courtyard teaching novices, who were far more dangerous than they realised. Some had progressed to metal blades, but the sharpest weapon on display was D'arzenta's commentary. Dino avoided the *maestro* where he could and excused himself early when he couldn't. The Orfano hurried through Demesne to reach House Contadino on the far side, not pausing to greet acquaintances or engage in idle chat. Massimo and Bruno were waiting for him beside the latter's wagon, now repaired. A handsome silver-black mare had been tethered to the wagon, paid for with Dino's coin.

'Bruno was just telling me you let him sleep in your old apartment.' Massimo clapped a hand about the Orfano's shoulder, favouring him with a broad grin. 'I had no idea you were a hotelier.'

'Try not to tell everyone,' Dino said in a stage whisper. 'It's a very exclusive establishment. I'm trying to keep the hoi polloi out.'

'My lord, you've been most generous.' Bruno bowed, his arm strapped up in a new sling. Dino had provided the man with good food, a barber and a change of clothes. 'If there is anything I can ever do for you ...'

'Only one thing,' said Dino. 'If you hear anyone say the Orfani don't care for the lives of the *cittadini* please tell them otherwise. I know we're not well liked on the estates, but my sister and I are not the fearsome *streghe* of late-night tales.'

'I think people would much less afraid if they knew you for true.'

'Where are you heading?' asked Massimo.

'House Di Toro, back to my family.'

'Safe journey then, Bruno.'

Screams erupted outside the gates as the swordsman shook the farmer's hand.

'Twice in three days.' Dino drew steel, feeling the familiar calm descend on him even as his heart kicked in his chest. 'Our new friends are clearly audacious.'

'New friends?' Massimo flicked a concerned glance back and forth between the gates of the Contadino courtyard and Dino, who was already advancing toward the source of the furor.

The two guards on the gate were quickly overwhelmed, outnumbered three to one. The courtyard, home to the many granaries of House Contadino, descended into chaos as *cittadini* charged in all directions. Dino ran forward, feinting with a low strike before opening his opponent's shoulder. The grey rags parted just as the flesh beneath was split in a streak of crimson.

'*Vai al diavolo*,' whispered the grey man. Dino replied with steel, silencing him for ever. Another of the raiders dodged to one side, entering the courtyard unchecked. Dino prepared to give pursuit only to find himself engaged by another, this one swinging a club.

You said about thirty of them?

Yes, my lord.

Bruno's answer from two days past.

Dino parried a strike from the club but failed to notice a matching weapon in the other hand. It smacked into his left shoulder, knocking him back a step. Massimo was holding two raiders at bay with a series of slashes almost too fast to follow. Dino's attacker pressed in again, but found his first club caught in the Orfano's open hand. The second followed but the hand holding it was neatly severed. The man cried out, staring at the stump of his ruined arm, eyes frozen with feverish disbelief. Dino finished him with a thrust and a grunt, wiping his blade on the rags.

'Shut the gates!' he bellowed. 'Someone shut the gates!'

Massimo dispatched one opponent, only for another to take his place before the swordsman had recovered himself. Dino dashed into the melee, mashing the pommel of his sword into the back of one head, then slashed down with an overhead strike. White shards of ribs were clear to see as he opened the grey raider from shoulder to hip. The doors to the courtyard began to close, but more raiders piled in, fetid ashen shadows bearing the halberds of slain guards. The grey men sprinted past the swordsmen, intent on the spoils of the Contadino stores.

'Where are the guards?' complained Dino, knocking aside a rusty blade.

The gates were almost closed when one more of the raiders broke through. Dino frowned. It was the veiled man from the forest. He took a moment to kill a fleeing page boy, then turned his dark gaze toward the Orfano. They closed at speed. Dino found his opening strike blocked by a dagger. He jumped to one side, lost his footing and rolled, all to avoid having his guts split open by the short sword held in a reversed grip. He'd barely regained his feet when the veiled man was on him. And then gone. Vaulting up into the air to land behind him. Dino dropped to one knee, turning his blade and thrusting back with both hands. There was a rip of fabric and a grunt. The veiled raider fell back. Dino rolled forward and onto his feet, batting aside a strike from another attacker. Three slashes later and the ragged man was lying in the dirt, blood dripping from deeps cuts that no amount of sewing would ever heal.

A sting across Dino's shoulder produced a wordless cry. He staggered and spun, blocked the next strike, and the next, and the next. The clash of steel sounded loudly over Dino's laboured breath. The veiled attacker pressed in, so close Dino could smell him. The short sword whipped about in a figure of eight, the style unusual and hard to predict, the dagger waiting in the left hand ready to parry any riposte.

'Into the teeth of the wolf,' snarled Dino. He stepped forward and mashed his forehead into the veiled man's face, catching him in the mouth. The veiled man clutched at his face, eyes clamped shut with agony. Dino didn't waste the moment of reprieve, taking his blade in both hands and drawing back for a killing strike. A jolt of pain from his wounded shoulder slowed his attack. The veiled raider threw himself forward, throwing his weight behind the parry, catching Dino's blade on the flat of his dagger.

'*Porca miserisa*,' grunted Dino, before the veiled man replied with a slash. Dino ducked under it. Almost.

Had he been standing further away the blade would have split his skull, instead the damage came from the crosspiece, which caught him near the temple and sent him sprawling. The world rocked, the sky blazed white. There was dust in his mouth, in his eyes. Dino rolled onto his back, veiled attacker looming over him, strike already falling, sunlight reflecting from the blade. Massimo barged into the raider, grabbing him around the waist.

'Massimo!' Dino pushed himself to his feet, head swimming with the nausea of concussion. His feet were a leaden jumble, the ground not where he'd expected it.

'Come on,' shouted Massimo, standing before him, face pale. 'Where did he go?'

'I don't know. And I don't care much either. We're leaving.'

The veiled attacker had melted into the chaos, leaving only blood and shock in his wake.

Dino recognised the *dottore* from the Verde Guerra but couldn't remember his name. The specifics failed to interest him as the needle pulled his flesh together. The cut crossed much of his left shoulder blade. It wasn't the first time he'd been wounded, but the stitching combined with concussion left him quiet and tremulous. Achilles climbed atop the bookcase, his usual redoubt when strangers entered the apartment. Fiorenza hovered nearby, boiling fresh water at the fireplace. She flashed concerned looks at the wounded Orfano and wrung her hands. Dino looked up at the mantelpiece, where the duke's stiletto lay. The gold engraving gleamed as blood dripped down his back.

'There's someone at the door, my lord,' said Fiorenza.

'Send them in. I'm not going anywhere for a while.'

Speranza entered, eyes red-rimmed, face pinched. She said nothing and saluted.

'*Porcia miseria.* It must be bad if you're being that formal.' He turned to Fiorenza. 'Can I have some wine? If I'm going to have bad news then I'd really rather—'

'Dino.' The voice that emerged from Speranza silenced him. Dino swallowed, chest suddenly tight. The image of Camelia bidding them farewell flashed across his mind.

'I'm done, my lord,' said the *dottore*. 'Get some rest. A week at the minimum.' The man stood and packed his things, departing without fuss. Dino stared after him, desperate not to hear Speranza's news.

'My lord, there were casualties.'

'Funny word for it, don't you think?' He forced a smile, but it withered on his lips. 'Nothing casual about dying.' He attempted to stand but the room lurched and shifted at the edges of his vision, threatening darkness. He slumped back onto the couch.

'Who died, Speranza?'

'Many guards, but I thought you should know, Signore Bruno was killed. He held two attackers at bay as Massimo brought you inside.'

The silence in the apartment was suffocating.

'He died to protect me,' whispered the Orfano. 'And Massimo?'

'Wounded. He should survive.'

Dino pressed a hand to his brow and tried to swallow. A terrible emptiness yawned inside. And not breath, or wine or warmth would fill it for days to come.

28

Convalescence Ends

— 13 Agosto 325

Dino woke to the familiar weight of Achilles padding across the bed. Sunlight streamed through the curtains, a blood-red kaleidoscope on his half-opened eyes. Motes of dust floated in the shafts of light, pinpricks of bronze and gold. Achilles shifted again and hissed.

'Hungry are we?' Dino pushed himself up onto his elbows, feeling stitches pull tight across his shoulder blade, a now familiar ache. Six days since the attack outside the castle. Six nights since the raid on the granaries. Almost a week of brooding on the fate of a farmer barely known.

'I suppose I should venture out; I can't stay here with only you for conversation.'

Another hiss and the drake slithered over the side of the bed, a blur of sepia-brown scales and whip-like tail. Dino followed the reptile with his eyes. Duke Fontein's stiletto lay on the floor. He'd placed it under his pillow after the attack, and yet there it was, waiting to be found. A proclamation of his guilt exquisitely manufactured in every way. He reached down to retrieve the engraved blade, turning the three tapering sides.

Tempo. Velocita. Misura.

His attention wandered to the glass of water on the dresser, yet another reminder of the duke. Perhaps he too would succumb to poison, yet he suspected his own death would be distinctly more violent.

'I need to speak to some people before I go entirely insane.'

Achilles yawned, turning a flinty gaze on the Orfano.

'I think we both need to.'

Dino scratched at stubble. He was rank with sourness, both of body and spirit. One he could sluice off with water, the other would remain with him long after he wished it otherwise.

He had just finished dressing when a knock sounded at the door. The Orfano eased a dagger from his boot, concealing it in the small of his back. Achilles bolted across the room, scurried up one leg, then clawed his way to perch on Dino's shoulder.

'Careful, you ugly brute,' muttered the Orfano as he opened the door.

'Not quite the greeting I was expecting.' Speranza smiled at him from the corridor.

'I was talking to my friend here.' Dino jerked a thumb toward the drake. 'He seems to have forgotten I was stitched up barely a week ago.'

'How is it?'

'Uninfected. It seem small mercies do still exist.' Dino ushered her in with a flick of his head. The messenger watched him secrete the blade in the side of his boot.

'Not taking any chances?'

'None at all.' Achilles jumped from Dino's shoulder to the armchair and coiled a tail about himself, closing his eyes.

'I've barely seen you this week.' The messenger smiled. 'I was worried you'd run away to join a troupe of players.'

'If only that were true. Imagine roaming the countryside, performing to the minor houses and estates. No politics, no intrigue, no struggle for a republic.'

'No hot water, no beds, no charming messengers.'

'I don't pay you to dismantle my pipe dreams,' replied Dino.

'You don't pay me at all,' said Speranza.

He nodded, too tired to smile at the banter. At least she'd dropped the formality.

'The Domina sent this.' She produced a length of rolled parchment from a battered leather tube secured to her *bandoliera*. Dino took it, noting the fine quality, the purple sealing wax.

A moment's hesitation. He had no wish to be the Domina's lapdog again, nor her hound. He placed the missive on the mantelpiece, on the same spot Duke Fontein's stiletto had occupied just six days previously.

'I believe it's of some import, my lord.'

Dino said nothing and considered staying in his apartment after all. Achilles slithered off the armchair, padding across the room to curl about his boots, before hissing at the messenger.

'Be quiet.'

'I thought you should know,' said Speranza in a respectful hush. 'I took word of Signore Bruno's death to his family at House Di Toro.'

Dino nodded but failed to find any appropriate words. He suspected they would sound trite even if they found his mouth.

'He is survived by a wife, a daughter—'

'And a son,' said Dino, tone leached of intonation.

'Yes, Drago. I delivered the wagon and the horse to him. I explained what happened. I mentioned your name, of course. He was grateful for everything you'd done for his father.'

Dino nodded and lifted the cataphract drake from the floor with a tender hand.

'You know Signore Bruno's death wasn't your fault, Dino. He chose to defend you.'

'Thank you. That's all, Speranza.'

'No one could have foreseen the attack.'

'You are dismissed.' The Orfano didn't take his eyes from the drake. The messenger retired from the room, reluctance at every step. Dino stared at the Domina's missive, dearly wishing he could burn it.

It was well known throughout Demesne, and all of Landfall, that House Erudito had the finest kitchen staff of the great houses. The tastes of the *professori* were refined, in some cases gluttonous, requiring a special level of culinary art. Despite this, Dino rarely took breakfast in House Erudito, preferring instead the kitchen of Camelia in House Contadino. He emerged through the stone arch to find its staff taking a mid-morning break. A *caraffa* of diluted wine had been prepared for the many cooks and porters. Camelia sat at the centre of the chatting assembly, a golden-haired queen. A chopping board laden with unsalted bread and olive oil were being picked at with enthusiasm.

'Dino?' She broke into a smile. 'I didn't expect to see you here. Shame you had to bring that awful reptile into my kitchen. Is he clean?'

Achilles turned his back on the cook until he was riding Dino's shoulder back to front.

'Now you've offended him,' said Dino, a ghost of a smile on his face.

'What brings you here?'

'This is one of my favourite places in the whole castle, you know?' He slumped down on a stool. 'I'd spend all day here if I could.'

The staff eyed each other warily. They had not forgotten the Orfano's chiding following the funeral.

'I doubt you'd fit in, Dino.' The cook grinned at him. 'We work for a living down here.' Camelia crossed the room and grabbed him by the collar, planting a kiss on each cheek. Her staff scurried away or found chores in need of completion. 'Would it have killed you to send word?' She gripped his shoulders with both hands, checking him over.

'Things trying to kill me is why I've not been around much.'

'I'm sorry, poor turn of phrase.'

'I'm fine. I've been in my room all week.'

'You had me worried sick.'

'And you I. There was a terrible moment when Speranza visited my apartment. I thought that … Are you sure you won't come to live in the castle?'

'Dino.' She held up a warning finger.

'I mean it. You could have Lucien's old apartment. There'd be more than enough room. It's warmer—'

'Dino! I said no once, and my answer hasn't changed.'

'But it's such a long walk and you'd be safer in here, with us.'

'Safer? Do you really think so? "In here" is where all the trouble is. I'm much safer outside, thank you. Now is there anything that you're wanting?'

'Is it lunch time yet?'

'That's more like it. Just promise me you'll avoid getting killed today.'

'That's easy.' He tapped the pommel of his sword. 'I make that promise to myself every morning.'

Revisiting the courtyard opened up a selection of memories he'd preferred to forget, like splitting a thick scab, the wound below just as tender. Achilles abandoned him, keen to be free of the shade so he might sun himself. He perched atop the kitchen porch like a miniature gargoyle.

'So much for companionship,' muttered Dino.

The Orfano sat on the same barrel in the same corner of the courtyard. He ate his food from the same wagon-wheel table, trying to decide where Bruno had spent his final moments. The cobbles were stained dark red in a handful of locations, each a possible marker of where the farmer had fallen.

'Hell of a thing.'

'Morning, Nardo.'

'Wish I'd been here.' The messenger tucked his thumbs behind the thick leather of his sword belt. 'You healed?'

'Still sore, but I can't stay in my apartment for ever.'

'Huh.' Nardo leaned against the porch, eying the four guards at the gates, which were half closed. A team of carpenters were busy repairing a granary door on the far side of the courtyard. 'Word has it you aren't in the best of humours today.' Nardo tamped moondrake leaf into his pipe, mouth a downturned arch.

'It seems people spend a lot of time wondering what mood I'm in.' Dino dropped his fork on the plate with a clatter. 'Maybe if they knew what I know they'd spend less time speculating.'

The messenger said nothing. Dark circles and stubble revealed the man had been worked hard of late. He lit the pipe and blew out a plume of blue-grey smoke, eyes still set on the carpenters.

Dino took a sip of beer and set the mug down. 'Something on your mind, Nardo?'

'Huh. I was about to ask the same.' Another toke from the pipe.

'There's always something on my mind lately.'

The messenger blew out another plume of smoke, eyes still set on the far side of the courtyard. 'And Speranza? Is she on your mind?'

'Speranza?'

'One day you're thick as thieves, the next you've can barely got ten words for her.'

'I …' Dino opened his mouth to speak, but Nardo had turned to him, a stern cast to his tired features. '*Misura*. Measure. Can also mean consistency, no?'

Dino's mind raced to the stiletto, the word etched along the blade. His stomach tightened. 'Consistency?'

'Think on it.' The messenger departed, leaving the Orfano to sweat in the shade of the bloodstained courtyard.

'And you're giving this to me only now?' Stephania eyed the earring Dino had found at the cemetery. 'A little late, isn't it?'

'I'm sorry, so much has been going on …'

The sun made the pearl blaze amid the gold. They were standing on Stephania's balcony again, where it was difficult to be overheard.

'I heard about the attack.'

'They've doubled the guard. The *capo* is drilling them every afternoon.'

Achilles dismounted from Dino's shoulder and scampered to the parapet.

'Do you recognise it?' He gestured at the jewellery.

'Few could afford such work.' Stephania hesitated. 'Where did you find it?'

'In the cemetery. Two riders were handing over a letter to some grey raiders in the woods.'

Stephania's eye's widened in shock. 'That would explain how Erebus is getting his letters in and out of Demesne. Did you see who they were?'

'No. They wore cloaks and I couldn't get close enough.'

Something like relief crossed Stephania's face.

'So who could afford jewellery like that?' he asked.

'Duchess Fontein for one.'

'It wasn't her,' said Dino. 'Someone younger.'

'Lady Allattamento is well known for her love of gold.' Stephania turned the earring over in her hands. 'It could well be an heirloom. Perhaps Erebus is recruiting from among the minor houses?'

'Or perhaps it was Erebus I saw in the woods behind the cemetery? Perhaps Erebus is a noblewomen?'

'It seems unlikely,' said Stephania, not taking her eyes from the earring.

'Perhaps I've underestimated Lady Allattamento all this time. It would make sense – her son led the attack on Anea.'

Stephania nodded, lips pressed together tightly, eyes revealing only anxiety.

'Are you unwell?' asked Dino.

'Forgive me, I'm not myself today.' She forced a smile. 'I need to rest.'

She pressed the earring back into his hands before leaving the balcony. The cataphract drake and the Orfano looked at each other as the pearl gleamed in the sunlight.

29

Ravenscourt Waiting

– 14 Agosto 325

Shouting and the shuffling of feet greeted Dino as he entered the Fontein practice yard. Ruggeri and D'arzenta were drilling soldiers, many of whom hadn't seen combat since the Verde Guerra. Soldiers who had spent the last seven years avoiding any serious exertion, years growing soft, drinking and chasing skirt, accepting the odd bribe to look the other way. Dino looked out over a sea of scarlet and black tabards. He'd half a mind to march them into the sea just to be free of the smell. Ruggeri crossed the courtyard and saluted.

'Are you well, my lord?'

'Still drawing breath. How goes the training?'

'As ever, slow and painful.'

'Pain is a great teacher, as Virmyre says. More painful if you're struck by the enemy, I assure you.'

'Of that there can be no doubt, my lord.'

'The *capo*?'

'Has been standing in as *maestro* during your recovery.' Ruggeri flashed a look over his shoulder, then took a step closer. 'He's not much of a *capo*, I grant you, but he does know how to drill the soldiers.'

Too bad he doesn't know how to lead them, Dino wanted to say, but kept the comment to himself. Ruggeri saluted and pressed on with his duties. Dino edged around the men. They took turns to attack each other with wooden daggers and clubs, imitations of the weapons used by the grey raiders. Massimo was teaching a small intake of boys the rudiments of duelling in the far corner of the yard. The eldest of the novices was perhaps eleven.

'Pay attention, young bravos. This is Lord Dino.' Massimo smiled broadly. 'Erudito in name, Diaspora in heart. There are few swordsmen in all of Landfall who are his equal, and fewer still who can claim to be his better.'

'Witchling.' The word came from the back of the crowd. Dino struggled to keep his expression neutral.

'And that concludes today's lesson, gentlemen.' Massimo eyed the young nobles, no trace of humour remaining. 'When you return tomorrow I'll want the name of the novice who just insulted my friend.'

Guilty looks and mutters of complaint.

'Think on that tonight as you take your rest. Should you fail in this task I will have you mucking out the Erudito stables every week until I have that name.' The boys stared back, expressions ranging from sullen to petulant. 'You are dismissed.'

Massimo left the courtyard, throwing a crimson jacket over his shoulder as he went. Dino regarded the boys with a wintry look before following the swordsman's lead. They headed up spiralling stone stairs to a compact refectory large enough to accommodate ten men. A rough wooden table was accompanied by equally crude benches. The modest room was dominated by a portrait of Duke Fontein, a rushed affair in a chipped frame. Dino suppressed a shiver as the painting glowered at him.

'Good to see you.' Massimo poured a cup of water from a jug, holding it out to the Orfano with a smile. Dino took what was offered and flushed slightly as his fingers brushed against Massimo's.

'I see the old prejudices are still breeding true among the *nobili*,' said the Orfano, gesturing out of the window at the practice yard. A new class of novices had trooped in, picking fights among themselves.

'You know what they're like.' Massimo poured himself a drink. 'All bright steel and entitlement. I detest teaching, but Margravio Contadino said it would be good for me.'

'And is it?'

'Well, I haven't killed any of them yet.'

'Difficult with a wooden sword.'

'You have no idea, but I do keep trying.' Massimo rolled his shoulders.

'I was hoping for a fencing lesson of my own.'

'First day back?'

'Exactly. I need to work out the kinks.'

'Why me?' Massimo smiled, holding Dino's hand steady as he refilled his cup. Dino flushed again. 'There's any number of swordsmen who would gladly spar with you.'

Dino couldn't decide if he was being taunted or not. 'You're the only person I can trust to draw steel who doesn't want me dead, you know?'

'I can believe it, but don't you think you exaggerate, just slightly?'

'I don't know any more. I trust Ruggeri –' Dino shrugged '– but I can hardly ask Margravio Contadino, can I?'

'Maybe you should. It might lighten his mood.'

'I'm hoping it will lighten mine.' Dino paused, glancing into his cup, remembering the poison he'd used on Duke Fontein. 'Did the *margravio* sell any of his estates?'

Massimo regarded the Orfano. Dino could sense the swordsman weighing his loyalties.

'I'm sorry, I shouldn't have asked.' Dino looked away to the window and forced a smile. 'All this spying for the Domina has addled my brain. I barely know friend from foe these days.'

'No matter.' Massimo waved aside the misstep and sighed. 'I don't think it's your shoulder that's the problem.'

'How so?'

'Your trust and your confidence have taken the greater wound. Come on, let's practise.'

They trained inside, in one of the smaller rooms on the third floor that rarely saw use. It had become a dumping ground, stacked with wooden dummies, broken practice swords, a shield fractured from use. A ripped tabard had begun to grow mouldy.

'Hardly the respect I'd show my own house colours,' noted

Dino. 'And to think of all the trouble Lucien went through to earn the scarlet and black.'

'Real loyalty is hard to find any more.' Massimo looked down at the detritus. 'Like I said, it's all bright steel and entitlement. Personal glory at sword point.'

'There's precious little glory lately.'

'But we do seem to live at sword point.' Massimo snorted a laugh, lips curving in a smile loaded with resignation. Dino found himself doing the same. Massimo never failed to lift his spirits.

'I never thanked you for saving my life,' said Dino.

'Nor will you. That honour goes to Bruno.'

'But it was you who prevented the killing stroke, you who dragged me from the courtyard.' Dino shook his head. 'We only went out for a drink.'

'That's when you need armour the most, my lord.' Another smile. Dino laughed and felt the tension drain out him.

They started at the very lowest level, working up from positions and guards that Massimo had taught just minutes earlier in the courtyard. Slashes and strikes, thrusts and ripostes. Scabbards were discarded, jackets hung from practice dummies as the moves increased in complexity.

The clash of steel on steel provided a backdrop of bright sound. The sun reached its zenith, shining through grimed windows. Soon they were stripped to the waist and sweating freely. Dino kept his forearms bound lest Massimo see the strangeness of the dark blue tines. The swordsman declined to mention the Orfano's deformity or even take notice of the bandages.

The practice continued. Dino found his eye drawn to taut muscles moving beneath olive skin; Massimo possessed not an ounce of fat. From firm forearms to lean yet defined biceps, the thick sweep of his deltoids, the firmness of his jaw. He was a study in anatomy, and a perfect one. A flash of memory: standing at Cherubini's door, seeing other hard bodies entwined, sweat-sheened in candlelight, the soft murmur of ecstatic voices. Dino pushed the thought aside and threw up a parry, stumbling as he did so. He glared and bit off a curse, lip curled back in a snarl.

'Dino?' Massimo had retreated with a furrowed brow, eyes beneath full of concern. 'Is it your shoulder?'

'My shoulder's fine; it's my concentration that's weak.' Dino rubbed at his forehead. 'I've been idle too long.'

Massimo turned away and Dino's eyes were drawn to his narrow waist, wide shoulders featuring pale pink lines – practice scars – across the muscles. His gaze descended the firm ridge of his spine to his britches and the tight roundness of his buttocks. Dino looked away, overwhelmed by arousal and shame.

'Have some water.' The swordsman held out the jug. Dino approached, tiredness washing over him. 'You're very pale – we should take a rest.'

'I'm fine,' mumbled Dino, feeling anything but.

'This business with Bruno has really got under your skin.'

Dino took a swallow from the jug.

'Didn't do such a great job of protecting him, did I? And there he was, one arm fractured, fighting with a pitchfork.' Dino's mouth curved in disgust.

'He fought for you because he believed in you, for what you did for him. Most of the *cittadini* get nothing but scorn from the *nobili*. Speranza told me the *capo* accused him of conspiring with the raiders.'

Dino nodded. 'It was at that point we had a disagreement.'

'Exactly, and the *capo* exemplifies the relationship between the *nobili* and those in the fields.' Dino had never seen Massimo so animated.

'But you're *nobile*. You don't behave that way.'

'No, I'm Esposito.'

Dino shrugged. 'That's just a name though.'

'The Orfani aren't the only children found on the steps of the great houses. Orfano is a special distinction for children with your ...' He waved a hand a moment, struggling for the word. Dino glanced at his bound forearms.

'Lineage?'

'I was going to say gifts, but it's the same thing.' Massimo looked at him. 'Dino, what do you suppose happens to the children, *cittadini* children, who are left on the steps of the castle?'

Dino shook his head, barely able to believe he'd not considered the possibility before. Weren't all normal children born to families who wanted them, who loved them? Hadn't he grown up wanting to be like normal people?

'*Esposito* means "to place outside",' said Massimo. 'I'm an orphan, Dino. Not Orfano like you, but ... I have no one. Contadino is my family now.'

'I had no idea, Mass. I'm so sorry, I just assumed ...'

'My upkeep, my schooling, my lessons with the blade: everything I am I owe to Margravio Contadino.'

They stood less than an arm's length apart. Dino could smell the swordsman's earthy scent. 'We're more alike than I ever imagined,' mumbled the Orfano. He took a step forward, daring himself closer. Massimo remained, saying nothing. Dino began to tremble, unable to take his eyes from the swordsman's lips.

'My lord?' This from the far side of the room. The two men staggered apart. Nardo stood in the doorway with a sour look about him.

'The Ravenscourt is waiting on you. The Domina sent you a summons yesterday.'

Dino recalled the note on his mantel delivered by Speranza, still unopened.

'*Figlio di puttana.*'

'Huh. I suggest you make haste. Change is coming.'

30

Reverie

– *Marzo* 319

The Year of the Diaspora 319 ushered in a great many things. Snow initially, which coated the land in a hush of perfect white. The building work outside Demesne halted. Dino was glad of a reprieve from the sounds of industry. Hammers, saws and shifting timber provided a chaotic percussion, punctuated by the curses of labourers. Life inside the castle would never be the same once the work was complete; the town of Santa Maria was fast flourishing beyond the walls of Demesne. There would be no deep silences around the vast edifices of the great houses. The King's Keep – now called the Central Keep and the Ravenscourt under Anea's tenure – would preside over a bustling town. Only the yearly snows might dampen the people's spirits, but the days of brooding silence were at an end.

The melt arrived the month after, but few if any could say they felt the warm breath of spring, only the plaintive calls of ill news. Grey clouds dominated the skies, threatening rain. An entire train of wagons had gone missing in the Foresta Vecchia, and all who rode with it had yet to be found. None expected the teamsters to return. The last vestiges of winter would account for any not lost to what awaited among the pines.

The long road to the south-east ran through the heart of the ancient forest and was the only link to San Marino. It was commonly believed that those who travelled through the mass of trees took their lives in their hands. People entered and emerged, or were lost; there was no other outcome. Travelling with companions offered no protection. All would arrive, whole and safe, feeling they had enjoyed Fortune's favour, or none at all. The Foresta Vecchia did not care for stragglers or survivors. And so the people of the Diaspora remained unaware of what waited beneath the great pines. Small wonder the king had forbidden entrance to those solemn trees since time immemorial.

The loss of the wagon train precipitated war, although what they would fight was yet to be determined. Duke Fontein had roused the Ravenscourt with an admirable display of sabre-rattling previously unknown in Landfall. People had gladly voted to send their sons and fathers to vanquish the unseen. Virmyre summarised the mood perfectly: they were chasing shadows. It was only fitting that House Fontein should begin the campaign in the month of *marzo*. March. Mars. The bringer of war.

The Verde Guerra they called it, the Green War, on account of fighting beneath the evergreen trees of the Foresta Vecchia. In truth it would be remembered not for the foliage, but for how untested they'd been, ill equipped and poorly led. This much became apparent, even to a sixteen-year-old Orfano.

Dino had begged Anea to let him join the campaign. She'd flatly refused, unwilling to lose her little brother in Duke Fontein's war. Then a change of mind. A supply train was heading to the front under the stewardship of Margravio Contadino. Two regiments of soldiers had departed a week earlier and required a resupply of provisions. Margravio Contadino appeared in person requesting the Orfano's services as an *aiutante*. This simple act breached etiquette in ways Dino was only dimly aware of and would never care about. No Orfano had ever acted as squire to the nobility. All that mattered was that he was going to war, although none really believed a regiment of bandits or pirates awaited them in the Foresta. The idea was ludicrous. Dino suspected Virmyre's influence in Anea's sudden change of heart but refrained from comment, struggling to contain his delight.

Margravio Contadino's retinue included Nardo, Massimo, two grizzled teamsters and an anxious, withdrawn *dottore* in his early twenties. The retinue was accompanied by a large and odious wolfhound. Retinue. The word filled Dino with a deep and ecstatic excitement. He'd not been part of anything before, save belonging to the order Orfano, which enjoyed little respect or prestige. This, as Massimo later pointed out, was not strictly true. Dino did, after all, also belong to House Erudito, which was much loved by many in Landfall. Dino conceded the point as he always did when challenged by Margravio Contadino's swordsman. Massimo was four years his senior, sporting the broad shoulders and stubble of a fully grown man, things Dino envied him for. Envy would later transmute to fascination, loath as he was to admit it. The swordsman dutifully took the Orfano under his wing. Dino happily settled into the role of protégé, despite having kills to his name. Massimo, as far he as knew, had never drawn a blade in anger.

The day of the departure arrived. The two teamsters and Nardo took the reins of three great wagons piled high with good things. The remainder had mounts, acting as outriders. No sooner had this proud party set out than the sky unleashed a heavy rainfall and all feared they would never be dry again. Dino quickly revised his opinions on retinues, squires, wars, campaigns and supply trains. He found himself dreaming of roaring fires, nesting drakes, plates of gnocchi and a well appointed training chamber. A dry training chamber with a much repaired roof.

The sun, such as there had been that day, slunk toward the horizon as the rain dwindled and finally relented, clouds spent. A farmstead emerged from the downpour. The party found itself in a rough piazza boasting a barn, well and stable. A suitably anxious-looking sheepdog slunk away from the wolf-hound, tail tucked firmly between its legs, ears flat to its head. Two men emerged from the farmhouse, wary and unbowed. Both held pitchforks in a way that said nothing of straw and less about farming.

Nardo introduced the party, making mention of substantial remuneration for a night's dry lodging and feed for the horses. Dino clutched at his collar and shook out his hat, hoping Nardo's entreaty was sufficient. The farmers agreed with furtive looks that revealed the coin mentioned was indeed substantial. They set to receiving their guests with cheerful fervour. Margravio Contadino dismounted and shook hands with the men of his estate before snatching a look at the sky, which threatened more unpleasantness before dawn.

It was a fine enough evening despite the rudeness of the dwelling. The change of clothes lifted Dino's spirits considerably, as did a rabbit stew that benefited from a great number of carrots, parsnips and the judicious use of herbs. A good dark bread was sawn into thick slices and served with butter and wine of dubious quality. That it was watered down offended no one. The kitchen was crowded with men who shared drink and good humour in equal measure, simply glad to be free of the impending rain. Even the *dottore* abandoned his disapproving pout, entering into a spirited discussion with the farmers. Dino found his eye drawn time and again to Massimo, who sat opposite.

Massimo, ever ready with a quip to lighten Nardo's dour observations, complimented the farmers on their fine stew. It was Massimo who noted the spare bowl, enquiring who had earned the spare portion. The farmers, brothers as it turned out, revealed their grandfather was asleep in a back room and would soon wake famished and cantankerous. The farmers fell quiet at the mention of their patriarch and it was Massimo again who filled the silence with more banter. Nardo joined Margravio Contadino for a smoke on the porch while the teamsters washed the plates. Massimo and the *dottore* checked on the horses. Dino, for want of anything better to do, fetched water from the well.

The farmstead was ankle deep in mud and worse. Dino hoped the first casualty of war would not be his dignity. He had no wish to fall face down in the foulness underfoot. The second bucket was full, progressing up the well shaft by means of a worn and age-smoothed handle when Massimo appeared. The swordsman hefted the bucket to one side, flashing a perfect grin at Dino, who could only stare back, lost for words.

'I'm glad we don't have to sleep outside tonight,' said the swordsman as the wind caught the trees, bringing the first spots of new rain.

'Two farmers and a single grandfather. A household of men.

Not much of a family,' Dino commented, surprised at the bitterness in his own voice.

'Better than no family at all,' replied Massimo. His usual gentle humour was much diminished, but his curiosity was awakened. What was it like growing up Orfano? Did Dino wonder after his parents? How had he found his way in a world tense with intrigue and rife with subterfuge?

Dino had no revelations for him.

'It's the only life I've ever known, much as the farmers have only known life on the farmstead, I expect.' The Orfano flashed a sullen look at the rain clouds. 'As for my parents – my mother, I mean – I try not to think of her.' Dino stumbled with the telling of it, neither of them believing the claim. 'Discovering I'm related to Lucien and Anea made things easier. I was less thrilled about being related to Golia, but one never chooses family, only friends.'

Massimo smiled and Dino took a shaky breath. He rarely spoke of such things.

'Perhaps when all this is done, this Verde Guerra, we'll call each other brothers,' said Massimo. 'Brothers in arms.'

Dino would live with these words in his heart for all the years to come.

31

A New Republic

– 14 Agosto 325

Dino entered the Ravenscourt, Massimo following at his shoulder. They were both unkempt, shirts unbuttoned, jackets slung on moments before entering. The sweat of their travails glistened on skin, Dino's brow beaded with perspiration, Massimo's hair damp. The crowd drew back, all eyes on the Orfano and swordsman. The pair approached the dais feigning a show of bravura, reluctance following at their heels. Duchess Prospero grinned behind a fluttering fan, silken gown revealing every curve of her voluptuous frame.

'So good of you to join us,' she cooed.

'We were sparring.'

'A pretty name for it.' The duchess flicked her gaze to Lady Allattamento, who covered a smile with a fan of her own.

'The only name for it,' replied Dino.

'I see you're suitably attired for the Ravenscourt,' said the duchess. The *capo* sniggered and folded his arms.

'And you for the bedroom, Duchess.' Dino curled a lip. 'I hear that's where you do most of your business.'

A half-dozen sharp intakes of breath. The duchess's eyes narrowed and she forced a tight smile. 'I do *so* enjoying gaming with you, my lord.'

Dino turned his back on her.

'Do I look to be in a gaming mood?'

'Just promise me you won't kill anyone,' replied Massimo.

'I can't promise anything, least of all that.'

Dino crossed to where the Contadinos stood with Nardo.

'This is very irregular, Lord Erudito,' said Medea quietly

without meeting his eye. Dino said nothing, jaw clenched, fists the same.

'Apologies, my lord.' Massimo sketched a bow to his master. 'Lord Erudito and I were training, in light of the recent—'

'Very good, Massimo.' The words confirming anything but. 'Don't let it happen again.'

A susurration of commentary issued from the gallery above, joined by pointed comments from the floor of the Ravenscourt. Dino nodded to Nardo, hoping for an ally in the crowd. The messenger looked away, face blank. Chagrined, Dino smoothed down his shirt and began to button his jacket, a sneer on his lip. His eyes alighted on Stephania, a vision in purple and black despite the heat. She curtsied to him with a smile touching her lips. Behind her were the familiar faces of her retinue, her black-haired messenger and her maid Mea. Added to these was a figure Dino barely recognised, such was her transformation.

She was dressed in a modest yet immaculate long-sleeved gown of purest white. A cord of pale blue encircled her waist, matching her headscarf and slippers. Her face was veiled with white, just as it had been the day he'd met her in the cemetery. No trace of the gutter prophet remained, only the mismatched eyes, piercing him with their strangeness. That a disciple of Santa Maria had gained entrance to the Ravenscourt was unprecedented. That she escorted Stephania, not Medea, was stranger still.

Duchess Fontein stood to the right of the dais, a column of black. Grief suited her poorly, making an already sallow and pinched woman ghoul-like. Her maid Isabella stood behind, hands clasped neatly. She blinked and looked down at her feet as Dino met her gaze. Maestro di Spada D'arzenta escorted the duchess in lieu of the duke. Speranza stood behind the *maestro di spada*, not sparing Dino so much as a glance, eyes fixed on the dais.

Even the ancient and infirm House Datini had attended: the viscount and his wife stood apart from each other. It was no secret they lived separately. The viscount was in his middle seventies, his wife nine years younger and profoundly deaf.

And on the far side of the hall, clinging to the few shadows of the Ravenscourt, was Lady Allattamento. Her attire, unlike her holdings, was not diminished. She retained an abundance of gold and precious stones. Dino studied her ears, wondering at the pearl he'd found in the cemetery. Her daughters stood behind her, Stella and Viola, joined by a third woman Dino failed to recognise.

Virmyre appeared at Dino's side, resting on his black-enamelled stick. He stroked his beard, eyes narrowed. His frock coat was black silk, embossed with tiny ravens in dark silver. A turquoise sash cinched his waist, declaring him for Anea and House Diaspora, as if any might doubt it.

'I'm not familiar with this new fashion you've adopted,' he said, appraising Dino's attire.

'You wouldn't understand.' Dino raised an eyebrow. 'You're quite old.'

'Well, there is that. What are they calling this? *Arrufato?*'

'I don't know the old tongue like you do.'

'Because you're so young.'

'What does *arrufato* mean?'

'Dishevelled.' Virmyre's blue eyes twinkled with mischief.

'Ah, I deserved that.'

'It is ever the duty of the aged to comment on the younger, who know not their actions.'

'I think I preferred it when you were in the lab.'

'On that at least we can agree. I'd be spared this frock coat and be able to work in shirtsleeves.'

All present chafed with impatience, exchanging sour quips and wishing for relief. The door at the back of the chamber was pushed inward with a grunt of wood on stone, disgorging the scarlet form of the Domina. Her eyes lingered on Dino for a second as she took her place at the front of the dais. The silver staff slammed down, once, twice, three times.

The room dropped to one knee, heads bowed.

Anea, more gaunt than Dino remembered, entered, dark circles under her eyes harrowing in the bright light. She wore white and turquoise, a poor choice for someone so pale and clearly unwell. Anea took her seat and the nobles stood.

'As you are no doubt aware from the invitations I sent you –'

the Domina let her gaze fall on Dino, who folded his arms '– Lady Aranea Oscuro Diaspora wishes it that the hereditary titles of Demesne and the roles they serve be divided.'

'You chose a hell of day to be late,' muttered Nardo. Dino struggled not to swear.

'As such there will be a new council,' continued Russo. 'This will be known as the Grand Council and be made up of ministers from across Landfall. Initially these will comprise the commander of the guard, the ministers of agriculture, commerce, academia and apothecaries, and the head of the church.'

Dino's eyes darted to Stephania and her pet prophet. He wondered if she'd anticipated this outcome. Or perhaps Anea was making a play of her own. He couldn't say the idea of giving political power to the nascent church appealed much.

'In addition –' the Domina struggled to make herself heard over the buzz of discontent '– the Grand Council will have seats for the position of Majordomo or Domina, and the mayors of both Santa Maria and San Marino.'

Another buzz of excitement from the gallery. Duchess Prospero exchanged a sour look with Duchess Fontein.

'All of these positions will be elected by the people.' The Domina smiled.

The chamber was filled with the clamour of outrage. Faces pinched with indignation complained, while meeker souls struggled to comprehend what was unfolding. Dino pressed a palm to his mouth to hide his smile. The duke's death had prompted Anea to hasten her timetable for a republic. Some good at least might be derived from the killing.

'Order!'

This took some time.

The room settled, a surly acquiescence tangible in the airless chamber.

'The existing *nobili* will retain their lands and properties. Ministers will be entitled to apartments within Demesne. These positions will be voted for in the autumn. All are welcome to run for ministerial positions provided they have a proposer and a second.'

Duchess Prospero moved apart from her clique. The Domina nodded to her and the gallery fell silent.

'Lady Diaspora, you are ever the visionary, but I fear you have failed to account for ignorance in this instance.'

Anea raised her face, green eyes piercing the duchess from above the white veil.

'Surely the good people of Santa Maria, and of San Marino, are unable to read. Literacy is the domain of the learned, therefore it should be the *nobili* who vote on such important matters.'

Duchess Fontein, the *capo* and various hangers-on joined together in polite applause. Anea began signing and the Domina translated again.

'The instance of ignorance is with you on this occasion.'

Duchess Prospero stiffened, smile evaporating in a moment.

'Had you stepped outside the castle you would be well aware that Santa Maria has a library. There is also a school, set up by my brother, Lucien Marino. The people are more than capable of reading a list of names and placing an *x* by those they think suitable to govern.'

Throaty laughter and more commentary from the gallery. Dino wondered if his sister had gone too far. Duchess Prospero had not withdrawn, a tight smile on her lips, conceding the point but not the argument.

'There is one more position in Landfall that is hereditary. I wonder if you are so keen to divide your title as Orfano from your role as ruler.'

No applause this time. The chamber was pinioned by anticipation. A cloud passed over the sun and for once there was a moment of shade. Anea stood, immaculate but frail, tired yet imperious. Her clever fingers began to sign, the words given voice by the Domina.

'Let any who wish to place themselves in competition with me do so. I will gladly use the opportunity to prove my quality. No one has striven more completely than I to serve the population of Landfall.'

Anea paused to look over the nobles, many of whom withered under her gaze.

'The vote for the leadership of Landfall will be the first

vote taken by the people. We will give them a voice; we will hear them speak.' Her scouring gaze came to rest on Duchess Prospero, who fanned herself and feigned boredom.

'Let the first day of *ottobre* be the date of the elections.'

Anea waved to the gallery and swept from the room through the door at the back of the chamber. The Domina followed.

'I suppose you think you're dreadfully clever,' said the *capo*. Dino had failed to notice Guido sidle up to him through the crowd, intent on his sister's departure.

'Dreadfully clever? Not really. I just have to be more clever than you.'

'Surely a clever man would have a few more allies.'

'I don't have to fuck my allies to ensure their loyalty.'

'I'm not so sure,' replied the *capo*, flicking a glance toward Massimo.

'Are you unloading in Duchess Fontein now?' countered Dino.

Guido's mouth twisted. 'You knew about this, knew that my becoming Duke Fontein would be pointless.'

'Perhaps,' said Dino, wishing he'd consulted the Domina upon receipt of the letter.

'You filthy Orfano,' whispered the *capo*. 'Your time is over. You were an experiment. Nothing more.'

'My lords.' It was Virmyre who'd laid a hand on Guido's forearm. The *capo* was now grasping the hilt of his blade, lips peeled back from his teeth. 'I think perhaps this conversation is concluded.' Virmyre looked up to the gallery. Sure enough, three score staff and *cittadini* looked down at the unfolding hostility. 'It would be poor form indeed to spill blood in the Ravenscourt, especially with so rapt an audience.'

The *capo* stalked away, the few remaining nobles clearing a path for him as he passed through the double doors.

'I see you're as popular as ever,' rumbled Virmyre.

'It's my natural charisma combined with my comic timing.' Dino shrugged. 'I'm unbeatable really.'

'If only that were true.' Virmyre shook his head.

'Will you be back soon? From this damned science of yours?

We need you, and her.' Dino gestured to the door Anea had retired through. 'Landfall needs her. I need her.'

'I know,' replied Virmyre, looking troubled, 'but there's so much to learn, Dino. And there have been problems.'

'Problems?'

'It's fine. You must understand, the king kept so much from us. There are hints at advances we can only begin to imagine, and not just in medicine.'

'It didn't do the king much good.'

'The king was insane.'

'Have you seen Anea?' Dino leaned in close to the *professore*. 'She's hardly the picture of health these days.'

'True enough. I'll see to it that she rests.'

'You keep a close watch on her, Virmyre. I only have one sister. I'd prefer it if she didn't see out her days in the *sanatorio* for the wrong reasons.'

'You could look in on her yourself.'

'With everything that's going on in Demesne?'

'I'm sure you could find time in your busy schedule.'

'It didn't go so well the last time I dropped in, did it? She could barely spare five minutes.'

'That was unfortunate. We—'

'It'll be more unfortunate if there's no Ravenscourt to come back to. Tell her we need her back on the throne, where she belongs.'

Virmyre nodded, making his way across the vast chamber of the Ravenscourt.

'So, a republic then?' Massimo raised his eyebrows.

'Looks that way,' replied Dino with a scowl. 'One duke dies and the whole island falls apart.'

32

Stephania's Plight

– 15 Agosto 325

'Your fascination with this establishment constantly puzzles me.' Dino looked around the piazza, then inspected the contents of the wooden mug. The *taverna* was busy but the proprietor had cleared a table. Guests such as the Contadino swordsman and his Orfano friend could not be turned away. The near-white sun blazed down, unimpeded by cloud, the air dry and still.

'It never hurts to be among the *cittadini*,' said Massimo. 'The *nobili* might be more honest if they stepped beyond the castle walls occasionally.'

'On that we can agree. I'm still undecided about the *taverna* though.'

Massimo smiled. For a second Dino could forget the whole tawdry business of Demesne. He looked across the piazza to the statue of the saint, where a crowd of the very poorest of the *cittadini* had gathered. Stephania and the disciple of Santa Maria were giving out portions of bread and wizened vegetables. Four guards stood nearby showing the barest interest. The disciple caught Dino's gaze with her mismatched eyes.

'Rumour is that Guido was hoping to petition Lady Diaspora for the right to rule House Fontein.'

'Can you imagine it?' Dino rolled his eyes. '*Porca miseria.*'

'It seems the duchess was content to pass the title on to him.'

'But now Anea's reduced the influence of the major houses.'

Massimo nodded. 'No dukedom for Guido, but he's gained support among the minor houses.'

'How many houses?' said Dino.

Massimo shrugged. 'Hard to know.'

'He'll use that support to get himself voted in as commander of the guard.'

'The Fonteins were always shits,' said Massimo in a rare moment of bitterness.

'That's one bloodline I'm happy to see the last of,' said Dino, sounding anything but cheerful.

'You really think it's the end of the Fonteins?' Massimo snorted. 'You can't tell me the old duke didn't father some bastards. They say he was handy with more than just a blade.'

'He was feeding his length to Lady Allattamento for years.' The Orfano paused. 'Stands to reason his infidelity didn't stop there.'

Dino imagined a handful of illegitimate sons waiting to strike back against their father's killer. He struggled to breathe a moment before his thoughts strayed to the portrait of the woman in the duke's chamber. 'Curious that people always think of bastards as male,' he whispered.

'What?'

'Just thinking aloud.' Dino drank and was surprised. 'The wine's undergone a significant improvement since the last time we were here.'

'I brought it with me.' Massimo took a sip and smiled again. He was clean shaven as ever. Dino regarded Massimo's strong calloused fingers holding the wooden mug, his other hand clutching the girth of the bottle. His mind wandered. 'The whole of Demesne is laying bets on whether you and the *capo* draw steel before this voting takes place.'

'How are my odds?' asked Dino.

'I didn't ask.' Massimo refilled his mug. 'I wouldn't be surprised if all of Landfall was betting on the outcome. We should get in some more practice, and soon.'

Dino tensed, mind lingering often on the previous day's training session.

'Ever find yourself imagining what it would be like to rule Landfall?' said the swordsman in a quiet voice, a hint of mischief in his eyes.

'Bloody.' Dino flashed a vicious smile. 'All the more reason not to do it. I wouldn't wish that task on anyone.'

Massimo's attention was drawn by the crowd of paupers. His eyes widened, then narrowed.

'Is that ...?'

'Lady Stephania Prospero.'

'Another convert to the cult of Santa Maria,' said Massimo.

'Or she's making a very cunning play to become mayor,' said Dino after a pause. 'The cult has been positioning itself as the champion of the downtrodden. What better way to attract votes from the *cittadini*?'

'Stephania's not the only one who's aligned herself with the Marians,' said Massimo.

'I know. I made some enquiries.' Dino shrugged when Massimo looked surprised. 'I'm a spy – it's what I do.'

'Who else?'

'Houses Elemosina and Di Toro have been making contributions to the poor.'

'That's no great surprise,' replied Massimo. 'I imagine Medea asked in such a way they couldn't refuse.'

Elemosina and Di Toro were both minor houses that had enjoyed a long relationship with the Contadinos, having rooms in that very house.

'Would it surprise you that House Sapiente is also paying into the cult's fund. Namely for the construction of the church itself.'

'I though Maestro Fidelio was taking pains to keep House Erudito politically neutral?'

'But religion isn't politics, is it?' replied Dino, taking a sip of wine. 'And Fidelio doesn't know what his minor houses do behind his back. House Sapiente in particular were strong supporters of Cherubini.'

They looked across the piazza. Stephania continued to give out food with a smile and a kind word for all.

'She'd make a good mayor,' said Dino.

'Margravio Contadino would be happy with that. Shame she isn't younger and Luc a bit older. That would be a political marriage to be reckoned with.'

'I wish,' said Dino, knocking back more of the wine.

'Seems you're wishing for a great many things lately.'

'And if wishes were wolves ...'

'We'd all be lying around with our throats ...'

'Ripped out.' They laughed. It was a common saying in Landfall since the Verde Guerra, but not popular at court.

'Where did the guards go?' said Dino rising to his feet. He shielded his eyes with the flat of his palm.

Massimo knocked back some more of the wine. 'I'm sure they're close by,' he said with a shrug.

'Not close enough. Come on. I'll bring the wine.'

They were halfway across the piazza when the raiders appeared. If the guards were close at hand they were dead already. The maudlin crowd scattered, an unkindness of ravens taking to wing. Someone fell, a loaf of dark bread tumbling from their grasp.

'*Tempo. Velocita. Misura,*' whispered Dino.

Massimo drew his blade and surged ahead. Dino followed, drawing his own steel, surrendering to the surge of adrenaline. Three men in grey saw them, detaching themselves from the group, perhaps a score in total. One bore a halberd liberated from a Fontein guard. He levelled the pole-arm at Dino and ran at him, only to fall on his arse as the wine bottle bounced from his forehead.

'You didn't have to throw it,' complained Massimo as he parried an incoming blow. He slammed an elbow into his opponent's face.

'Sorry,' grunted Dino.

'Such a waste,' grumbled the swordsman. Massimo's following slash opened the man up, leaving him on his knees, armfuls of purple entrails spilling out. He stared at his undoing with shocked fascination.

The raiders were too busy filling sacks to care about the noblewoman in their midst until she drew the knife. The metal glittered in the daylight.

'Stephania, no!' Dino shouted over the din. The Orfano lashed out with his blade, stepping past his next opponent, not bothering to finish him. A raider set aside his pillaging and advanced on Stephania, face unreadable beneath the hood. Dino pressed further into the chaos of bodies, Stephania still several feet away. He would not reach her in time.

The first halberd strike went high. She threw herself back, stumbling over the table. The halberd slammed down, splitting the tabletop as she rolled away from the opposite side, now strewn with splinters. Dino leaped onto the table and stamped a foot on the shaft, trapping the weapon. The man didn't have the sense to release the pole-arm; Dino split his head open for his stupidity. A shower of gore erupted across the pristine white of the disciple of Santa Maria, who threw up her arms to shield her face, shrieking in horror. Dino hopped down from the table and offered his hand to Stephania, speechless with shock. He pulled her upright.

'What's happening?' she asked, eyes dulled with confusion.

The Orfano lunged past her, thrusting his steel into the back of a raider engaged with Massimo. The man jolted upright with a scream, twisting. Dino clawed a free hand around the man's throat, thrusting the blade deeper. The tip emerged from the man's chest and the scream became a wheeze. Massimo parried an incoming club with his knife and unleashed a savage riposte with his sword, taking the man's arm off at the elbow.

The raiders fled, each clutching a sack loaded with food.

'Back to Demesne,' grunted Dino, grabbing Stephania by the elbow. 'Make sure she gets to safety,' he shouted at Massimo, indicating the gore-spattered disciple. The swordsman nodded and they headed back through streets filled with panic.

'I don't understand,' said Stephania over and over.

The quickest way into Demesne was through the Contadino courtyard, but Dino had no wish to go there, instead leading them beneath the triumphal arch where House Contadino stood alongside House Prospero at a flat run. The double doors that led to the Central Keep lay ahead, imposing and impregnable. The pommel of his weapon beat a staccato summons. He turned to check they hadn't been followed. Massimo trailed them by several feet, escorting the disciple. His tabard had been laid open at the shoulder, the white shirt beneath now dark with blood.

'*Figlio di puttana!* Open the door!'

Raiders darted past the triumphal arch. Smoke now hazed the blue sky. More shouts and screaming could be heard, the clash of steel.

Wood groaned and hinges complained. An old face appeared in the gap, whiskery and gap-toothed.

'My lord?'

'Good man,' breathed Dino. The four of them hustled into the cool darkness of the Central Keep.

They didn't stop until they found themselves in Stephania's apartment. Massimo and the disciple had vanished along another corridor. Dino gasped down air with his back to the door, still clutching his blade, sweat starting to cool. He unbuttoned his jacket and locked the door. Stephania collapsed onto a divan in her sitting room, staring glassy-eyed.

'I need a drink, and so do you.' He crossed the room to where a cabinet stood in an alcove. A *caraffa* of red wine waited with a cluster of glasses. He made to pour but his hands were shaking.

Stephania approached, soft hands easing the *caraffa* from his grasp. She'd let her hair down, dark brown tresses tumbling down the sides of her face. Dino surrendered the wine to her, watching her place it back in the cabinet.

'I wanted a drink ...' But the words dried up as she pressed herself against him, fingers tracing the lines of his face, so warm, trembling with frailty. He couldn't remember the last time anyone had touched him, held him.

'You came for me.' The words were no more than a breath barely formed.

'The guards, they abandoned their post.' Dino shrugged. 'I ...'

She tilted her head, pressing closer, arms slipping around his waist. Dino opened his mouth to speak and felt her tongue dart across his lips. The Orfano closed his eyes, wanting to surrender to the rise and swell of sensation, but the face in the darkness of his mind was not Stephania's but Massimo's.

He jolted away, face flushed, unable to breathe. Her eyes filled with confusion, shifted to accusation.

'I don't … Why won't you …?' The words died on her lips.

'I can't. I'm sorry.' He backed off a step, unable to meet her eye. 'I should go. They'll need me.'

'Dino, I'm sorry.' She held her hands out to him. 'I just …'

He made to leave, scabbard slapping against an armchair as he rushed to the door. Awkward seconds passed as he fumbled at the key in the lock, stumbling into the corridor, glad to be free of the wounded gaze of Lady Prospero.

33
Contadino's Request
− 16 Agosto 325

Dino spent the morning after the attack training some of Demesne's guards. There was no curse known to man he did not unleash upon them. The air in the practice yard was arid, the smells of sweat and leather drifting on the meagre breeze and the Orfano's impatience rose with the day's heat, threatening to become a searing anger. A handful of novices lingered at the edge of the practice yard, giving the *superiore* sullen looks. They'd hoped to see capable soldiers demonstrating the finer points of combat. Not a soul present wasn't aggrieved in some way.

'My lord,' said Ruggeri. He'd approached Dino as the guards took a moment to refresh themselves at the end of the session.

'How did we become so lax?' Dino scowled. 'After everything we went through in the Verde Guerra? They don't deserve to wear the scarlet and black.'

'These are not the men who abandoned Stephania Prospero yesterday.' Ruggeri flashed a look over his shoulder to make sure they were not overheard. 'You shouldn't punish them for the failure of others.'

The Orfano glowered, but mention of Stephania silenced him, bringing a wealth of misery with every syllable of her name. The soldiers filed out of the courtyard, more than a handful shooting wary or hostile looks at the Orfano as they departed.

'Demesne is afire with talk of your actions yesterday, my lord.'

'You would have done the same if you'd been there.' A flash

of memory brought the sensation of Stephania's lips to mind – and his inability to surrender to them.

'It was a brave thing,' continued Ruggeri, 'saving Lady Prospero and all.'

'Did we discover what happened to the four guards in the piazza?' asked Dino, keen to avoid further mention of the noblewoman.

'They were found in a side street with their throats cut. They paid a high price for their laxity.'

'There's nothing lax about those two.' Dino gestured to the far side of the courtyard where D'arzenta and the *capo* were locked in argument.

'Guido fancies himself for commander of guard in the elections,' said Ruggeri.

'But D'arzenta is worried he won't get the votes he needs.'

'D'arzenta worries you'll stand against him.' Ruggeri sighed. 'And what do you worry about?'

'I'm not paid to worry; I'm paid to teach.' Ruggeri shook his head. 'Are you going to give the novices the brunt of your bad temper this afternoon?'

'No,' Dino replied, not meeting the eyes of the *maestro di spada*. 'I think it best I retire for the day.'

'Take care, my lord. Get some rest.'

'Thank you, Ruggeri.' Dino turned from the empty courtyard and the fierce sun above to wend his way through the stifling corridors of Demesne.

The walk back to his apartment was uneventful. Dino shrugged off his jacket and hung it from the back of the armchair nearest the door. A *caraffa* of wine had been brought up, left on the sideboard with clean glasses. The previous night's empty bottle had been removed. It was of small consequence; didn't all the nobles drink a similar amount?

He was unbuckling his sword belt just as the bedroom door yawned open. He flung the belt up, scabbard and all, then caught the sword hilt and shucked the blade free in a circling motion. His opponent was armed only with linen.

220

'Fiorenza.' Dino released a breath. 'Forgive me. I'm on edge and wasn't expecting you.'

The maid smiled after a moment's hesitation, her gaze lingering on the blade. She clutched the bundle of bedclothes more tightly.

'I can't say I blame you in the light of yesterday. I only came for the sheets. I can come back later if you'd prefer?'

'It's fine.' Dino sheathed the sword. 'I'm going to rest. Have the afternoon for yourself.'

'Thank you.' Fiorenza made to exit, then thought better of it. 'Is it true you saved Lady Prospero?'

Dino nodded and crossed to the sideboard, not trusting himself to speak. He reached for the wine then paused before pouring water instead.

'She's very beautiful,' ventured Fiorenza.

Dino nodded again, unwilling to meet the woman's eyes.

'I'll see you tomorrow perhaps?' Fiorenza curtsied and left the room.

'She *is* very beautiful,' said Dino, but no sooner had the words passed his lips than the image of Massimo came to him. Achilles scuttled from under the couch and began the ascent up one leg.

'I wondered where you were hiding.' Dino reached down and hefted the reptile onto his shoulder. 'Perhaps we should train you with a blade. I trust you more than I trust the guards.'

Achilles blinked and flicked out a black tongue. A muted conversation was taking place in the corridor, one of the voices belonged to Fiorenza. Dino waited for the rap of knuckles on wood then closed a fist around the door handle.

'When did it become so difficult to enjoy a moment's peace?' he asked the drake in a whisper and opened the door.

'*Marchesa.*' Medea Contadino stood in the corridor, a look of relief on her face, almost as pale as the gown she wore.

'It is good to see you unharmed, my lord.' There was a tired, wary look in her eyes.

Dino gestured her in and bade her sit down. 'You really don't have to bother with the formalities. I'm long past caring. Wine?'

'No, thank you, Dino.'

'How is Massimo? He took a wound yesterday.'

'He's fine.' 'The *dottore* saw him. If you hadn't been there—'

'That's not the case. It was Massimo who invited me to the *taverna*. We defended Stephania together.'

'You're very honest, Dino, but the *cittadini* tell a different story. You're quite the hero, but I'm concerned that good reputation is about to be undone.'

'How so?' Dino frowned, wishing he'd had some wine after all. The water was tepid and tasted of grit.

'The *nobili* have long been fascinated by your friendship with Massimo, and after the other day ...'

'When we were late for the session of the Ravenscourt.'

'Exactly,' said Medea. 'We've barely recovered from the shock of Cherubini.'

'Cherubini wasn't hurting anyone.' Dino fell silent, the anger in his voice all too clear.

Medea looked away for a second. 'I didn't say that he was, nor am I offended by what he is, but many are and many find it disgusting.'

'And now they're talking about me.'

'Yes.' Medea laced her fingers and looked thoughtful.

'And I'm already disgusting on account of being Orfano.' His eye slipped to his forearm.

'Is there someone,' Medea paused and swallowed, 'some woman that you are keen on?'

'When would I have the time to court a woman?' Dino nearly stumbled on the words. It was not a question he'd asked before.

'I appreciate Stephania Prospero is somewhat older ...' Medea faltered as she saw the expression cross Dino's face '... and that her mother wanted her to marry Lucien, but she would be a good match, if only politically.'

'I'm not marrying in response to the first flurry of gossip. If people think me *invertito* they can call me out. I'll give them an answer in steel.' Dino looked down at his boots, well aware of how ridiculous he sounded.

'It's not the first flurry of gossip, Dino. I really do think you should marry. As an Orfano you can do as you please. You don't have to marry nobility if there's a woman among the *cittadini* who's taken your eye.'

'You're talking about Speranza.'

Medea flushed and said nothing.

'As if I don't have enough to worry about, now I have to consider a wedding and a bride.' Dino crossed to the sideboard and poured himself a glass of wine. It was larger than he intended, so he told himself.

'Any word from the town today?' he asked before taking a sip.

'Emilo and I went to the market. We felt a show of confidence might make people feel more at ease.' The visit had not been entirely well received judging by her tight smile. 'The rest of the town was unaffected. Fires were lit to create a distraction but it was the food they were after. The fires failed to take hold or were quickly extinguished by the *cittadini*.'

'That's fortunate.'

'Fortune had nothing to do with it. My husband insisted we buy a hundred pails after the first attack. We handed them out just this week.'

'If only the rest of the *nobili* were so prudent, or so charitable.' Dino released a breath. 'What happened to the disciple?'

'Agostina? She's safe. I have her at my apartment, recovering from the shock.'

'And you trust her?'

'She's not political, Dino. The people trust her; I trust her.'

'You can't blame me for being wary.' Dino sat forward, cradling his wine in both hands. 'An uninvited guest arrives at a funeral and ushers in a rain of ants ...'

'That wasn't her doing. You can't believe that, Dino.'

'I don't, but I'm a soldier. I dislike ambiguity as much I dislike disobedience. What agenda is she pushing?'

'Faith needs no agenda.'

Dino slumped into the armchair, sipping his wine as Achilles slithered down to the floor, coiling about his boots. Medea fussed with the sleeve of her gown.

'So are you going to tell me why you're here, or were you

hoping to make a convert?' Dino forced a smile but Medea was unimpressed with his attempt to lighten the mood.

'I need your complete confidence.'

Dino raised an eyebrow. 'I thought we were long past such assurances. I've always been a staunch ally of House Contadino.'

'This is different.' Medea narrowed her eyes. 'Duchess Prospero sent my husband a letter. She fears she is about to suffer a betrayal by a close ally. She wants to meet my husband alone to discuss coming over to our side.'

'Duchess Fontein has severed links with House Prospero?'

'We don't know for sure. It could be a disagreement with House Allattamento. We just don't know.'

'This is perfect.' Dino grinned. 'Duchess Prospero needs our help. I couldn't have wished for fortune like this.' He took another sip of wine.

'He can't meet her, Dino.' Medea's face was taut with worry, fingers tightly laced. 'She wants to meet in the woodland beyond the cemetery, for secrecy.'

'Small wonder you're anxious.'

'It bears the stench of a trap. And yet Emilio refuses to pass up the chance to make an ally.'

'What do you need?'

'Go with him. I know Massimo will escort him, regardless of whether they want him to go alone, but after yesterday ...'

'Massimo's wounded shoulder.'

Medea nodded and wrung her hands, eyes brimming with concern.

Dino stood and crossed to the fireplace. 'When?'

'The day after tomorrow.'

'Of course I'll go, Medea.'

She stood up and crossed the room, standing on tiptoe, taking his face in both hands. For a second he remembered Stephania in the very same pose just the day before. Medea pressed her lips to his forehead just as Camelia used to do when he were younger.

'I don't know what we'd do without you, Dino. I fear we'd all be lost.' She smiled with a sadness he found unbearable. 'Have you visited Stephania today? Is she well?'

'No.' Dino blushed scarlet. 'I suppose I should.' He knew he'd struggle to explain to Stephania why he'd shunned her kiss; he'd struggle more to make the journey to her door.

'I should return,' said Medea. 'Emilio will be worrying.'

Dino opened the door. 'You have an escort?'

'Of course. Nardo and Abramo are waiting at the end of the corridor.'

'You've got Nardo playing bodyguard?'

'I trust him.'

'And to think –' Dino smiled '– this was supposed to be my secret apartment. Seems all of Landfall knows where I sleep.'

'Let's hope not,' said Medea, then turned away into the gloom of Demesne's corridors.

34

Prospero Betrayed

– 17 Agosto 325

Dino left his apartment as the sun's first rays adorned the horizon with golden light. Another stifling, airless day, the sort that suited cataphract drakes and few others. Achilles perched, content and blood warm on his shoulder, tail curled around the collar of his jacket.

'I can't put off seeing any her longer,' mumbled Dino. Achilles tightened his grip on his shoulder and performed a slow blink of his onyx eyes. The Orfano descended the worn stone steps of House Erudito. He was in no mood to climb Demesne today, had no wish to pick his way across rooftops. His progress was slow, his desire to visit anywhere but House Prospero's seventh floor. Achilles hissed.

'I know, I know.'

The Orfano drifted through the workshops of House Prospero. Clogged and aproned craftsmen regarded him. Many nodded; all were curious. He commissioned a new suit on a whim, much to the surprise of a trio of tailors. That he'd chosen black damask in the height of summer was not remarked upon, nor that he'd abandoned his customary grey. His responses were stunted, his small talk atrophied, attention unfocused. The tailors took their cue and resumed their work, tight smiles and polite bows ending the stilted conversation.

This was the creative heart of Demesne, where clothes were sewn, furniture made, raw materials transmuted into wonders. Its blacksmiths and armourers had long since defected to House Fontein leaving a soft murmur of industry.

'My lord?' Stephania looked pale, not quite frowning. 'Strange to see you in House Prospero.'

'I ...' He glanced at his boots. 'I was just coming to see you.'

The craftsmen politely ignored the noblewoman and the Orfano in their midst, but Dino imagined every ear would be bent to the conversation. Stephania glanced around, unease on her face, appearing to read his mind. She gestured that he should follow.

Up spiral staircases they went, past narrow windows, hearing the scuttle of rats in the darkness. Before long they were standing on her balcony, Landfall a tapestry of green and gold before them, the dust brown roads winding to distant locales.

'I love it up here.' Stephania let down her hair, the rich brown of her tresses tumbling. 'I sometimes think the greatest treasure in Demesne is the view.'

Dino smiled, nodding his agreement, but words remained beyond reach.

'I wanted to apologise to you,' she said, hands toying with the slender purple cord that encircled her waist. Dino closed his eyes and shook his head, then massaged his brow with one hand.

'There's nothing to apologise for, Stephania. The fault—'

'I was presumptuous,' she added.

'You were overcome.' He dipped his head, unwilling to meet her gaze. 'Looking for comfort after the attack.'

'That's not true. I think of you fondly, my lord. You saved my life.'

'My lord?' Dino rolled his eyes. 'We've known each other for ever, Stephania. You of all people don't have to call me that.'

'Do you have any feelings for me, Dino? Any at all?'

'Of course, but ...' She had thrown him off balance. Her forwardness was unexpected. Words were so much harder to parry than blades. 'It's just ...' The objection twisted on his lips, almost burned on the way out. 'I'm so much younger than you.'

'And Lucien? Rafaela?' She'd prepared for this. Lord Marino's wife was older by a greater margin. Stephania had easily sidestepped his riposte.

'I wouldn't want people to think less of you for transferring your affections from one Orfano to another. We're brothers after all. Of a sort.'

'Ten years, Dino.' She struck back. 'Ten long years. Do you think I care what they say in the Ravenscourt?'

'At least we're past the formalities now.' A smile stole over his lips. She didn't return it.

'I'm serious, Dino.' The momentum was hers. 'I can't do all of this on my own. Why *should* I have to do this on my own?' She drew closer. 'I'll understand if there's someone else.'

He shook his head, as much to dispel the image of Massimo as to refute her suggestion. Achilles slithered from his shoulder and coiled around Dino's boots, glaring at the noblewoman.

'Is it Speranza?'

'What?'

'The Fontein messenger. Do you have ...' she faltered '... an understanding with her?'

'No. Nothing like that. Why does everyone think I'm bedding Speranza?'

'You spend a lot of time with her considering she's sworn to House Fontein.'

'My bed remains mine, and mine alone. I've ...' His turn to falter now, suddenly vulnerable. 'I've never shared my bed.' The words crushed him. Given voice, they seemed terrible and cruel. Stephania looked at him, a wistful cast to her features, features greatly admired throughout Landfall.

'Never?'

He shook his head, tried to swallow past the thickness in his throat.

'There's no reason for you sleep alone, Dino.' She turned as soon as the words had tumbled from her lips, each one finding its mark on him. The Orfano remained silent, watching her retreat into the cool of her apartment.

'That could have gone better,' breathed the Orfano. The drake looked back and Dino imagined deep disapproval in the stony eyes. 'It's not like she made it easy for me.' Dino looked away, regarding the town below, spotting the Domina in her familiar scarlet robes, escorted by six guards. A thought occurred.

Dino had all but run back to House Erudito. He rapped on the door and felt a moment's disappointment as a voice called out, 'One moment.' Dino waited for Fiorenza to appear. She was midway through her chores in the Domina's apartment. The door swung open and a smile touched her lips. 'Good morning. I'm afraid she's not here.'

'Ah, yes. I know.' Dino floundered a moment. 'She asked me to fetch something for her.'

'She did leave in quite a hurry. I'm almost done.'

'You can leave the key with me if you like. I'll return it to you this afternoon.'

'It's not a problem.' Fiorenza's eyes narrowed. 'I can wait.'

'There's really no need.' Dino forced a smile. 'There's a letter, and she's not sure where she left it …'

Fiorenza's look made it clear she did not believe, or have any intention of believing, him. Dino didn't bother to repeat the lie.

She reached into her pocket. 'I'll need them back as soon as you've found the letter, my lord.'

'Of course.'

'As soon as you're done, my lord.'

He flashed her a grin, but it was apologetic rather than sincere, embarrassed rather than grateful.

'Well, here we are again,' he whispered as the door clicked shut behind Fiorenza. He locked it, keen not to be discovered. The Domina's apartment was unchanged, disarray and clutter, buried beneath correspondence and statutes. He bypassed the broad desk of her industry and crossed to the bedroom. He was not disappointed, although the letters were not quite so carelessly left on display as before.

My dear Domina,

Please find the vials of tinctura *enclosed with this note. I hope you enjoy the benefits of them and they go some way to securing your agreement for the scheme I propose.*

It has come to my attention that Duke Fontein is preparing

to move against Demesne, perhaps even wishing to take
the throne for himself. This cannot be allowed to happen.
Fontein has ever been a truculent house, and the duke
continues this tradition. If he were to die now, without an
heir, it would provide stability for the years ahead. Think on
this.
    Sincerely yours,
     Erebus

Dino shuddered. The Domina had clearly stated the decision to kill the duke was hers alone, and yet the proof rested in his hands, pale parchment and spidery scrawl testament to her lie. Not an order, but a suggestion. Dino set down the note to find another hidden in the false bottom of a top drawer of the dresser.

My dear Domina,
    Your decision to remove Duke Fontein is brave and
admirable. All too often those in power fail to grasp
what needs to be done even when it is unseemly to do it.
Especially when it is unseemly to do it. You have far more
steel than those craven fools and I am pleased. Find another
vial of tinctura *enclosed as a measure of my regard for you.*
    There is one small problem. The duke sired a bastard. It
is thought the bastard lives within Demesne. If this bastard
were to learn of its heritage it could lay claim to the House
Fontein estates and become a formidable power. Rumours of
the duke's assassination are to be expected, but I am pleased
that he died in a sufficiently peaceful way. Your assassin is
skilled and not without talent.
    Apologies again for my continued absence, but know that
I hunger to attend the Ravenscourt most keenly.
    Sincerely yours,
     Erebus

Dino's mouth curled in disgust. He placed the letters back into the false-bottomed drawer, stealing a glance around the bedroom. Nothing seemed amiss. His fingers had curled around the handle of the door when the scrape of key on metal alerted him. The click of a lock, a collection of footsteps muffled by the rug at the centre of the sitting room. The low murmur of voices, the Domina and another. The apartment door closed behind them, then locked. Dino had no time to spirit himself through a window, instead pressing himself against the wall behind the bedroom door, which opened at that very moment. No one entered. Dino guessed the Domina stood on the threshold of her bedchamber.

'I would never have thought you timid.' The Domina's voice, sultry, challenging.

'I came to talk, not to fuck.' Dino recognised the voice instantly, so angry he could barely breathe.

'The duchess is playing a dangerous game,' continued the Domina. 'Salvaza can't possibly hope to put herself in contention with Anea to lead the republic.'

'Don't be so sure of Anea,' countered the *capo*. 'She's becoming every inch the reclusive king. The people haven't made the connection yet, but they will, and they'll turn against her. A few well placed rumours of growing madness and, well ...'

'Even with Cherubini gone, there's very little Anea can't do.' The Domina was all but purring now. 'The cult adore her. That she's Lucien's sister makes her a hero by association. It would be unfortunate if you were on the wrong side when the dust settles.'

'The wrong side?' The *capo* coughed politely. 'She wants to strip the *nobili* of everything. Everything they own and everything they've worked for.'

'Or had their vassals work for.' Dino could hear the mocking smile on the Domina's lips.

'An estate doesn't build itself, wealth doesn't grow on trees.' This defiantly from the *capo*.

'True. But in the republic you won't need a title to be rich, just the desire to work hard. And possess the right allies. We'll not take anything from you in return for your loyalty.'

'But the duchess—'

'Her time is over, Guido. Don't you think she should have married you by now? Rewarded you for ten long years of companionship. She's sneering at you, making a mockery of all those bright ambitions you once held.'

'It's going to cost you.' His words were icy.

'Name your price.'

'I want to be the next Duke Fontein.'

'That name will die out with the bloodline. Anea won't be turned from this.'

'I want to be commander of the guard. Dino must lose the vote.'

'That will be even more difficult to manage.'

'Those are my terms.' He sounded less sure of himself now.

'Why don't we talk further,' said the Domina, 'in my chamber?'

'I can't; I have lessons to attend.' Dino could almost hear the conflicting thoughts rattling around the *capo*'s empty head, like rusty chains pulling in different directions. 'I'll visit you tonight.'

The *capo* and the Domina left the apartment, leaving Dino shaking with anger and relief.

35

Anter Undeserved

— 18 Agosto 325

Dino presented himself at the Contadino apartments after a breakfast which he picked at without interest. Any appetite had been atrophied by the discoveries of the previous day. What schemes would the Domina pursue today? What letters would she receive? What orders would she give, or be given?

Maria opened the door, ending such ruminations. She was a woman in her late twenties with kindly eyes, possessing an aura of calm. It was small wonder Nardo had married her, smaller wonder still that Medea Contadino employed her as her housekeeper.

'Good morning, Maria.'

'Good morning, my lord,' she replied.

'Oh, how I love to be addressed that way.' Dino rolled his eyes.

'Don't start with that; you know this morning is formal. Come in before you cut yourself on that sarcasm you're so fond of wielding.'

The Orfano grinned.

The Contadino apartments were lavish compared to Dino's own, the repository of decades if not centuries of wealth. Today the sitting room was knife sharp with tension. Margravio Contadino stood at the mantelpiece, stern as ever. He nodded to the Orfano.

'My lord —' Dino bowed politely '— you've gathered quite an escort.'

It was true. Two men stood at the window wearing tabards of scarlet and white made bulky by the studded leather jerkins they wore beneath. Both wore dagger and sword, hung from *bandoliere*. As much as they were armed identically they couldn't have looked more different.

'This is my man Abramo,' said Margravio Contadino, an edge of pride in his voice. Abramo was a tall lean man with dark olive skin. The hint of a smile played at the edge of his lips. Dino knew of the messenger, a veteran of the Verde Guerra, by reputation. He was a keen admirer of the many maids who worked in Demesne, who admired him back on occasion, so it was said. Some gossiped the man was nearly impoverished feeding his many children. Abramo saluted, favouring Dino with a broad grin.

'Good to have you with us, my lord. I hear the roads are unsafe lately.'

'And not just the roads.' Dino smiled back.

'And this,' continued Margravio Contadino, 'is Marcell.'

Marcell was as stout as Abramo was thin, as pale as his friend was dark, possessing an entirely different humour. The stocky man nodded curtly. Dino noted Marcell was heavy in the shoulder and wore his hair cropped, hallmarks of the previous *superiore*. Giancarlo was ten years gone but still cast a shadow over the living, not least his students. Marcell had served during the Verde Guerra too, judging by the bronze sunburst medal he wore on his chest.

Dino's eyes shifted back to Margravio Contadino, now flanked by Massimo. Dino swallowed and cleared his throat. If Massimo's wounded shoulder troubled him he made no show of it. His white tabard was immaculate, edged in scarlet, grey britches tucked into polished riding boots, scabbard hanging from a *bandoliera* of thick brown leather. Massimo nodded, sober and dutiful. Dino drew in a breath and realised he'd give anything for the swordsman to remain within the safety of the castle. Small chance of that.

Medea entered from an adjoining room, an arm around each of her children. Luc Contadino regarded everyone with a wary gaze, as if the men in the room were there to threaten his father, rather than escort him.

'Please, Emilio, I beg you not to go.' Medea all but choked on the words. 'Will you not stay and protect your family?'

The bravos at the window looked away, embarrassed.

'I have to go,' said the *margravio*. 'Cherubini has been exiled, Duke Fontein dead in mysterious circumstances. I'd rather act than react.'

'You're *reacting* to a summons,' replied Medea, voice spiking with anger. 'This is a crude trap, and you're handing yourself over to them.'

'My lord,' interrupted Dino, 'I will follow you anywhere, but I agree with Marchesa Contadino on this matter. Even if the letter is from Duchess Prospero, and even if she is seeking an alliance, why not just meet here, in Demesne?'

'She's obviously scared for her life,' said the *margravio*. 'Her position is precarious – she's overextended herself. Duke Fontein's death has birthed a army of consequences.'

A knock at the door broke the flow of Dino's thoughts. Maria answered it. Nardo entered, removed his hat and bowed.

'My lord, I saw Duchess Prospero leave not more than thirty minutes ago. She was alone, carrying flowers, riding in the direction of the cemetery.'

'And the *capo*?'

'Training the men in the Fontein courtyard. He's scheduled to be there all day.'

'Strange the duchess should venture out alone,' grunted Marcell. 'Did she have a fight with her pretty boy?'

'I believe the *capo* has had a change of heart lately,' said Dino, choosing his words carefully. 'He's found a more influential patron to aid his ambitions.'

'Huh. Never thought I'd see him start thinking for himself,' muttered Nardo.

'Don't worry,' replied Dino. 'He hasn't. He's sided with the Domina, but I'm not sure if that's for the good.'

No one said anything. The Domina had done much to undo her popularity, especially with the nobles, who were bitter at the prospect of a republic and their dwindling power.

'Please, Emilio,' Medea again, her voice a fractured whisper, 'don't do this. Send someone else, anyone.' Silver tears tumbled down her face. Always a petite woman, her sadness reduced her further.

Margravio Contadino shook his head sadly, then knelt down and removed his signet ring. He took his son's hands and pressed the embossed metal into one palm. 'You must survive. If anything should happen to me …' The *margravio* swallowed and glanced at his ashen-faced wife. 'Take care of your mother and sister. Trust in Nardo and Maria. Trust Dino. Stephania Prospero will be a friend to you. Flee to the coast if need be, but you must survive.'

The boy, just eleven summers old, nodded solemnly, then clutched his mother. The *margravio* hugged his daughter, kissing Isabella on each cheek.

'*Bambini*,' was all he said, a catch in his voice.

The men filed out of the apartment, boots echoing down the corridor. Dino felt every footfall as if they walked over his chest. His reluctance to kill the duke had been well founded, but until now he'd only thought of the moral complications, never the practical consequences.

'Are you well, my lord?' Abramo had fallen into step beside him.

'As well as can be expected,' replied Dino. 'Are you as good with the weapon on your hip as you are with the one in your britches?'

Abramo grinned like a wolf. 'I know the hilt from the sharp end.'

'Well, that's a start.'

'Do you really think it's a trap, my lord?'

'I don't know what to think any more, only that Demesne continues to surprise me. And never in a good way.'

They were almost at the stables in the Erudito courtyard when Stephania found him. Dino glanced at Massimo, feeling guilt rise like a welt from a lash.

'There's so many of you. Is something afoot?'

Dino gave a tight nod, tried for a smile that wouldn't come.

'We're going to patrol the Di Toro estate,' he lied. 'Reassure people after the recent raids.'

236

She nodded, seeing the sense of it. The others were leading their mounts from the stable, checking reins and adjusting buckles. The courtyard was unquiet with the noise of horseshoes on cobbles.

'Dino, I'm worried for my mother.' Stephania didn't meet his eyes. She stepped closer. 'She came to me last night, said that she didn't feel safe any more, that she feared for her life.'

'She's not been tardy making enemies.' Dino's voice was flat.

'And not just her own life, but mine too.'

'Did she say why?'

'Rumours are growing of more assassinations.' Stephania lowered her voice. 'She worries they'll kill me to strike at her.'

'You're not going to be assassinated,' whispered Dino.

'She asked me to flee to the coast.'

'That's convenient for her. Don't you think she might just want you out of the way?'

'I believed her, Dino. I didn't want to, but she was so upset.'

'She's shed tears before.'

'Not like this. She arrived at my door full of contrition. We spoke until the small hours. What if they kill her, Dino?'

'Then you'll finally acquire the command of your house.'

Stephania stared back, one hand going to her throat, a frown drawing down her mouth. 'It's one thing to be estranged from one's mother; it's quite another to stand idle when she might be killed.'

Dino shrugged. 'I wouldn't know.'

She glared at him. 'Is now really the time to play the lonely Orfano?'

'Play?' The word writhed with disgust as it fell from his lips.

'Dino, I'm telling you I'm worried for the safety of my mother.'

'And I'm telling you that your mother will reap what she's sown. If she has any sense she'll stop this continued opposition to Anea and fall in line.'

'Fall in line?' Stephania's eyes flashed with anger, lips curling with indignation. 'Are we just supposed to follow mindlessly, like cattle?'

'Your mother was a known ally of Duke Fontein.'

'And that's a sound enough reason for her to die?'

'Don't you think you're being overdramatic?'

'My mother didn't send those three bravos to kill Anea.'

'Know her that well, do you?' Dino knew he should be trying to calm her but couldn't stop the surge of frustration that had found a target.

Stephania's eyes narrowed.

'Look,' he continued. 'I've reason to believe her association with the *capo* is at an end. Perhaps now is the time to build some bridges with her. You might even suggest she hands power over to you. That would be an elegant solution.'

'Before she ends up like Duke Fontein, you mean?' Stephania turned on her heel and swept through the doorway into House Erudito. Dino stared after her regretting every word.

'Your horse, my lord.' It was Abramo. He held out the reins and flashed a glance at the retreating figure of Stephania. 'She's a spirited one.'

'She gets it from her mother.'

'I meant the horse,' said the swordsman with a wry smile.

'Of course you did,' replied Dino, sliding one boot into a stirrup and swinging himself up.

Abramo had taken hold of the bridle and looked up at Dino. 'If I might make a observation, my lord.'

Dino raised an eyebrow, then nodded.

'A woman will forgive a man many things, but nothing wears down affection more quickly than being the target for anger undeserved.'

Dino swallowed and cleared his throat. He nodded again. 'It's a well observed remark.'

Abramo nodded in return, turned to his own mount and took the saddle. Dino rolled his shoulders, willing the tension from them, his muscles taut ropes. His eyes never strayed far from the Contadino swordsman. Nardo and Massimo were paying the stable lad a few *denari* for his troubles. Massimo flashed a tight smile and a nod before urging his mount across the courtyard until he was beside the Orfano.

'Stephania seemed agitated,' he said. 'Did you two fight?'

'You make us sound like lovers.' Dino scowled.

'I could think of worse pairings.' Massimo smiled and looked away.

A leaden weariness overtook Dino's heart. 'I'm not sure I'm the marrying kind, Mass.'

'Perhaps one day.'

'Perhaps one day I'll just leave this behind and live with the one I love near the coast. Just the two of us.'

'And compose poetry? How idyllic,' said Massimo. 'Who knew Lord Erudito was such a romantic?'

Finally the doors of the courtyard yawned open, four guards grunting with the strain.

'Come on. She'll still be here when you get back.' Massimo winked. 'You can argue some more then.'

The riders set their mounts to a canter and followed the north-eastern road through Santa Maria.

36

A Day of Thorns

− 18 Agosto 325

'Some trouble with Lady Prospero?' They had left the tight confines of the town and were heading along the road that led to the woodland behind the cemetery. Margravio Contadino had dropped back, drawing his mount alongside Dino, shrouded in thought.

'My lord,' Dino nodded. 'She fears for her mother. A reasonable instinct under the circumstances.'

Abramo and Marcell led the patrol, while Massimo rode alongside Nardo a few score feet ahead.

'And Stephania turned to you to protect the duchess?'

Dino nodded and released a sigh. Irritation plucked at him.

'You're quite indispensable, it seems.'

'Only when people need a bodyguard.' Dino scowled. The *margravio* turned his head sharply but said nothing.

'I meant no offence, my lord. Today is hardly akin to sitting in an armchair during the small hours of the morning.'

'No matter.' The *margravio* waved off the misstep.

'What happened to the sale of the villa?' Dino was all too keen to change the subject. 'Or did the transaction fall through when the duke died?'

'Far from it.' Margravio Contadino looked in the direction of the Schiaparelli estate, just visible in the distance. 'Lady Allattamento took possession of a well appointed villa, then gave it up to an undisclosed party.'

'How did you come by this information?'

'The notary told me, for a price. He couldn't tell me who

owns the place now, only that it doesn't belong to any of the great houses. Or any of the minor ones.'

Dino sighed again. Another thread in the unravelling tapestry of Demesne, another mystery to distract him.

'The money has been useful,' continued Emilio, 'but the affair was otherwise pointless. I should have listened to you, Dino. I fear you have a wiser head than I ever will.' A pensive look crossed Margravio Contadino's face. 'Do you believe there's any truth to the rumour that the duke was poisoned?'

Aside from being responsible? Dino wanted to say.

'I heard he was found abed with two empty wine glasses. The maid found a whore's small clothes in the room. I think the duke enjoyed an exciting end –' Dino shrugged '– but not a poisonous one.'

'It's a strange thing when so persistent a thorn is suddenly gone. I dare say I miss the *bastardo vecchio*.' Emilio gave a rueful smile.

'There are always more thorns, my lord,' replied Dino.

'And what thorns are troubling you?' The *margravio* regarded Dino from the corner of his eye.

'Thorns? The Domina for one. I'm trying to locate a conspirator of hers, someone who remains in the shadows.' Dino paused to consider the consequences a moment. 'Do you know of anyone calling themselves Erebus, my lord?'

The *margravio* shook his head. 'No. Is it possible the name's a cover for someone we know?'

'I suspect Lady Allattamento, but she lacks the finances to orchestrate a plot.'

'Plot?'

'I shouldn't have mentioned it. For all I know Erebus might be riding beside me.' Dino grinned, but the *margravio* didn't return it. There was an uncomfortable pause. 'I don't really think—' Dino started

'Medea mentioned a possible marriage to Stephania.'

Dino looked at the road, at the woodland that beckoned them onward; he looked anywhere but at the man riding at his side.

'She also said you were less than keen. I can't say I was

pleased when Medea made her intentions clear, but she really has been the best possible influence on me. Don't be too hasty to turn away someone who shows you kindness, Dino.'

The Orfano smiled, a mask over his misery. 'I don't love her.'

'Love thrives in all climates, and it grows in the most unlooked-for places.'

'That we can agree on,' muttered Dino.

'Your heart belongs to someone else?' pressed the *margravio*.

'I'm not sleeping with Speranza. Why does everyone assume I'm sleeping with Speranza?'

'It wasn't Speranza I was thinking of.' The *margravio* nodded up the dusty road to the riders in front, just four score feet away. Massimo, resplendent in white and scarlet, was chatting with Nardo, who scoured the countryside with a watchful gaze.

'I'm not sure I follow you, my lord,' said Dino, blushing.

'If I'm right, and I think I am, you'll need to be more careful in future.' The *margravio* had never looked more serious. 'Losing Cherubini was bad enough; losing the pair of you would be calamitous.'

Abramo and Marcell dismounted and began leading their steeds toward the woodland off to the side of the road. Nardo waited on horseback.

'Not coming with us?' asked Dino

'Huh. I'll wait here to check you're not followed. Not my idea. Margravio Contadino insisted.'

'Keep safe,' muttered Dino. Nardo nodded and fetched his pipe from a saddlebag. 'It's not me you need to worry about.'

Duchess Prospero had given instructions to meet in what was known as the secret graveyard, no longer a secret since Lucien's discovery of it. The graveyard lay behind the walled cemetery, hidden by trees. It was the final resting place of scores of Orfani, the Majordomo's dumping ground for those too twisted to live. Dino had visited it long ago with Virmyre, vowing never to return. So many lives ruined by the old king's meddling. It was no more than a clearing, with rude markers announcing each unfortunate life long since passed from memory. The graveyard was also the resting place of those Orfani who had died in vendettas over the centuries. Far better to be buried in obscurity than suffer a defaced headstone. The people of Landfall had rarely taken to the *streghe*, only tolerating their existence at the express wishes of the king.

The men entered the clearing, weeping willows providing a curtain of pale green. Taller oaks stood behind them, aged and verdant.

Abramo grinned back at Dino. 'I've been thinking.'

'Always a pastime fraught with peril,' said Dino.

'I'm sure I could accommodate Duchess Prospero if she needs a new lover.'

'Anyone is an improvement on the *capo*,' replied the Orfano, glad of the banter. Tension seared through him. The men pressed in among the grave markers, hands on weapons.

'I'll show her a real man, not like that pretty boy,' continued Abramo.

He stopped suddenly and shuddered. Dino frowned, thinking the man convulsing with laughter. Abramo turned to him, a knife hilt protruding from his neck. The swordsman slumped down onto the long grass and Dino ran to him, kneeling among the grave markers. The strength ebbed from Abramo as Dino clutched his hand, disbelief shocking him to stillness.

The veiled attacker from the courtyard emerged from the willows' languorous limbs. Other men in grey appeared from the trees, all armed, all eyes intent on the *margravio*.

'It seems I failed to heed your advice one time too many, Dino,' said Emilio, drawing his blade. The Orfano did likewise, counting their opponents. At least three to one by his reckoning. Massimo and Marcell fell in alongside their lord, Massimo sparing a glance for Dino.

'There are always more thorns, my lord,' repeated Dino.

The grey men advanced into the the graveyard.

'Into the teeth of the wolf,' said Massimo. Any hope in the swordsman's eyes dwindled as the Orfano shook his head.

37

Remembrance

– *Novembre* 321

Dino knelt before the dais of the Ravenscourt, one arm resting on his raised knee, the opposite hand holding his scabbard lest it scrape on the chequerboard flagstones. Squares of white and black surrounded him, making him a lone playing piece in a game he was still gaining the measure of. The nobles had gathered, dwarfed by the columns at the sides of the chamber. Those in the gallery were made small by the vast dome of the ceiling. The sun shone through the windows with a weak lambency; winter had done much to reduce even that mighty orb. Dino knew what it was to feel small. He closed his eyes, listening to the droning ceremony. The Domina's voice was the only sound, a sheet of dog-eared parchment clutched in her hands.

It was the eleventh day of *novembre,* Dino's foundling day. This fact had precipitated Anea's decision. Orfani did not enjoy birthdays like ordinary people; how could they? It was a staple of the Orfano legend that misshapen babies arrived, unbidden, on the steps of the great houses. Except Dino had not been found at the gatehouse of Fontein or Erudito or Prospero or even Contadino. Eighteen years ago today he'd been found, a small bundle of swaddling clothes and deformities, outside the King's Keep – as it had been known back then. This twist had added to his personal legend.

Little Luc they'd called him at first, on account of his keenness to emulate Lucien. He'd grown out of this stage, his legend becoming distinctly unique. He was Dino of the poisonous spines, Dino of the bloody tears, Dino the grey, on account of the suits he wore. And, more important still, Dino the prodigy – few his age had mastered the blade with such finesse.

Anxiety surged through him. Things would never be the same after today, the threshold of adulthood vast and imposing. True, all Orfani were children for a span of their lives, but no one dared call what they experienced a childhood. Perhaps adulthood would bring some surprises or just a continuance of a life already lived at the sharp edge of politics and intrigue. Before now he had simply been Orfano. With no other responsibilities, his only duty was of care for Anea, one he performed tirelessly. Now he was to have a role. Just as he'd moved out from Lucien's shadow, now, today, he would stand free of Anea's. The thought pleased him, and yet still he felt small.

Recently this smallness had manifested itself in other ways. Not in his physicality, how could it? Now eighteen and tempered by war, he'd never be a large man, but his days as a stripling were long past. Instead he endured a smallness of spirit, eroded by guilt. Why had he survived the Verde Guerra when so many hadn't? Eighteen long months of uncertainty beneath the trees, by turns freezing and sweltering in the shadows of those ancient pines. So many dead had spilt their blood to nourish those roots, dead like the sons of House Datini.

Dino regarded the remainder of that much-reduced house from the corner of his eye, feeling the familiar pang. Why had he been spared? Why had the war, which had killed indiscriminately, decided that two brave men should die and be missed by their parents? Dino watched them now. Viscount Datini was a white-haired man with a perpetually downturned mouth beneath a blunt beak of a nose. His mien declared there was not one thing in creation that pleased him. Certainly the deaths of his sons had not improved his demeanour. His eyes were so deeply sunken as to be likened to holes punched through the canvas of night, where even stars didn't dare shine. In his prime he'd been a swordsman the equal of Duke Fontein; now in his twilight he clenched his hands behind his back lest people see how much they shake. Viscount Datini had been made small by time and the fractured pride he clung to.

Viscountess Datini was a wizened yet curiously smiling

245

woman, as cheerful as her husband was dour. There was a gentle kindness to her eyes but she joined conversations infrequently. Many thought her deaf, yet she always affected the highest interest in others, nodding pleasantly to any who spoke to her. Viscountess Datini's ever-present smile had wavered in recent times. She had been lessened by the passing of her sons: two in the grave and the third outcast by his father. Dino wished there was something he could do for the viscountess. The fate of her sons had rested in the hands of the *capo*, who had fumbled the duty, diminishing himself in the theatre of war.

In one night Guido di Fontein had been reduced from fearless leader to inept popinjay, though few were surprised by the unmasking. That the two Datini brothers and a score of household troops died for this truth to emerge made a tragedy of the *commedia* that was the *capo*'s life. Had he been less drunk, less arrogant, less casual, he may well have sent reinforcements. Instead the *capo* had waited until the following day, claiming one more night amid the silent pines would not harm their chances. Except he'd been wrong, and now the sons of Datini were no more. Guido di Fontein, made small by his own incompetence.

All of these thoughts swam amidst the roil and swell of Dino's mind. The Domina reached the end of her peroration and bade him stand. She tied a sash of deepest scarlet around his waist once he'd gained his feet. Dino turned to face his peers. The Domina presented the new *maestro superiore di spada* to the Ravenscourt. Many had known this day would come, and many had been opposed to the appointment, not least Duke Fontein. Dino made eye contact with the man and nodded, a pretence of respect that none in the Ravenscourt believed. The duke made disparaging remarks behind his hand to Lady Allattamento. Duchess Prospero pouted and fussed at the *capo*, torn between frustration and chagrin in equal measure.

Anea stepped down from the dais and embraced Dino, fixing a silver medal in the shape of a star to his jacket. The silver bore an amethyst stone at the centre.

For bravery, she signed with her clever fingers, then pressed her veiled cheek to his in the semblance of a kiss. Dino's heart

246

swelled and he embraced her in return. This moment was broken by the fluster and bustle of Duchess Fontein. She'd been acid in her disapproval of Anea's appointment. That an Orfano should hold a rank in House Fontein was not welcome, especially with Anea's plans for a republic advancing with each passing year.

The nobles approached the new *maestro superiore di spada* to congratulate him, meaningfully or otherwise. Viscount Datini was the first, his wife following him. She embraced Dino in a break with etiquette that was remarked on for weeks after. Massimo, bearing a silver star of his own upon his jacket, also embraced him. They grinned at each other, scarcely able to believe they'd not been friends but two years ago. Now they were all but inseparable.

Viscount Simonetti loomed over the assembled well-wishers, a gentle smile and a warm handshake confirming his pleasure at the appointment. The library's archivist gave a small leather-bound book to the Orfano, a primer on tactics. Lady Allattamento performed a curtsy so small Dino wondered if she'd caught her heel on her gown. He smiled in response, ignoring the insincerity that fell from her lips, her words pretty and meaningless.

Maestro Cherubini clucked and cooed. He beamed with pride, entreating all to fete the young *superiore*.

'Hasn't he grown while away in the south?' pointed out the *maestro*. 'Hasn't he filled out into a fine young man?' They all agreed he had while carefully avoiding any mention of the war itself or the many lost souls who had failed to return.

Margravio Contadino bowed and managed a gruff smile.

'It's long past time you had some proper duties. One day we'll look back on when you were a mere *aiutante* with a smile.'

'I hope so,' said Dino, but it would be many years until he could speak of the war lightly.

'We can all sleep a little easier in the years to come knowing you'll be teaching future generations to fight,' said the *margravio*. This turned out to be a false prophecy: just six months later Dino would be almost fully occupied keeping Anea safe.

Attending lessons and teaching students would take but a small part of his time.

Medea embraced him lightly, favouring him with a kiss on each cheek. She had to rise to her toes to do so. She'd adopted him in all but name since his return from the Verde Guerra. Luc Contadino, just seven years old but in full possession of his father's gravity, bowed deeply and fell in beside his mother.

Medea smiled. 'Perhaps one day you'll learn the blade from Dino,' she said to her son. The young noble stared at the new *maestro superiore di spada* with a strange expression. Dino imagined he saw mistrust in the boy's eyes. It seemed even the title of *superiore* would not rid him of the Orfani's dire associations.

The moment of unease was undone by Virmyre. 'If a layabout wine-supping noble has to be awarded the position of *superiore* then it's best it's you, I suppose.'

'Those of House Erudito, well known for their love of wine, should not be so hasty to cast aspersions on others.' Dino smiled. 'Least of all those going about their daily business armed.' This brought a polite ripple of laughter from the crowd.

The nobles filtered away from the Ravencourt to a feast hosted by the Contadinos. Massimo sat beside him making jokes while the *margravio* regaled the guests with tales of Dino's time as his *aiutante*. But not company nor wine, not the medal nor the title, could dislodge the discomfort Dino felt. While the Verde Guerra was at an end, there would be no real peace. This simple truth had been written large like graffiti in Luc Contadino's eyes. Anea's plans to make Demesne anew would be met with hostility. Violence and madness would make the very greatest of them small given time.

38

Esposito Lost

– 18 Agosto 325

The men in grey had gained much from their raids on Demesne. Many were armed with halberds liberated from fallen guardsmen.

'Fall back,' grunted Marcell, but it was a futile suggestion. There was no safe path of retreat, no place to fall back to. They were surrounded.

'I'll kill Salvaza Prospero for this myself,' grated Dino from between clenched teeth. He batted aside a clumsy thrust from a pole-arm.

'You may not get the chance,' replied Margravio Contadino.

Marcell had downed an opponent and was parrying strikes from two more. The quiet clearing was now alive with the sound of steel ringing on steel, urgent grunts of exertion, the wheezing rasps of the dying.

'Mass, get behind me,' said Dino, eyeing his friend's wounded shoulder.

'I'm fine,' came the terse response. The swordsman threw up a weak parry, narrowly avoiding a halberd heading for his vitals. Dino sized up their opponents, looking for a gap in the circle they might break through. Hope was in poor supply.

'What do you want?' bellowed the *margravio*, but no one replied, least of all the veiled and hooded attacker from the courtyard, who appeared to be directing the grey men. He stood on a fallen tree, staring at the four swordsmen with glowering intensity. The previous attacks had been predicated on the need for food. The only outcome sought today was death.

Margravio Contadino's party was now hard pressed on all

sides, in a small circle, fending off a ceaseless number of savage swings. Abramo lay several feet away, face down, the grass around his throat slick with blood. Marcell succumbed next, taking not one but two halberds to the shoulders. Dino heard rather than saw it. Stifled disbelieving grunts shaken from the veteran, collarbones shattered. Dino dared a glance over his shoulder to see Marcell sink to his knees, unable to parry the next attack, and the next. His head was split asunder, coming apart in a shower of gore.

Dino cursed.

Another attacker used the moment of Dino's distraction. The Orfano turned back to find a halberd levelled at his chest, blurring forward. His left arm snapped out, the bound forearm meeting the wooden shaft at an angle, the tines providing a measure of armour. He knocked the blade up and aside, his hand closing down on the weapon, clamping shut even as his right hand thrust his sword forward. There was an agonised yelp as the sword emerged from the ragged man's back. Dino felt steel grate on ribs, knowing it was lodged fast in the man's chest. He relinquished his grip on the blade, spinning the halberd around his hand in a blur. Another attacker found himself bereft of his head a heartbeat later. Dino lunged forward, abandoning the *margravio* and Massimo, breaking free of the encirclement. The attackers faltered, unsure how to proceed.

'My lord, this way,' shouted Dino. He regretted it immediately. Margravio Contadino turned toward Dino's path of escape. A halberd smashed into his shoulder. His attacker struck again, knocking the *margravio* to his knees. Massimo cried out, his blade falling in a sunlit glare of steel. The sword cleaved through the wrist of the man responsible, but it was too late.

Margravio Emilio Contadino stumbled to his feet, bent double, a savage slash across his broken ribs, now slick with crimson. Massimo knocked aside two more killing blows, desperate to delay the inevitable death of his master. The swordsman split another attacker's face open, a soundless howl of fury on his lips. Dino ran forward to gather the wounded lord in his arms, but was separated by yet more attackers. For one hateful second the *margravio* locked eyes with the Orfano.

'Run, Dino.' He coughed blood. '*Avanti.*' His head was severed in a single strike. Dino stumbled back, almost losing his footing as he knocked over a grave marker. So much death.

Massimo broke into a flat run, disappearing through the trees pursued by six men, rags flapping about them like diseased skin. The veiled and hooded leader looked on, immobile at the edge of the clearing, arms folded across his chest. If he had orders to kill Dino he appeared unwilling to execute them.

Dino ran, fear a jagged song playing on his nerves. Frustration snagged at his boots; shock made a knot of his stomach. The willows sighed and shuddered in the wind, roused by the ecstasy of violence. The woodland was oppressive with shadow, occasional flashes of sunlight blurring Dino's vision, threatening to blind him. His flight was long and panicked, thrusting him into a meadow, gasping for breath. He dared snatch a look behind. Shapes and colours beneath the trees coalesced into figures, lurching, sprinting.

Dino dropped the halberd, fleeing across the yellow grasses of the meadow, waiting for the moment his flesh would fall prey to implacable steel. Nardo waited ahead, astride his mount, holding the reins of Dino's. His face was marked with questions.

Margravio Contadino dead. And Massimo too most likely. The thought almost brought Dino to his knees, momentum carrying him on. He vaulted the hindquarters of the mount, landing in the saddle with such force he nearly slipped past the horse's neck. Thighs grasped at the horse's flanks, hands clutched at reins. The beast complained, then took off. Nardo looked on astonished and silent.

Dino struggled to find the stirrups, cursing, clinging on, desperate not to fall to the road below, as it slipped past under hooves that beat the dust into tawny clouds. With each beat he was carried away from where Margravio Contadino had fallen.

And Abramo.

And Marcell.

And Massimo emerged from the woods breathless and

ashen-faced. Dino veered in to meet him, the horse leaping the fence beside the road into the meadow. Nardo followed, his own blade free of its scabbard. The first of the pursuers broke free of the trailing limbs of the willows, lunging after Massimo. Dino's breath caught in his throat, chest constricted. The Contadino swordsman hadn't seen his pursuer. Dino put his heels to his mount, the horse surging forward. He reached for his sword but found nothing: the blade remained lodged between a dead man's ribs. Dino gritted his teeth and trampled the attacker into the long grass. The impact near shook him free of the saddle; a curse slipped his lips. The horse's momentum carried it past the grey man, but it sagged a second later. Dino wheeled around to pull Massimo up into his arms. Nardo had engaged another of the attackers, but the man's halberd was proving dangerous to both horse and rider.

'Mass! *Porca miseria!* Get over here!'

Massimo stumbled toward him, confusion crowding his features, his gait stumbling and unsure. Dino reached down, pulling the swordsman up with a grunt. His hand came away bloodied.

'Picked up a few more scars,' said Massimo with a weak smile, arms folding around Dino's waist. So many times had Dino wished for this, but never under such hateful circumstances.

'Nardo!'

The messenger didn't waste time trying to finish his opponent, content to let the speed of his mount protect him. They fled from the woodland edge as more and more attackers in grey spilled from the shadows.

'*Dottore!* Someone fetch a *dottore!*'

The horses were all but forgotten, abandoned in the Contadino courtyard. Dino carried the wounded swordsman in aching arms. The pain in those strong limbs was as nothing to the fear that racked his chest.

Don't die on me. Don't leave me here.

A silent prayer to any who might hear it, even Santa Maria herself. They stumbled through Demesne, porters and cooks' faces stricken with shock and concern. None looked more stricken than Massimo, who had slumped from the saddle, eyes closed, into the arms of Dino.

'A *dottore*! Please!'

Dino pressed on, out into the rose garden, from which shocked courtiers fled. Others remained, desperate to know Margravio Contadino's whereabouts. Windows opened on all sides of the garden, on all floors of Demesne. Faces appeared beneath pointed arches, regarding the unfolding tragedy, hands pressed to mouths and chests, powerless and aghast.

'Don't leave me here alone, Mass. You can't leave me.' He was whispering now. Blood-red and cloud-white roses surrounded them, roses the colour of Massimo, bleeding freely from uncounted wounds, staining his tabard. The swordsman's face was paler than Dino had ever seen it.

'Please don't die on me. I'm begging you.'

Massimo's eyes fluttered a moment but remained closed.

'A *dottore* for my friend.' He'd meant to shout, but the words were no more than sobs.

'Put him down here. We'll improvise some bandages.' Nardo was grim-faced, dusty from the road. He gestured to the centre of the garden, where the calming gaze of Santa Maria looked over a congregation of flowers.

'Please don't leave me,' repeated Dino like a mantra, not realising the words escaped his lips. Massimo's eyes opened slow, his gaze unfocused. Staff emerged doorways, some brave enough to investigate further. They edged closer among the roses, eyes intent on the fallen swordsman, watching the Orfano hold back tears, regarding the messenger, whose face foretold the outcome.

'Please don't leave me,' whispered Dino. He'd sunk to his knees in the shadow of Santa Maria, clutching the swordsman in arms slick and red. 'Don't you leave me, Mass.'

'I'll always be here for you.' The tiniest of smiles creased the corners of Massimo's perfect mouth. How many times had Dino's eyes lingered on Massimo's lips, barely hearing the words, only watching their shape and curve.

'I never told you—'

'I know.' Massimo laboured a weak cough. 'You never needed to; I always knew.'

'How?'

'The way you look at me. No one else ever looked at me like that.'

Dino tried to swallow, stomach hollow and collapsing, his chest like rubble, heart fractured at the centre.

'Don't leave me, Mass. I couldn't bear it.'

'I'm not going anywhere.' The swordsman smiled, impossibly serene, his eyes wet with unfallen tears. Dino bowed forward, pressing his lips to the beautiful man in his arms, but when he opened his eyes there was just the body of a swordsman – another casualty, another corpse, another funeral to be planned, another name to be added to the rolls of Demesne's history.

'Mass?'

Nardo dropped to one knee, reaching out a tentative hand for Dino's shoulder. That simple touch told him the very thing his mind would not accept. Could not accept.

'Mass? Please. I'm begging you. I'll do anything. Anything you ask, just don't go.'

'It's too late, my lord.' Nardo's voice cracked with the telling of it. The Orfano shook his head, clutched the dead man tighter, eyes pressed shut, willing the tears away.

'No, I won't allow it.' His voice was like gravel scratching on wood.

'He's gone,' whispered Nardo, 'There was nothing we could do.'

'Where's the *dottore*?'

The *dottore*, when he arrived, could do nothing but shake his head sadly.

'I'm sorry, my lord,' was all he said. Dino was numb and broken. By now the windows of the rose garden were packed with every stripe and rank of person that inhabited Demesne. They had all borne witness, not just to the loss of life but the loss of love. Scandalised whispers would come later, but for now the gossiping tongues were silenced by the outpouring of Dino's grief. Until tomorrow it mattered not that he'd loved a man, only that he'd been parted from him in such a brutal fashion.

Camelia appeared, viewing the scene with tears frozen in her eyes. One arm curved around the Orfano's shoulders. She hauled him up and led him step by step through Demesne to House Erudito. He'd yet to open his eyes, blinded by grief, the sight of Massimo's serene smile etched into his memory.

'I never told him I loved him.'

Camelia could say nothing, only wipe the bloody tears away as they appeared at the corners of his eyes in greater and greater profusion.

39

The Brooding Drake

– 25 Agosto 325

The wine glass hit the door, shattering into a hundred jagged slivers. Many of the pieces that fell to the floor were coated with dregs, tiny bloodstained blades. The door had seen its fair share of projectiles over the last seven days. Other glasses had been thrown, a wine bottle and three books. All had followed the same fate, now forgotten on the floor. Drink combined with anger had seen a stiletto cast at the offending portal, impacting hilt first. This proved fortunate, else the blade be stuck firm for all to see, a painful marker of a time that would haunt Dino long into the future.

The summons issued from the door yet again, the rapping loud and raucous. Achilles hissed and pushed his head beneath his tail. Dino cursed under his breath. There was nothing else left to throw, bar the bottle of Barolo in his hand, half full.

'If you think I'm wasting this on—' The knock interrupted his slurred soliloquy. *'PORCA MISERIA!'* he bellowed, then lurched up from the couch like a windblown scarecrow. He almost lost his footing on the short walk to the door. The knocker was keeping up a steady percussion now, the sound driving Dino to murderous intentions.

'WILL YOU PLEASE FUCK OFF?' he bellowed through the door. The rapping continued unabated. Dino struggled to fit the key in the lock, finally dropping to his knees so he might finally fill the offending keyhole. He opened the door still kneeling, peering through the gap. A familiar face waited in the corridor above him.

'Are you deaf, old man?'

'Profoundly. Now stand up, you little shit.'

To his great surprise Dino found himself doing just that. Virmyre entered, giving the Orfano a long and withering look. He turned his attention to the apartment and folded his arms, one hand straying to his chin.

'Well, I'm glad the rumours of your decline are unfounded.'

'I'm fine,' said Dino, holding on to the couch for support.

'Yes.' Virmyre looked at the room with distaste. 'Interesting interpretation of "fine".'

'Interesting how?' Dino slumped against the arm of the couch and tried to swallow. He felt as if he were suddenly plunged back into his schooldays. Virmyre had ever been a stern teacher, his reprimands legendary.

'Well, I hadn't thought the word included such descriptors as unwashed or unshaven.'

'So I took a few days off from—'

'And the apartment?' Virmyre took in the desolation. 'Is deep and unrelenting squalor the new fashion?'

'I didn't feel like letting Fiorenza in.' Dino's voice withered with each exchange.

'And the fact you smell like you took a shit in your britches.'

'I do not smell like I took a shi—'

'Shut up, Dino.'

'I just ...' He gagged on the words, his chest filling with the all too familiar pain of his grief.

'I know,' said Virmyre, laying one hand on his shoulder. 'I know. Go to your chamber.'

A bath had been prepared by a team of maids before Dino was fully aware. He'd sat on the bed while Virmyre urged him to drink coffee.

'Is this to sober me up?'

'No. All the coffee in Landfall couldn't achieve that miracle. Besides, that's a myth. Coffee keeps a drunk awake, which means they're a good deal more manageable. I simply want you to stay awake long enough to perform your ablutions.'

The staff departed the wreckage of the bedroom, shooting

wary looks at Virmyre. He nodded to them with his usual stern demeanour, then locked the door.

'I'd throw those britches from the window if I were you. I couldn't give them to the laundry staff in any good conscience.'

'They're not as bad as all that.'

'How about we burn them and I'll never mention it again?'

Dino peeled off the offending garment and slipped into the wooden tub, gasping as the heat of the water seared his skin. Virmyre seated himself on a stool, drawing a straight-edge razor from inside his jacket.

'Well, get some soap on your face then. You really don't suit a beard and I'm not here to help you kill yourself.' Virmyre eyed the razor, the blade reflecting the sunlight. 'However, I must congratulate you: you're doing a remarkable job of that by yourself.'

'I'm not killing myself.' Dino frowned. 'I've only been drinking. What time is it?'

'Around seven,' replied Virmyre, tilting Dino's head back. 'In fact seven seems to be a number you're rather keen on.' The blade was pressed to his face and began to scrape the whiskers from his cheek. 'Seven days cooped up, wallowing in your own foulness. Seven breakfasts untouched. Seven dinners not eaten. Seven messengers turned away.'

Dino could feel waves of disappointment emanating from the older man.

'I just want to be left alone,' he protested between scrapes of the blade, now working at his throat. Virmyre held his head firm with his free hand. He was sitting so close that Dino could smell scented soap and laboratory chemicals.

'You've also missed four funerals.'

Dino tensed against the man's grasp but stayed still. The insistent scrape of steel on stubble, the only sound in the room, suddenly deafening. The suffocating grief in his chest became a dull spike.

'Couldn't you have killed off another three people? Just to round it out to that seven I'm so fond of?'

'I considered it.' Virmyre sighed. 'But there are so many worthy targets I rather lost my focus.'

Dino said nothing, allowing the news of Massimo's burial to filter through his mind. There was the usual sting of denial, a hot flash of anger to no avail. Only resignation remained. He'd never see the Contadino swordsman again, never spar with him, never drink with him, never hear his voice. He tried to swallow and couldn't. Wanted to breathe and at the same time wouldn't have cared if he'd never drawn another breath.

'It does get better,' said Virmyre in a quiet voice.

'Really?' Dino couldn't keep the sneer from his lips. 'When?'

'When you start facing it and stop hiding behind the drink.' Virmyre still had a hand on him, still patiently scraped the blade over his beard, now thinning with each stroke.

'I don't want to face it.'

'And the alternative is what? Staying here? Drinking yourself to an early death? Refusing to eat, like some damn fool lovesick teenager?'

Dino broke free of the man and turned to face him, lip curled back. If Virmyre was surprised he refused to let it sully his features.

'And what do you know about losing anyone? You've never loved; you're as bad as Anea and her infernal machines.' Dino stood up, displacing a good deal of bath water onto the floor. Staggering out of the tub, he snatched a towel to hide his nakedness, fully aware how ridiculous he must look. 'Please, if you're such an expert, tell me all there is to know.' His teeth were bared now, fingers balled into fists of frustration, the yawning emptiness of his stomach knotted with anger. Virmyre's gaze was steady, face impassive. He rinsed the blade, dried it on a small towel and folded the razor neatly.

'My wife died in childbirth the night Lucien appeared on the steps of the castle. My son died too.'

It was as if a great hand had placed itself on Dino's chest and pushed down. He slumped onto the bed.

'I may be an educated man but I'm no *dottore*. And I'm no midwife.' The words were evenly paced – no inflection, no emphasis, just the pleasant rumble of Virmyre's baritone sharing his most intimate defeat.

'Angelicola was supposed to deliver the baby, but he was

busy. It was different back then. There were hardly any *dottori*, and most were reluctant to leave the houses they served. Not one came to us. I lost the most precious woman in the world and the boy too.'

Dino's shoulders slumped, head bowed.

'Where was Angelicola?'

'Delivering Lucien.'

'Oh.' No word existed to respond to such a revelation. Dino wished he'd remained silent.

'So you see –' Virmyre's voice was a calm hush '– I know quite a lot. About death. About blame. About guilt. Powerlessness. About missing someone so badly you'd rather forget their name. Easier to persuade yourself you never knew them that way, easier to pretend they had never existed.'

Dino pressed a fist to his mouth, forcing down the sobs of his own despair. 'I'm so sorry. I never knew.'

'Few do. It's not one of my favourite topics of conversation. And it was a long time ago now. But I do know, Dino. And I also know each day is an improvement on the last. But only if you face it, accept it. Only if you take it into your heart and not let it poison you.'

'They took him from me.' Dino whispered the words so quietly he doubted Virmyre had heard.

'I know. And Emilio too, and those brave swordsmen, and a dozen *cittadini*. We'll get them, Dino. We'll bury every last one of the them, but only when you pull yourself out of that bottle.'

Dino nodded, every muscle tense, holding in the desolation.

'Now get back in the tub and let me finish what I've started. Massimo would be horrified if he could see that beard.'

The sitting room had been restored to its former glory by the time Dino had bathed. The glass on the floor was swept up, the bloodied rags of his grief spirited away; everything had been neatened and brushed, dusted and wiped clean. A barber was waiting, setting to work on Dino as Virmyre sat at the dining table reading a book. The *professore* idly worked his way through the remaining wine while Dino concentrated on

260

not throwing up. The barber had mastered the age-old art of remaining silent, only his scissors disturbed the quiet.

'Do you *have* to drink that?'

'It would be a shame to waste it.' Virmyre regarded the wine, breathed in the bouquet. Dino's stomach turned. 'And besides, if I drink it I know you can't. So I'm doing you a service really.'

'How selfless.'

It was then he noticed Virmyre had come without a walking stick. Age no longer slowed his steps; the grey in his hair and beard was much reduced; the lines of that craggy face were softened. It were as if time had withdrawn from the man, taking its erosion with it.

'You look …' Dino fumbled for the word '… well.'

'It's true, I am markedly more vital these days.' Virmyre gave a small shrug and sipped his wine. 'I've been sleeping better. Eating better too.'

'What did I miss?'

'During your hiatus?' Virmyre eyed the barber, clearly weighing his words. 'Nothing you couldn't guess at, I'd wager. Demesne is in uproar, of course. Medea is accusing Salvaza of laying an ambush for her husband and consorting with the raiders. Salvaza is denying everything, but her position is precarious. The *capo*'s silence is scandalising everyone. Stephania frets and House Erudito makes polite but empty gestures.'

'What does Anea make of all this? Has she convened the court?'

'I've not seen Anea since the whole business began.' The words were like flecks of ice, Virmyre's eyes wintry.

'What?' Dino almost started from the chair. The barber paused his labours.

Virmyre cleared his throat. 'She fell ill and retired to her apartment here in Demesne. I assumed you knew.'

Dino shook his head. 'So the Domina is left in charge, trying to keep everyone from killing each other?'

'Yes, although she's as rare a sight as you are these days. She's not returned any of my messages.' Virmyre stroked his beard and the barber shifted position. The scissors resumed their work, and brown hair fluttered to the floor.

'What of Medea?'

'She's taken Emilio's death very badly. She adored him, of course. Maria has moved in with the children and is taking care of them full time.'

'I told him not to go,' mumbled Dino.

'Some are saying Medea may not come back to herself.' Virmyre seemed to utter this comment reluctantly, almost an aside. He looked through the window at the thin clouds stretching to nothing against the evening sky.

'What does that mean? "Come back to herself"?'

'They say her mind may have gone.' Virmyre turned back to him, a frown above his pale blue eyes. 'The staff are unwilling to leave her in her own company. She's been worried about you, of course, on the occasions she's lucid. Everyone has been worried about you. Well, everyone except me. I always knew you were a drunk.'

'Thanks.'

'I just didn't realise you were too stupid to eat while getting drunk. Amateur.' Virmyre shook his head.

'Can we talk about Nardo? I feel we've already covered my failings.'

'Good point.'

'Is he well?'

'He feels terrible about the death of Emilio, naturally, but also the two swordsmen and—'

'That's ridiculous,' interrupted Dino. 'Nardo would likely have been killed had he ventured into the woods. It's a miracle that Massimo and I got away.'

The barber stopped cutting.

'I mean …' Dino swallowed. 'I mean …'

'Are you nearly finished?' Virmyre looked at the barber, who spent a moment on some finishing touches and departed without fuss. The *professore* closed and locked the door after him. He circled the Orfano and settled into the armchair opposite.

'I mean got away from the woods,' continued Dino. 'I didn't realise how badly wounded he was.' He wasn't speaking to Virmyre now, just letting the words pour out. 'I pulled him up onto my horse. My hand came back bloody, but I'd seen him wounded before. He always recovered. He couldn't die. Not Massimo.' Dino crossed his arms, clutching himself, almost forcing the words out of a chest now leaden. 'And his arms grew weaker and weaker around my waist. We were riding so fast. I knew I had to reach Demesne, reach a *dottore*. He was barely holding me at all by the time we got back.'

Dino's vision had pinked at the edges, his malformed tear ducts feeding blood across his grey eyes. The room was turgid with sadness and regret seen through a filter of red. Dino took a deep breath and pressed his eyelids shut.

'So what do we do next?' Perhaps duty would free him from the inertia of sadness. He hoped so; anything to stop feeling so desolate.

'I'm going to pay a few calls on the houses,' said Virmyre, 'take the temperature of the various parties. See if I can't prevent things from boiling over.'

'I'll come with—'

'No, you won't.' Virmyre stood in front of him, hands clasped behind his back. 'You're going to see Nardo and take him out for a meal at the *taverna*. It would do the pair of you good to come to turns with what's happened. You need to get out of this awful apartment – get away from these hateful old stones.'

Dino nodded and wondered where he'd left his sword. It mattered not. The world outside was daunting in a way no steel could reassure him against.

40

Rumours

– 25 Agosto 325

'I'm just saying you need to be careful. People are asking a lot of questions following what happened in the rose garden.' Nardo directed his gaze into the wine glass. His face was deeply lined, dark circles accentuated by its paleness. He'd barely laid eyes on Dino for the hour they'd sat together.

'I lost my best friend,' the Orfano all but snarled.

'I know that.' Nardo looked up at him a moment but couldn't sustain it, his eyes returning to the dregs of the red wine. 'It's just … you two were very close, and that sets people to talking. Especially with all that business with Cherubini and all.'

They were sitting at the usual table outside the *taverna*. A circle had cleared around them. A corona of privacy. Or revulsion. The innkeeper's hospitality was strained – he appeared only when summoned. Dino didn't care for the look in the man's eyes or the abrupt manner of the service.

'The *maestro* should never have been sent away,' said Dino.

'Huh. The *maestro* should have kept his house in order,' countered the messenger.

'And that's what I've to do is it? Keep my house in order?'

'Hell, Dino. It was a figure of speech.'

The walk from Dino's apartment in House Erudito had not been a pleasant one. The staff he encountered looked at the Orfano with surprise that quickly darkened to mistrust. His reception at House Contadino was no better. Camelia was absent, denying him even the comfort of a friendly face. The kitchen staff's whispers were audible the moment he turned his back. This was the punishment Cherubini had endured, the loss of face in a thousand painful increments.

'New sword?' said the messenger. The Orfano nodded and laid the weapon across the table in front of him. The pommel was a snub-nosed drake cast in silver. The hilt was snug with soft leather dyed turquoise.

'Virmyre commissioned it while I was ...' He gestured toward his apartment.

'Drunk.'

'Recovering.' There was a note of warning in his voice. 'I've called it Achilles.'

'Give you a good deal, did they?' Nardo regarded the black-enamelled scabbard.

'You think anyone in House Fontein is going to give me a good anything?'

'Huh.'

'So what *are* people saying?' Dino could barely bring himself to ask the question, syllables tripping over his lips, a reluctant mumble.

'Everyone saw, Dino. Those that weren't standing in the doorways were hanging from the windows. They saw him die in your arms. They saw how upset you were. What do you suppose they're saying?'

'He was my friend.'

'Huh. Not my business who you're friends with, but people are idle. Most of them are just waiting for some intrigue to gossip about.' The messenger produced his pipe, turning the stem over and over. He made no move to smoke; only occupy his restless hands.

'It's no secret there are men in Demesne who remained unmarried,' said Dino. He looked away to the piazza, sullen. 'Some are too ugly, some too sour.' He took a sip of wine to fortify himself for what he would say next. 'And the rest maintain the fiction they've yet to meet the right woman.'

'Huh. In Demesne? Certainly. But out on the estates? Such men are beaten, they're disowned; some are forced to move on, others never get a job worth their talents.' The messenger glanced at a passing serving girl. His eyes shifted to Dino, who flashed a look at her.

'She's very attractive,' said the Orfano without inflection.

'And you're a terrible liar.'

Sounds from the piazza filled the silence between the two men. Catcalls and insults, laughter and feigned outrage, a few stubborn market traders bellowing their wares.

'They'll find something else to speak of this time next week,' said Dino, gaze directed at the rough wood of the table dividing them.

'No, they won't. This is going to stick to you like pitch. And it won't be over in a week, or even two weeks.'

'What do you mean?'

'Some of the *sergenti* have called for your resignation as *superiore*.' The messenger looked up from the pipe, which rested between his fingers, his face hard, eyes the same. Dino took a slow breath of the warm night air, then sipped his wine.

'They wouldn't dare,' he replied, words lacking conviction.

'They're saying it's because you never teach, but that's horse shit. They want you out because of this business with Massimo.'

'There was never any *business* with Massimo.'

'I believe you. I do. But people love to talk.'

'What happens with House Contadino now?' asked Dino to sidestep the impasse.

'Huh.' Nardo shrugged. 'Medea is expected to rule until Luc is old enough.' The messenger's face twisted into a grimace. 'Hell of a thing for a boy to lose his father like that.'

'We didn't lose Emilio; he was taken from us, just as Massimo was taken from us.'

'And Marcell and Abramo.'

'Yes, those too.' Dino remembered Abramo, so confident, so loyal.

'I should have been there, not tending to the horses at the side of the road.'

'It wouldn't have made a difference.'

A familiar leaden feeling filled his chest, the bitter tang of regret at the back of his throat. The only sound he could hear was the thundering of hooves, the only sensation Massimo's arms about his waist. And there was the smell of blood; it clung to him like the fading tendrils of a nightmare. Now the hushed crunch of footsteps on gravel, Massimo's boots dragging. Sounds of sobbing.

The messenger stood and cleared his throat, ushering Dino back to the present.

'I should get back. Maria will need help getting the children to bed.' Nardo frowned and looked away. 'Isabella isn't sleeping.'

'She's not the only one.' Dino blinked, and when his eyes closed he saw only Massimo, laid out among the roses of the Contadino gardens.

'You coming?'

'I think I'll stay here for a while longer,' said the Orfano, indicating the unfinished wine. 'I'm not sure those walls will make me feel any safer tonight.'

Nardo nodded and turned on his heel, disappearing among the crowds of Santa Maria. The *cittadini* were determined to have a good time despite the unfolding disasters of recent months. Perhaps in spite of the disasters. The mood was almost hysterical, heightened but hollow. Dino kept drinking, hand never far from the drake-headed sword.

'And that sets people to talking.' Dino slurred his imitation of Nardo's words and rapped his knuckles on the door of the Allattamento apartment. His other hand was occupied with a bottle, a now familiar accomplice.

'Virmyre will kill me when he discovers I'm drunk again.' He shook his head and tried to focus on the door. 'Still, better him than these other fuckers. At least he'd make it quick.' Dino's mumbling filled the corridor, which was empty save for two brave mice and a long-case clock, its rich mahogany almost invisible in the darkness, polished brass reflecting the candlelight. The pendulum moved with a velvet grace. The Orfano knocked again, louder this time.

'How long does a man have to wait to get—' The door opened, revealing a worried face, one hand clutching a shawl at her throat, nightdress reaching her ankles.

'I was expecting a bit more flesh on display.' Dino grunted a laugh and stumbled forward. The woman placed one hand against his chest, gentle yet firm, stalling his progress. There was something familiar about those deep brown eyes, an indignation to them.

'What do you want?' He didn't know her name. Doesn't matter; probably better like that, he thought.

'What do you think I'm here for? This is House Allattamento, isn't it?'

She ushered him in, gesturing to a couch.

41

Nobility, Vendetta and Revenge

– 25 Agosto 325

He'd imagined House Allattamento differently, the women attired in silk, feeding grapes and goblets of wine to older, moneyed men. He'd imagined the cries of lovemaking coming from the bedrooms as men took their pleasure. Instead the room was devoid of all decoration save the furniture. The girl was quite alone.

'Why are you here, my lord?' There was something familiar about the girl, but Dino struggled to place her.

'Where is everyone?'

'Lady Allattamento has taken her daughters to the country-side. She thinks it safer there and I agree with her. I'm to join them tomorrow.'

'But ...' Dino let this sink in. He suddenly wished he were sober. 'I thought they sold themselves? How ...?'

The girl gave a derisive snort and shook her head.

'What?'

'That rumour came about purely because Duke Fontein visited so often. He and Lady Allattamento were lovers. For a time. Her daughters are far from chaste but they're not whores. Surely you of all people know the power of rumour?'

Dino blinked. 'I don't understand.'

'We brought girls in off the street to cater to the more ... insistent callers. Do you really think Lady Allattamento would sell her own daughters to every *sergente* and *nobile* with coin to spare?'

'And what about you?'

269

'Is that what you're here for?' Full lips smiling without humour. 'To lie with a woman?'

Dino felt his cheeks blaze scarlet. He managed a stiff nod.

'I thought you preferred the company of fighting men. So brave, so masculine.' Dino felt the sting of her taunt through the haze of his drunkenness. 'So loyal,' she continued. 'And yet here you are.'

He set down the bottle. Still he said nothing.

'Lord Dino Erudito, finally wanting to sample the pleasures of the fairer sex.' She brushed the sides of her breasts with her palms, the nightdress stretching over her curves. He didn't care for her sneering tone nor the cruel curl of her lip. The room spun as he pushed himself to his feet, his focus wavering. She looked up from her seat on the couch, defiant.

'And you think I'm the woman to give you an education?'

'What's your name?' he grunted, keen to say something – anything. Wasn't she supposed to cater to his every need? Instead every word was a challenge.

'Giolla di Leona.' She stood up and laid one hand against his chest. 'And I'm not a whore either.'

'Fuck me,' he breathed. Not an exclamation but a command.

'Sit.' He obeyed, wine-leaden limbs pulling him down into the softness of the couch, scabbard angling awkwardly, the drake-headed hilt staring back in disgust.

Giolla stood over him, easing the shawl from her shoulders, not taking her eyes from him. The fabric fell to the floor, gathered about her naked feet. Her smile remained mocking, eyes intent on his own, ready to observe the direction of his gaze. Then the nightdress, fingers working at the buttons, struggling out of it, pushing it past her ripe breasts and down to her waist.

'I'll bet everything I own that my nakedness does nothing for you, *my lord*.' These last two words were caustic and sour. The nightdress joined the shawl on the floor, revealing lithe legs and the tangle of her sex, the soft sweep of her stomach.

'Oh no,' moaned Dino and pressed one hand to his forehead.

'Let me guess. Too drunk, my lord? Or are you finally going to admit your true nature?'

Dino shook his head. 'You're the girl from the painting.'

270

Giolla stiffened, eyes widening, then she snatched up her nightdress, hurrying back into it.

'What did you just say?'

'You. That's where I've seen you before. You're the girl in the painting.'

'How do you know about the painting?'

'Because I've seen the fucking thing.' He glowered at her. 'It looked a bit rushed, but it's absolutely you. No question about that.'

Giolla's face became ashen. She gathered her shawl and busied herself with it before turning to him. 'So it was you.'

'What do you mean?' Dino shifted on the couch, pulling at his shirt. She said nothing, eyes accusatory, frown deepening, mouth a taut line. 'What do you mean, "it was you"?' he pressed.

'Duke Fontein never let anyone into his chamber. He came here when he lay with Lady Allattamento. Even Duchess Fontein never visited his chamber. It was sacrosanct to him.'

'What are you talking about?' But Dino knew it was too late.

'Only four people know of the existence of that painting – myself, the duke, his maid and the painter, Delfino Datini.'

Dino struggled to breathe. 'I saw it after he died.'

'No, you didn't. Because I had the maid bring it to me.'

'I ...' The words died on his lips. He was too drunk to lie, sick with deceit, too tired to maintain the pretence.

'You poisoned him. Didn't you?'

Dino said nothing, shame a boulder on his chest, crushing the air from his lungs. He had left the duke's stiletto on the mantelpiece as a marker of his guilt. He'd wanted to be found out, wanted blame and reprisal to absolve him. He'd staggered to House Allattamento to prove himself a man, finding only an assassin instead. And a drunk one at that.

'I'd have done the same,' Giolla said. 'He planned to kill both you and your sister.'

'You knew?' whispered Dino, incredulous.

'Of course. I knew him well. We were very close at the end.'

'Were you lovers?'

Another cruel smile, another dismissive snort. Dino

wondered if she'd ever experienced happiness. The taint of cynicism lingered on her every word and expression.

'Duke Fontein was my father.'

Dino pressed his eyes shut and cursed himself for a fool. He pressed one fist to his mouth, unsure what words would spill from his lips next.

'I suppose you'll want revenge for what I did?' He was aware of the knife hidden in his right boot, the sword sleeping in the scabbard, but he'd never killed a woman before. He had no wish to start tonight.

'Revenge.' The word was laced with futility. Giolla sat down, a sad smile crossing her face. 'He sent my mother away to House Marco. We weren't poor, but it was a far cry from life in Demesne. I had no idea who he was at first – just a stranger on a horse come to visit, and even then rarely. My mother adored him, of course.' Giolla sighed. 'And I despised her for it.'

'How did you come to live in House Allattamento?'

'My mother died when I was thirteen and the duke took me into the staff. I'd never been so lonely –' she crossed her arms '– even surrounded by all the people in the castle. I was too common to be taken seriously, no good for anything but cooking and cleaning. But the duke paid for my tuition with House Erudito. Lady Allattamento taught me etiquette.'

'When did you find out?' Dino knew the pain of uncertainty all too well. 'About your father, I mean?'

'Four years ago. He told me one night – late, drunk, as you are now. Imagine, a poor girl from the countryside discovering her father is one of the most powerful men in Demesne. He promised me the world, of course, on condition Duchess Fontein never discovered my identity. He always thought he'd outlive her.'

'Small chance of that. She's like a gorse bush without the personality.' This at least made Fontein's daughter smile. Her shoulders were bowed, as if her confession weighed on her.

'I'll not tell a soul,' offered Dino, wanting to make some small amends.

'It's no matter. I'm leaving tomorrow, and that will conclude the whole tawdry business.' She shrugged and pouted. 'House Fontein will die out and there'll be few if any to mourn it.'

'We're still left with the fact that I killed your father.' He sat forward, lacing his fingers. 'Revenge is a staple of the *nobili*, vendetta their daily bread.'

'True enough.' She shrugged. 'But what can I do to you that's not been done already?'

The Orfano shook his head. 'What do you mean?'

'You're all but abandoned by your sister, and the Domina is perhaps the least trustworthy person in Demesne right now.'

He nodded, desolation mounting in his chest.

'Your best friend has just been killed, if indeed you were only friends.' She should have gloated over that but instead only managed to look sad. 'The *maestro* has been exiled, Margravio Contadino killed, his wife on the edge of madness.' She drew a bleak picture, and he could refute none of it. 'And me? I'm just the bastard of a dead man who plotted against the throne. What do I care who lives or who dies? You call this nobility?' Now she was sneering. 'I call it a sham. There are *cittadini* in the fields who behave with more dignity and compassion than any bloodline of Demesne.'

She stood, the truth of her words sharper than any blade, cutting him deep.

'Take your nobility, take your vendetta, take your revenge. I want none of it. You want to be absolved? Forget me, forget everything you know about me. Let me disappear into the countryside tomorrow. Let me live out my days in peace.'

Dino pushed himself to his feet, painfully sober, words foreign to him, silence his only friend.

'And you.' She looked at him with eyes full of pity. 'You can stay here and suffer the consequences. That's your punishment, my lord. As if losing Massimo wasn't punishment enough.' She went to her chamber and locked the door, leaving him wondering what new tragedies would be ushered in with the dawn. And if he would survive them.

42

The Domina's Secret

– 26 Agosto 325

Dino stood atop the roof of House Erudito watching a cart meander along the eastern road. Landfall appeared reduced and toy-like from this vantage point, although the games that played out were anything but happy ones. Very few would be setting out from Demesne at such an early hour. The Orfano swallowed in a throat dry with hangover, temples a dull pain from the previous night's excess. Dino knew with absolute certainty who drove the cart, diminished as he was. He knew exactly where Giolla di Leona was heading, just as he knew he'd never see her again. Her words from the previous night returned, a mocking echo.

Let me guess. Too drunk, my lord? Or will you finally admit your true nature.

A vision of Massimo came to him – among the roses, covered in blood, a serene smile touching his perfect lips.

'Huh. Doesn't seem so long since Cherubini headed out.'

Dino hadn't heard the messenger approach. He stood some twenty feet away, leaning against a chimney stack, fingers stuffing the bowl of his pipe with moonleaf.

'It's a month,' said the Orfano, failing to keep the sadness from his voice. Dino turned his eyes back to the departing form of Giolla. 'To the very day.'

'Hell of a thing. Seems like we could use him right now.' The messenger nodded at the cart on the road. 'Friend of yours?'

'No. Just the last of the Allattamento household leaving Demesne.'

'Huh. Giolla.' Not a question.

Dino nodded. 'Did you know her?'

'Not really.' Nardo shrugged. 'Was told she was a distant cousin of mine when I was younger. Everyone seems to be joined by blood in Demesne.'

'Blood shared or blood spilled.' Dino's eyes remained fixed on the cart.

'Those two aren't always so different.' The messenger blew out a plume of grey smoke then nodded toward the horizon. 'She was taken in by Lady Allattamento not long after she was brought to House Fontein. Not much reason to speak to her after that. Always an unhappy sort.'

Dino shook his head. Duke Fontein had hidden his bastard right beneath their noses, even providing her with false relatives. A grim smile of grudging respect creased his lips.

'How did you know I'd be up here?'

Nardo shrugged. 'Seems like a good place to come to get perspective on things. Quiet up here without the ravens, though.' The messenger took a drag from the pipe, breathed out a mist of smoke and cleared his throat.

'What happened to them?'

'Fewer and fewer of them with each passing year after Lucien left. No one paid them much mind, and then they weren't here any more.'

'Seems the *nobili* are going the same way,' replied the Orfano. Nardo dragged on his pipe and for a moment the two men were content to let the growing heat of the sun suffuse them. Though neither of them would confess it, the night's chill had left them restless and out of sorts.

'What was said at the *taverna*—'

'I'd rather not talk about it, Nardo.'

'No business of mine who you lie with.' The messenger looked down at his pipe, a wisp of smoke twisting and coiling. 'I'm just ... I just find it strange. You've always been a friend to me, and we've always carried out our duties. No reason we can't be friends still.'

'But?'

'But there's other people who won't see it the same way. They'll try and make you leave just the same as Cherubini.' He

275

nodded toward the cart trundling east. Dino's mouth twisted in response, sadness pressing against his sternum like a fist.

'Anea won't let them send me away,' he said after a pause, but there was little if any conviction to the words.

'What will you do now?'

'I'm still a *maestro di spada*. I should go and teach, although I doubt any of House Fontein will be pleased to see me.'

'Huh. Into the teeth of the wolf,' said the messenger.

'And knock them out, every one,' replied Dino, eyes lingering on Giolla di Leona's cart.

Demesne had altered, a subtle alchemy, a shifting of architecture. Perhaps the very air had been transmuted in some way? Emilio Contadino's death had ushered in an age of darkness despite the summer's glare.

Guards in Fontein livery stood to attention at street junctions and gatehouses, slouching postures replaced with alert poses. Those who had been transparently bored wore looks of stern wariness. None of the soldiers had ever taken to Dino, who was too much the product of privilege, too strange as an Orfano yet envied for his position. Added to this list of sins was the rumour.

Invertito.

The slur was spoken aloud in darkened corridors as he passed, but when he turned he found only empty space. The authors of the insult were already drifting beyond another corner, another door, another curve of House Fontein's dark walls. The rumours would settle down in time. The tormentors would soon tire of their game. He hoped.

The *capo* emerged from a door many feet ahead, immaculate as ever and bearing a look of contentment. He greeted a trio of guards on their way to morning practice and joined them. Dino slowed to remain undetected. Today might be the very occasion Guido drew steel against him. There would be no allies to stand beside the Orfano, no one to risk his life for the rumoured *invertito*. The doorway led to a place indistinct in Dino's memory, if he'd ever bothered to investigate it before.

It was an unremarkable-looking portal: sturdy oak, frame

stout, handle, lock and studs all cast in black iron. More unremarkable still for remaining unlocked, an opportunity afforded by Guido's lack of attention. Simply because he couldn't remember what was on the other side, Dino unhooked a lantern from the wall and went through. The corridor beyond was merely a landing, steps falling away into gloom. Whatever business had occupied the *capo* lay underground. It was damp here, despite the best efforts of the blazing sun and the drought that besieged the castle. There was a rank note on the air that spoke of things dying; Dino hoped he'd encounter nothing more sinister than decomposing rats.

A sliver of gold light ran across the floor ahead showing every imperfection of the rough flagstones, a sliver that escaped from under a door. Dino slowed his pace and lifted his heels lest his boots announce him. The lantern was switched to his left hand and held behind, while his right reached across his waist to curl about the drake-headed hilt of his sword. A soft mumble of conversation reached his ears. He urged himself closer, straining to hear. A score of ants scurried about, throwing tiny shadows across the light emerging under the door. They had no task other than foraging, as far as Dino could tell, yet they moved with steely assertion. And they were large, far larger than any ants he'd seen in the long months of drought and infestation. The Orfano resisted the urge to capture a specimen, rewarded with the words of the Domina, heard despite the heavy oak of the door between them.

'As you can see, I've put the money Lord Erebus provided to good use.' There was a pause before she continued: 'I had to pay five of House Fontein's finest blacksmiths in order to be ready in time. I also needed to buy their silence, one of Demesne's more expensive commodities.'

Dino waited, expecting another voice to reply, but nothing came. His mind raced, wondering what lay beyond the door. Something undoubtedly made of metal, but what? And shown to whom?

'Now that we have this many we can tell the Ravenscourt. There will be some unrest, but I'm confident we can contain it.'

The Domina's one-sided conversation was odd. Was her companion someone who needed no words?

'Anea. What have you done?' he breathed, wanting to draw back, wanting to retreat to the stairs and the door that waited at their summit. He should be outside in the sun, teaching the blade, not trapped here underground, new secrets threatening to swallow him like a landslide.

'The assassin is no longer in my employ. His fortunes are in decline, and his position becomes more precarious by the day.'

Dino's blood ran cold. *In decline.*

'He'll be a vocal opponent in the times ahead, but he's a *maestro di spada*, nothing more.'

The Domina had no need to iterate Dino's title to Anea. Whoever she spoke to couldn't be her.

'I'd rather consult Lord Erebus before acting with haste. There's always a chance he'll come over to our side.'

Another pause.

'Stranger things have happened in Landfall.'

The golden sliver of light faded from beneath the door, leaving the Orfano with only the company of ants. The Domina and her silent accomplice had left by another exit unknown to him. Dino waited for long minutes before trying the handle with a cautious hand. It was locked, of course, likely bolted. The Domina's secret would remain so for a little longer at least. Frustrated, the Orfano headed to a training chamber and practised alone. He'd need his skills soon, of that he had no doubt.

'I'll show you decline,' he said as he concluded each exercise.

43

The Myrmidons

– 27 Agosto 325

Nardo found him the following morning, occupying the same perch above House Erudito. The Orfano sat cross-legged on a sloping roof beneath an eggshell-blue sky stained with gold. Achilles dozed in his lap, basking in the rising sun.

'Someone else leaving?' asked the messenger.

'I couldn't sleep.' The dark circles beneath Dino's eyes spoke the truth of it. He'd spent most of the night failing to discover what the Domina was hiding behind lock and key. 'I came to watch the sun rise.'

'You were missed at House Fontein yesterday.'

'I doubt it.'

Nardo shrugged.

'Not smoking your pipe?'

'Huh. No time. We have to go.' The messenger nodded toward the great dome at Demesne's centre. 'The Ravenscourt is coming to session.'

Dino raised his eyebrows but said nothing. Achilles yawned and stared around, expression flinty.

The Ravenscourt was as full as Dino had ever seen it. The gallery teemed with *cittadini*, all focused on their betters below. The court itself contained representatives from every house. All ranks were present, from the lowliest messengers and pages to those with titles and illustrious family histories. The *capo*, surrounded by four bravos wearing House Fontein colours, regarded Dino with a drowsy smile.

'Huh. What's got him so smug?'

'I think we'll know by the time this session is done.'

'No Duchess Fontein,' remarked the messenger.

'Perhaps she's drowning her sorrows, or her self-pity.' Dino couldn't keep the bitterness from his tone. His regret for the dead duke had faded, as if Giolla had scoured the guilt from him. It was no absolution, but that she understood his motive made the burden easier to bear.

'You could have dressed for the occasion,' grunted Nardo.

Several courtiers stared, openly gossiping. Dino silenced them with a glare. His appearance – jacket unbuttoned, shirt rucked, hair messy – was attracting attention. Daggers peeked from the tops of his boots; the scabbard he wore was an open invitation to the careless or the brave. A sombre suit of black damask indicated his mood, only the sash of turquoise at his waist declared his loyalty. In truth he found it harder to wear Anea's colour with each passing day.

'Not so many friendly faces,' said Nardo.

'Those divided and those ruled,' commented Dino. The new *maestro* of House Erudito was present, but Dino couldn't recall the man's name. A swarm of *professori* stood harrumphing, all stilted small talk and awkward asides. Dino felt another pang of regret for the outcast Cherubini.

Stephania, flanked by her messenger and maid, offered a curt nod. The disciple of Santa Maria stood close, mismatched eyes calm above her veil. Her fingers counted out rosewood beads in a measured, unhurried fashion. Dino forced the sneer from his lips. She was only alive due to Massimo's efforts.

Camelia stood with Nardo's wife, Maria, doing their best to represent the much-depleted House Contadino. The Orfano and messenger approached, and Camelia took a moment to kiss Dino on each cheek. A few nobles spluttered, muttering under their breaths, becoming close-mouthed under Dino's unflinching gaze. His hand on the pommel of the drake-headed blade was ample incentive to fall silent.

'You're getting thin,' chided Camelia.

'I'll be sure to visit soon for a good feeding.'

'Make sure you do; I've been worried about you.'

'You're always worried about me.'

'That's because you're always in trouble.'

'I can't deny that.' He smiled and felt the warmth of Camelia thaw the frost on his heart.

Medea's absence was keenly felt, although paling beside the loss of Emilio. Medea at least had the opportunity to recover from her despair.

'How are the children?' Dino gave a tight smile.

'They miss their parents,' replied Camelia.

Duchess Prospero stood alone, hands clasped demurely at her waist, chin tucked in. She stared at the dais from underneath her brow, mien intent but neutral. The darkness about her eyes spoke of sleep lost to the ravages of worry; her gown was unusually conservative.

'She looks lonely, no?' said Nardo from behind a raised hand.

'It's an act,' replied Dino.

'Huh. How so?'

'She could have brought a messenger, pages or a maid with her.'

'But?'

'But she chooses to stand alone. Perhaps she's looking vulnerable in the hope someone will come to her rescue.'

'Never thought I'd hear the word vulnerable used to describe Salvaza.'

'No one stays strong for ever.'

Dino's eyes sought his sister, wondering how deep the cost of the king's machines had been. Anea sat on the oak throne, looking much improved but different to how Dino remembered her. Had it really been so long? Had the endless hours of research wrought some subtle change to her features?

'She looks different,' he whispered to Nardo.

'Huh. She looks like she's eating again. Not before time.'

'She was dreadfully thin,' agreed Camelia.

The Domina stood at one side of the dais, silver staff in hand, new scarlet robes immaculate, the circular biretta making a merely tall woman an imposing one. She too looked in better health, less tired certainly. The Domina was flanked by five figures shrouded in robes of grey. Dino searched the sea of anxious

281

faces sweltering in the morning heat. Not a single halberd rose above the assembly; no breastplates gleamed amid the throng.

'Someone missing?' said Nardo.

'There's a distinct lack of House Fontein guards.' Dino's subdued spirits sank further; Virmyre too was absent.

The Domina's silver staff boomed three times. A breathless hush descended, the nobles dropping to one knee in unison.

'This session is now in progress.' The Domina's voice rang to the edges of the Ravenscourt, lost only to the great dome that rose above their heads. Dino's eyes were drawn back time and again to the five grey-robed figures. Sweat prickled at his brow. The Domina stretched open a rolled parchment and began to read.

'In the light of recent attacks and the repeated failure of House Fontein and Margravio Contadino to protect our granaries, I have decided to create a new army to protect Demesne.'

Agitated words ran amok across the Ravenscourt. Emilio's death was still painfully sharp for his allies. The gallery was a scandalised susurrus.

'Furthermore, it is the order of Lady Diaspora that a curfew be introduced between sunrise and sunset in Santa Maria.'

Another round of seething whispers, more words unleashed from incredulous mouths.

'Where are you getting your new soldiers from?' shouted a man in the gallery. The Domina ignored him. Dino's eyes were now locked on the figures behind the Domina. A terrible certainty gripped him, holding him fast in the dizzying heat of the Ravenscourt. The chamber was now drunk with outrage. The silver staff boomed down on the dais. Once. Twice. Three times. The Domina passed an excoriating gaze over the assembly.

'These are the wishes of Lady Araneae Oscuro Diaspora. It is her wish we join together in this time of hardship.'

'What of House Fontein?' This shout from the gallery brought a murmur of support.

'We spoke of this,' Dino said quietly to Nardo. 'Spoke of creating a new army, one we could trust.'

'The days of that house are at an end,' the Domina all but snarled, fixing the *cittadini* with an icy gaze.

'What do you mean, "new army"?' Nardo frowned.

'Watch.' Dino nodded toward the dais.

One by one the robed figures revealed themselves. All wore unnatural, insect-like dark brown breastplates and sleek helms. Short swords were belted at the hip, scabbards enamelled in matching dark brown. They stood at wary attention, thin wiry limbs under heavy grey garments.

'Did you know about this?' asked Nardo, an edge of mistrust to the whisper.

'No! Of course not.' Dino frowned. 'I'm as shocked as you are.'

'They're not Fontein guards?'

The Domina was struggling to make herself heard over the din. 'And how much does it cost to outfit a new army?' bleated one of the nobles.

'You need to talk to Anea,' said Nardo. Dino chewed his lip, ignoring the messenger's angry glance. How had he not seen this coming? How had they kept such a project secret?

'I'm not sure I know her any more,' admitted Dino. 'All that time spent in the *sanatorio* has warped her senses.' The crowd around them jostled. Dino locked eyes with Anea, but the look she returned was devoid of recognition or interest. He held up his hands and flashed a series of gestures.

We need to talk.

Her brow creased in confusion and she turned her eyes to the Domina.

'Our new guards are called the Myrmidons. They will answer directly to me. There will be no more violence in Demesne, no more raids.' She was all but shouting now. 'We will pull togeth—'

Dino didn't hear the rest of her words. His eyes had found the gallery, which was thinning fast, anxious glances thrown over shoulders. In perhaps a quarter of an hour word would have spread throughout Santa Maria. And then, at the far end of the gallery, he spotted the reason for the *cittadini*'s hurried exit: one of the Domina's new Myrmidons. He wore two short swords across his back and lacked the sleek helm of his comrades, instead opting for a veil. His dark brown hair was ragged, long and tied back. Dino almost drew his blade on instinct. The veiled Myrmidon looked down, meeting Dino's gaze with dispassionate eyes.

'He was in the woods when Emilio was killed,' breathed Dino, 'and he nearly bested me in the Contadino courtyard.'

'Who?' Nardo was all but crushed against him as the Ravenscourt descended into chaos. More of the Myrmidons had appeared, looking all too keen to wield the weapons given to them by the Domina. Anea rose from the throne and exited by the back door, a wall of Myrmidons protecting her from the calls and protests of the court. The *capo* and his retinue made to leave, but not before Guido closed with those loyal to Contadino.

'It seems neither of us will become Duke Fontein,' said the *capo* with a smirk.

'It does seem that way, doesn't it?' replied Dino, too shocked to form a more biting response.

'I heard you failed to protect Margravio Contadino. How embarrassing, what with you being *superiore*.'

Dino lunged forward, but the bravos at Guido's side interposed themselves.

'We all make mistakes, Dino.' The *capo* grinned.

'And what will happen next time you fail?' asked Dino. 'Do you think she's the kind to suffer fools gladly?' Dino flashed his eyes toward the Domina, Guido stiffening as he followed the direction of the Orfano's gaze. 'Do you think she suffers fools at all? You're being played, Guido.'

The *capo* spent a moment constructing a riposte, but the moment was gone and he knew it. He swept out of the Ravenscourt, his bravos shouldering those too slow or too proud from his path. There was a fresh outburst of agitated voices.

'I preferred it when he was keeping company with Salvaza,' said Nardo.

'I trust him less now he's taken up with the Domina,' added Maria.

Dino and his companions pressed through the crowd,

reaching the dais to discover the Domina had departed. He flashed a look up to the gallery, but the veiled Myrmidon had gone. The Ravenscourt had begun to empty.

'What does this mean?' asked Camelia. 'For us? For House Contadino?'

'It means we're all fucked,' said Dino.

'What do you mean?' pressed Nardo.

'I mean if Anea has turned Demesne over to the Domina and these ... Myrmidons, then there's no telling what she has in mind for the remaining *nobili*.'

'She wouldn't—' said Maria.

'Her mind has gone.' Dino spat the words. 'The machines, the king's secrets. I warned Virmyre. I told him to keep her safe.'

'She wouldn't kill the children,' protested Maria.

'Demesne is no stranger to killing children as they sleep,' replied Dino, remembering his childhood.

'I'll go to them now,' said Nardo.

They left together, crossing the polished marble of the Ravenscourt with anxiety gnawing at their heels. They were almost through the doors when a Myrmidon appeared. Dino made to draw but Nardo stilled his arm. The newcomer entered, summoning those guarding the Ravenscourt with a guttural shout. The grey men marched out in their deep-brown armour, boot heels tramping on flagstones.

'Where are they going?' muttered Nardo.

'To put down a riot,' whispered Dino.

They watched the unrest from the windows of Lucien's old apartment. The town had fragmented into those trying to escape and those venting their rage at a change none had agreed to. Camelia clung to Luc as Maria held Isabella, shielding her eyes. Nardo and Dino looked down at the town powerlessly. The gates of all the great houses were locked and barred. All the portals to Demesne had been reinforced to repel the raiders, who now protected them with a spiteful zeal. Fire licked at the wood only to be doused with the buckets so thoughtfully provided by the now dead Margravio Contadino. The whole affair had the taste of a cruel joke gone terribly wrong. Pitchforks lay discarded in the street, their owners face down on cobbles slick with blood. By nightfall the anger had dissipated, its cost counted in lives.

'I have to speak to Anea,' said Dino.

Nardo nodded, too shocked to say anything meaningful. 'Hell of a thing,' was all he whispered.

44

Slaves to Duty

– 28 Agosto 325

The day after the riot was a day of tense silences. No words of consolation could salve what had befallen Santa Maria. Dino stalked the corridors of Demesne with a hand on the hilt of his blade. Myrmidons stood at the main gates of the great houses and the Central Keep. There was no way to determine just how many of the armoured soldiers existed. All individuality was scoured away, faces unseen beneath curving helms. They barely registered Dino's passing, adding to his pique.

The Orfano killed two long hours training with the new blade, the drake-headed hilt a comfort in his hand, onyx eyes amid the silver scales. Dino paused to catch his breath, sweat a bright sheen across his torso. Massimo had partnered him the last time he'd ventured to the abandoned practice room; now his killers guarded Demesne.

Massimo.

The name continued to weigh heavy on his heart. He lashed out with the sword, striking through the very thought, turning away from it. He began working through the steps, just as he'd done the day he'd sparred with the Contadino swordsman. The simple stances and slashes of novices evolved into the parries and feints of the adept. Finally he practised the combinations and ripostes of the master swordsman. All of his awareness was consumed by the weight of the steel, the balance of the blade, the rise and fall of his breath. Individual movements became an extended fluid motion, weaving a nimbus of destruction about him. Grief abated, frustration diminished, the drake looked back from the pommel and glittered. If death should find him tonight he would be ready for it.

The door opened with a creak of protesting hinges, announcing Nardo.

'I went up to the rooftops looking for you,' said the messenger.

'Thought I should practise. I can't lose my edge at a time like this.'

'Huh. I think we've all lost our edge of late.' Nardo checked the corridor, then closed and locked the door. 'I feel like there's some greater force at work.'

'There is,' said Dino sheathing his sword.

'Want to share what you know?'

Dino recounted what he knew of Erebus, how he used *tinctura* to buy influence with the Domina, how Duke Fontein's assassination had been the express wish of the Domina's mystery correspondent.

'You've been playing this close to your chest.'

'Sorry.' Dino shrugged. 'I asked Stephania and Massimo for help first; I should have included you.'

'What does Stephania make of it all?'

'Not much, just speculation.'

'And Anea knows all of this?'

'I don't know. I've not spoken to her in weeks. Longer than weeks, in fact.'

'Well there's an opportunity to change that. I've had word the House Fontein maids have been cleaning a room all morning. Her furniture is being moved over there as we speak. Tailors and seamstresses from House Prospero have have been summoned.'

'Anea's moving to House Fontein?'

The messenger nodded. 'The Domina is on the move also.'

Dino advanced toward the door, full of purpose. Nardo laid one hand against his chest lightly.

'Slow down. She's surrounded. They're all there – the Domina, a *dottore*, that veiled bastard, a couple of Myrmidons guarding the door. Viscount Datini and Simonetti appear to be part of the cabal too.'

'I need to speak to Anea.'

'Huh. Better you speak to her alone, if you can.'

Dino nodded, then let out a frustrated sigh.

'Wait until nightfall.' The messenger clapped him on the shoulder. 'And keep that thing sharp.' Nardo gestured at the sword. 'You're going to need it.'

Dino spent the afternoon slumped in an armchair in one corner of the Contadino apartment. Maria went about her chores and the children played quietly or read from books; neither of them spared the Orfano much interest. Dino was grateful. He dozed in the chair with his sword across his lap, the drake slumbering on his shoulder. Camelia arrived, making a fuss, before the five of them took an awkward meal together. Luc and Isabella remained silent throughout. Maria and Camelia spoke of mundane things so as to not upset them. It was a vain effort; everyone at the table knew how dire their situation was. Dino counted off the hours, waiting for his chance to see Anea.

'You're up to something,' said Camelia as they cleared the dishes away.

'Everyone in Demesne is up to something,' replied Dino. Achilles flicked out a black tongue.

'Do you want a clip round the ear?'

'I always forget how direct you are.' Dino grinned.

'I'm more than happy to remind you.' Camelia smiled back.

'I'm going to try and speak to Anea tonight.'

'Oh,' said Camelia, stopping her chores.

'Yes. Oh.'

'What will you say?'

'I want to find out who's manipulating her. There's someone behind the scenes with an agenda and I mean to unmask them.'

'Do you have any suspicions?'

'I did wonder if Lady Allattamento might be the culprit, but she's left the castle. Duke Fontein is dead, but his wife could be responsible.'

'Do you really think so?'

'No.' He plucked at his lip. 'I did wonder if Salvaza might be the problem, but she wouldn't order the death of Duke Fontein. It doesn't make any sense, you know?'

'Things stopped making sense months ago.'

'True enough.' Dino drew in a breath, feeling the tension in his shoulders. 'It can't be the *capo*.'

Camelia snorted in disdain. 'He only thinks with his britches.'

'Perhaps it's someone we're not aware of, or someone who's been away from Demesne for a few years.'

'You can't mean Lucien.' Camelia frowned.

Dino blinked and shook his head. 'No, of course not. Why would he seek power here when he has power enough in San Marino?'

'You should send word to him. He'd come and help.'

'I already have, but the messenger hasn't been seen in weeks.'

'Promise me something.' The cook circled the table and drew close. She smoothed back his hair, tucking some stray strands behind one ear as if he were no more than seven or eight years old.

'What is it?'

'This person you're hunting, are they responsible for Lord Contadino's murder?'

'I'm not sure. That finger seems to point toward Salvaza.'

'Well, when you do know who is responsible ...' Camelia hesitated '... make sure you kill them.'

Dino nodded, Camelia's request had all the hallmarks of an assassination about it. It would be a just killing, but a killing all the same.

Evening had darkened the streets of Santa Maria, the west side of the town caught in the deepening shadows of Demesne itself. The window revealed a horizon the colour of an angry wound. Dino waited for the land to scab over with darkness. The stars appeared only dimly, witness to an unhappy town cowed by the violence of the riots. The brightest of them shone amethyst, a vengeful eye in the firmament.

Anea passed from her sitting room to the bedroom, a slump to her shoulders telling of a day loaded with frustrations. She had dismissed her maids some hours earlier. The tailors and seamstresses had departed with measurements and a good deal of coin. Anea had grown weary of the Domina too, who had insisted on lingering late into the night. This much Dino had determined by lurking on the windowsill, an ear pressed to the lead-latticed glass.

The door to the apartment was guarded by two Myrmidons. Dino had passed along the corridor earlier, disguised as a Fontein messenger. A hat and a tabard was all it took. A further two Myrmidons patrolled the corridor itself, pausing at the tops of the staircases, deterrents to any who might loiter.

Anea stood by her bed. A single candelabrum held five waxy columns, each bearing a tongue of flame. The Silent Queen moved to regard herself in the full-length looking glass, turning her head this way and that as if looking for some blemish. Dino found her at once familiar and unknown. There was something new about her, some intangible change that he could not pin down. She reached her hands to the nape of her neck, preparing to untie the veil hiding the lower part of her face. All these years and Dino had never enquired, never discovered what lay beneath. They'd been close, but it seemed that relationship had been discarded as if it were no more than a soiled rag. It was then that she spotted him behind the door of her chamber. Dino had lain in wait for over an hour. He pushed the door closed, a sidestep and a twist of the wrist locking it shut.

'It seems you and I have a few matters to discuss.'

Dino caught sight of himself in the looking glass: the drake-headed pommel reflected the candlelight; everything else about the Orfano was darkness.

Anea hadn't turned to face him, but was tracking his progress by reflection. Her arms slid together across the gentle curve of her stomach. Her eyes were drab olive, not the brilliant jade he remembered. Had nostalgia cast her in a more favourable light?

'I see your pet Myrmidons are guarding your door.'

A single nod.

'It would have been nice to know about their formation ahead of time. I am the *superiore* after all; the soldiers answer to me.'

Not my idea. The gestures were basic, the words roughly sketched in the air. *The Domina told me we could not trust you after the death of Massimo.*

Dino clenched his fists. 'She has that much right, at least.'

The Domina suggested we employ the raiders ... rather than fight them. I could see no outcome that would not leave ... scores of dead.

'We have scores of dead. From the riots.' His words were like a slap. Anea shivered in the silence that followed. 'We had scores of dead from their raids. People, innocent people.'

It would have been far worse if we had tried to fight them.

Dino failed to keep the sneer from his face. Anea refused to turn, as if conversing with his reflection might lessen his anger. He'd expected a more spirited discussion than this. Her responses were placating, not the forthright intelligent ripostes of the Ravenscourt.

'Why come back at all? The Domina is running the place – into the ground in my opinion. An army of armoured murderers, the *nobili* in disarray: perfect for the coming of your new republic.'

I came back to rule.

'You call this ruling?' His anger seethed with each syllable, burned with each word.

Remember the Majordomo?

Dino couldn't easily forget the Majordomo, the Domina's predecessor. A looming giant of a man wrapped in grey robes no better than rags, the droning voice of the Majordomo had conveyed the will of the king since time unremembered.

'You know I do.'

Remember how the king was absent, a recluse? Remember how it felt like the Majordomo was the ... authority? How none spoke against him, how everyone ... scurried to do his bidding?

'He was repulsive. People were afraid of him.'

But in time we forgot the king. He became an abstract, a concept.

'Lucien wouldn't agree; he saw him with his own eyes.'

And what did Lucien say?

'That he was a changeling, a monstrous changeling, demented by his paranoia, corrupted by power.'

That is why I came back. I am not an abstract ... I will not fester in the dark. I will rule, and the way in which I do so may not be to everyone's taste.

This at last was beginning to sound like the Anea he'd once known, even if the silent language she used was stilted. It was as if she had only recently learned the many gestures, signing at half speed, pauses overlong.

'I'm surprised you could drag yourself away from your beloved machines to spare us the time.'

A person could waste a lifetime trying to ... decipher the king's secrets. We have advances enough for the time being.

Dino raised an incredulous eyebrow. The Anea he had known would never have been satisfied.

'What caused this sudden change?'

What do you mean?

'You've been researching those machines, uncovering their secrets, for a decade. Now you're asking me to believe you're going to abandon them, just like that.'

I have Virmyre to tend to the sciences. He is no doubt shackled to the king's machines as we speak.

'Where is he?'

I do not know. She made the words slowly, as if unsure how, or what to say. *In the* sanatorio, *I expect. Where else?*

'Turn around.' The words were not to be dismissed or disobeyed. 'I said turn around.'

The Anea he knew hated the word *sanatorio*, hated the associations with that building. She hated the dark history that overshadowed her precious library. The woman in front of Dino turned. She was the right height, her eyes the right colour; certainly she retained the frosty countenance Anea was famous for. She thrust out her chin, eyes hardening above the veil.

Any other questions, or are you quite finished?

'Just one actually.' He stepped closer to her, and closer still. She wore the same perfume, her hair the same sun-drenched blond, caught in a plait that reached down her spine. And yet a difference lingered at the limit of his senses, some indefinable quality, a maddening ambiguity.

'Who is Erebus?'

Anea's eyes widened in shock for a second before she feigned a puzzled frown.

'He's the author of some letters to the Domina. And he's not shy of making demands.'

293

I do not know that name. Her fingers trembled as she signed the words. She swallowed, her breathing quickening.

'You're lying.'

I do not know—

'You're lying!'

Dino raised his hand to grab her, to shake her by the shoulders, then pulled back at the last second.

I swear to you. She took a step back.

'Erebus funded your army of killers. Did you think the Domina financed that many weapons, that much armour, simply by raising taxes?'

What else do you know about this Erebus?

'Only that I can't find him. If he is even a man. You could be the author of the letters for all I know.'

I am not.

'If you are,' said Dino, 'I'll kill you myself.'

Anea laced her fingers, green eyes full of anger. They stood, staring at one another, an arm's length apart at the very most. Dino's disgust rose like bile.

'I don't know what happened in the *sanatorio*, but you should have consulted me – on Erebus, on the Myrmidons, on Duke Fontein.' Dino reached beneath his jacket and pulled out a turquoise sash, tossing it to the floor. 'Return this to me when you think to include me on your plans. Until then, stay away from House Contadino. I'll kill anyone who raises a hand against them.'

Dino turned and unlocked the door, yanking the handle with a snarl on his lips. He had almost passed from the room when he spared her a glance over his shoulder. His anger fled, leaving him with a chasm of loss.

'I feel like I don't know you any more.'

Anea stared back, gaze resolute, posture rigid, fingers woven together. Who or what had worked its way beneath the skin of his sister? What animus guided her thoughts?

Dino stalked away from the apartment, hand brushing the drake-head pommel of his sword. Boot heels sounded loudly on the flagstones, yet Anea's door had yet to close, the lock yet to click. He turned to find her staring after him, not with the eyes of a distant sister but the gaze of a stranger.

45

Decline and Seclusion

− 28 Agosto 325

There were two of them, dark outlines against the bulk of the old *sanatorio*. The curving helms and breastplates gave them away even in the night. Their swords may well have been used to quell the protests, the blood of the rioters wiped clean from the steel. Dino had no doubt the Myrmidons would turn him away. The Domina would brook no interference, nor suffer the undoing of plans so carefully laid by Erebus the unseen.

The Orfano circled to the east, hurrying down deserted streets that had seen frustration crescendo into violence just the day before. Detritus lay across cobbles like wreckage thrown up by the tide. The streets parted − a quick sprint, body bent low − and then he was climbing the ivy that clung to the *sanatorio*, fingers seeking handholds, boots finding purchase on the many ledges and overhangs of narrow windows. He would not be denied the truth, even if his own sister was taking pains to keep it from him. The dire influence now commanding her thoughts would not prevent him from discovering Demesne's affliction.

Erebus.

Even the name was like poison, and poison was just a chemical like any other. Who better to advise on the use of chemicals than a scientist? A scientist shackled to the king's machines, by Anea's reckoning.

Dino climbed easily, a sneer on his lips as two more Myrmidons patrolled below, oblivious. He was another shadow among the foliage, which now quivered in the night's breeze. A final grunt of exertion and he was over the lip of the roof among gargoyles who had witnessed the previous day's bloodletting.

The time spent in Anea's apartment had not been wasted. He had not merely lain in wait to ambush her with questions. A quick search had turned up a iron hoop bearing five keys. He knelt down on the conical roof beside the hatch and tried the first key. The metal slid into the dark hole, failing to turn either way. The same was true of the second key. He fumbled in the darkness for the third, remembering the last time he'd been up here. Achilles had led him to the *sanatorio* rooftop. He cursed under his breath and tried the third key: too large for the hole. The fourth key was bent and no amount of straining or colourful language would return it to usefulness.

Dino looked to the star-strewn heavens. He should entreat Santa Maria to bestow good fortune upon him at a time like this. Small chance of that.

'I'm getting into this building, one way or another.'

The fifth key turned in the lock; the Orfano grinned.

The upper floors were deserted. He'd expected as much but dared to believe he might find Virmyre at work on his beloved machines. The darkness was held back by the guttering lantern he'd chanced upon in Anea's sitting room. Doorways lay ahead like despairing mouths, leading to cells that had once housed the afflicted. Not a soul stirred, not a voice broke the silence, just legions of devices in flinty grey and obsidian black. They stared into darkness with amethyst eyes that glowed like stars. Dino recoiled, confident the machines could do no harm yet profoundly wary of the secrets they held.

Curiosity snared him, and he crossed the threshold to a larger room, three cells with the walls knocked through. Lantern light crept along edges and smooth surfaces. At seven feet long it was the largest machine he'd ever seen, like a sarcophagus and just as deep, created from glossy black material. Grooves ran along the edges, smooth to the touch, while the top was a pleasing convexity. A questing finger found a small disc of glass inset at one corner, but the signature amethyst light within was extinguished.

The contrivance yawned open, causing Dino to jump back, afraid of what it might unleash. His sword was free of the scabbard, his stance low, heart hammering a staccato in his chest.

Nothing emerged.

Dino stepped closer, but the sarcophagus held stale air and nothing else. Anything that it had once contained had since been removed. The Orfano cursed the machine and pressed on, chiding himself.

The staircase spiralled down into the heart of the *sanatorio*, offering more gloomy corridors, more darkened cells. Dino tried to imagine what the hateful building must have been like when at capacity. Had the inmates cried out or languished without complaint? Had they even been aware of their confinement? The echos of those captive women lingered still, even after a decade, but not as sound. Melancholy had a made a home of the *sanatorio*.

'Hello.' A greeting from the darkness. Dino crossed to the nearest closed door and peered through its barred window, spotting a figure sitting on the floor, back to the wall, knees drawn to its chest.

'Oh, you've stopped drinking long enough to find your own arse. Did it take just one hand or both?'

Dino struggled to contain a smile. Virmyre's barbs were all too welcome despite their situation.

'I've certainly found an arse; I may yet start drinking.'

The huddled form rose to its feet, edging closer to the light that flickered around the bars in the door. The familiar face of the *professore* looked at Dino.

'I'm afraid I've nothing to offer you. My cellar is lacking. Please forgive the state of my rooms; my maid has been greatly remiss of late.'

The cell held a narrow cot, and a fetid reek cloyed the air.

'I see confinement hasn't dulled your tongue, or your wit.'

'I sharpen it with a whetstone and hide it in that bucket of excrement. It's the one place the Myrmidons don't look.'

'Ingenious to the end.'

'I have no intention of ending,' intoned Virmyre.

'Care to tell me how you ended up in here?'

'The Myrmidons, of course.'

'Anea just told me she didn't know of your whereabouts.'

'Then we have to suspect that the order for my confinement came from the Domina.'

Dino held the light up and narrowed his eyes. The *professore* looked in good health, despite his circumstances. Dino again noted the smoothing of the crow's feet that had lined Virmyre's face. His lips looked fuller, his brow uncreased.

'What have you and Anea been dabbling with?' asked Dino, aware of the many machines on the floor above.

'We call it *tinctura*,' said Virmyre.

Dino's eyes widened. That word again.

'What is it?'

'*Tinctura* is the appellation for a pharmacological mixture the formula for which we found written inside the king's machines.'

'I should have known.' Dino's mouth curled in disgust. 'Those machines will be the death of us.'

'Quite the reverse. We made up a batch and tested it.'

'On who?'

'Myself, at first.' Virmyre shrugged in response to Dino's incredulous scowl. 'There's not exactly an abundance of volunteers for the king's secrets. Especially when you consider the king used to administer *tinctura* to himself.'

'How?'

'Two drops of the mixture in each eye. At first I thought it was a stimulant, nothing more, but there are other qualities.'

'Go on.'

'According to the king's notes, *tinctura* stops the degradation of bodily tissues and regenerates portions of the brain. A side effect seems to be a lessening of empathy and an aversion to sunlight.'

'That would explain the king's decline. And seclusion.'

'Quite. And also why Anea and I were so keen to continue research.'

'But you stopped taking it?'

Virmyre nodded.

'And Anea?'

'I'm not sure.' Virmyre looked away. 'She hasn't been herself for some time. She was taking it twice a day. I insisted she take some rest, which is what she has appeared to do. Now I can't be sure.'

'And you were sending this *tinctura* to the Domina?'

'No.' Virmyre shook his head. 'We never told the Domina about it.'

'Well, someone did. Someone called Erebus.'

Virmyre grasped the bars of his cell. 'Have you seen this Erebus?'

'No, but he corresponds with the Domina, giving orders couched as favours. *Tinctura* is how he buys her obedience.'

'It would certainly explain her behaviour,' rumbled Virmyre.

'She's been mired in suspicion and resentment for some time. A lessening of empathy just makes her more ...'

'Dangerous.'

'I was going to say inhuman, but that would be rich from an Orfano.'

'You're a lot more human than most out there.' Virmyre flicked his gaze beyond the end of the corridor, insinuating Demesne. 'And you've always struggled for what was good for everyone, not just pursued your own comfort.'

'Comfort?' Dino snorted with contempt.

'I heard fighting in the streets yesterday.'

Dino nodded. 'The Domina produced the Myrmidons, her new army. After so many months of raids the people were angry. Understandably so.'

'And Anea?'

'She sat on the throne, barely moving.'

'I see.' Virmyre's face remained impassive, his voice betraying the responsibility he felt.

'Is it permanent? This lessening of empathy.'

'I can't be sure.' Virmyre sighed. 'The quantities she was taking ...'

They lapsed into silence until a jagged spike of anger rose in Dino's chest.

'I trusted you to watch over my sister,' he whispered, 'not allow her to become an addict.'

'We didn't know what we were getting ourselves into,' admitted Virmyre.

'And now look at you.'

'So do you plan on rescuing me – like a damsel?' said Virmyre, but the line sounded strained to Dino's ears. 'Or were you merely seeking counsel?'

The Orfano produced the keys he'd stolen from Anea. Each proved useless.

'Well, at least I can work on my memoirs,' said Virmyre.

Feet scuffed on flagstones in the depths of the *sanatorio*.

'Here comes the solution,' whispered Dino, drawing a dagger. He passed it through the bars of the door.

'Just in case.'

Dino discarded the lantern in an empty cell, orange light spilling out, wavering on black flagstones. He watched from the shadows of the curved corridor, waiting inside another open doorway, barely breathing. The Myrmidon emerged from the stairwell bearing a lantern of his own, his other hand holding a tray of food. Dino eased a dagger free of its sheath, the usual cool detachment settling upon him. The Myrmidon faltered in the corridor, confused by the second source of light. He edged to the cell where the bait had been set. The Myrmidon stepped into the cell with an unintelligible grunt.

Dino needed no further invitation. He rushed along the corridor, willing his boots to silence as he closed the distance. The Myrmidon, vision much reduced by his helm, failed to see his attacker. There was a muffled thump as bodies impacted. Dino's arm circled the larger Myrmidon's neck, even as the tip of the knife slid over deep brown armour, failing to find a gap. The Myrmidon wore a gorget to protect his throat. The tray fell to the floor with a dull clatter. Food spilled wetly. Another thrust. A strangled grunt of shock from the Myrmidon. The sound of steel scoring metal armour.

Dino growled bitter curses. The Myrmidons were armoured front and back. The expense must have been prohibitive. How had the Domina managed it?

An elbow slammed into Dino's sternum, staggering him. He gasped for breath that would not come, switching the dagger to his left hand even as he gagged. The Myrmidon collected himself, drawing his sword and lashing out, adrenaline speeding the blade. Dino caught the swipe on the flat edge of the dagger, feeling it bend. His own sword came free of its scabbard with practised ease, slashing for thighs less protected than the Myrmidon's torso. Blood welled from a deep cut. An intake of shocked breath from his opponent. Dino tensed, then mashed the pommel of his sword into the jaw of the helm, hoping it would connect with his opponent's mouth. The Myrmidon did not call out, if he was able to. What strangeness lay beneath the armour? Did he sport tines along his forearms? Did he weep bloody tears? Could he climb preternaturally? Were they not both descendants of the king? Myrmidon, Orfano, creatures essentially the same, divided by accident of birth. Might it have been Dino who wore the armour had the skeins of fortune spooled differently? This single moment of compassion slowed Dino's blade; the Myrmidon responded, undeterred by such thoughts.

The blow caught Dino across the brow. Seconds of crawling panic followed until he realised he'd been punched, not slashed. He reeled all the same, body slamming into the wall behind, stone glancing off the back of his skull. He parried the following strike largely on instinct, thrusting his dagger into the Myrmidon's unwounded leg. Another grunt. Dino dropped his sword and seized his opponent's helm, slamming it into the wall. Desperate flailing moments, resistance from the wounded Myrmidon, a rising swell of hate as Dino recalled Massimo fleeing through the woodland. He kept slamming the Myrmidon's head against the wall, lost in the mindless jerk and thrust of it. How many times had they struck Massimo as he sought to escape? And then he was standing over the inert body of the Myrmidon, the acid taste of regret in his throat.

'I think he's quite dead now. You can get me out!' Virmyre's voice was a harsh and desperate whisper. Dino knelt beside the body, relieved to find a leather cord, a brass key glinting dully in the lantern light. 'Quickly now!' Virmyre's eyes were fixed on the short corridor leading to the staircase. Dino unlocked the cell door and took up the Myrmidon's lantern, staring at the fallen man, unsure if he was dead or simply unconscious.

'There'll be another at the main doors. Two more are

patrolling outside. I'm not sure I can overcome them with so much armour.'

'How did you get in?'

'I climbed.'

Virmyre nodded. 'I should have known. You Orfani never use a door when there's a rooftop nearby.'

'Come on. We'll find a rope. I'll get you back to the Contadinos.'

'No, you won't.' Virmyre laid one hand on Dino's shoulder. 'Go back the way you came. I'll remain here. There are things I need to do.'

'With the machines.' Not a question.

'Yes.' Virmyre was unable to meet his eyes. 'I'd prefer it if the Domina didn't help herself to all of my hard work, much less this Erebus you speak of. There are other things here besides *tinctura*.'

'And you'll not be persuaded?'

'I appear to have become predictable in my old age.'

'Let me help you; let me wait for you at least.'

'Best you get back to Medea and Nardo. And Stephania. It's my fault this *tinctura* has been used. Perhaps I can prevent other evils ruining Demesne.' Virmyre took up the Myrmidon's sword in the lantern light. 'I'll keep this, if you don't mind.'

'Take it. More of them will be along soon.' Dino sighed. 'How will you escape?'

'I'm a scientist: I'll think of something. Go now, before more of them come. Watch for me at House Contadino. I'll be with you by dawn.'

The Orfano turned away, leaving Virmyre with scarcely more freedom than when he'd entered. He couldn't help feeling they were both prisoners, chained by the brooding influence of Erebus.

46

Vengeance Stirs

− 29 Agosto 325

Dino woke with the dawn, if indeed he had slept at all. Virmyre's wish to remain in the *sanatorio* had haunted him through the night. That the *tinctura* could reverse the ravages of time was equal parts unnatural and unholy. Still, he'd take a subtly changed Virmyre over no Virmyre at all.

Achilles pulled himself up onto the bed and glowered from beneath a scaly brow.

'I hope he manages to escape,' muttered the Orfano. 'We could use the help at House Contadino.'

Dino watched the pale disc of the sun ascend into Landfall's faded skies. He rarely drew the curtains these days, better to see assassins who might perch on window ledges. The Orfano rose with reluctance, cold water from the basin sluicing away the dregs of his languor. He dressed quickly and without care, more concerned for the weapons he carried than any sartorial finesse. Clothes were the tools of the court; he had only a need for steel. A scrape and click from the sitting room set his pulse to a staccato, a dagger fetched itself to his palm before he'd drawn breath.

'My lord?' A familiar voice, kind and calm.

'Fiorenza?' He passed through the doorway to the sitting room. 'I'd assumed you'd stop calling in.'

'No, my lord. The Domina has no need of me any more.' She bowed her head. 'I came to see if you still require my services.'

'Yes, of course. Are you well?'

'As anyone can be, my lord. Strange times − there's much that's difficult to make sense of.'

Achilles scuttled out from under the couch, and the woman knelt down. 'And how are you, young man?'

The drake yawned, hesitated, then clambered up into the maid's lap.

'He likes you.' Dino smiled. 'We both do. I'd be delighted if you stayed on as my chambermaid. Perhaps in time we can talk about finding you a position within House Erudito that makes full use of your talents.'

Fiorenza looked from the drake to the Orfano and released a contented sigh.

'But not right now; there's too much in Demesne that needs resolving.'

'I understand. I've heard ... things.' She forced a smile then turned her attention to the drake.

'What? What have you heard?' He should have been blushing as he said it but felt only anger. He wanted to know the full depth and range of the gossip. If Virmyre was unholy for meddling with *tinctura*, then wasn't he just as unholy for desiring to lie with men? Not *men*, he realised. Only Massimo.

'I heard about what happened in the rose garden.' She looked down, lacing her fingers in front of her. 'I'm sorry. He was a good man.'

'I suppose Demesne is rife with rumours about me.'

'Perhaps, but you've always been good to me. It's no business of mine who you've feelings for.' She cocked her head to one side; an impish smile appeared. 'Another lord may have tried to be overfamiliar with me. That's one worry I'll never have with you.'

Dino smiled at the simplicity of it. Hadn't Duke Fontein sired Giolla on just such a maid, and one in the employ of his own house?

'And are you well, my lord?'

'I think we're well past titles now, Fiorenza, don't you?'

'Dino –' she stepped closer '– you've endured a lot. Is there anything I can do?'

'Bring Massimo back.' He shrugged, voice cracking as he mouthed the words, struggling to smile through the pain.

'I hear there are stiff penalties for necromancy in these parts.'

She returned his fractured smile with a gentle one of her own. 'And I promised Mother I'd only practise hearth magic.'

'It's probably for the best.' He grinned. It had been a long time since he'd enjoyed such nonsense. 'I always preferred hearth magic.'

'What will you do today?'

'Try and keep those dearest to me from harm, much the same as any other day.'

'Well you'd best get to it then,' she said, gesturing to the door. 'And you'd best take Master Achilles here. I want to sweep and clean.'

The Orfano took his drake, settling the reptile on one shoulder.

'Thank you, Fiorenza.'

'Take care, Dino.'

Down spiral staircases lush with silence, past stilled clocks, pendulums inert. Demesne had run out of time, or perhaps was outside time. The days were blurred and indistinct with oppression, nights sullen with anxiety. Events occurred with ever-increasing frequency and intensity, uncaring of polite schedules or long-held routines.

Tempo. Velocita. Misura.

The sconces of House Erudito were miniature cataphract drakes cast in bronze. Now they grasped only darkness, claws empty of candles, the floor beneath spattered with spent wax. Dino wondered at this as he emerged onto the rooftops to take the air. Erebus had truly ushered in a new dark age. It was only when Dino had the roof's terracotta pantiles underfoot that he felt anything approaching calm, glad of the sun's bright rays overhead. Nardo sat on a ridge of the rooftop landscape, already smoking.

'Hell of a thing,' said Dino.

A plume of blue smoke jetted from Nardo's half-cocked smile. 'It's the small rituals that keep us human. Huh.' He took another drag on the pipe.

'Has anyone presented themselves at House Contadino this morning?'

A shake of the head. 'Not when I left. Expecting someone?'

Dino nodded. He hoped leaving Virmyre in the *sanatorio* wouldn't be the cause of a new regret. He already possessed a score of those and they were all too heavy a burden.

'Maybe this one's for you,' said Nardo, pointing the stem of his pipe at the eastern road. A single rider approached, horse galloping.

'I don't think so,' replied Dino. 'I was hoping for Virmyre, and last I saw he was on foot.' The messenger and the Orfano stared at the lone rider. 'Do you know who it is?'

Nardo shook his head and squinted from under the flat of his hand. 'Purple and black.'

'House Prospero then.' Dino's lip curled. 'I wonder what schemes the duchess is hatching. She must be desperate now Guido's abandoned her.'

'Desperate doesn't begin to cover it,' growled Nardo. 'I'll see that *puttana* dead for her part in Emilio's assassination.'

The rider approached the outskirts of Santa Maria, which had roused itself, irascible in the heat. Some few townsfolk went about their tasks, wary and with haste. A column of House Fontein guards marched through the town, insects in scarlet and black. All carried pole-arms and bore sling bags. Two wagons followed at the rear, a cluster of women keeping pace with the mules.

'What are they up to?' said Dino, nodding toward the soldiers.

'Leaving, I reckon. Huh.'

Dino turned to the messenger, incredulous.

'The Domina ordered the House Fontein guards to become part of the Myrmidons last night,' said Nardo. 'They refused. D'arzenta resigned with twenty men.'

'And those?' Dino pointed at the troops passing through the subdued streets of Santa Maria.

'The remaining few soldiers with balls enough to walk out of here. They might even be led by Ruggeri. Difficult to see.'

'Where will they go?'

'Who can say?' The messenger shrugged.

Dino stared down at the winding streets of the town as if they might offer him some way out of the maelstrom of intrigue and discord. All he saw was a long fall to a quick death. There was a glimmer of appeal to it.

'Let's get down there.' Nardo tucked his pipe away.

'Virmyre may yet turn up,' whispered Dino. 'And Salvaza Prospero might yet see retribution.'

Nardo fixed Dino with a hard look. 'Huh. Stranger things have happened in this old pile of stones. I've not lost faith in them yet.'

The messenger and the Orfano were met by Maria, who oversaw the children and the morning repast. Medea was still abed. She had yet to rise before noon since Emilio's death. Maria and Nardo had slipped into the shoes of parenthood with ease. Luc and Isabella were sullen but well behaved, accepting their new guardians with stoicism.

'You really should eat something, Dino,' said Maria as the men sat at the table. 'You're like a bag of bones.' He obeyed, but neither his heart nor his stomach was in it.

'Has Virmyre surfaced this morning?'

'I've not seen him,' replied Maria. 'He's probably tinkering with those awful machines.'

'He said he'd be here. Said he was done with them.'

'Is that so?' Maria frowned. 'You saw him?'

'Last night. They had him locked up in the *sanatorio*.'

'It was only a matter of time before they used that place for its old purpose.' Maria's face was pinched with anger. Dino couldn't blame her. The whole building was an affront to the women of Landfall. Nardo remained close-mouthed, turning a spoon over and over between his calloused fingers.

The children left the table, keen to be free of the messenger's silence. The Orfano's brooding didn't help.

'We could try and gain entry,' said Nardo as Dino regarded the dregs at the bottom of his mug.

'To the *sanatorio*?'

'Where else.' His fingers continued to worry at the spoon. 'We should at least try and rescue him.'

'Virmyre will have been found.' Dino sighed. 'I killed a guard. Other Myrmidons would have looked for him, would have discovered Virmyre's cell empty. After that it would be mere hours until they captured him.'

'What business did he have that was so important he couldn't leave with you?'

'The machines, of course. What else?'

'Huh.' Nardo discarded the spoon with a clatter. 'Trust Virmyre; he knows what he's doing.'

Dino nodded but felt anything but agreement.

47

Medea's Justice

– 29 Agosto 325

The morning was spent in the rose garden, teaching Luc Contadino the rudiments of duelling. Master and student clutched two rapiers; heavier swords would come later. The boy's enthusiasm had yet to manifest. Dino stuck to the task, providing an abundance of praise in the hope the pupil might warm to both subject and teacher. They practised on the east side of the courtyard, immersed in shadow, far from the statue of Santa Maria. Dino couldn't abide being near the thing.

'As far as I'm aware I'm still *maestro superiore di spada*, and you're the head of a great house.' Luc parried the strikes and struck back, but there was no velocity to the attack, no passion, not even anger. The movements were perfunctory at best.

'*Tempo. Velocita. Misura,*' Dino chanted. 'I'd be remiss if I didn't at least try and teach you something of value.'

The boy remained sullen, steeped in silence and expression blank.

'Fencing sharpens the mind, Luc. It makes the clutter and din of the every day fall silent, quietens the wants of the heart and the needs of the mind. All becomes one with the blade.'

The boy offered nothing, not even acknowledging the *superiore's* words. Dino wondered if the boy's eyes contained an accusation. Was there judgement in those eyes or merely reluctance? Wasn't Dino the very *maestro di spada* sent to protect Emilio on his foolhardy venture? Hadn't he been Medea's great hope to defend the boy's father from the schemes of Salvaza Prospero? Dino's passion for the lesson dwindled, and he dropped to one knee.

'I never explained ... about your father.' He opened his mouth but found the words he was about to say trite, unsuitable. His apology progressed no further. Luc threw down the rapier and turned on his heel, fleeing through the red and white blossoms of the rose garden, back through the double doors.

Dino regarded the rapier, throwing his own down to join it in the gravel. The weight of his sword remained; he'd not be able to divest himself of that weapon so easily. Nor did he want to. There were still debts of blood to repay, and he would see every last drop paid in full.

Take your nobility, take your vendetta, take your revenge. I want none of it. You want to be absolved? Giolla di Leona's words came back to him. The easiest route to absolution would be found in revenge. It would be ugly, petty, stained in blood, but what else was there? Giolla had the truth of it.

Dino looked up from his musing, wondering why Luc Contadino had fled. It would be no bad thing if the boy never took up arms, never drew a blade in anger, never fought for survival. Was it possible the boy would never thirst for violence or seek to avenge his father? It was a faint hope, one that would likely evaporate in the heat of the sun.

Dino drifted to the centre of the garden, regarding the hallowed statue, careful not to trespass on the spot where Massimo had died. The bloodstained gravel had been replaced with new chips of stone but the job had been done badly. Flecks of dark brown remained: not the honest hue of earth and mud but the rusty tone of blood long dry. Dino raised his eyes from stained gravel to sculpted saint. The sun scorched him from a cloudless sky, making the air an arid fume Dino had no wish to breathe. It was hard to believe he'd lost his love here, amid the roses. A love not given time to flourish. True, the roots of it ran deep, but he'd never know the beauty of its colour or the richness of the scent. The roses themselves were browning in the oppressive heat, the edges of delicate petals desiccated.

'Pity you couldn't intervene.' He addressed the blissful saint in a whisper. 'He was right here at your very feet, within arm's reach. There were few more noble, more selfless, more dutiful in all of Demesne. None more beautiful in Landfall. Not to me, anyway.' So much blood. The memory of it stained him even now.

'But it's the nature of prayers to fall on deaf ears.' His lip curled, fingers clenched into fists. 'Anyone who says different is dreaming.'

If the saint took offence she didn't show it.

'Do you know what I've been praying for?' Dino turned at the voice and found himself face to face with Medea. She was wild-haired, attired only in a silk nightgown of midnight blue, damp with sweat as if from fever. The gown clung to the recesses of her spare body, thin with grief. Her eyes, always a store of kindness amid the harsh realities of Demesne, harboured only darkness. She'd woven a rose stem around her forearm, the thorns puncturing her soft flesh. Tiny rubies of blood glittered on olive skin. Her hand clutched a stiletto, the ricasso etched with the house motto, a word on each side of the triangular blade, each a foundation of the Contadino way.

Dovere. Lavoro. Fedelta.

Duty. Labour. Loyalty. The watchwords of those who toiled in fields.

'My lady.' Dino sketched a bow and realised how ridiculous they must look.

'Do you know what I've been praying for?' she repeated, a faraway cast to her eyes, deeply unsettling.

'I can't say.'

'I've been praying for Salvaza to die.'

Dino was addressing someone who looked like Medea but at heart was a stranger. Were any of them the people they had once been? Hadn't grief and suspicion wrought parodies from the proudest, tragedies from the honest?

'Sometimes I dream of strangling her,' continued Medea, 'or putting out her eyes with my thumbs.'

Dino swallowed, struggling for words.

'Other times I think of knives, or swords, or axes. A beheading would not be so very grotesque, certainly not for the architect of Emilio's murder.'

'We can't be sure tha—'

'It was her letter that summoned him.'

'Forgery is not so very difficult to—'

'In her own hand.'

Dino's thoughts conjured Stephania in the courtyard the very hour they'd departed for the foolhardy rendezvous. He hoped she'd not been party to her mother's plans. Medea took a step forward; the acrid tang of the unwashed assailed him.

'I want her dead, Dino. And I want you to do it. I don't care how.'

'I'm not sure I could acquire poison without arousing suspicion.' Dino retreated a step. 'Not after Duke Fontein.'

'I said I don't care how. If she wakes with a dagger in her heart all the better.' Medea came closer still. 'At least people will know that to cross Contadino means death.'

'My lady, Medea, listen to yourself. These aren't the words of a Contadino, they're not words you'd even dare whisper.' He retreated another step.

'I thought you at least would have the stomach for this.' The disdain in her voice was unbearable. 'Are you not capable? Have you not killed?'

Dino thought back to the many raids of the last few months, the raiders he'd slain. He thought of the single Myrmidon he'd killed in the depths of the *sanatorio*, mashing his head against the wall until he stopped moving. He thought of Duke Fontein, eyes rolled back in his head, mouth agape, poison slowing his heart.

'I've killed. But never women. And rarely in cold blood.'

'Do you think me cold, Dino? Feel my skin, Dino.' Medea proffered an arm, thrust it forward, a weapon. 'Do I feel cold to you? Do I?'

Dino made no move, as if contact with her might infect him with the darkness she carried.

'I'd say not. I've been consumed by a fever. I mean to have my cure by way of Salvaza Prospero's death.'

It was as if a malignant spirit had expelled Medea Contadino's soul, taken her over. Dino scarcely recognised the gaunt apparition, much less her murderous entreaty.

'Will you kill her?' she pressed.

'There's no sense to it. She's not a danger any more. Salvaza is just as at risk as the rest of us.'

'I don't care for threats to come, I care for justice. I want justice for Emilio.'

'What you're speaking of sounds a lot like revenge.'

Medea showed no sign of having heard him.

'Isn't that what *you* want? Justice.' The repetition of the word hammered his resolve, shattering his resistance.

'Of course. But—'

'Well stop pouting in my rose garden and set to it.'

'I just think that—' He got not further.

'There are scores of rumours circling you, Dino. None of them kind. Hardly the sort of rumours a man of your skills would want.' Medea's eyes gleamed. 'But as an assassin ...' She smiled. 'No one would dare speak ill of you.'

'I'm not an assassin, Medea. I'm *superiore*. I teach, I don't kill.'

'You killed during the Verde Guerra.'

'That was different, that was war.'

'You killed when the men in grey raided Demesne and Santa Maria.'

'I was protecting people, not seeking a fight.'

'Who else, Dino? Who else has succumbed to the finest swordsman in Landfall? That's quite a title for someone so reluctant to kill.'

'I can't just walk up to Salvaza and kill her in cold blood.' His voice was all but a broken whisper.

'I expected more of you, Dino. Did Emilio mean nothing? Didn't Massimo die in this very place?'

The Orfano looked down. Medea's cruel petition had forced him back, his boots now planted on the very spot where his love had died. Dino looked up, fresh sweat prickling across his scalp, down his spine, on the palms of his hands.

Don't leave me, Mass.

'We should consult Anea,' he said, the words weak. The odious task would not be so easily deferred.

'Anea is gone.' Medea's seething was replaced by a more

forlorn tone. 'You know only too well that she serves herself; she cares nothing for us.'

'I can't do it, Medea. I can't. I can't be an assassin for you.'

Medea made no acknowledgment, turning away, gliding back to her apartment on naked feet.

'There'd be no way of undoing such a thing once it's done,' he called after her, but she continued on her way. Dino looked down at the gravel beneath his boots, choking down the rage that kicked and roiled in his gut. He couldn't kill Stephania Prospero's mother, he couldn't kill the woman who had engineered Massimo death.

The finest swordsman in Landfall? Medea's words haunted him long after she'd departed. *That's quite a title for someone so reluctant to kill.*

The evening summoned a blood-warm breeze as the sun drenched the horizon in scarlet and orange. Clouds burned magenta. The trees in the town sighed with discomfort, parched and browning leaves desperate for rain. The people of Santa Maria journeyed home from their travails, downcast and cowed. The taverns were watched by pairs of Myrmidons, mute and immobile. Customers seldom stayed long, keen to be among their families.

Dino watched all of this from the roof of House Contadino, hunkered down with arms wrapped about his torso, belt weighted with sword and stiletto. The smaller weapon was plain and businesslike, undecorated and unrecognizable. The single-minded hatred that consumed Medea's soul had infected Dino. He felt it spreading icy fingers through his chest.

'Huh. Thought you were a gargoyle for a moment there.'

Dino turned, wanted to smile by way of greeting to the messenger but managed only to chew his lip. He turned his eyes toward the horizon.

'Hell of a thing Medea's got you doing.' Nardo's hands fussed at his pipe, spilling twists of moonleaf.

'She told you?'

'Didn't need to.' The messenger tamped the weed into the

bowl of the pipe. 'Only one reason a women deep in grief leaves her bed and comes to you.'

'Am I so obviously an assassin now? Is this what the Domina has made me?' The first question was spiked with anger, the second forlorn.

'You're whatever you choose to be, Dino. You don't think of me only as a messenger, do you?' He lit and dragged on the pipe and narrowed his eyes.

'I think of you as a father to those children. Luc will certainly need someone reliable like you in the years ahead. He's going to be angry. He'll be rash.'

They waited, the messenger calm amidst his smoke, the assassin a coil of tension on the roof's edge.

'Do you need anything?' Nardo cleared his throat and shifted his feet.

'Only darkness, and that's contingent on my friend there.' Dino nodded toward the sun, gradually being consumed by the lip of the world.

'Things are going to be more complicated when your friend there rises tomorrow.' Nardo blew plumes of smoke out of his nostrils.

'I warned Medea as much, but she won't be turned from her course.'

'And what of your course?'

Dino pursed his lips. 'I want Salvaza dead for Massimo. Being in the rose garden reopened the wound. I want her dead for Emilio, and Abramo, and Marcell. I've no doubt her hand bears the blood of Bruno too.' Dino thought back to the night the farmer had given his life so that he might live. Was he not worth avenging too? Did he not deserve justice as much as any lord or swordsman?

'When you list her sins in lives it's difficult to mount a defence,' replied Nardo.

'And are you?' Dino stood and pulled the stiletto from the sheath, his eyes settling on the point, which was bathed in the bloody light of the dying sun.

'Am I what?' The messenger frowned and blew out another jet of smoke.

'Trying to mount a defence for Salvaza? Didn't you stand here just this morning and say you wanted her dead?'

Nardo looked away to the horizon, then nodded.

'And do you still want her dead?'

The messenger nodded again, then turned on his heel, entering the corridors of Demesne, back to the fatherless children placed in his care.

48

Recollection

– Agosto 322

The first assassination attempt came just six months into Dino's tenure as *maestro superiore di spada*. A lone attacker gained entrance to the bedroom by an open window. What surprised Dino most was that the attempt was quickly followed by a poisoning, which also failed. More surprising still was that he was not the target of either.

Anea had survived, but only just.

The Ravenscourt descended into uproar. Demesne all but seethed with speculation, the people of Landfall fearing for their Silent Queen. When Dino's fury abated he found himself adrift on a sea of worry. The students he trained were duly assigned to D'arzenta and Ruggeri. Neither protested, but their silences were equally strident. Dino's desire to teach evaporated, his every waking thought now bent to one purpose: the safety of Lady Aranea Oscuro Diaspora. The months crawled along like a hound in summer heat, possessed of a similar temper and bearing a stench much the same. Dino was almost brought to his knees with exhaustion, unable to trust anyone besides himself. Virmyre, much concerned for the Orfano, suggested Anea visit San Marino at short notice. Such a visit would give Dino a much-needed reprieve by putting Lady Diaspora beyond the reach of assassins.

It was on the third day of Anea's absence that Dino received a missive. The note, asking for a fencing lesson, was delivered by an unfamiliar messenger in Prospero livery. He'd have dismissed the request had he not grown bored of idleness. Achilles padded about the apartment, tail swishing with reptilian restlessness. Dino regarded the note anew. That the author was Stephania Prospero decided him. He'd barely seen her since returning from the Verde Guerra. The opportunity to reacquaint himself was a welcome one. They had been close once. She had never cared that he was Orfano; that he made her laugh was enough.

Dino left the apartment with a firm stride, savouring a relief he'd not felt since his appointment as *maestro di spada*. Achilles looked down from his shoulder, onyx eyes inspecting each guard they passed. Once in the training chamber the Orfano procured two rapiers, setting one by the door and unsheathing the other. He'd not used such a light blade in years, but soon recalled the parries and stances. Feet found their paces, muscles adjusted to the new weight, eye following the velocity of the strikes. He began to sweat, grinning with the exertion, unbuttoning his shirt, jacket removed on account of the heat. Achilles stared with indifference, perched on a practice dummy upholstered in dust.

Dino was now eighteen and no longer a child. More than that he was a veteran of the Verde Guerra and *maestro superiore di spada*. Stephania was twenty-five. Older, certainly, but not outrageously so. The rapier flashed in the sunlight, reflecting back his distorted face along the narrow blade. He'd spent so much time committed to soldiery he'd not considered anything else. Didn't men court women? Didn't couples marry? Was he required to sleep in Anea's armchair for the rest of his days? Or endure the loneliness of his bed?

All of these thoughts stretched and coiled like sleeping drakes in sunshine. He pushed himself through another combination of thrusts and slashes, parrying imagined blows, forming ripostes. Dino was well acquainted with death – the creatures of the Verde Guerra had taken their tithe from Demesne – now he sought the bright spark of life.

There was no doubt Stephania was a light in the firmament of Landfall, sought after by many, but remaining distant due to her title. Dino liked her well enough, though thoughts of women seldom crossed his mind. Another button unfastened, he smoothed down his hair and made sure his sleeves covered the hated tines sprouting from his forearms. Politically it would be a sound partnership, winning over a worthy ally to Anea's cause. Then anxiety struck him like a thunderbolt, suddenly aware he knew nothing of women, much less of seduction.

The door on the far side of the chamber interrupted his thoughts, rattling and scraping in the silence of the summer afternoon. Dino blinked in surprise.

Duchess Salvaza Prospero entered and took up the rapier so thoughtfully left by the door. She fixed the Orfano with a pout. 'You could at least try to mask your disappointment, Dino.'

'Apologies, Duchess. I confess I wasn't expecting you and ...' The words ran down like a slowed clock.

Another pout from the duchess, an insouciant shrug. She sauntered to the centre of the chamber, every swish of her hips a mocking challenge. Salvaza wore a simple riding skirt, good sturdy boots and a blouse that would not impede the motion of her arms. It was not in the mode of the gowns she so often wore – yards of rich fabric yet none providing much in the way of propriety. There could be no doubt she had dressed for a fencing lesson.

Dino had been played. And he was not alone in noticing attire.

'How you've grown, Dino. No longer the mischievous urchin of the House Contadino kitchens. Why, you're almost undressed. I hope I'm not interrupting some assignation? Did you have some agenda beyond training this afternoon?'

This was a curious reversal. He looked down to find himself sweat-dewed, chest visible. The duchess laughed, strutting a circle around him. Then the question.

'Were you deceived by the handwriting of the letter?' The duchess smirked. 'Perhaps you thought the signee was Stephania instead of Salvaza?'

There was no need to reply, only look abashed and fasten his shirt. The duchess responded by cooing behind one hand. Her laugh would have been irritating from one half her age; her giggle was at once grotesque and theatrical. She stepped closer, dragging one index finger over the sweep of his chest, causing the fabric of his shirt to go taut.

'And may I ask what designs the Lord Dino Adolfo Erudito has on my daughter?' Are they respectful? Political? Marital?' A pause, a simper. 'Carnal?' She smoothed the fabric of his shirt, favouring him with a smile at once cruel and lascivious.

The Orfano said nothing, each question a white-hot knife pressed to his flesh. The plan to seduce Stephania now seemed as remote as it was ridiculous. Had the duchess planted the idea in his mind before entering? Might she be an enchantress with the power to shape thoughts? Dino stepped back beyond the range of lingering fingers and his own childish imaginings. He cleared his throat. Salvaza drew her rapier a few inches from the scabbard, studying the forte of the blade. She settled into a first position, drew and sighted down the length of the weapon.

Then came the confession, each revelation a slash that threatened to cut him to the bone, leaving him bleeding across the flagstones of the training chamber.

'I was married off to Duke Prospero at sixteen while very much in love with Emilio. I had to choose politics over the desperate yearnings of my womanhood. We courted in secret up to the very week of the wedding.' She dipped her eyes a moment. 'To this day I can't be sure if Stephania was a child born of Prospero. Certainly she lacks any of Stephanio's attributes.'

Dino locked his eyes on the flagstones, looking for some way out, some way past the duchess. He drew his own rapier, the scabbard clenched in his left hand, ready to parry should he need it.

'Emilio,' she purred, 'much tortured by the union, left for the fields of the Schiaparelli estate, keen to be free of Demesne. He did not return for three years. Not even for *La Festa*. When he finally returned it was as if Medea had been waiting for him. So began a long and careful campaign. She all but served herself to him on a platter, until he couldn't but help notice her.' A sour twist stole across the duchess's lips. 'Medea nursed his fractured heart, soothing his anger until life became bearable again.'

Achilles stirred on the practice dummy, aware of Dino's discomfort. The drake stretched, tail coiling. The sun made no concession; Dino felt as he were all but boiling. Still he gripped the rapier, and still Salvaza cast her secrets like thrusts and slashes that he could not avoid and would never parry.

'Emilio's union with Medea was in turn a torture to me. Seeing him with his younger, pretty wife was a splinter I've never been able to rid myself of.' She sighed, passing a weary hand over her face. 'The things we do for politics – for duty,' she added, looking genuinely miserable.

'If you had truly loved Emilio you would have married him,' he countered.

The duchess laughed in his face. 'Are you so naive?' An able riposte. 'A romantic without any sense of the real world?'

Dino sidestepped this: 'Is it not more practical to pursue the one you love? Failing to do so only ends in regret –' he chewed his lip a moment '– which in turn is self-defeating.' These words sounded solid to his own ears, yet he knew he lacked conviction. What did he know of pursuing love?

She struck back: 'Of course I loved Emilio, but love is for paupers and scoundrels, perhaps poets in their happier days.'

Dino had hated her for that, cut back: 'And your own unhappy marriage to Duke Prospero? Surely that resulted in your affair with the *capo*?' The words rang like steel, and the duchess took a step back. Dino pressed his advantage, keen to maintain the momentum.

'Might you be married to Emilio this very day had you followed your heart? Instead you're burdened with a halfwit lover who only craves the position you could award him.'

The duchess withdrew, disarmed, and threw up her hands.

'The affair is mutually beneficial.' Each syllable struggled past the tightness of her smile, neither of them believing the words she formed.

The Orfano pressed in for the coup de grâce. 'I know full well the *capo* has journeyed to the coast with Anea. Not out of a sense of duty, but in a fit of pique.' He shook his head. 'You refused to marry him. Again.'

Salvaza set down the rapier on the varnished floor, clapping slowly, glowering behind her hands. 'Your sources are rich indeed, and well informed.'

'I have no sources. The whole castle speaks of nothing else, my lady.'

Not beaten, the badly wounded duchess responded one last time: 'Promise me one thing.'

Now it was Dino's turn to shrug.

The duchess pressed on all the same. 'Promise me that, if you find love, you'll not let anything come between you – not duty or station or expectation. You may be my opponent, Dino Erudito, but I wouldn't wish my fate on my most hated enemy.'

Dino watched the duchess leave the training chamber, unsure of who had really won; certainly they both bled freely. Achilles had no answer for him, wrapping a tail about himself protectively.

49

Ravens Returned

– 29 Agosto 325

Dino was well acquainted with the location of Duchess Prospero's apartment; he'd spent a score of nights eavesdropping there. The duchess had never concerned herself hiring soldiers; small need when she'd entertained the *capo* all these years. Now her protector was absent, and with him the protection of House Fontein. Dino approached with stiletto in hand, confident none would prevent him. It would not be such a great task to kill a sleeping person, he lied to himself. One simple thrust then pull the sheets over eyes full of shock and accusation. There would be fleeting seconds of struggle, but they would pass.

Clocks across Demesne announced the hour, eleven muted and discordant chimes. He welcomed the din, knowing it would cover the sound of his footsteps and the betraying groan of floorboards. With every step his hatred swelled; every corner turned summoned a vision of death. First Abramo, a knife in his throat, face down in the long grass. Then Marcell, head coming apart in a welter of crimson. He'd seen the face of Margravio Contadino all too often in his nightmares. It waited in the darkness, etched behind his eyelids. And finally Massimo, bleeding out among the roses with his perfect smile. Dino's lip curled in a snarl, the fragments of his heart grating together. All these deaths the consequence of one letter, the work of Salvaza Prospero. He gripped the dagger more tightly. He could kill Salvaza Prospero. He *would* kill Salvaza Prospero. He must. Massimo had not cried out for revenge with his dying breath, but there would be no solace while Medea Contadino stalked

323

Demesne. It were as if she she walked beside him now, a taunting Erinyes, her words the judgement of the Dirae.

The Orfano lingered by a window in the corridor, waiting for the light beneath the duchess's door to darken. The lattice of glass at his shoulder revealed stars. Clouds edged into view, snuffing out its perfect silver until only a sliver of the moon remained, lambent and muted. The light beneath the door was extinguished. The killing beckoned.

The clocks chimed again, their dull clamour announcing midnight and the last day that Duchess Salvaza Prospero would draw breath. Fingers sought the iron key within his jacket. It had long lay unused, a forgotten item in a dish on Stephania's mantelpiece, buried beneath other oddments. The key represented a way home for an estranged daughter, a gesture of reconciliation from a parent who had long since given up hope. Stephania's growing disgust with her mother had ossified, the key remaining forgotten by all. All except Dino, who had palmed it during a seemingly innocent visit.

The lock clicked, oiled hinges silent as Dino pushed the door open with velvet-gloved fingertips. Fortune was smiling on him, it seemed. The sitting room was much as he'd imagined it, lavish and baroque. Soft furnishings in violent fuchsia were subdued by the darkness. Thick curtains, undone in tiny increments by moths and vermin, held back the night. It was trove of objets d'art, every surface bearing treasures ornate and unique. Statuettes stood beside porcelain, nestled amid pottery, under canvases that showed pastoral idylls. The paintings were a cruel hypocrisy to Dino since the duchess had only ever held disdain for those in the fields. Now Dino would repay the feeling.

The door to the bedroom was ajar. If the duchess was afraid of assassins she erected no obstacles to them. She may well have instructed the *capo* in the arts of love, but he'd failed her with lessons in security. Dino padded into the room unchallenged by lock or guardian, taking in the scene. Her chamber was every inch a boudoir, at once feminine and gaudy, a maiden's dream of romanticism that had failed to mature. Dino sneered. It resembled a room from a fairy tale, yet the kiss he bestowed would not awaken the sleeper. She lay on the bed. A candle remained lit, burned down to a stub on the cabinet beside her. A single rose wilted in a slender vase, thorns brown and sharp. Dino blinked and saw Massimo on dry white gravel, watched over by an uncaring saint. The icy fingers of Medea's revenge curled around Dino's spine, forcing the air from leaden lungs.

An open book lay beneath Salvaza's hand, the other at rest on her considerable breast, swaddled in silk. Brunette curls spread across the soft cream of the pillow. The great economic heart of Demesne at rest, dreaming of riches and intrigues, or perhaps of simple survival.

A single pearl lay on the bedside cabinet bathed in the guttering glow of the candle, an eye filmed with rheum. Dino knew with certainty why this one remained alone: he'd given its match to Stephania. He'd all but forgotten the misplaced earring at the cemetery. His desire to find the owner of the jewel had been occluded with each death and act of violence. The tiny weight of gold and pearl stared back at the Orfano, further proof of Salvaza's treachery.

Sweat spread itself across his palms, making his velvet gloves damp. The stiletto was now an extension of him, heavy in his grip, heart the same in his chest. He whispered Massimo's name, drawing up the weapon in two hands, spreading his feet wider than the breadth of his shoulders. The killing blow needed to be perfect. He swallowed in a dry throat. The moon gleamed from the blade.

Tap. Tap, tap.

The point of the stiletto wavered as Dino's eyes sought the source of the sound. A raven perched on the window ledge, tar black and full of muscular purpose. If the bird woke the duchess, she might scream or, worse yet, beg for her life. He had no wish to hear Salvaza's plea.

Tap. Tap, tap.

Dino's eyes flicked up again. Another raven had alighted on the window ledge, but this was a minor consideration beside the apparition that caught his eye. Framed in mahogany was a perfect portrait lit from the side by golden candle light. He knew it to be a looking glass but his was not the reflection that stared back. Lucien regarded him from the glass, ashen-faced.

They'd always shared a resemblance, but the likeness now was uncanny: the locks of his hair an echo of Lucien's own, the same leanness of limb, a liquid grace in each movement. Even the cut of his jacket.

If not the weapon.

Lucien had never been without a blade, though he'd never wield something as mean as a stiletto. He'd sneer and call it for what it was, the tool of an assassin. Dino looked down at the sleeping duchess and took in a shuddering breath, keen to be free of Lucien's condemnation.

Tap. Tap, tap.

Once again his gaze was drawn to the window. Now a handful of ravens stared back, accusatory and truculent. Why had they chosen tonight to return? Dino failed to ignore the looking glass and Lucien's sneering disapproval, withering under that terrible judgment. What would the older Orfano think if he were here now? Hadn't Dino himself nearly been killed in his bed by assassins as a youth? And now he stooped to the very tactics of his enemies.

Tap. Tap, tap.

The reflection shook its head, distaste sketched in the set of its mouth, eyes hard and accusing. Disappointment showed in the set of the shoulders. The reflection offered no disparaging words, had no need to. Dino was fully aware of Lucien's verdict.

Assassino. Murderer.

Tap. Tap, tap.

The room spun. Dino struggled to remain standing. His breath faltered, pulse fluttering, uneven. Was this sorcery or had he succumbed to the madness that had claimed Anea? Would he know if he'd slipped over the edge of sanity into the abyss of paranoia and suspicion? Why, after all these years, did Lucien appear now? Dino unravelled beneath the weight of questions, yet one more remained.

Tap. Tap, tap.

Would Massimo have approved of killing women in their sleep? The reflection shook its head once more. Dino's grasp on the stiletto faltered, and he lowered his arms, turning away from Salvaza to sit on the side of the bed.

'Guido? Is that you?' Her voice was a whisper. He didn't answer, couldn't answer for the knot of frustration and loathing tied at his throat.

'Who's there?' Panic now, her sleepy whisper giving way to alarm.

He had no reply for her. Struggling to sit upright, he held down racking sobs. He had fallen so far.

'Dino? What are you doing here?'

He turned his head to glance at her over his shoulder through the red-tinged film clouding his sight. Tears blossomed from misshapen ducts, spilling scarlet down his face.

'You're bleeding,' she gasped.

'Not bleeding. Weeping.' His voice was the rasp of cemetery gravel. Thoughts turned anew to the rose garden and of Massimo.

'Why are you here?' No trace of the arrogant, smirking, assured Duchess Prospero, just a woman of middle age attired in nothing but silk and fear.

'Retaliation,' replied the Orfano. 'For Emilio. And Massimo.'

'You're here to kill me?'

'It was your letter, your handwriting, your work.'

'I was blackmailed, Dino, I swear ...' Silence crowded in about them. The candle flickered, the flame drowning in wax.

'So you admit to writing the letter?'

'Yes, but I never meant for Emilio to be killed. We were lovers once, after all.'

'I know. You told me, but that hardly makes a difference in Demesne.'

'I still cared for him,' she remonstrated.

'But you wrote the letter.'

'Yes, at the insistence of ...'

He had yet to face her, the stiletto a cold weight in his hand, bloody tears wet on his face.

'Who made you lure Emilio to the ambush?'

'I've never met him. He calls himself Erebus.'

Dino twisted around so fast the duchess flinched away, pressing herself against the headboard. Her eyes were frozen

327

on the point of the stiletto, one hand at her throat, the other held out to ward off his wrath.

'Erebus?'

She nodded. 'Please don't kill me. He threatened to kill Stephania unless I ...'

The candle flickered and died. A long moment passed as Dino considered the revelation, shrouded in darkness. It made murder no less repulsive. He fumbled on the cabinet and lit a new candle, then resumed his seat at the edge of the bed.

'You sent Emilio to his death to protect Stephania?'

Another nod. 'Erebus began writing to me months ago. At first he promised support for Duke Fontein and myself. We were anxious Anea was going to launch this republic of hers and leave us with nothing. The duke was ever opposed to her taking power, especially from such a young age. It was he who recruited the three assassins.' Her eyes drifted to the stiletto in his hand.

'And then Anea stripped Lady Allattamento of her holdings,' said Dino, 'confirming the worst of your fears. The end of the *nobili*.' He could see the tapestry of causality woven together in front of him.

The duchess nodded again. 'Fontein decided more action was needed but died before he could put any plans into place.'

'And then the Domina stole your plaything, and you were bereft of allies.'

'The Domina?' Salvaza's face creased with incomprehension.

Dino wiped his bloodied eyes on his sleeve. 'The *capo* was always a dog. He'll serve any master who will feed him. For a time that was you, but you wouldn't grant him a title, so he started sniffing around the Domina.'

'What will happen to me now?' The duchess's eyes lingered on the stiletto blade.

The Orfano shrugged.

'Are any of us safe?' she whispered.

'Not with Erebus manipulating everyone, and I suspect he is. The Domina's been receiving her own orders, ones running contrary to yours.'

'Divide and rule,' said Salvaza, pushing herself up from the bed and drawing a shawl around her shoulders.

Dino stood and slunk toward the door.

'You need to do something for me.' The duchess had regained some composure, a note of steel returning to her tone.

Dino couldn't hold back the bark of laughter that escaped his lips. 'You should be grateful to be alive. I was sent to kill you, remember?' Dino looked down at the stiletto as if trying to convince himself it were true. He glanced back to the looking glass expecting to see Lucien, but the older Orfano had fled with the waking of the duchess.

'But you didn't kill me. You've always been the best of us, Dino. Wouldn't you rather be protector than assassin?'

'I think the proof is in the action, or inaction.' Dino shrugged. 'Tell me what you want.'

'Stephania, beyond the reach of this Erebus. Take her away. Take her to San Marino, and place her under the protection of Lucien.'

'I can't leave the Contadinos—'

'Erebus has neutralised the Contadinos for the time being. Stephania has no one and stands for everything Anea was trying to achieve before she went mad. Erebus will surely kill her next.'

The stirrings of purpose awoke in him and he was glad for it, glad to feel something other than the constant dread and grief of the last few months.

'Save my daughter, Dino. Take her away from all this, from Erebus. And yourself too.'

'I'll need the letters from Erebus.'

'I ... I burned them. I burned all of them.' Her mouth twisted. She wrung her hands and looked away.

The Orfano laid the stiletto on a dresser near the door, his fingers lingering on it a moment before he looked up.

'What are you doing?' asked the duchess.

'I don't need this any more.'

50

It Has a Name

– 30 Agosto 325

Dino hurried back to his apartment in House Erudito, listing in his mind what he would take to San Marino. There was something pleasing about constructing a list: horses, saddles, feed, a sturdy cloak, a good loaf and some cheese, water and wine and so on. It was not the list that concerned him, but Stephania; she'd likely refuse to leave. A way to persuade her eluded him but she was open to reason at least. The same could not be said of Anea, but she was not the woman he had once known.

His mind turned to the ravens and to Lucien's ghostly appearance in the looking glass. He dismissed it as trick of the light and nothing more, the conjuration of a mind driven to extremes. Demesne had long been a breeding ground for infirmities of the mind. He pushed on, focusing on the task at hand. He'd put Stephania beyond the reach of Erebus. That the Domina was his puppet was without question, and by extension the *capo*. Dino wondered if he too was fulfilling some part of Erebus' plan. No way to know for sure, he decided; only by leaving could Dino secure his own release from his machinations.

Footsteps, hurried and uncaring, the runner choosing velocity over stealth even in the small hours of the morning. Dino tensed and drew his sword, but no sooner was the steel beyond its sheath than he was knocked to the ground. A dark blur careened into the wall with the impact but no curse or yelp sounded in the darkness. Dino snatched a glance from the dusty floorboards. He had not been the only assassin abroad at this hour. The figure regarded him, its face obscured by a veil. A short sword in a scabbard remained undrawn, for now.

Dino forced himself up from the floor and retrieved his blade, a metallic tang of blood infusing his mouth as adrenaline presaged the violence to come. A veil could be worn by anyone, but Dino knew with certainty who looked from behind it: the Domina's pet Myrmidon. He struggled to his feet, switching the blade to his right hand. The corridor would hamper his choice of attack. He found his balance and held out the sword, but the veiled man fled, swallowed by the gloom. The Orfano let out a long and emphatic series of curses that said much about the parentage of the departed assassin. With no opponent to face, Dino resumed his progress, keen not to be drawn away from his purpose: protecting Stephania Prospero.

A figure waited outside his apartment, peering into the darkness, bearing a lantern held high.

'Dino? Tell me you didn't do it.'

'What are you talking about?' It was Speranza, and even by the tawny glare of the lantern he could tell she was ashen-faced. 'What are you doing here at this time, Speranza?'

The messenger looked at him, searching every contour of his face for an answer. Her shoulders were hunched and her body spoke only of tension, as if she might flee at any moment. She drew her sword slowly, the very sword he'd given her on the day of Cherubini's departure. An old sword and scabbard with a loose chape. A cast-off blade that had lived in the back of a cupboard for years. It was not the finely crafted weapon of a noble, had not been handed down to him as a valued heirloom, worth very little. And yet it would kill him all the same.

'The Domina sent me. Tell me you didn't do it.'

Dino swallowed, unsure of what he was being accused of. His mind flashed up an image of Duke Fontein's stiletto on the mantel.

Tempo. Velocita. Misura.

He couldn't get the measure of the woman before him, and things were moving far too quickly to comprehend.

'Tell me.' Her jaw was tight, knuckles white on the hilt of the blade.

'You mean the duke?'

'I never cared for the duke. I had no loyalty to him.' She held out her sword, point hovering a foot from his face. 'You know full well that's not what I mean. Did you do it?'

Dino's eyes drifted, taking in the thin sliver of light escaping around the door where it stood ajar. The lock had been smashed.

'I didn't kill Duchess Prospero,' he said, feeling ridiculous. Speranza was a messenger, he *maestro superiore di spada*, and yet here he was answering her questions at sword point.

Speranza shook her head incredulously. 'Do you think this a game?' A snarl of anger made her look feral in the half-light. 'Are you toying with me? Have you become as mad as Anea?' The tip of the sword thrust forward a few inches. He held his ground, felt his anger pique and uncoil.

'Who is it you think I've killed exactly?' he grated, patience exhausted. The messenger looked at him with mute fury. 'To hell with this.'

He stepped inside her guard, batting aside the blade with his forearm, tines beneath jacket and shirt protection from the blade. His hand locked her wrist, pushing down, grasping vice-like.

'What it is this about, Speranza?'

She jerked back but found herself held fast.

'Fiorenza,' she whispered with tears in her eyes.

The maid lay on the floor by the hearth, the familiar handle of Duke Fontein's stiletto jutting from her chest. Anguish pierced Dino. Erebus had claimed the life of one more innocent.

'Tell me you didn't kill her,' said Speranza from behind, a note of pleading in her voice.

'Why would I smash the lock to my apartment? Why would I return now? What possible reason does the *maestro superiore di spada* have for killing his maid?'

'The Domina said she was with child, and that—'

'Mine?' He laughed bitterly. 'I think we have both heard the rumours often enough to know that's unlikely.'

'So it's true then? You and Massimo?'

'It hardly matters,' he whispered, still unable to speak the words of his otherness. 'This is the Domina's work. Fiorenza worked for her. There's no doubt she would have overheard a few choice secrets, some embarrassments. What better way to silence them for ever? And in my apartment.' Dino stooped to take the weapon from the breast of the girl who had shown him nothing but loyalty. The stiletto came free of the wound with a sucking sound. He hoped it had been a quick death. Hadn't he just set aside a weapon of assassination in Salvaza's chamber? Now he'd returned to find himself haunted by another.

'And what better weapon than the keepsake I used to torture myself all this time? It's perfect.'

'If not you then who?'

'Her Myrmidon, of course. The one with the veil.'

'Marchetti?'

'It has a name?' Dino sneered. 'He ran into me in the corridor as I returned from House Prospero.'

'Dino, I'm sorry. I should never—'

'What else did the Domina say?'

'That I was to report back to her ...'

She got no further, the sound of boots echoing from the corridor beyond. Not the *stamp-stamp* of a lone runner, but the sustained rumble of many urgent feet.

'The window,' he grunted, eyeing the smashed lock of the door, knowing the room was indefensible. He dragged one heavy armchair to the doorway and pushed it closed. It wouldn't hold for long but might give them a moment.

'What?' The messenger eyed him, incredulous and wary.

'Climb for the roof or the nearest open window. Now, Speranza!'

The sounds in the hall were no longer limited to the thunder of footfalls, but had been joined by the jingle of buckles and scabbards, the sounds of Myrmidons hastening his end, the sounds of enemies he could not hope to overcome. The window swung open, slamming and clattering against the shutters beyond. He held out one hand, imploring the messenger to follow him.

'But I can't ...'

'You were supposed to report back when you found Fiorenza dead. You didn't. That makes you my accomplice, or incompetent. Either way your life is forfeit.'

She followed him onto the ledge and they began the ascent, heartbeats loud in their ears. He took a moment to close the window, in order to leave no indication of their escape route. Dino had always known his Orfano heritage had given him a facility with climbing, another gift he had in common with Lucien. It was easy to take such a gift for granted until forced to climb with someone who lacked it so completely. Speranza struggled to find handholds amid the masonry.

The sitting room filled with the sounds of armoured bodies searching and tearing apart furniture for the duke's stiletto, gore-slicked and thrust beneath Dino's belt. It sounded like a stampede. There would be no return to his apartment now; Dino had only the clothes on his back and the sword on his hip. The ascent was long and agonising, harder with each moment the climb consumed. Dino guided Speranza's hands, whispering encouragement while hoping the Myrmidons below would not emerge and scale the walls, although their armour alone made this unlikely. He hoped. Windows stared out from Demesne, regarding Landfall like sullen eyes. Dino and Speranza continued with stifled curses, losing their fingers amidst the ever-present ivy which stained the masonry in a deep crimson.

The lip of the roof provided a final obstacle to the messenger, who stood on a ledge below, haggard and spent. Dino flowed up and over the edge, one leg becoming entangled with his scabbard for a second. He looked seven storeys down to the clutter of Santa Maria, then back to the messenger.

'Come on, you're almost there. Not much further.' He extended his shoulders beyond the roof, lying flat with his arms stretched down.

'Just go. I'll break the window.'

'Don't be foolish. The noise will bring the Myrmidons. Come on.' He waved her on.

She raised her hands but there was no strength there, no resolve. He grabbed her hands and heaved, feeling his shoulders sing with the pain of it, but Speranza, all gritted teeth and desperate eyes, slithered out of his grasp. She dropped back onto the window ledge, transfixed by the long drop to the cobbles below.

'Just leave me here.'

'They'll kill you, like they've killed everyone else.'

'Just go, Dino.' He heard her voice in the night, and also the crack as she said his name. He watched her for a moment and stood up, curses escaping his lips into the darkness. Then inspiration.

His sword belt did not have the strength of rope, nor was it particularly long, but Speranza clung to it nevertheless.

'Brace your feet against the wall, lean back and walk up,' Dino hissed.

'This is the last time I jump out of a window with you,' replied Speranza through her teeth. Foot followed hesitant foot as Dino hauled and swore and sweated. Finally she all but collapsed over the edge onto the rooftop, daring herself to look over her shoulder.

'Nothing but a long fall and a short ending,' whispered Dino beside her, wrapping one arm about her waist.

'I'm sorry about ... I didn't really think you'd killed her.'

'Yes, you did. It's exactly what the Domina wanted you to think. She's getting very good at that sort of thing.' Dino released her and shrugged. 'Even I don't know what to think any more.'

'What will you do?'

'Leave. There's nothing else for it.'

'And the Contadinos?'

'They're no threat to anyone now. And I can't protect them while they remain within the walls of Demesne. Medea won't leave.'

'I'd like to help you. What do you need?'

'Three horses, saddled, in the Contadino courtyard.' He chewed his lip. 'What will you do?'

'D'arzenta said I was welcome among his company. I'll go to him. I've no love for Duchess Fontein, and even she can't keep me safe from this insanity.'

Dino nodded. 'Waste no time. Good fortune.' He turned

away toward House Prospero and the unwelcome task of persuading Stephania to accompany him to San Marino.

'Why three horses, Dino?'

He stopped and turned. 'Because I'm getting Stephania Prospero away from this place, and I've not given up on Virmyre yet. He's still alive, I know it. I'm going to put both of them beyond the Domina's reach, away from Erebus.'

'Who's Erebus?' Speranza asked.

'If I knew that I might be able to find him. And kill him.'

51

The Ravenscourt Defiled

– 30 Agosto 325

Dino had spent much of the summer clambering across Demesne's rooftops in the dark, but always in the service of the Domina and always on behalf of Anea. Or so he had thought. The revelation that Duchess Prospero had been manipulated was obvious with hindsight. That Duke Fontein had also received letters in that spidery hand provoked little surprise. How much of Dino's spying had occurred at the behest of Erebus? The idea of being a pawn in a vast and unknowable game was like a splinter in his mind. Worse still that the rules might change the instant he learned them.

Dino cast his gaze to the stars emerging from cloudy concealment to look down on Demesne. Again he saw a single amethyst eye amid the deep blue of night, reminding him of the king's machines in the *sanatorio*. Dawn would arrive soon, sunlight fading each silver pinprick and its malevolent purple kin. The new day brought only the promise of death, the best Dino could hope for a fast horse. At present he could not win, but he might outrun defeat; ultimately there could be no victory while Erebus drew breath.

The great houses of Demesne radiated out from the Central Keep, each a spar of a cross. Dino's journey from House Erudito to House Prospero took him across the centre of the immense edifice. Past the Ravenscourt. He had almost left the pregnant curve of the dome behind when a dark bird alighted, seemingly calling him back. The raven glowered and skipped about in an agitation of wings, never settling for long before calling out anew. Dino eyed the raven with caution, wary step following wary step until he was close enough to see into the Ravenscourt itself. The chamber was lit brightly by thick candles in wrought-iron stands. Pristine cream drapes hung from the walls. Into this twilight came Fiorenza's killer, now attired in the armour of the Myrmidons but shunning the helm for his preferred veil.

Marchetti.

The Orfano's lips peeled back from his teeth in a snarl, unable to tear his eyes away from the graceful shadow that slipped across the black and white tiles. Marchetti drew his sword and knelt before the dais, head bowed, assassin turned supplicant.

Dino's fingers curled around the hilt of his own sword, mind racing through the corridors of Demesne, tracing the fastest route to the hated Myrmidon. However, these thoughts were overturned completely as Anea rose from the throne, clad in grey and black, hair a golden dishevelment. Stillness had shrouded her from sight. The breath snagged in Dino's throat at the sight of her, now a stranger to him. She glided across the floor and trailed her fingers across Marchetti's shoulders, circling the assassin until she stood before him. Fingers slipped beneath the assassin's chin, raising his veiled face to hers. He stood slowly, sword forgotten on the floor. Anea backed away, one finger hooked over the Myrmidon's breastplate, an inverted beckoning. Marchetti stumbled after her, his previous grace reduced to hapless shamble. And then she was back on the throne, drawing up the hem of her dress, pulling the gown up to the valley of her thighs, which parted. Dino sobbed with shock and incomprehension, realising his sister was truly lost to him. Marchetti knelt before his queen, all trace of supplication vanished. Her hands were now at his belt, pushing into his britches.

Dino fell back, appalled.

The raven had ceased its harangue and was now attending to its feathers, apparently keen to be occupied lest it see the rutting on the throne. Dino pressed one hand to his mouth and dragged down a shuddering breath. And then he was running, desperate to be out from under the gaze of the stars, desperate

338

to be away from the pairing below, which approached climax. Had he imagined it as he had imagined Lucien in the looking glass? He couldn't bear to return for confirmation; he would rather burn the Ravenscourt that be forced to lay eyes on his sister's most intimate betrayal.

Dino ran until the rooftops threatened to trip him. He ran until his lungs felt like tailoring unstitched, bright seams of pain in his ribcage. He ran with the metallic tang of blood at the back of his throat, knowing he would never outrun this quirk of his biology, just as he could never hide from his preferences. He arrived at the balcony of Lady Stephania Prospero stripped of everything except purpose. He would put her beyond the reach of Erebus.

'Dino?'

He had no answer for her, only the painful drawing of breath and the taste of Anea's betrayal.

'Come in, quickly.'

She opened the door to the balcony and ushered him in, turning the key in the lock once he was inside. He drifted to the middle of the sitting room, chest rising and falling, limbs leaden. His head spun with images of Anea that he fought to banish. Then a moment of surprise. Stephania circled him warily until she stood with her back to the door leading to the corridor. She held a stiletto. Her lack of experience with weapons did nothing to quell his disbelief. Or his wariness.

'They're saying you killed Fiorenza with the blade you took from Duke Fontein.'

'I didn't kill Fiorenza.'

'Interesting,' she said. 'I believe you.' But the stiletto remained pointed toward him. 'And Duke Fontein?'

He nodded, then chewed his lip, pressing his fingers into the palms of his hands until his fingernails cut.

'And are you here for me now?'

'Yes,' he said, hoping she might go with him without dissent. Her eyes widened; the grip on the stiletto tightened. 'No, not like that!' He held out one hand to placate her, keeping it far from the hilt of his sword. 'I'm here to rescue you,' he whispered. 'To take you away from here. We've all been played.'

There was a rap on the door so hard it all but knocked Stephania to the floor. She glared at Dino as if this too were his fault.

'Lady Prospero?' The whining tones of the *capo*. Dino began to draw his sword but took his hand away when Stephania's frown deepened. She made a shooing gesture with one hand and approached the door. Dino crossed to her bedchamber on the balls of his feet.

'Yes? I'm here, Guido.' Dino grinned. This sudden lapse of formality would wrongfoot the idiot *capo*. Guido knew only too well Stephania insisted on using his title when forced to mention or address him at all. Dino closed the bedroom door, but not before seeing Stephania slip one strap of her nightgown off her shoulder. She turned the key in the lock and opened the door, the other hand still occupied by the stiletto, now in the small of her back.

'Lady Stephania?' The *capo* all but choked, as would any man presented with such a vision. Any except me, thought Dino.

'So good of you to check on my safety. I'm perfectly fine, as you can see. Oh, and you've got lots of Myrmidons with you.'

Dino chewed his lip to refrain from swearing.

'Could we possibly search the apartment, Lady Stephania?'

A pause. Dino caught his breath. The next sounds would determine his future. He eyed the window and hoped it was unlocked.

'Of course,' said Stephania. Dino could hear her smile as she said it, hear the curl of those lips so desired by the men of Landfall, 'but why don't you come back in the morning. It's not seemly to enter a woman's apartment when she's in a state of undress.'

The *capo* made noises. Undoubtedly intended as words they emerged from his mouth strangled embarrassments.

'Why don't you post a pair of your Myrmidons outside, just to make sure no one enters. I don't feel safe any more.' This last pandered to the *capo*'s sense of rightness. He snapped out some orders, grateful to have something to do.

'I shall return come the dawn for a thorough inspection,' he blurted, full of new purpose. Stephania giggled and the *capo* subsided into half-apologies, undone by his own double entendre. The door closed; the lock clicked; Dino released a breath.

The noblewoman entered her bedchamber and regarded the Orfano, who sat on a wooden chest, a blanket box of some craftsmanship. The stiletto shone bright in her hand as she closed the door behind her. Her fingers turned the key and Dino's thoughts returned to Virmyre, trapped in the *sanatorio*.

'What do you mean, *played*?' Stephania whispered.

'Played?' Dino's heart was still hammering in his chest from his near-discovery and Stephania's artful dissembling.

'You said we were being played.'

Dino nodded. 'The Domina, your mother, Duke Fontein, they all received letters from one calling himself Erebus. He set them against each other.'

'As if they needed any encouragement.' Stephania rolled her eyes.

Dino nodded, unable to deny the truth of it.

'It's possible Erebus suggested things that may have remained undone.'

'Like Margravio Contadino's murder?'

Dino nodded again, a cold pang of guilt in his heart. 'And the *maestro*'s expulsion.' Now a smothering of shame. 'The Myrmidons are undoubtedly his work ...' He sighed, tangled in skeins of speculation, choked with suspicions.

'How can I be sure all of this true, Dino? How can I be sure you've not descended into the same labyrinth of madness that Anea now occupies?'

For a second he was on the rooftops again, staring down into the Ravenscourt as his sister rutted with Fiorenza's killer.

'Dino?' Stephania's frown deepened, her impatience clear. The Orfano reached into his jacket, bringing out the letter from Duchess Prospero to Margravio Contadino. The lure that had led Emilio to the graveyard. He proffered it with care, keeping his hand clear of his sword lest she misread his intent and stab him. Stephania unfolded the missive and devoured its contents.

'Interesting but there's no mention of any Erebus,' she said.

'I've spoken to Salvaza tonight. She said Erebus threatened to kill you if she failed to get Emilio to the graveyard.'

'And you believe her?'

'Didn't she warn you of the self-same thing before Emilio died?'

'She said I was in danger; she said we both were.'

'And you believed her. Why else would you lie to me about the earring? You were covering for her, hoping you could extricate her from the mess she had made.'

'I don't know what you mean.' Stephania's eyes strayed across the room to where the pearl in gold rested on her bedside cabinet.

'Fine. Whether you recognised it or not –' Dino sighed '– it hardly matters.'

'I'm not sure I ever really knew my mother,' she admitted. 'She's not the sort of person who enjoys the company of women; she's only happy when she's fluttering around men.'

'She loved Emilio once.'

Stephania's eyes widened; her mouth by contrast became pinched.

'They were lovers when she was very young,' he continued. 'Your mother has many faults, but she'd never put him at risk. Not unless she had no other choice.'

The duchess's words from their afternoon in the training chamber revisited him like a faded whisper: *To this day I can't be sure if Stephania was a child born of Prospero. Certainly she lacks any of Stephano's attributes.* Dino studied Stephania, searching for a trace of Emilio in the lines of her face – her brow, her nose – but any evidence of her paternity remained concealed, if it existed at all.

'You can't ask me to trust her, Dino.'

'She sacrificed Emilio to save you,' he replied. 'You may not want to believe she's capable of any good, and I don't blame you, but she'd never have anyone killed.'

'How can you be so sure?'

'Because that's what she had Duke Fontein for. Salvaza is strictly political. Fontein was dangerous not just because of his influence but because he preferred more direct action. He was a killer. That's why I killed him.'

Stephania lowered the stiletto, shoulders slumping, leaning her back against the door. Her chin dropped, eyes closed. Her lips trembled with the force of all she held back. That she might be Emilio Contadino's daughter was one secret Dino retained. He'd not add to her burdens on a night like this.

'She asked me to take you to San Marino,' he said after she'd had a moment to absorb everything.

'And you trust her?'

'Trust is too strong a word, but I believe it's a good idea.' Dino crossed the room and touched Stephania on the shoulder. He found himself looking into deep brown eyes holding back tears that deserved to be shed. She fell into his embrace, not as a lover, but as a child orphaned by Demesne. By politics. By the twisted machinery of service and rule. He may have lost one sister, but he had surely gained another. She dashed away unformed tears and set herself to dressing, reaching into a lacquered wardrobe.

'There's one more problem.' Dino rubbed at his forehead.

'Which is?'

'You asked the *capo* to post two Myrmidons outside your door.'

She nodded, unconcerned, as if having two heavily armoured thugs within twenty feet was nothing, then shucked off her nightgown.

Dino turned away out of habit. 'I'm not sure I can take both of them without attracting undue attention.'

'I know that,' she replied.

After a minute he turned to find her wearing men's riding britches, a blouse and thick jacket. Small clothes were packed into a bag.

'Perhaps we could lure them in one at a time, or ...'

'You'll need this,' she said, holding out the tabard of a House Prospero messenger. He took the garment and struggled into it, then found himself presented with a tricorn bearing a purple feather.

343

'The disguise is good,' he admitted, 'but they'll undoubtedly recognise me up close.'

'Dino,' she said with a mischievous smile, 'how important would you say I am?' She'd wriggled into a messenger's tabard of her own.

'Well, you're the next duchess of House Prospero, if I can keep you alive.'

'Which means?' She buckled on a wide belt of deep brown leather, then retrieved a fencing sword in a battered scabbard.

'An entire house, the economic heart of Demesne, is yours to command one day. Assuming your mother hasn't spent all of its reserves on inappropriate dresses.' This last earned him a smile.

'Fairly important then?' She raised her eyebrows, smirked, then sketched a bow before placing the tricorn upon her head. Dino nodded, unsure of where she was taking this line of conversation. Stephania opened the doors to a second lacquered wardrobe. It was not filled with clothes. It was not filled with anything as far as Dino could see. The future Duchess Prospero hauled up a trapdoor set in its base. She turned to him, looking about as smug as he'd ever seen her.

'So it stands to reason I can escape my own chamber by means less obvious than the front door. Don't you think?'

'I think I love you, Stephania.'

'Only if you weren't *invertito*.' He knew she'd said in jest but it stung all the same. 'Sorry. Love is love.' She embraced him once more, a light kiss on his cheek to complete the apology, and then they were fleeing down a ladder, wondering if they'd survive the dawn.

52

The Faces of Messengers

– 30 Agosto 325

The secret route from Stephania's chamber descended through cobweb and darkness. It was a place of tight corners and rough stone, a graveyard for dust, a repository for whispers long forgotten. How many secrets and arguments had echoed in these places between walls? Dino's nerves were frayed from being hunted, the feeling persisting even here. They were in a hidden place, obscured from view yet far from safe. They climbed down ladders or else used the ancient timbers of Demesne to take them ever lower, following a route unremembered by all except by ancient architects.

And Stephania.

'How do you know this place so well?' asked Dino.

'My father showed me. He said the great houses were a good deal more hostile toward each other during my grandfather's rule. This route is from that time.'

They emerged into the empty kitchens of House Prospero, yet to awaken to the day's labours. Only the scurrying of mice across floorboards broke the silence. Dino imagined he could hear the endless crawl of a thousand ants, infesting every corner of Demesne, searching out every crumb of comfort.

'We should take something for the road,' said Stephania. They searched the pantries and took a small selection of food. The desire to leave pressed upon them.

'Where did you get that thing from?' enquired Dino, tapping the scabbard attached to her belt with an index finger. The sword had a swept hilt of admirable craftsmanship, but the metal was dull and grimy. The canvas of the scabbard was worn and bare, the chape loose. Much like the weapon I gave Speranza, he thought.

'It was my father's,' replied Stephania. 'He was never much of a soldier. I found it in his office one day and begged him to let me have it.' She brushed her fingers over the hilt, tender as a lover. 'He could never deny me anything.'

'Do you know how to use it?'

'I had some lessons, but my mother found out and made me stop.'

'When?'

'Shortly before I was sixteen.' Stephania raised an eyebrow. 'She said it was unladylike.'

'Show me,' said Dino, withdrawing a few steps.

'What here? In the kitchen?' Stephania pouted.

'You don't go looking for the fight; the fight comes looking for you. And it doesn't care too much for the when or the where.'

She drew, holding out the sword with an arm that hadn't lifted anything heavier than a quill for some time.

'Again, but bend your knees. Try not to turn out your feet out so much. This isn't ballet.'

'Thanks for the reminder.' She re-sheathed the sword and tried again, drew perfectly. A slash, a thrust.

He caught the tip of the blade in a gloved hand and flashed a grin at her. 'You're full of surprises, aren't you?'

'Let's hope I don't actually have to use it,' she replied.

Soon they were stalking through House Prospero, entering the circuitous corridor that embraced the Ravenscourt. Dino pushed a gloved hand into Stephania's. She squeezed, though whether it was meant as reassurance or came from anxiety wasn't clear. They hurried onward.

'Have you seen Anea?' Stephania whispered.

'Yes.' How could one word be so hard to say? As if a hand had clamped around his throat.

'Did you speak to her?'

'I tried. She's not the person I knew.' Thoughts of Anea's betrayal were a phantom that haunted every shadowed corner. 'I think ...' The words faltered. He knew what he wanted to say, just couldn't stand the speaking of them. 'I think one of the Myrmidons has influence over her.' Perhaps Anea had seen something of herself in Marchetti. Perhaps she'd been lost to the ravages of *tinctura*.

'This Erebus you mentioned?'

'No, he's called Marchetti. The man who killed Fiorenza.' A thought occurred. 'It's not inconceivable that they're the same person. It would explain a few things.' Dino felt his hate for the Myrmidon swell until he could barely breathe.

'This Marchetti would have to be some sort of genius.'

'He's a genius with the blade,' admitted Dino, 'but I'm not sure I see him as an expert on intrigue and subterfuge. Perhaps I underestimate him.'

'Dino.' Stephania squeezed his hand. 'Up ahead.'

Two Myrmidons stood to either side of the Contadino gate-house.

Stephania paused and tugged his hand. 'Let's find another way.'

But the Myrmidons had seen them, raising blunt-faced helms to the messengers, who stood hand in hand with a sack of plundered food. Dino held his breath and heard the thick pounding of his heart. His instinct was to reach for his blade, but his hand gripped Stephania's instead.

The Myrmidons nodded, made no attempt to accost them. The disguises had done their work. The messengers hurried on, safely wrapped in tabards of purple and black, heads bowed beneath the peaks of their three-cornered hats.

The rose garden was a balm after the stark and haunted corridors of Demesne. The night's darkness had not yet relented, soothed by the soft light of the sickle blade moon.

'You don't seem concerned about leaving,' whispered Dino as they passed through the blooms of red and white.

'I have *so much* to stay for.' Stephania flashed a crooked smile.

'Difficult to argue with that logic.' Hadn't he too yearned to be away from here for months, even years? Hadn't he wanted to leave with Cherubini upon his expulsion? Surely any trials in San Marino would feel like blessings after the nightmares of Demesne.

They were halfway across the rose garden, circling the statue of Santa Maria, when the voice called out to them. Dino's hand went to the hilt of his blade; Stephania lurched back in surprise.

'Think I know the faces of every messenger in Demesne, and yet I've not met these two before. Huh.' This from one night-shadowed corner. A tiny spark of light seethed orange, moonleaf in the bowl of Nardo's pipe.

'We must stop meeting like this. People will talk.' Dino flicked out a lazy salute, unable to keep a smile of relief from his face.

'They'll talk about you,' replied Nardo, standing. 'I'm married.'

'They already talk about me,' said Dino, no bitterness, just matter of fact. Nardo nodded to Stephania and she favoured him with a smile.

'Found new employment, my lady?'

'Dino has taken me on as his apprentice. We're off to seek our fortunes in San Marino.'

'Can't say I blame you.'

'And why are you awake so late?' she asked.

'Got something for you,' said the messenger, holding out a sack. Dino took it, felt the contents shift and writhe.

'What in nine hells?' He reached into the sack and broke into a smile. 'Achilles, you little bastard!'

'Huh. Bastard difficult to catch too, especially after the Myrmidons had ransacked your apartment. I hoped you'd come this way.'

'Best to keep him in there for now,' said Stephania, peering into the sack. Beady black eyes stared back, as unimpressed as Dino had ever seen them. The moment of their departure stretched, became leaden with so many unsaid words.

'You're ... you're not going to talk me out of it?' said Dino.

'Hell of thing to be accused of murdering your maid. I think it best you flee now and come back some other time. You might want to come back with Lucien and a few score armed men.'

'I'll be sure to pass that on to him,' replied Dino, trying to imagine war between the two towns.

'What will you do?' pressed Stephania.

348

'Same as always. Keep my head down, look out for Medea and the children. I'll try and persuade her to move to House Albero once she's well, then send word to you. But for now there's no reasoning with her.' The messenger eyed the pair, stony-faced as ever, then coughed and gestured Dino closer with one finger. 'Come here.'

Nardo swept the Orfano up in a burly hug he'd never have expected.

'Get your scrawny *invertito* arse to the coast and keep out of trouble, if you're able. I'll see you again.'

Dino nodded, unable to reply. Stephania kissed the veteran messenger on each cheek and led Dino inside. After a time they emerged into the courtyard beyond.

Four horses waited in the shadows of the Contadino granaries. Speranza was mounted, shoulders hunched from the pre-dawn chill or tense with prospect of discovery. Likely the latter, Dino guessed. She had changed her clothes, dressed in a riding skirt and travel cloak, better to escape the notice of those looking for a Fontein messenger.

Dino walked as casually as he dared, every instinct urging him to run. Speranza soothed her mount toward the gates of House Contadino without a pause, hoof beats echoing from the walls. Either she hadn't recognised them or had no wish to take her chances with the escaping Orfano. It mattered not. She paused for a moment at the well and cast a glance over her shoulder, but Dino failed to decipher the expression on her face. The Myrmidons at the gate hefted the cross bar and tugged on the handles. Santa Maria waited beyond the walls, townhouses shuttered to keep out the night. A solitary lantern hung from a shop sign, a beacon of warmth threatening to gutter out. Speranza passed under the arch of the gatehouse, nodding to the Myrmidons as she left. They made no gesture, returning to the light of a brazier which threw long shadows over the cobbles like clutching fingers.

'Where is she going?' whispered Stephania.

'To join D'arzenta, most likely. And Giolla di Leona too, I'd guess.'

'Giolla? Who is she?'

'No one.' The Orfano shook his head. 'No one who matters.'

Dino walked to their mounts and checked them over, Stephania did likewise. The smell of leather and horse was thick on the air as Dino watched the Myrmidons with a surreptitious eye. The gate remained open, awaiting their departure. Stephania said nothing, pushing her wealth of tresses under her tricorn lest they reveal her. The staccato of hooves faded as Speranza passed through the town, leaving Dino with the sound of his heart, now loud in his ears. At least the messenger of Fontein would escape the death that stalked the corridors of Demesne so freely. Dino hoped D'arzenta would treat the woman well.

The Orfano pressed Duke Fontein's stiletto into Stephania's hand, gold etched writing gleaming in the darkness.

'I already have a sword. What am I supposed to do with this?' she said with obvious distaste.

'Use it. On them, or yourself if you want to avoid being captured alive.'

'Interesting.' She wrinkled her nose. 'That's not much of choice.'

'Choices are the luxury of those in power.'

'Dino, I've never killed anyone before.' This in a voice made small by the quiet.

'With any fortune you won't have to. Here,' he handed her the sack, 'Take Achilles. Come on. *Avanti.*'

They mounted as one. Dino spent a second regarding the spare horse meant for Virmyre. It would likely be standing here still come the dawn. He couldn't worry about that now; escape was at hand. The horses carried them across the courtyard. With each *clip* and every *clop* Dino yearned to remove himself from the malign influence of Erebus. Stephania lowered her chin, the tip of the tricorn throwing a darker shadow over her face. The Myrmidons made no move from their place at the brazier. The horses were just feet from the gate. Dino's hands were tight on the reins, jaw clenched, stomach a coil of anxiety.

A crowd had gathered outside the gates, indistinct in the darkness. The lantern above the shop sign had guttered out. Dino flicked his gaze to the Myrmidons at the brazier, who roused themselves but made no move to apprehend the disguised Orfano, instead troubling themselves with the bar that would secure the gates once the riders had passed.

'Dino,' hissed Stephania. The Orfano glanced up and felt his heart sink. The crowd beyond the gates was no crowd at all. A dozen Myrmidons levelled halberds at the horses. The *capo* stood at their centre, raising a lantern to his perfect, smirking face.

'Going somewhere?'

53

Fiorenza's Requiem

– 30 Agosto 325

The only light issued from the man who held up a lantern as if it were a crown. Guido di Fontein, *capo de custodia*, grinned.

'My Lord Erudito.'

'Guido. Strange to see you awake at this hour.'

'I take my duties very seriously.' The *capo* preened.

'Perhaps the Domina's abed with some other bravo tonight?'

Guido's smile slipped before he pushed back his shoulders. 'Lady Prospero.' The *capo* inclined his head. 'It would seem I won't be carrying out that inspection of your apartment after all.'

'I'm sure you'll survive the disappointment.' Her words were acid. 'It's not as if you're unfamiliar with the bedrooms of House Prospero, is it?'

The *capo* winced. 'I'll need to ask you both to dismount. You're no doubt aware I am to apprehend you for the murders of Duke Fontein and your maid, Dino. What was her name?'

'You *know* what her name was, just as you know it was Marchetti who killed her.'

'Oh yes. Her name.' The *capo* smirked. 'Uh, Fiorella?'

'Her name was Fiorenza. Did you give Marchetti the order or was that the Domina?'

'Such lies.' The *capo* scowled. 'I knew you were pathetic, Dino; I never thought you'd stoop to killing women.'

'I don't know.' The Orfano flashed an unfriendly smile. 'I could stoop to killing you.'

The Myrmidons advanced with their halberds, causing the horses to rear. Dino regained control of his steed with gritted teeth, Stephania turned her mount expertly, trotting back to the courtyard, hooves clattering on the cobbles. The Myrmidons passed through the gate, fanning out into a semicircle, halberds pointed at their quarry, dull spikes in the gloom of the courtyard. The gatekeepers waited until their kin had passed through, then pushed the heavy studded doors closed. Dino swore as the bar fell into place with a dull thump. There would be no escape now. The *capo* passed the lantern to a subordinate and drew his blade.

'If you will not dismount we will kill the horses.'

'If you so much as touch my horse I will string you up, you perfumed fop,' said Stephania.

Orfano and noblewoman stepped down from the stirrups, chagrin weighing on them as feet alighted on cobbles. Stephania clutched the sack containing Achilles to her chest. A Myrmidon closed and drew a sword.

'Leave them!' The *capo* managed a note of command he'd never master with more human soldiers. 'The Orfano killed my duke. I will have my revenge on him in person.' He drew his blade to reinforce his intent.

'The Domina ordered the duke to be killed, you idiot.'

'Dino should receive a trial,' called out Stephania.

'We're long past the sanctuary of law,' grated the Orfano.

The Myrmidons had the sense to back off, spreading out to let the *capo* have his entertainment.

'I've been training for this moment a long time.' The *capo* smiled.

'I rather hope so, for your sake' said Stephania sweetly.

Dino pushed the messenger's tabard over his head, knocking the tricorn off in the process. He drew a knife from his boot and cut through the sleeves of his shirt, revealing his bandaged forearms. Two more jerking cuts and the bandages lay in pools of spooling fabric.

'Showing your true colours?' sneered the *capo*. Dino looked down at the dark blue tines growing from each forearm. How many mornings he'd bound them so as not to draw attention to his otherness.

'They're sharp, you know,' said Dino calmly. He tested one

tine with his finger . 'You might say I've been dealing with pricks my whole life.' He smiled at the *capo*. 'I really can't see why you'd give me any trouble.'

The *capo* surged forward, two slashes the same tempo followed by a thrust that was sudden but not unexpected. Dino stepped beyond the range of the first two attacks and parried the third with his dagger, every sense intent on Guido: his footwork, the set of his shoulders, the direction of his eyes, his grip on the hilt and the positioning of his blade. He drew his own sword, the silver drake pommel now familiar under his gloved fingers. Dino flashed a terrible smile, eager for the violence to come. It was all for nothing, of course. Even if he defeated the *capo* he'd be cut down by the Myrmidons, just as Emilio had been. This thought leaked through his mind and caught fire like oil from a lantern.

The *capo* turned aside his opening thrust but almost lost his footing such was Dino's fury, a slash threatening to remove one leg at the knee. Guido flinched away with widening eyes. He batted off another slash that would have opened his face and bisected his pretty nose. A grunt, a curse, a flash of steel. The fighters parted and circled each other. The *capo* drew a dagger from his belt and rolled his shoulders. Dino snorted a derisive laugh; Guido was struggling to find his rhythm.

'I've always hated you. You, Lucien, Anea, even Golia. All so smug and sure of yourselves. Eradicating the Orfani is an ambition I've long nurtured.'

'I've often found ambition exceeds ability. In your case doubly so.'

The *capo* thrust. Dino responded with a low slash at his front leg, easily avoided. They stumbled past each other, the backhanded swing that would have opened Guido's vitals deflected by a dagger. The fighters pivoted and came about. A thrust at the *capo*'s face. This deserved a full parry with the sword; everyone knew how handsome Guido was, not least himself. Dino took advantage, landing a solid kick between the *capo*'s legs. He was rewarded with a muffled cough. It was a petty move but a deserved one.

'*Strega* scum.' Guido staggered back with tears in his eyes.

And then Dino fell on him like a raven, threatening to rip the *capo* apart in tiny increments.

'You can't eradicate the Orfani, you idiot.' Dino thrust again, found his blade turned aside by the dagger once more. 'Myrmidons, Orfani; they're all one and the same.' A slash, opening the *capo* across one shoulder, jacket tearing, resistance as the blade met leather beneath. 'All twisted ancestry from the same source.' The blade found its mark again, sank deeper. 'Only the titles make us different.'

'The Myrmidons answer to us,' sneered the *capo*; 'they answer to the throne.' He slashed back, but it was a reckless backhanded strike. Dino ducked beneath it, then parried the returning slash as if it were no more than practice.

'They answer to humans,' sneered Guido. 'They know their place.'

Dino's mouth twisted. Demesne hated difference. The nobility sneered at the *cittadini*; those fully human were unnerved by the Orfani; women were treated as slaves or objects by men; the majority felt disgust for Cherubini and his preference. All were united in their hatred of the Myrmidons, and the Myrmidons no doubt harboured their own grudges. Landfall did not encourage difference, did not welcome individuals. Soon it would be as uniform as any ant colony. A colony designed by Erebus.

The two men clashed, coming together and drawing apart, circling, then lunging again with awful intensity. Guido's dagger, the instrument of many parries, gouged Dino's side beneath his ribs. Stephania cried out, her voice rising above even the pitch of the clashing steel. The Orfano staggered back, throwing up an arm protectively at the sword falling toward him in a blur. The steel slashed down at a shallow angle onto the blue tines of his forearm, snapping them, smashing through, but not cutting the flesh beneath.

Dino chewed off a curse.

The *capo* struck again, shocked his blade hadn't severed Dino's arm; the attack he launched hasty and ill prepared. Dino took the hilt of his blade in both hands, steel clashed upon steel before he made a circling motion ending in a sharp flick. The *capo*'s sword was wrenched free, skittering across the cobbles. Guido stood before the Orfano empty-handed.

'Her name was Fiorenza,' hissed Dino.

Dino's overhead strike was caught on the flat of Guido's dagger. The metal snapped and the *capo* was forced to his knees. A seasoned fighter, he used the opportunity to draw another knife from his boot, surging to his feet. Dino raised his left arm and backhanded the noble across the face, rending pretty skin with tines. Guido stepped back in horror then slumped to his knees, a whimper escaping his shivering lips. His grip on the knife slackened in numb fingers.

'Witchcraft,' whispered the *capo*, lips turning blue.

'Perhaps,' said Dino, breathing heavily, 'although I tend to call it poison.'

The *capo* clutched at his throat as it began to constrict, each breath more tortured than the last.

'My maid's name. What was it?'

'*Vai al diavolo*,' wheezed Guido.

Dino ran him through the chest with his sword and watched the man's eyes widen in shock.

'Her name.'

'*Puttana.*'

Dino drew his blade from the *capo*'s chest, a wet rasp in the awful silence. He twisted the steel as it came loose, eliciting a shriek from the defeated *capo*. The Orfano leaned in close. 'Her name was Fiorenza, you fuck.'

The *capo* tried to stab him in the chest with the dagger, the strike weak and unfocused.

Dino caught his wrist with ease. 'Say it.'

Still the *capo* tried to stab him, face purple, veins blue against his skin. Dino's grip was absolute. The dagger trembled but came no closer to its prize.

'Her name was Fiorenza.'

'Just another whore,' wheezed the *capo*, 'in a maid's uniform. They're all whores, Dino.' He flashed a look of hatred at Stephania. 'Salvaza, the Domina, all of them.' He clawed down another breath. 'But you wouldn't know. You've been too busy fucking men.'

356

'Duty makes whores of us all,' whispered Dino. He stepped back from the *capo* and watched him die. Watched the poison surge through every vein.

The Myrmidons showed little concern for the loss of the *capo* but remained in a loose semicircle around the fugitives.

Stephania pressed herself to the Orfano and looked down at his forearm, eyes rich with concern, mouth a twist of worry. She took his arm and regarded the smashed and broken tines.

'Don't worry about those,' he said wearily. 'They always grow back. How is Achilles?'

'Still wriggling,' she replied, hefting the sack. He picked up his tabard, pulling it on under the blank gaze of the Myrmidons and their curving helms. Stephania took his hand and thrust out her chin.

'I command you to stand down.' They made no move, might have been carved from granite for all of her imperiousness.

Stephania attempted to lead Dino toward the gates, but the points of halberds prevented her. They found themselves pressed up against the well, the Myrmidons closing in around them.

'Won't you let us go? We just want to leave,' she pleaded. No response, but neither did the Myrmidons seek to harm them. 'Why aren't they attacking?' she whispered.

'Because they know what I know,' said Dino. 'Them and me, we're not so different. Just on different sides.'

It was then that the Domina appeared with Marchetti at her side. Dino felt his blood run cold. He eyed the veiled Myrmidon and saw someone whose anger eclipsed his own, someone eager to carry out any atrocity, someone with no compunctions, someone prepared to kill women. The Domina muttered to the assassin, and Marchetti nodded then drew his blade and crossed the courtyard.

'We don't have to stay and fight,' whispered Stephania.

'What are you talking about?' replied Dino, not taking his eyes from the assassin.

'There are tunnels beneath Demesne; we can find another way.'

Dino eyed Stephania, remembering the promise he'd made

to her mother. Marchetti was close now, perhaps twenty feet away. The moon shone from his blade, his eyes reflected silver.

'Are you ready?' said Dino.

'Of course.'

The Orfano lifted Lady Stephania Prospero over the side of the well and dropped her, throwing himself after.

54

A Drowning

— 30 Agosto 325

Dino fell, the well shaft a blur of grey and an occasional smear of green. Moss most likely. A vision of Emilio in the graveyard flashed before his eyes. Again. The cold water stunned the air from his lungs. He kicked for the surface, a glimmer of light his only hope, paddling with one hand, the other clutching the sword. He broke the surface and gasped down air, floundering. A quick look confirmed his fears. No Stephania.

A dim light filtered down the shaft, the pale moon penetrating even here, deep below Demesne. A *maestro di spada* drowned in a well, drowned beneath the very castle he sought to protect. *Hardly the stirring victory a real swordsman yearns for,* muttered the shade of Duke Fontein in his ear.

'Shut. Up,' the Orfano grated, then began to slip beneath the water once more. A flash of light from beneath, the silver pommel of his sword reflecting the moonlight. The weapon he'd spent a lifetime mastering was going to drag him to the bottom. What he depended on for his survival now a tool of his demise. He kicked and cursed, boots full of water, slowing his efforts. His chin dipped beneath the water again, a mouthful swallowed, then coughing. He redoubled his efforts but the messenger's tabard added to his sodden weight. He was beneath the water now, looking up from below, snatching breaths when his mouth breached, swallowing yet more water when he timed it wrong. His kicks slackened.

Something snagged his collar; the light came closer, air caressed his skin. He dragged a shuddering breath and coughed and hacked on the exhalation. A shape in the water beside

359

him, lithe and strong. Then an arm around his neck slender and cold. Surge and lull, surge and lull through the water. He blinked and sampled life by way of small gasps.

'Hold here.' Stephania guided his hand to a ledge and then pulled herself out. She was a faint outline in the darkness, gleaming wetly. After a moment she relieved him of the blade, then pulled him from the water.

'Where did you go?' he said between coughing fits.

'I was making sure Achilles didn't drown in the sack. Seems I should have been more worried about you. Could you wait a little longer before committing suicide?'

'I wasn't committing anything; we need a sword if we're going to escape.'

'I thought Anea was stubborn.' Stephania rolled her eyes. 'Seeing you cling to that sword makes me think it's a family trait.'

'It's one of my more attractive qualities, you know?' He tried for a smile but surrendered to a racking cough instead.

'Perseverance is attractive; stubbornness is something else entirely.' Stephania shivered. 'They're not the same.'

'Pedant.' He grinned, flushed with adrenaline, trembling with shock. 'You took your time, didn't you?'

'Don't mention it, my lord.' She stood and found her weapon and boots in the darkness. 'I can throw you back in if you'd prefer?'

He shrugged, busying himself with Achilles as she dressed. The reptile took his place on Lucien's shoulder, clinging to the nape of his neck. A scaly tail slid under his collar, seeking warmth.

'It's nice to see you too,' whispered Dino, laying a hand on the reptile's flank.

'Are you hurt?' asked Stephania.

'No. Mercifully.' He pressed a hand to where the *capo* had gouged him, then stood with care; the ledge was not wide. 'Thank you for saving me.'

Stephania gave a shrug as if it was of no consequence, a pouting smile betraying her pleasure. His eyes grew accustomed to the reduced light. The chamber they occupied was round, like so many of the training rooms of House Fontein. The roof swept up to an inverted funnel narrowing into the well shaft. Its stone walls were immaculate and smooth, the joins almost too fine to see. He removed a sodden glove and traced a line with a fingertip.

'This place is ...'

'Huge,' supplied Stephania, now dressed except for her tabard. 'I had no idea structures like this existed.' Certainly there were no columns holding the courtyard aloft.

'Are you ready?' asked Dino. 'I think there's a way out over there.' He pointed to a small oval of deeper darkness in the curving wall of the chamber.

A blur from the well shaft startled them. Falling, flailing. A splash and a series of ripples. A figure breached the surface and turned its head this way and that, face lost to shadow.

'Marchetti.' Dino struggled to remain on the ledge. He waited, sword ready, as the figure sank below the surface. A hand clawed up, paddled, sought purchase. Marchetti slipped below once more. The water was now churning around the drowning Myrmidon. Dino guessed the assassin had discarded his armour before his plunge into the underworld. The water's motion settled to a bob and swell. Bubbles broke the surface in profusion.

'I'm not so inclined to rescue Fiorenza's killer.' There was a darkness to Stephania's voice that Dino hadn't heard before.

'Neither am I.'

'Come on.' Stephania gazed at the middle of the cistern, the water now still. There was no trace of the fallen Myrmidon. 'You can let this vendetta go, Dino. He's gone.'

They exited the chamber, shivering and wet.

The passage was cramped, the stone rough and unfinished. A spiral staircase ascended into darkness. Sounds of dripping and the burbling of rivulets filled their ears. Sodden boots scuffed at steps blindly as they climbed, hand in hand, Dino leading the way. Cobwebs dragged at their faces and clung to shoulders. The air turned rancid, then became entirely unwholesome. Light filtered down and the Orfano and noblewoman emerged into the warm, golden glow of lanterns. They stood on another ledge, looking through endless rows of archways vaulting the ceiling above. Demesne pressed down, the weight of so much stone like a guilty conscience. A rank sea of pale brown water extended in all directions.

'Where are we?' whispered Stephania. Achilles roused himself from his torpor and blinked in the weak light.

'The Majordomo used to imprison those he wanted rid of in a place beneath the castle.' Dino's voice was hushed. 'It was called the oubliette, but it wasn't really a chamber or even a series of cells. Lucien told me it was more akin to catacombs where the prisoners preyed on each other.'

'That's hideous.'

'It gets worse. Lucien said the oubliette was knee-deep in water. The king poisoned the water with some chemistry called Lethe, which dissolved their memories. In time the prisoners were unable to remember their own names.'

'Why are there lights?' Her hand squeezed his, her voice a whisper.

'I don't know. Lucien described it as black as pitch. Massimo always suspected the grey raiders came from beneath Demesne. Perhaps he was right.'

They stepped down into the filthy water, glad when it reached their thighs and no further. Infrequent lanterns cast their light across ancient stonework. A face looked down from the keystone of every arch. Dino assumed it was the king's. No one would recognised him, the many years he'd spent in seclusion had put paid to that. All carvings of the king had been chiselled into oblivion on the upper floors, but no mason had ventured here, and for good reason. Long shadows wavered and stretched on the water.

Muted cries of distress and mourning echoed through the oubliette. Dino pulled Stephania to the shadow of one column, holding a finger to his lips. They peered around its edge as one, eyes wide with curiosity.

A woman staggered through the waterlogged cavern, a trail of flotsam bobbing in her wake. She was hunched and gaunt except for the dome of her stomach, stretched with her unborn, the flesh pale. A head slumped between pockmarked shoulders, pallid and hairless scalp revealing veins of purple and blue. Her face was lost to shadow. A ragged skirt hung from her hips, trailing in the water, impeding her progress for the small dignity it afforded.

'The poor woman,' breathed Stephania. Achilles hissed, unnerved by the squalid figure. The sound caused the creature to turn. And it was a creature, no more than a parody of a woman. Stephania pressed a hand to her mouth, mute with revulsion. What had turned to face them bore no eyes nor any semblance of a human visage. The upper head was smooth, the nose a blunt snub, the mouth beneath resembling nothing so much as mandibles from an insect. The creature cast around blindly for the source of the noise, then turned back and headed deeper into the catacombs.

'What is it?' whispered Stephania.

'There were previous generations of Orfani. Many generations. They died through assassination –' he curled his lip '– or vendetta.'

'And that?' Stephania gestured to the pregnant wretch that waddled and swayed through the rank tide.

'Not every Orfano was fit for public view. Some were too strange, too twisted or too broken. They were exiled by the Majordomo or cast down here. That would certainly explain why there are so many Myrmidons, especially if they've been breeding.'

'Which they obviously have,' supplied Stephania, unable to keep the disgust out of her voice.

The creature continued her lonely pilgrimage, heading toward an archway. It was darker there, and the pale shouldered not-woman disappeared from view.

'Should we follow her?' said Stephania, liberating a lantern from the column they hid behind.

Dino nodded reluctantly and slowly. 'Can you see another way out of here?'

Stephania shook her head, pressing her body against his. 'I'm glad you hung onto the sword.'

'I'm glad you saved me from drowning,' he replied with a sad smile.

They waded to the archway and passed through into the gloom beyond. Stephania raised the lantern and they were astonished to find Duchess Fontein standing before them. Her dress floated on the water's surface like a series of black blisters; her eyes were glassy, her movements languid. One hand held a *caraffa* of red wine, the other smoothed back her dust- and web-matted hair. The spark of recognition was absent as her eyes met Dino's, as if she sleepwalked.

'For my Lord Erebus,' she explained, lifting the wine. 'Won't you join us?'

'What are you doing down here?' asked Dino.

'House Fontein is at an end. The world moves on. My husband is dead and I am cast down.'

'But why?' asked Stephania.

'If I can't rule above, perhaps I'll rule from below.'

They were just a few feet from the duchess now. Of the pregnant wretch there was no sign, Dino grateful to be spared seeing her again. Duchess Fontein turned, gliding away from them through the water, her dress dragging behind her. It was then that Dino realised the walls were writhing in a slow sinuous motion, almost imperceptible. Grey twisted bodies were entangled and wrapped about one another. He stared and felt revulsion hollow him. Countless misshapen creatures squirmed. Here a crooked limb embraced a corpulent stomach, there a hunched back pressed against a ragged head.

'What are they doing?' whispered Stephania.

'Keeping warm, I expect. They're more like animals than people.'

'Insects, you mean,' said Stephania.

'Yes, like a nest of ants.'

A tortured ecstasy consumed them all, their grotesque faces strangely peaceful. It was a communion of flesh that transcended the sexual.

'Dino.' Stephania's voice was a stricken whisper. 'Look up.'

A vast and hideous form hung above the tableau of knotted bodies, suspended on six jagged chitin legs. Its torso was encased in a mottled shell, and it had a bulbous segmented lower section. The head, curiously human in scale, was obscured by a Myrmidon's helm which featured two shear-like blades, mandibles in steel.

'Santa Maria have mercy,' said Stephania beneath her breath. Dino found himself thinking the same.

'The House of Fontein is at an end,' said the duchess in a dull monotone. She drank from the *caraffa*, the wine spilling over her chin. The rest she discarded in the water before approaching the wall of bodies.

'We have to stop her,' said Stephania.

'Her mind is gone,' said Dino, unable to tear his eyes from the noblewoman in black. The duchess reached the mass of twisted flesh and was quickly subsumed. There came the sounds of tearing fabric, a whimper, a sigh. The limbs parted and pulled at her. Malformed hands inserted her into the writhing chaos. She gave herself without reservation, sparing Dino a look of despair and resignation. And then she was gone, lost from view behind the infernal sprawl of bodies, hands covering her eyes, her mouth. Dino choked, unable to credit what he'd seen. Stephania sobbed beside him.

'Ah, women. Always so frail.' This from the aberration hanging from the ceiling. 'But their bodies, so malleable. So fertile. So laden with promise.'

Dino and Stephania exchanged a glance; neither had thought for one moment it would speak.

'Come now, Lord Dino. Sire a new generation of Orfani with your pretty companion. The Lady Stephania, yes?' The voice was a flat drone, one not heard for decades but familiar all the same. 'Sire a new generation and I will make you a king, the Myrmidon king.'

'I know you,' grunted Dino with certainty. 'You're the Majordomo.'

He was answered by a hollow wheeze that took much too long to abate.

'Yes, once I took that name.' The head beneath the curving helm nodded slowly. 'I took that name more closely to my heart than my own. I forgot myself in service to the king. Ironic that I should have to come to the oubliette to remember myself, is it not?'

365

'Lucien killed you,' Dino snarled. 'He told me he killed you.'

'Lucien began something he could not finish. I have been free of the king's shadow for ten long years and I have remade myself. More than that, I have remembered myself. I am Erebus.'

55

Mourning

– 11 Novembre 314

Dino would always look back on that winter day with a mixture of feelings, none of them good. None save the redeeming fact that Virmyre had sought him out.

'I just don't think it's healthy for you to stay here,' intoned Virmyre from his position near the mantelpiece. Dino sat on the windowsill of his sitting room, knees drawn up to his chest, eyes locked on the rivulets of water as they streaked across the glass. His breath steamed the panes until he broke his introspection to wipe the window with the sleeve of his nightshirt. Achilles nestled about Dino's shoulders like a scarf, occasionally looking up at the *professore* with a studied disinterest.

'I'll be fine,' said the Orfano. 'I'm just not in the mood to be around people.'

'That's what concerns me,' replied Virmyre.

It had been four days since Duke Prospero's funeral. The rain had continued to fall since that day, not torrentially, rather a lacklustre drizzle that showed no promise of ending. The clouds, so pale as to be near invisible, edged across the heavens in a stately procession. The Orfano looked over his shoulder at the older man, then ordered his scattered thoughts.

'How is she?' he said, so quietly the words were almost drowned by the patter of rain.

'Distraught, of course.'

Dino and Stephania had stumbled across the corpse of the duke, seemingly fallen to his death by way of a spiral stone staircase. It would not have been a quick death, Dino suspected. The stentorian duke was a barrel-shaped man, but even the padding of his vast appetite had not saved him from the fall. His neck had snapped, head resting at a cruel angle on the cold stone floor. Dino had never seen a corpse before, much less the corpse of someone he knew.

'Is there anything I can do?' asked the Orfano, knowing the answer before he finished the question.

'She simply needs time.' Virmyre, famously impassive, looked concerned. 'The loss of a parent is always difficult, and under such circumstances more harrowing still.'

The rain continued to fall and Achilles swished his tail. The *professore* banked up the fire for want of something to do.

'I can't say I ever really liked him,' said Dino. 'He was a buffoon really. Always yelling at the top of his voice—'

'He was partially deaf, Dino.'

'I know. What I was going to say, was that whether I liked him or not, it was no way for a duke to die.'

'Dukes are just people, like anyone else.' Virmyre sat down in an armchair and crossed his legs. 'I'm not sure death cares much for titles or birthright.'

'I disagree: they're not like anyone else. How can they be? Dukes are symbols to their houses. Dukes are figureheads. Dukes, for all their sins, deserve a better death than a tumble down a staircase and a broken neck.'

'I'm not sure I agree,' rumbled Virmyre, his hand straying to his beard. 'If you're saying the deaths of dukes are meant to mean something, then you'll be disappointed.'

Dino stared into the crackling flames but felt no warmth, nor the desire to reply.

'Besides,' continued Virmyre, 'there's at least one duke I'd help to the top of a staircase.'

'I thought you were supposed to be a good influence on me? I'm only eleven.'

'Life is full of disappointments, Dino. I'm afraid it was only a matter of time before I joined that long and illustrious list.'

'Stop trying to cheer me up.' Dino grinned. 'Can't you see I'm in the middle of some perfectly good brooding?'

'You're an amateur,' replied the *professore*, eyes twinkling.

'Now Lucien, there's an Orfano who can brood for the kingdom. I dare say he can brood for the entire island.'

The mention of the older boy's name scoured the humour from Dino's face.

'Still angry with him then?' asked Virmyre.

Dino looked away. Achilles pushed his snout against the curve of his neck, tail set to a metronome swish.

'And you won't illuminate me as to the source of this rift?'

'I … can't. It wouldn't be seemly.'

'Seemly?' Virmyre raised an eyebrow, but the Orfano refused to be drawn.

'Surely this is just a cross word over a favourite sword?'

'If only it were that mundane.' Dino caught himself, frowning because he'd said anything at all. 'I can't speak of it. I won't speak it.'

'Then I shall leave you to your thoughts, Master Dino. I'll be dining in the main hall tonight if you need to unburden yourself.'

'Thank you,' managed the boy on the windowsill, eyes locked on the glass and its panorama of rainswept countryside. The trees were like phantoms, indistinct in the rain, waiting to accost lonely travellers. Virmyre departed, the door closing quietly behind him.

Memories of the event swirled like a column of autumn leaves whipped into motion by the wind. *La Festa* was supposed to be a happy time, and Stephania had wasted no time acquainting herself with the wine. Now all that remained of that night was a sour aftertaste, one that promised to linger all too long. Dino stood and placed the cataphract drake on the bookcase with care.

'Try and stay out of trouble. One of us should, at least.'

Achilles grasped the edge of the shelf with his foreclaws, pushing his wedge-shaped head forward to regard his master, a gargoyle in miniature.

'At least I can trust you not fall down any stairs.' The cataphract drake blinked and hissed.

Dino dressed in warmer clothes, muttering to himself as he bound up his tines in linen. Virmyre was right: he would succumb to madness if he remained in his apartment. Better to go out into the world beyond his door than be a prisoner of his apartment. The Orfano belted on a sword, then slipped a dagger into the top of each boot. Duke Prospero may well have slipped due to his own clumsiness but Demesne was rife with rumours concerning assassins. One simple push was all it would take. Dino would not be caught unawares if the assassin sought him out, nor would he be unarmed. Finally, he slipped on a jacket with slashed sleeves and vertical piping. He'd had it made on a whim, the black silk all too appropriate, prescient even.

Demesne had been trapped in a collective malaise since the duke's death. There was a feeling of melancholy in the air which haunted every doorway and staircase, each dusty corridor and dimly lit hall. The cloisters were gloomy and rain slicked places promising chilly air and little else. Only Duchess Prospero served as any counterweight to the pervasive sadness. She had not troubled herself by playing the grieving widow; few if any would believe the performance no matter how well she played it.

Dino wandered for an hour or more before finding himself at the lonely spot where Duke Prospero had met his end. A more unremarkable place one could not hope to find, a rarely used stairwell with only cobwebs and shadows for decoration. Flowers had been laid: posies bound in twine from common folk, larger offerings from the nobles. All the blooms had surrendered to the first touches of decay. A solitary lantern cast a gentle light over the floral tableau.

Dino recalled the shock and disbelief that had overtaken Stephania as she recognised her father. She hadn't been able to bring herself to touch the supine body. Dino had done so in her place. The chill of waxy skin could not be banished by hearth or bathtub, no matter how hot the fire or scalding the water. He recalled his own revulsion, the knife edge of panic. Afterward he had blamed himself. If only he'd taken the time to speak to the duke at *La Festa,* perhaps even offered to escort him home. Ridiculous of course – the blame unwarranted, a child's guilt.

Dino shivered in the corridor amid the dying flowers.

Something moved at the limit of the lantern's light. The Orfano staggered back a step before his training asserted itself. He dropped into a fencing stance, blade halfway out of its sheath.

'*Figlio di puttana*,' he snarled.

The Majordomo emerged from the gloom, dappled with light from the lantern, eyes concealed by his hooded robe, weathered face betraying nothing.

'I did not mean to startle you, Master Dino.'

'What are you doing here?' asked the boy, failing to hide the accusatory tone in his voice. He withdrew another step, letting the ceramic blade slide back into its scabbard.

'I have been looking for you for much of today.'

The Domo passed under a stone arch, stooping as he came closer. A head taller than anyone in Demesne, he moved with a stately grace, wrapped in robes that had long forgotten their colour. He was a figure painted from a palette of rain clouds and ashes. A wiry long-fingered hand extended from one voluminous sleeve to clasp an oak staff. Tawny amber the size of a child's fist served as its headpiece. A dark shadow indicated something trapped amid the resin, but Dino had never drawn close enough to discern it. Tatty rope held the fabric of his attire together at the waist. There was a faint smell of libraries about him, as if he folded himself up and slept between leather-bound tomes, although none knew where he rested or even if he slept at all, just as none had seen the king they all served. A solitary fly buzzed mournfully about the cowl of the king's steward but failed to elicit any irritation from the gaunt man.

'So strange to find you alone, today of all days.' The Domo's voice was a drone, deep and resonant.

'I'm not sure I understand you. Did I miss some ceremony or observance?'

The Domo wheezed a few times before holding his free hand up to his mouth to wipe some spittle away. There was a hacking sound that made Dino wince, then came the disquieting realisation the Domo was laughing.

'An observance indeed,' said the Domo finally. The fly ceased orbiting the hooded head, settling into a crease of the ragged vestments. 'It is your birthday, Dino.'

The Orfano sneered as if he'd just been slapped, locking his eyes on the dark place within the cowl.

'I have no birthday, as you well know.'

'My apologies.' The Domo inclined his head, a faint smile appearing on his parchment-like lips. 'Your foundling day is what I meant.'

'Hardly a cause for celebration,' said Dino, folding his arms.

'Another year older, another year of wisdom accrued, another year survived,' droned the Domo. 'There is much to celebrate.'

'Celebrating my foundling day feels obscene. Should I throw a party to acknowledge my missing parents each year?'

'Being an Orfano is hard, I grant you. I too know the pain you speak of. It is why I have sought you out with this small token.'

The Domo took a step forward and extended his arm, fingers uncurling around a heart of amber the match of the one that topped his staff. Dino's reluctance was all too tangible, from the scuffing of his boots as he stepped forward to the hesitation as he plucked the prize from the Domo's palm. Dark beads glittered in the amber. Not beads.

'There are ants in here,' he said reverently, the amber held in the steeple of his fingers.

'I have always admired ants,' said the Domo. 'So industrious. Rarely giving a thought for themselves, only working toward serving their nest. Able to shoulder the heaviest burdens.'

'That doesn't sound like much of life,' complained Dino. 'It sounds like slavery.'

The Domo closed his hand into a fist and withdrew it, thin lips curling with distaste.

'How is one so young so dedicated to the path of selfishness?'

'The only path I'm on is one of survival.'

'Ah, you speak of the duke.'

The Domo and Orfano were joined in silence as they regarded the flowers.

'Is it true he was assassinated?' said Dino, unable to drag his eyes away from the wilting blooms.

'Demesne does not harbour assassins.' The Domo tightened his grip on his staff.

'Anyone could have slipped away from the party. It would have taken only minutes to trail the duke to the top of the stairs.'

'You speak as if you have experience of such things,' grated the Domo, taking a step closer. 'Perhaps the perpetrator stands before me?'

Dino, newly twelve, shrank.

'I'm no assassin. I'll not kill anyone unless they meet me with steel in their hands.'

'Good. We need more like you, Master Dino. Young, opinionated, with strong values.'

Dino couldn't decide if he was being mocked or not. There was an ambiguous quality to the droning chords of the Domo's voice that concealed as much as it imparted.

'Need me for what, exactly?'

'Perhaps you should find a staff. You could mount it with the amber I have just given you, make a staff the twin of my own.'

'Why would I do that?' asked Dino, dreading the answer to the question even as he was compelled to ask it.

'Ageless as I am, I will not exist for ever. I am ever watchful for someone to continue the great tradition I have been sworn to.'

'You should ask Lucien. He's older than I am.' It wasn't the most subtle of evasions, but Dino had not expected to be ambushed so thoroughly.

'Lucien's destiny follows another path; yours appears infinitely more—'

'I'm not sure I want to serve a king I've never met.'

The Domo shifted his weight, the interruption a rankle.

'He might be a figment for all we know.' This bald declaration brought forth more of the Domo's hateful laughter.

'The king is quite real, I assure you. Perhaps you'll see him one day.'

'But only if I become your apprentice?'

The Domo nodded, the great dome of his head moving slowly beneath the dusty cowl, his eyes remaining unseen as ever.

'I'll think on it,' replied Dino, recalling the times he'd seen Duchess Prospero playing for time, dismissive and petulant.

'Do not think on it too long.' The Domo stooped, pushing the blunt wedge of his face toward Dino's own until the Orfano feared he might be consumed beneath the hood. 'It is not an offer I make lightly, or often.'

'Why don't you ask Anea?' whispered Dino.

'Women have no place in the ruling of Demesne.'

'But hives are ruled by queens.'

The Domo straightened. 'I have changed my mind. I have no need of an apprentice after all.'

Darkness swallowed the Domo as he withdrew, staff beating out the tempo of his stride like the seconds of an ancient clock. Dino listened to the sound recede. Only when it was beyond the limit of his hearing did he let himself breathe.

56

Bloodline

− 30 Agosto 325

'Dino, please, get me away from here.' Stephania's hand clutched at his with painful intensity. 'It can't be him. It can't be,' she repeated. Achilles hissed.

Bodies from the grey wall of limbs began to peel off, becoming distinct, separate creatures. They ran the gamut of deformity: atrophied limbs, empty eye sockets, mouth parts no more than withered mandibles; swollen and corpulent, emaciated and sinewy. These were the unwanted children of the king's designs, the failures of experiments that had brought blight not fruition. Dino wondered how many were down here. He couldn't possibly fight them all, broken as they were.

'Lucien was supposed to rule.' Erebus' voice was deep and penetrating, resonating around the chamber. 'Golia was a monster we used to frighten the people into obedience, a blunt instrument; Lucien was the intelligent one, but Anea put her filthy ideas of a republic into him. Anea and that whore chambermaid.'

More bodies were shed from the wall of undulating flesh. Wretches in various stages of pregnancy were disgorged, waddling forward, ripe to deliver yet more twisted progeny into the world. Stephania stared at them appalled.

'None of us wanted to serve the king,' moaned Erebus, his voice a maudlin dirge. 'How we hated him, how we feared him, how we longed for a new way of life.'

Dino turned. The lanterns behind them were being extinguished one by one; soon the only source of light would be the lantern Stephania clutched. Her breathing was ragged and quick by his ear.

'Your father's sword,' said Dino, 'I think you're going to need it.'

Stephania switched the lantern to her left hand and drew, the tip of her blade hovering above the surface of the rank water.

'How sharp is that thing?' grunted Dino.

'More than your wits, less than my sarcasm.'

'Good to know,' replied the Orfano.

'Hundreds of years he reigned,' complained Erebus; 'decades I served, catering to his insane schemes, providing for his obsessions.'

Stephania pressed herself back to back with Dino, prompting another hiss from Achilles. She turned her head as the reptile abandoned Dino's shoulder for her own.

'What's he doing?' she whispered.

'Seems like he's laying odds on which one of us will get out of here alive,' replied Dino.

'How *do* we get out of here?'

'I don't know. Maybe we can persuade him to tell us?'

'You're not serious?'

'I can't fight all of them.'

Stephania stiffened, the lantern she held remaining steady, a reprieve from the darkness of the oubliette. 'We are *not* going to die down here, Dino.'

He wished he could murmur an assurance, but the chances of escape had dwindled with the light. Bodies loomed at the edge of the lantern's nimbus, daring themselves to press in further. Blind eyes and twisted limbs sought them out but remained unwilling to risk injury. Dino and Stephania held out their swords, promising death to any venturing too close.

'Let us go. There's nothing to be gained by keeping us here. You've taken Demesne.' Dino hated every word as he said it, hated having to bargain, to beg.

'Let you go?' Erebus wheezed and rattled, clearly amused. 'But you're so valuable, Dino. Your bloodline could provide the most interesting results. Come, my boy. Join me.'

'I'm not your boy, and I'm not your fucking experiment. There'll be no bloodline.'

'Pity. You and your Prospero bitch could sit on the throne and manage the people – with my guidance, of course.'

'Call her that again and I'll cut your throat.' Dino meant it, anger hot in his veins. The grotesques had become still. Silence descended about them. Dino peered into the darkness for some way that might lead them out of this Stygian place. There was none.

'Golia failed me, unable to play his part.'

'Do you ever stop whining?' shouted Stephania.

Erebus ignored her. 'Lucien failed me, unwilling to rule.'

'Lucien never failed.' Dino surprised himself with the passion of his rebuttal. 'He's the best of us.'

'And where is your brightest and best now?' Erebus stretched the words, twisting them with his scorn. 'Not here beside you. He fails you with his cowardice.'

Dino regarded Erebus, his grey eyes glittering with hate. Here was the architect of so much suffering, just an arm's reach away. All the deaths of the last few months could be traced to his design, including Massimo's.

'And now you have failed me, Dino. Failure and disappointment, is this all you bring to my court?'

The Orfano pulled Duke Fontein's stiletto from Stephania's belt. 'I'm sure I've got something you can have,' he said, dropping to a squat then launching himself up.

Dino angled his sword around behind Erebus' helm, anchoring him in place; his legs scissored around the monster's torso, clinging on fiercely. His left hand jabbed at the join between armoured chest and human head. A sick tremor passed through Erebus as the stiletto sank into his neck. Insect legs trembled, and Orfano and aberration collapsed into the fetid water. Stephania leaped clear of the tangle, barely keeping the lantern above the surface of the water. A lone creature staggered toward her, only to collapse as she ran it through the chest.

'Get away from me,' she gasped.

The grotesques shambled back, confused and awed by the fall of Erebus. Dino struggled to escape from beneath the writhing mass as Erebus' legs thrashed in the muck, throwing up water and the sediment of centuries of misery. The water was up around Dino's neck, one of his legs remaining trapped beneath the bulk of the unholy creation. Erebus dipped his head forward, the blades of the helmet descending. Dino jerked back and to one side to avoid a slashed throat, the water up to the corners of his eyes, lapping over his mouth. The Orfano turned, looking in vain for Stephania, trying to find the source of the light, desperate to see she was not being consumed by the horde, swallowed alive as Duchess Fontein had been.

Erebus coughed and flailed, lurching up. The light swung around the chamber at lunatic angles as Dino pushed himself to his feet. It was then he realised why Erebus had risen so quickly, abandoning his chance to drown the Orfano.

Stephania had mounted the back of the monstrosity; riding it like a wild horse. With no reins, she grasped the stiletto embedded in the aberration's neck. She pressed it deeper, thrust harder, the wound weeping pale fluid turning blue. She clung on, her other hand still fastened to the lantern. Achilles remained clamped to her shoulder, onyx eyes squinting in the melee, tail wrapped about Stephania. It was then Dino saw it. Erebus had positioned himself under a hole in the ceiling, making himself a living door to the underworld of the oubliette.

'Stephania! Above you! Jump.'

She looked up, nearly losing her precarious position on the lurching six-legged horror. Grotesques closed in on every side. Dino lashed out in a wide sweep that split the face of two attackers and buried the blade in the chest of another. There were hisses and wails, the stink of excrement as a shock wave of pain rippled through the disfigured. Another lurched forward, only to be greeted by the sharp tines of Dino's forearm sinking into the pallid muscles of its chest. It fell back, clutching half a dozen poisoned wounds.

'Stephania. Jump!'

She stared back stricken with indecision.

Dino took his blade in both hands and removed the head from an attacker bearing a rusted blade. Its skull splashed into the water and bobbed, looking back with a single baleful eye. Others squabbled in the muck for the blade.

'Go. Now!'

She jumped, throwing the lantern through the hole before her, abandoning her perch on the back of the monster. She caught the lip of the hole, long seconds slipping away as she hauled herself higher. Achilles leaped from his perch and scurried away. Her shoulders pushed through, then her hips. The riding boots scrabbled for purchase and then she was gone. Dino checked himself, staring down those who looked ready to attack. Erebus was spent and wheezing, the hilt of the stiletto protruding from his neck.

'Not good enough,' grated Dino, wishing the thrust had found the jugular. Erebus lurched to his insect feet and lumbered away into the darkness, the grotesques closing up behind him. Dino lunged forward in pursuit but was shoved back by a wall of limbs. A tawny crescent of light flickered from the hole above, but of Stephania there was no sign. Dino roared in fury, resigned to death, frustrated he wouldn't destroy the source of Demesne's corruption.

The grotesques withdrew, dragging the whimpering wounded in their wake. Dino stood with an eye on the pale yellow light above, waiting for salvation from above, knowing they'd be hunted down by the Myrmidons on the surface. He clutched his sword, arm aching, waiting for more danger to emerge from the twilight. His breathing became calm, the waters stilled and silence crept closer. Dino called out to Stephania, eyes fixed on the hole in the ceiling and the faint smudge of light that lingered there. No reply, no response. Perhaps she had fallen and knocked herself unconscious? Were there Myrmidons up there?

How long he waited he couldn't say, time meaningless in the oubliette. Relief infused him like sunshine when the light finally came. Somehow she'd circled around and was approaching from the direction of the well chamber. The lantern light bobbed closer, bringing with it a glint of steel.

'Stephania? I hope you've looked after Achilles.'

The bearer of the lantern remained silent.

57

In Chains

– 30 Agosto 325

Stephania!' He smiled. 'Seems like you're quite a bodyguard. That's twice in one day you've saved me.'

Still no reply.

'Stephania, can you remember the way back?'

The first glimmer of doubt, of curiosity, of anxiety.

'Are you hurt?'

The lantern came closer, shedding light over the figure who carried it. Dino felt a twinge from the dagger cut in his side. It was not Stephania but Marchetti who approached, stripped to the waist, face concealed behind his veil. Dino suspected he knew why, and why the assassin never spoke. One hand brought light, the other death; Marchetti had clung to his sword as keenly as Dino had to his. In this at least they were alike. Dino suspected the Myrmidon had followed the sounds of violence.

At least Stephania had escaped. He hoped.

The Domina's assassin hung the lantern from a rusted bracket by the archway, drew in a deep breath and rolled his shoulders. Dino pushed aside the pain of his wound, trying to draw on the anger he felt for Anea, finding only the enervation of betrayal.

Marchetti approached, circling, assessing, blade held out low, eyes keen. Dino shrugged off caution and opened with a flurry of thrusts and slashes, hampered only by the water, which dragged at his feet and legs. Marchetti turned the strikes aside, ducking beneath the last of them, turning the motion into a deadly riposte. Dino threw himself beyond the range of the blade lest his throat be opened and fell back beneath the water, struggling to regain his feet. Marchetti waited. Clearly he possessed some modicum of honour.

'Pity you didn't extend Fiorenza the same courtesy.'

Thoughts of the slain maid quickened Dino's blood. He unleashed another series of attacks, feinted and mashed a fist into the veil, eliciting a grunt of pain. The Myrmidon responded by driving the pommel of his sword into Dino's wound. The Orfano staggered, sickened by the pain. Now it fell to him to parry, Marchetti like a autumn gale, his advance irresistible. The Myrmidon's sword whipped about like silver leaves, every motion a blur that promised oblivion. Swords tolled like bells, rang like anvils. Dino imagined he could hear the rattling of chains, as if the damned themselves were close at hand, desperate to be free.

Something under the surface of the water troubled Dino's foot, causing him to pause and shift his weight. The distraction was enough for Marchetti. The Myrmidon's blade swung upright, clutched in both hands. Dino stared, waiting for the strike that would cleave him to his breastbone. He raised his sword arm, knowing it was too late.

Achilles slammed into Marchetti's veiled face, the drake's claws clamping each side of his head, tail constricting the neck of the Myrmidon. Marchetti stumbled back, off balance, dropping his sword, which sank beneath the rank tide.

'Dino, quickly!' Stephania's face looked down from the hole above. A length of heavy chain fell from the gap in the ceiling. The metal links, each as thick as his wrist, splashed into the water.

Marchetti gave a stifled grunt and clawed the reptile from his face, opening bloody gouges at the corners of his eyes. Dino stooped to rescue his pet, then landed a kick on the Myrmidon's hip, sending him sprawling back into the water.

'Dino, quickly. I think Myrmidons are coming.'

The Orfano sheathed his sword and started climbing the the heavy chain – not easy with boots full of water, even more difficult with a bedraggled cataphract drake clinging to one shoulder. His wound slowed him, the pain in his side agonising.

Marchetti bobbed to the surface and lurched upright, coughing and racking. He was unarmed. Dino knew he could finish him.

'Dino!' Stephania reached down with a hand. She was smiling with tears in her eyes, desperation and hope competing on her face.

He could finish Marchetti, avenge Fiorenza and Emilio and Massimo.

'Dino! Please, come on! I need you.'

He climbed. He slipped. He tightened his grip. He climbed again, the rust on the chain helping him to gain purchase on the links. He was close. A glance confirmed Marchetti had recovered his blade. The chain rattled and swayed below him as the Myrmidon pursued. Dino took Stephania's hand and pulled himself through the hole, staggering to his feet though it cost him dearly in pain.

'I thought I'd lost you,' she breathed with relief.

Dino stood on trembling legs, the pain in his side an insistent throb. And in the corner of his eye, rising through the floor like the abdead, was Marchetti. Dino spun and wrenched his sword from the scabbard. The sword came free with an upward slash that caught Marchetti in the face, ripping the veil and whatever lay beneath. The Myrmidon fell back, hands and feet slipping, through the breach in the floor. His head hit the side of the hole as he fell, the sound terrible and final in the silence of the oubliette. The assassin splashed into the water, which subsided over his body and was still.

Stephania hugged Dino fiercely.

'Mind my tines! I don't want to poison you.'

She hugged him anyway, eliciting a gasp.

'What is it?'

'My side, you're squeezing the wound.'

'*Porca miseria*. I'm sorry. Sorry.' She tore lengths of material from her tabard and made a crude bandage. The sound of ripping fabric made Dino uneasy. Once she'd treated his wound she turned her attention to his forearms, binding them tight.

'Just in case,' she explained.

Dino nodded, regaining his breath. 'Did you just throw my pet drake into a sword fight.'

382

'Of course not!' Stephania frowned. 'He jumped off my shoulder as I leaned over.'

'Is there anyone in Demesne who isn't rescuing me today?'

'Anyone else would be grateful.'

'I'll be grateful once I'm sure I'm not bleeding to death.' Dino blinked a few times and looked around. 'Where are we? How do we get out of Demesne from here?'

'I'll show you.' Stephania looked around uncertainly. 'I think I found a way out.'

'Just pull that chain up from the hole.' He gestured weakly to the floor. 'We don't need anything else coming up from down there.'

They set off, Dino with one hand pressed to the cut in his side, the other draped around the shoulders of Stephania, who struggled under his weight. His eyes were heavy, his feet unresponsive. There was no part of him that wasn't bruised or cold or wet. Stephania had stashed Achilles beneath the ragged remains of her tabard in order to keep the drake warm.

'Pay attention now. We have to go down.'

Dino opened his eyes wide. 'Down?' Stone steps lay before him, each further one less distinct in the gloom. 'We need to go up, Stephania.'

'Trust me. There's a passage deep beneath Demesne. I just have to find it.'

'We should go up—'

'And be caught by Myrmidons the minute we're seen?'

She started down the steps, dragging him with her. It was pointless to resist. Dino concentrated on walking, content just to remain conscious.

'I thought *you* were supposed to be taking *me* out of Demesne.'

'I am,' he grunted. 'I'm just feigning weakness to confuse our enemies.'

'Interesting. You're very good at it.'

'I've had lots of practice.'

It was easy to smile but the wound bled a little more with every step. It wasn't deep, nor fatal, but it was enough to set his head spinning with the loss of blood. He couldn't resist the heaviness of his eyelids and was almost sleepwalking.

The jostling strain of walking stopped. Stephania said nothing, prompting Dino to open his eyes, fearing the worst. They were in a low-ceilinged chamber, floor deep with dust. A thrum vibrated through the soles of his boots, as if the room was singing a wordless lament. Black rectangles of glossy black stood before them in orderly rows, ten abreast, each around seven feet tall. Each featured a single amethyst light off centre at the top.

'Looking glasses?'

'More of the king's machines,' said Dino.

'How can you tell?'

'I've seen smaller ones and one like this in the *sanatorio*. That's where Anea keeps them. They have the same purple light.'

'They look so smooth.' It was true. Each was three feet wide, smooth and flawless, elegantly curved, a perfect abstract sculpture. 'Wait here,' said Stephania. She set the wounded Orfano down on a step.

'Like I have a choice.'

Stephania approached the nearest of the devices with the lantern held aloft. The glass reflected her face stretched across the convex surface, but she could also make out something inside. Something terrible.

'Don't touch it,' urged Dino. 'Come away before something happens.'

'Like what?'

'I accidentally opened one of these in the *sanatorio*.'

'What was inside?' She was breathless with curiosity.

'Nothing. It was empty, and the light had faded from it.'

'Do you know what these contain?'

'No. Can you see what's inside?'

Stephania looked through the glass and shuddered. 'I can't really tell, but there are legs, lots of legs.' She took a step back. 'Insect legs like Erebus had.'

'Do you think they're alive?' he asked.

'Difficult to know,' she replied 'There are so many. Do you think it's an army?'

Dino didn't answer.

Stephania returned to him and pulled the Orfano to his feet, eliciting another grunt of pain.

'How many of the *cittadini* do you think have abandoned Santa Maria?' she asked.

'Not nearly enough,' said Dino. 'Everyone will die if he unleashes these ...'

'You can't know for sure they're the work of Erebus.'

'Who else?'

'You did say they were the king's machines.'

He nodded. It was all too convenient to lay the blame for everything on Erebus. The strangeness infesting Landfall stretched back centuries.

She all but carried him through the sarcophagi chamber, lit only by the baleful eyes of the machines. The purple lights lent the scene a surreal cast, held back in part by the flickering light of Stephania's lantern. Dino was glad of it, and for Stephania. He counted ten rows, with at least another ten to get past. They were over halfway across the room when the basso thrum changed in pitch.

'Do you hear that?'

Dino nodded, dread chilling him more than blood loss.

'Keep going.' Even his words sounded dusty, as if Demesne had infected him. Stephania pressed on, damp boots kicking up drifts of dust and web. A doorway beckoned, an opening of deeper darkness in the purple twilight.

'I told you there was a way out.' She looked pleased.

'You just didn't mention we had to sneak through a mass grave to get there.'

'I don't think they're buried,' she said; 'I think this is where they're grown.'

'At least if they were buried it would mean they're dead,' he muttered.

'Well, let's not wake them,' she whispered. They hurried on.

'Where are we?'

'An old sewer tunnel.' She was breathing hard, tiring under his weight. 'Now forgotten.'

'So how do you know about it?'

'When you're as rich as House Prospero you can afford anything. Even old maps that House Erudito find boring.'

Dino struggled to see beyond the nimbus of golden light Stephania bore. He was hoping the illumination might keep them safe even as he lost consciousness.

58

A Rising Storm

− 30 Agosto 325

Dino woke on a narrow cot in a spartan chamber, the walls plastered and whitewashed. A small figurine of a woman holding a child stood on the bedside cabinet: Santa Maria calm and kind in white marble. A candle as thick as his wrist burned with a pleasing steady light. His fingers traced the edges of bandages tightly wrapped; blankets smothered his body with gentle warmth. Simple unbleached cloth adorned the bed. There was no trace of extravagance, nor was there any dirt; someone had kept the room fastidiously clean. Each breath brought the tiniest hint of lavender.

Memories returned in flashes. Being bathed in clean water and scrubbed by a trio of veiled women, then a sharp pain he could not escape as they stitched him together and drowsiness as a preparation did its work, lulling him to sleep. And through it all the presence of Stephania, anxiety evident on her face, mouth a trembling line beset by anguish. She had refused to let it take her over − not while he remained conscious anyway.

Dino shifted onto his unwounded side, curling up into a ball. His entire body ached, heavy like a composite of granite and lead, like a gargoyle from the rooftop of the *sanatorio*. He wondered if Marchetti had died in the waters of the oubliette. Perhaps he was still down there, unable to remember himself or the way out.

A face appeared in the doorway.

'I'm awake,' he croaked, throat raw.

'Good. It's night again. We should try and slip away before

dawn.' Stephania sounded tired, but there was resolve in her voice. Her red-rimmed eyes showed her sadness at leaving.

'Where are we?'

'The chapel of Santa Maria. They found the tunnel when they dug the foundations for the courtyard. A larger church will be built in a year.'

Dino grunted and pushed himself up onto his elbows. 'I suppose you found this out from your pet disciple?'

'She's not my pet. But if she hadn't told me about the tunnel we'd still be trapped beneath Demesne.'

'I still don't like it.'

'Your feelings on the Sisters of Santa Maria are well known. You should probably show some gratitude though. They saved your life.'

'I think that accolade goes to you.'

She shrugged, forcing a pouting smile, a ghost of her old self returning.

'When did you decide?' He gestured toward the figurine on the nightstand.

'That I believed?' She folded her arms and looked downcast.

He nodded and regretted asking her.

'I'm not sure,' she said after a pause. 'The idea of an infinitely kind and maternal divine being is an attractive one.' A sad smile overtook her. 'Especially with a mother like mine.'

'Salvaza may have her faults but she did charge me with escorting you to safety.'

Stephania shrugged, unable to accept her mother's good deed. 'That's worked out really well, wouldn't you say?'

'It's all going to plan perfectly, you know?' Dino grinned.

Stephania returned the smile before her eyes narrowed. 'Don't you ever wonder about your mother? Who she was, if she might have survived.'

'I try not to.' He sat up straighter and grimaced. 'We'll need new clothes,' he said, keen to change the subject. 'Every Myrmidon in Demesne is going to be looking for two House Prospero messengers.'

'I've already thought of that. I'm going to dress as a Sister of the San Marino convent. They're under the protection of Lucien. The Domina wouldn't dare interfere.'

'There's another order?'

'The Sisters are more popular in San Marino than they are here.'

'Maybe I don't want to go there after all.' He sat right up and shuffled around until his feet were on the floor. 'So do I get to dress in a veil and wimple too?'

'If you like –' Stephania suppressed her mirth '– but it's probably best you ride with me as a man. Even the Sisters have armed escorts.'

New britches, boots, a shirt and a leather jerkin waited for him on a wooden chair at the foot of the bed. His sword rested in its scabbard, now battered, the enamel chipped. Dino identified with it all too readily.

'Resourceful these Sisters of yours.'

'They are, and there's more. Come on. *Avanti.*' She left.

He dressed. His body foreign to him, each movement a trial of discomfort, a test of pain. Pulling on the clothes elicited some choice expletives before Stephania thrust her head into the room.

'You are on consecrated ground, you know.'

'If Santa Maria is so forgiving she won't mind some off-colour language.'

'Dino.'

Stephania scowled. He shrugged, then winced. 'I'll be out in a minute.'

The clothes fitted, more or less. The boots were a pair of his own, although how anyone had got into his apartment to retrieve them he could only guess at. He attached the sword to the belt, and it was then he noticed the drake-headed pommel had been polished. They'd gone to a lot of trouble. He turned, eyeing the marble figurine.

'Sorry about the profanity.'

He paused. With one deft motion he swept the figurine from the cabinet, slipping it inside his jerkin.

'No reason you have to stay here with these boring Sisters.'

The figurine said nothing, which Dino took as a mark of consent.

The antechamber to his room was bathed in candlelight from two candelabra, each bearing a half-dozen candles. Stephania was engaged in conversation with Agostina, Achilles perched on one shoulder, as stern and unblinking as Dino remembered.

'I see you've stolen my drake.'

'He's clung to me all day, even dozed with me.'

Dino extended a hand to the reptile, traced his brow with a finger.

'After all I've done for you, and you leave me the minute a pretty girl shows interest.'

Dino nodded to Agostina, who bobbed a curtsy in return, her mismatched eyes unnerving even now. 'My lord.'

'I'm not sure I'm lord of anything any more, so you can dispense with the formalities.'

'You will always be a lord in my eyes,' she replied. 'You saved Stephania and myself during the raid in the piazza.'

'Massimo saved you,' he reminded her.

'Because you asked him to.'

'What will you do now?' he asked the Sister.

'The same as we have ever done; the people need us now more than ever. Taxes creep up, working hours are long, and I don't expect much help from our ruler.'

'She's lost to us.' There could be no mistaking the bitterness in his voice. 'Corrupted by Erebus and Marchetti.' He cleared his throat and looked away. 'I don't know if there's anything left of the Anea I used to know.'

'It can't be helped,' said the disciple. 'In the meantime, these are yours for the road ahead.' She turned and proffered a thick riding cloak. Saddlebags packed with food lay on the table beside her.

'This is excellent,' Dino said.

Stephania smiled. 'I called in a few favours with people I know I can trust.'

'Risky –' Dino regarded the supplies '– but preferable to eating anything from the Foresta Vecchia.'

Stephania had changed into the white robes of the order,

olive-green wimple denoting her membership of the San Marino branch. The disguise was undermined by the cataphract drake perching on her shoulder, but Landfall had seen stranger sights than this. Stephania completed her outfit with a white veil.

'My lord.' The disciple crossed the room, gesturing with an open hand to a large sword secured to the wall. 'We would be honoured if you would take this with you. It was stored in a crate beneath Demesne for many years.'

'I'm not surprised. It looks antique.'

'Dino,' chided Stephania. He approached the sword, masking his disdain with winces from his wounds. The blade had been sharpened, polished to a mirror finish. There was blue tint to the steel.

'The Sisters are keen that you take it,' said Stephania.

'Fine.' He pulled the blade down from the wall, taking a second to become familiar with the heft of the two-handed sword. It wasn't as tall as him, but it wasn't far off either. The weight was prodigious. 'I'll take it, if it will spare their feelings.'

'It's the sword of a templar,' added Agostina.

'I'll take the gift but leave the title if I may. I'm still smarting from the fact I'm not *superiore* any more.'

Stephania shook her head and pursed her lips. Dino indicated the door, thinking it best to leave before he caused any further offence.

Outside the chapel three Sisters waited for them. Spots of rain fell from the sky, few at first and then with greater frequency. Dino mumbled his thanks to the robed women and earned himself another sharp look from Stephania. A pair of fine roan horses had been acquired and were saddled. Lightning flashed in the distance, a single column of light like a jagged lance thrust into the horizon. Dino took a moment to stare, waiting for the roll of thunder to rumble toward them. The rain increased and Dino cast his gaze over Santa Maria. Demesne loomed over the townhouses, a behemoth threatening to crush everything beneath its careless feet. The Orfano pulled his hood up and shivered. Stephania mounted her horse with the help of some wooden steps.

'Are you going to stand there all night?' asked Stephania.

'We're really leaving, aren't we?' Reluctance weighted each word.

She gave a tight nod and looked away.

'I was supposed to save Anea.'

'I know,' soothed Stephania, 'but you can't save people from themselves. She's taken a different path. And besides, you've saved me.'

Dino mounted his horse like an old man, fearing his stitches would come apart. The bandages held fast, a reassuring tightness around his gut. He'd laced the leather jerkin as tightly as he dared. Stephania spoke her thanks to the Sisters, who signalled back with their hands.

'They've learned the silent language?' he asked with a curt nod toward the veiled women.

'They've taken a vow of silence,' supplied the disciple. Dino struggled not to curl his lip. 'They're saying some Myrmidons left Demesne through the triumphal arch just a few minutes ago.

Dino and Stephania put their heels to the horses' sides and set off at gentle walk. A deep hush covered the town, broken only by the pattering of the rain and the susurrus of trees yet to lose their leaves. The coming autumn would finish what the drought had started. The distant green of the spring was a cherished memory. A few of the townhouses were boarded up. Dino guessed they were owned by *cittadini* who had fled following the riots. The horses continued, the clatter and ring of their hooves loud in the silence of the night. It was inevitable they would attract attention; even thunder could not mask the noise of their departure. The edge of the town was lit by braziers and the odd torch held aloft by a Myrmidon. Dino knew the outline of them in the darkness all too well.

'This doesn't look good.'

'When does it?' asked Stephania.

'So much for not interfering with a Sister of the San Marino branch.'

'Shut up, Dino.' Achilles hissed.

A Myrmidon commanded them to halt, hand held out. Dino counted twelve of them strung out in a loose line.

'Just go,' he whispered, the words sour on his tongue.

'We can't.'

'Not we,' he said through gritted teeth. 'You. You, just go.'

'But Dino ...'

'Your mother told me to get you away from here. That's what I'm doing.' The two-handed sword came out of the sheath across his back. The dull scrape of the metal sounded strange to his ears, the weight unfamiliar in his hands, perfectly balanced for all that.

'I'm not leaving you.' The words were matter of fact but had no effect on the grim-faced Orfano.

'Yes, you are. Take this with you.' He handed her the drake-pommelled sword, silver flashing in the night. 'Look after it, you know.'

'Dino, come on ...'

The Myrmidons had drawn closer, were almost upon them, halberds levelled. The majority had singled out Dino and the huge weight of metal that he held in his hands.

'Just. Go. Stephania.'

She had no reply, her eyes locked on Dino's. Another flash of lightning lit tears at the corners of her eyes. The rattle and boom followed a few seconds later, unsettling the Myrmidons baffled by the lone Orfano threatening violence. Dino slid from the saddle with a pained grunt, then raised the sword above his head.

'Take my horse,' he hissed from clenched teeth. The sword came down in a savage arc that rent a breastplate and everything under it.

'Go now!'

Stephania took the reins to Dino's steed and pressed her body low to her own mount, urging it on with coaxing whispers. The horses leapt a low fence, racing across a field until she met the road. Dino watched her leave with a bitter smile. The great sword rose again, promising a harvest of blood to all who approached. It was unthinkable he could defeat them all, even with such a weapon.

The Myrmidons closed in. Chaos erupted.

The nearest Myrmidon thrust in with his pole-arm, only to have the weapon smashed from his hands. Dino grinned and hefted the sword.

'You stepped into my parlour. Fuckers.'

The blade fell, and rose again.

59

Correspondence

− 31 Agosto 325

Mother,

By the time you read this I will be many days on the road to San Marino. Days paid for with the blood of Lord Dino Adolfo Erudito. I should be thanking you for charging him with the mission to escort me from Demesne, but in truth I feel nothing but grief. He had such a torturous last few months of life. That he should lose so many friends and comrades is truly awful, and in no small part your responsibility. I have lost a dear friend, and Landfall is missing a noble protector. Think on that next time you begin your schemes.

Was there really no other way to defeat Anea's wishes? Was aiding Duke Fontein's coup necessary? Your complicity with Erebus has ushered in a dire period for Landfall. A decent person might try and redress that balance.

Despite his long opposition to you, Dino asked that I accept you wanted me safe, hence my writing this letter. I would not be writing it for any other reason. I am staying at the Terminus Inn on the road to San Marino. The two brothers that run the inn have regaled me with stories of the various persons who have stopped here, Margravio Contadino among them. I feel I'm treading in noble steps. The brothers assure me this note will find itself to Demesne, and to you, once I am safely away from here.

In time I hope you will make a similar journey, if only to escape Erebus. Dino was sure that Anea was only mad, not evil. Perhaps if you could remove Erebus she might be

restored in some way, though that task sounds insuperable.
Erebus is monstrous and has numberless minions in
Demesne's catacombs. I should know, I have seen them with
my own eyes.

I do not expect to return. Please watch over Medea and
the children — you owe them that much.

Your daughter,
Stephania

Coda

The Best Revenge

– 19 Settembre 325

Three riders emerged from the Foresta Vecchia clad in cloaks filthy from the road. Both mounts and mounted were spattered with mud. Darker stains spoke of hardships greater than the weather, their journey paid for in sweat and sometimes blood. Pine needles clung to them, dark memories of the forest itself. The trees stretched into the skies, rustling in a wind that troubled their upper branches. The forest was an implacable wall of dark green, tall and sinister in the mist, which conspired to mute even the dull thuds of the horses' hooves. The only other sound to break the hush was a plaintive call from a solitary raven looking down with interest at the newcomers.

The foremost of the riders was Durante Corvino; a quiet man, he had taken the veil of Santa Maria, a curious choice for one of his gender. He was never without his riding gloves or the matched swords that hung from each hip. His hood was pulled up to ward off the occasional showers, but in truth he preferred it that way. The town of San Marino was no stranger to him, and he urged his horse onward, made keen by the promise of a hot bath and clean sheets. These he could depend on, being as he was an *aiutante* to the man who rode a score of feet behind.

Delfino Datini dozed in his saddle. The last five weeks had been taxing ones; there was no resource he owned that hadn't been strained. Patience, stamina, politeness, even his purse was much diminished. And, though he preferred not to admit it, his bravery had been put to the test also. He feared there would be a dash more grey to the salt and pepper of his hair, which was in great need of a cut. That he'd run out of moonleaf had further dampened his mood. He roused himself and looked to the horizon, where San Marino lay a half mile from the cliff tops.

'We're here, my lady,' he said, a ghost of a smile touching his lips.

Lady Stephania Prospero might well have been a man. The ride had hardened muscles; any softness of feature had been scoured away by the ancient forest. Her plaited air was filthy from the journey. A sword with the pommel of a cataphract drake sat on her hip, meticulously clean despite the forest and the many nights she'd slept under the stars.

'Is this it?' She dared to let hope kindle inside her. 'Is this finally it?'

'Yes,' said Datini with a single nod. 'And I've never been happier to see it. San Marino.'

Stephania regarded the town with awe. It was unlike anything she had seen. It resembled nothing so much as three upturned saucers, each a pavilion a mile across at least. The huge structures glimmered in the autumn sunlight like seashells, cream and coffee brown, accents of iridescent cyan dancing on their curved surfaces. Masts reared into the sky at their rims, bearing sails in turquoise, brown, grey, black and white, each bearing seven triangles picked out in a contrasting colour. Not sails, she realised, but banners, the flags of Duke Lucien's new houses.

'Artigiano, Terreno, Scolari and Vedetta,' said Datini.

Towering over the striated pavilions was a tower that defied logic. It looked skewed somehow, as if it were made of metal heated and twisted like the wrought-iron gates so familiar around Demesne. Sections of the building spooled away, becoming buttresses that nestled in the earth like the roots of some vast pale tree. Moss had adhered to the tower's base and flourished, consuming the seashell colours in dull green. The tower tapered upward, terminating in four blunt points carved at sloping angles.

'Is that the lighthouse?'

'We don't call it that any more,' said Datini with a wary cast to eyes.

'It must be over twelve storeys tall,' she breathed.

Datini nodded. 'Closer to fifteen.'

'Does Lucien live there?'

Datini shook his head. 'Nothing lives in the tower; it's a place of ghosts.'

More familiar-looking buildings huddled beside the pavilions, these obviously built by human hands – townhouses and shops, taverns and stables. Each was painted a pastel hue, complementing its neighbours yet distinct all the same. Streams spanned by wooden walkways and bridges ran between the pavilions. Lanterns hung from sturdy poles. A trio of youths was in the process of lighting them for the night to come. The riders drew closer, consumed with equal parts relief and exhaustion.

'It's beautiful,' breathed Stephania.

'It's more than beautiful,' replied Datini; 'it's home.'

They rode on in silence, Stephania drinking in the sight of the town. So different to the drab streets of Santa Maria, free of the looming shadow of Demesne. How was it possible to feel like a foreigner on the same island? she wondered.

Corvino led them on, his horse circling the nearest of the pavilions, heading toward the one which lay closest to the cliff edge. The sea remained hidden beneath a dense fog.

'Is the weather always this gloomy?' asked Stephania with a note of pique.

'Winter's arrived early,' replied Datini. 'It's cooler than usual for the time of year.'

They passed under the broad roof of the pavilion. None of the buildings inside was higher than three storeys, strange after the height and bulk of Demesne. Sisters of Santa Maria went on their way in groups of three or four. *Cittadini* called out to the riders, greeting them warmly, waving at Datini with enthusiasm.

'Are you well known here?' asked Stephania.

'I'd hope so: I used to lead House Vedetta.'

Stephania regarded him and shook her head. 'I thought you said were a painter?'

'I did. And I am.' Another smile, an almost apologetic shrug.

'And House Vedetta ...'

'Are Lucien's scouts.'

'And you led them?'

'I did. Then I became bored.'

Stephania rolled her eyes. The man was infuriating. They approached the centre of the pavilion, a clearing among the houses and shops. A profusion of archways and alleys led off in all directions. In the middle was a vast dais with words carved on its side in letters longer than her arm. A circular table surrounded by scores of high-backed chairs dominated the platform. Men and women were locked in discussion, the finery of their robes displaying their wealth or flamboyance.

'This is how Lucien rules?' Stephania could not bring herself to believe it.

'This is the main assembly,' said Datini, dismounting. 'We do things differently by the coast.' Another smile. Stephania found herself keen to be shown to somewhere private where she could finally be free of the man. She dismounted slowly, legs stiff, back aching. Corvino took the reins of her horse, nodded politely, then led the mounts away.

'Doesn't it get cold?' she enquired.

'You'd be amazed how quickly meetings conclude when people would rather be indoors.' The voice, one she'd not heard for a decade, came from behind her. The words they'd parted with had been unkind at best. She corrected herself. The unkind words had belonged to her. His had been of explanation, and apology.

Lady Stephania Prospero turned with a leaden heart.

Standing before her was Duke Lucien Marino, long hair concealing the absence of ears. His pale blue eyes were as haunting as ever, a look of concern creasing his brow above a straight nose and fine cheekbones. He wore an immaculate frock coat of deep brown with turquoise embroidery, trousers of the same. A short sword rested at his hip, medals adorned his breast, and his jaw was clean-shaven. No wonder Stephania had been keen to marry him, yet the woman who owned his heart stood just behind Lucien.

Rafaela wore her years with ease – she had a handful more

than her husband, though none would guess it. Dark hair was caught in a circlet of silver run through with beads that twinkled in the light. Her skirt, a rich turquoise that complemented the short jacket she wore in a deep brown, reached her ankles. Rafaela gave a tight smile and nodded politely.

And behind her was the great bulk of Franco, a large man made more impressive still by the breastplate he wore and the great halberd he clutched. His hair was still the same iron grey she remembered, his face a rich tracery of creases, most of them laughter lines. He beamed at Stephania.

'Welcome to San Marino,' said Lucien. 'I wish you were here under happier circumstances.'

'As do I,' she replied, a twist of grief on her lips.

Lucien looked to Datini and then back to Stephania. 'Where is Dino?'

She shook her head, a tightness in her chest she was all too familiar with.

'Where is he?' Lucien's urgent tone caused heads to turn nearby and the main assembly to cease their chatter.

'My lord –' Datini stepped forward '– Lord Dino was lost before we could reach Demesne. We had word he died amid a dozen of the enemy.'

'The enemy?' repeated Lucien, full of incredulity. 'Who is the enemy?'

'Anea is, and she has an army,' supplied Datini.

'Is this true?' Lucien stepped closer to Stephania. She nodded, felt the sting of tears. The road had given her an abundance of time to grieve and yet tears for Dino remained. She unbuckled the sword and handed it to Lucien.

'Virmyre had this made for him. Dino called it Achilles. He'd want you to have it, I'm sure.'

Lucien took the weapon, fingers trembling as they gripped the scabbard. He opened his mouth to speak, but nothing emerged.

'He died fighting so I might escape.'

'Killed by my sister's own men?' Lucien, always pale, blanched. Rafaela pressed one hand to her mouth, eyes stricken. Franco laid an arm about her shoulders.

'Anea is not who she once was,' explained Stephania. 'She's under the influence of one called Erebus, but you'd know him better as the Majordomo.'

'That's impossible,' muttered Lucien, but the words lacked conviction and all who heard them witnessed his discomfort.

'You said you killed him that day,' pressed Stephania.

'I did. I ... No man could have survived the wounds I inflicted.' Lucien shook his head in disbelief. 'I did everything but run him through the heart.'

'Well, I've seen him with my own eyes.' Stephania took an uneasy breath, the memory unsettling her. 'He lives beneath Demesne like a growth, like an infection, and Anea and the Domina are both in his power.'

'And the people?' asked Rafaela, her voice thick with emotion.

'The people suffer, those who haven't fled to the country-side. I wonder how many have lost their lives trying to journey through the forest.'

No one answered her.

'Is there anyone I love still alive?' said Lucien in a quiet voice.

'When I left, yes. But for how long?' She shrugged. 'Nardo suggested you take a few score soldiers to Demesne, but I'd say you'll need more than that to restore it to sanity.'

'Is that the course we're on?' asked Lucien. 'War?'

'That's up to you,' she replied. 'I told Dino that the best revenge is to live well. And that's what I'm going to do, though I worry for everyone I left behind.'

Stephania bobbed a curtsy and turned away, not knowing what direction she was heading in or even where she would spend the night, losing herself in the concentric streets of San Marino. In time she settled on a bench outside a *taverna*, killing time with a bottle of red from the Previdente vineyards. Achilles, who'd slept most of the journey in the hood of her cloak, chose that moment to rouse himself.

'Don't look at me like that,' muttered Stephania. 'If you were human you'd be drinking too.' Achilles blinked and scuttled into her lap.

The evening unwound, Stephania lost to remembering the Orfano who'd given his life to save hers. What would Dino say now, were he idling at the *taverna*, celebrating the end of a long journey? Thoughts turned to friends distant, friends alive and those passed on. The *cittadini* of San Marino avoided her, favouring the stranger and her reptile with a wary looks when they bothered to notice her at all. She kept drinking, one finger tracing the rim of her cup. Strange to be out in the street by night and not see the sky. The pearlescent pavilion provided shelter from the rain, heard faintly, but did nothing to take the chill from the sea breeze.

Datini appeared across the street, a tender look in his hazel eyes, concern in the set of his mouth. She nodded to him, and he approached, still grimy from the road.

'I'll show you around tomorrow, but what say we get you into a hot bath?' he said. 'Then we'll find somewhere for you to bed down?'

She nodded, throat too constricted by grief to agree.

'I know I'm hardly your first choice for a friend,' he continued, 'but I reckon I'm all you've got.'

Achilles abandoned her lap and clambered up Datini's leg until the scout lifted the drake onto his shoulder.

'You'll do just fine,' she said, forcing a smile. 'Just don't go rushing off to get yourself killed. I've had quite enough of that lately.'

'I think I can keep a promise like that.' Datini smiled and offered his hand. Stephania stood and took a deep breath, linking her arm with his, following him to where her life might begin again.

Acknowledgements

Huge gratitude to Matt Rowan for level-headed support and Matt Lyons for meticulous test reading.

Thanks to Simon Spanton, Gillian Redfearn, Sophie Calder, Charlie Panayiotou and all at Gollancz for their hard work and friendliness.

Leopard-print kudos to my agent Juliet Mushens and thanks to Sarah Manning and the Agency Group.

I've crossed paths with many authors in the last year, inspirations, imbibers of intoxicants, and fine folk: John Hornor Jacobs, Edward Cox, James Oswald, Joe Abercrombie, Rebecca Levene, Daniel Polansky, Scott Lynch, Elizabeth Bear, Jon Wallace, and, as ever, Tom Pollock and Jen Williams.

Many thanks to Goldsboro Books for making me feel so welcome, Forbidden Planet Southampton, and the many Waterstone's book sellers who chose *The Boy with the Porcelain Blade* as a recommended read.